STORM AGAINST
THE WALL

STORM AGAINST
THE WALL

Fannie Cook

To my friend
HELEN TODD
who read the beginning
and demanded more

When the blast of the terrible ones Is as a storm against
the wall.

The story and characters in this novel are fictional.

CONTENTS

PART I

1904–1910

… my life, or my father's family …

SAMUEL I

CHAPTER I

THE CHILDREN AND Aurelia, their mother, were still eating when Hans Kleinman pushed his plate forward and tapped at a letter taken from his inner pocket. It was addressed in English script learned in a German school; slender loops solemnly frivolous.

"It looks like your writing, Papa," Marc said. The boy's voice was soft with praise, as if all his father did was excellently done.

Papa spoke across the table to Mama. "A visitor must be made welcome. This man comes a long distance. From Germany. He is now in New York. He is my sister Martha's husband."

Marc stopped eating. Papa's eyes were peering at Mama strangely. Too light for the brunette skin, they were blue like a German's, round like a child's.

Mrs. Kleinman's eyes were small, brown, busy eyes looking everywhere and nowhere. The spoon fell from her fingers and clattered onto the plate.

"When will he get here? Why is he coming? What's his name? Say something, Hans!"

Now Marc felt certain the time for laughing had come. Papa always laughed when Mama ordered him to speak. Then Mama would laugh. And the children too.

But Papa only continued to frown at the opened letter. "He comes tomorrow. In the afternoon he will visit the World's

Fair . . . . In the evening he wishes to call upon my family. 'To pay his respects.' He writes politely, Mama."

The swift look between Hans and Aurelia was more than the usual telling of parental secrets. There was a larger mystery in it and the resolve to be brave.

Until this moment aunts and uncles and cousins had been Mama's brothers and their wives and children. Papa's family was only a list of German names which he would chant upon request to ease a cut finger or a bumped head.

Mama's eyes stood still in anger. "Why is he coming? Why?"

"Wool cloth. His firm has a display at the Fair. He comes on business."

Papa's face again became contented. It was a round face with round features, a child's face no longer young.

Suddenly gay, Mama clapped her little hands. Jumping up, she nearly tipped over her chair. "Marc is as usual dreaming. Before the store closes, run, Freddy, get me a yeast! And a piece of citron. Raisins!" she called after him from the kitchen door. "Lots of raisins. I'll pay tomorrow."

Papa didn't hear the worry in her voice as she said she would pay tomorrow. Only Marc heard and knew that her lower lip was tucked for a second under the shining upper teeth, and that she shook her head in self-rebuke. Papa's eyes were seeing people in a far-off country.

Before Freddy's Indian whoops had dwindled down the alley Mama was entirely happy again. She laughed aloud when the large earthen bowl she pulled from the shelf rattled against the pie pans, making them tumble and roll and chatter.

Papa said proudly, "What a dinner that will be!"

The smoke from his cigar stretched in a flat gray cloud across the room above their heads. No air came from the opened window to disturb it. Because the evening was warm, only one gas jet was lighted. The twins were in the kitchen helping Mama. Papa and Marc were alone.

"Papa, is this a nice man?"

"It is to be hoped. After all, he has married my favorite sister. He is father to her children. Martha must love him. . . . I hope she loves him. In Germany it is necessary to love those within your walls."

Marc's eyes explored his father's placid features for the little tweaks which were not placid. "Why, Papa? Tell me why."

Mr. Kleinman leaned back in his armchair. All day he had been a little man selling shoes, hurried by his customers, harried by Mr. Kemper, his boss, but here with Marc he was a man whose opinions counted.

"In Germany life is not friendly for a Jew. Beyond his doors he is not welcome. It is therefore important that in his home all be sweet and kind. It is necessary. It is all a man has. You are a lucky little boy to be born in America."

"Why was Mama afraid of the man?"

Mr. Kleinman chuckled. "For eleven you are a smart fellow."

"She was afraid."

"You must always love your mother . . . . It is hard not to love a mother."

"Didn't you love your mother?"

Even when Marc wasn't excited his eyes seemed too large for his face. Now, spreading with unbelief, they seemed to make the head too heavy for its thin neck.

"In Germany the world is always punishing a child for being a Jew . . . . My mother sided with the world."

"Tell more, Papa."

"My father was a dealer in hops. Once a year he made a trip into Nürnberg to sell his crop. There it was the rule that the Jew had to wear a yellow badge to let Christians know he was a Jew. Our neighbors, when they went into the city to sell their hops, did not wear such a badge. It was my mother who always pinned it on him—without a word or a kiss. ... At school once I got into a fight with the *Bürgermeister's* son. If I must fight, she said, I must fight with a Jew. She whipped me—very hard .... But it was when she made my sister Carolina marry Isaac that I could no longer—— Carolina was in love with a handsome fellow from the village. Even I who was too young to know about love could see that something between them had made her like a princess."

"Isaac?"

"Isaac!" Papa scoffed. "An ugly old man with six children! His wife was dead. She had been our mother's sister. He was Uncle Isaac to us. We didn't like him. He was cross and stingy. A rich man, stingy!"

"Mother said Carolina would have bread; she could do without love. Carolina was only sixteen. It was a famine year. Bread was very important that year. But when Carolina left home on Uncle Isaac's arm, she was sobbing, a pretty girl sobbing .... After that I tried but I couldn't love my mother."

"Why was Mama afraid?"

"They did not want me to marry her. They wanted me to marry a cousin's niece. Very rich."

"And ugly like Isaac?"

"A beautiful girl with wonderful red hair. I met her here in America. She looked at me with eyes like Carolina's looking at Uncle Isaac. I had not come to America to have a sobbing bride on my arm. My mother in Germany wrote to me, a scolding. My father sent a stranger—a lawyer, he was—to argue with me. I kicked him out. They said things about Mama."

"Will you kick this man out too?" Marc bent to look under the table at Papa's short legs which nevertheless could kick out those who spoke against Mama.

"If he says things about Mama, of course." Papa was smiling now. "But he will not say ugly things. He is friendly, surely. Very likely Martha just wants to know how I am. We must be kind to her husband. I am glad he is coming. It is time."

In St. Louis in 1904 a man as respectful as Hans did not sit down at his table in shirt sleeves. After dinner, when the cigar had been smoked, was the proper time for removing outer garments. He took off his coat, his vest, his tie, his stiff collar with the turned-back wings.

The shirt clung moistly to his shoulders. He carried his garments upstairs. Soon water could be heard and Hans sputtering and sighing with pleasure as he dashed it against his face.

Marc stood in the dim hall listening. He amended the story. This time the little boy in Germany snatched the yellow badge from his father's coat. He chased Isaac away from Carolina, led the pretty girl into the arms of the handsome fellow in the village, and stacked their doorway high with loaves of bread.

When Hans came downstairs he was wearing a shirt open at the neck. His dark hair was neatly brushed.

He stood on tiptoe to turn out the low gaslight.

"The mosquitoes need not be invited in," he mumbled.

But he forgot to pat Marc on the shoulder as he passed. He did not ask whether Freddy had come back. Nor what the twins were doing. Nor why Mama didn't come away from the hot kitchen. He went out on the porch and sat alone on the green slatted bench, pulling deeply at his cigar. Marc knew that at times his eyes were narrowed against the smoke and at other times they were wide, staring back into a world which he could not forget and hated to remember.

The next morning Mrs. Kleinman got up early. Her little round body was neat in a black-and-white house dress and red apron. Papa said, "Aury, you look pretty," but she told him she had no time for such nonsense.

She rushed about from room to room as if something had to be done in each at the very same moment. For a while she added flour to the yeast now risen; then she pulled all the parlor furniture toward the middle of the floor so that Mamie Lee would see that she must clean back of things, and all the while Mama was calling out orders:

"Hans, wear your good suit!"

"Ruth, Bertha, come down here at once!"

"Freddy, I need something from the store!"

"Marc, stop that reading! Come down here and cut the grass!"

"Hans, wear your good tie!"

In her voice, which pretended anger, there was also joy. Her husband saw how it was with her.

"Mama," he said, "I have not yet had the pleasure of meeting Gustav Cramer, but I am certain he will not look under your rug for dust."

The children roared at Papa's joke. Ruth, the livelier of the twins, pretended to be Gustav Cramer, a haughty, stern man who bent stiffly to peer under the rug. Then the others also were Gustav Cramer, haughty and peering, one Kleinman child at each of the four corners. Proud of his success, Papa stood at the door trying not to look too pleased. He was a neat shining little man, slightly potbellied.

After Papa left, Mama put all the children to work. She said it was harder than doing things herself. All morning she scolded through her happiness. When Freddy said it was Marc's turn to go to the store, she retorted, "All right, then you cut the grass and bathe Rags!" When Marc, hearing, said going to the store was much less than bathing Rags and cutting grass, Mama answered, "All right. I'll bathe Rags and he'll be my dog. I'll give him to the dog catchers."

She was more stern with the girls. They were seven, and she was angry at them for being toothless on this important day. A week ago, desperate to make them look better, she had their hair bobbed. It was a new style and the man at the shop had said they would look chic. Instead they looked uglier than ever. Only Papa still thought them pretty. He admitted yes, bobbed hair did remind him of the bobbed tails of horses, but not on the twins. On them it was pretty.

Certainly this morning it was not pretty, only tangled and sprawling into their eyes. So that when Ruth shook her head to protest against dusting the scrollwork of the ebony screen, Mama gave her a little slap and said she was a stupid girl or she would see that it could be made into a fine game. Pulling the silk dust-cloth through, Mama made it whine and sing; she kept time with her foot and whistled a song to match. After that both Ruth and Bertha wanted to dust the screen, but Mama told Bertha to go back to the cut-glass in the kitchen. That, too, was a game, not just ammonia and weeping eyes.

Mama grew crosser every minute because Mamie Lee should have come by now, and in Mama's heart was a tornado of terror lest she fail to arrive.

When the floor of the back porch at last moaned under Mamie Lee's feet, Marc's quick steps followed. He wanted to hear what Mama would say when she discovered that Mamie Lee again had brought along a grandchild. This one, newly born, rested lightly in the crook of Mamie Lee's big arm, its head a red-brown ball.

Before Mrs. Kleinman noticed the baby she said, "Mamie Lee, I hope you brought your serving apron. Mr. Kleinman's brother-in-law will be here for dinner. Mr. Kleinman comes from a very particular family. We—— My God, Mamie Lee, why did you bring the baby today?"

"He ain't gonna worry nobody. I had to bring him. He ain't got nobody but me."

"You!"

"Yaas'm. His papa's my Orvell. His mama, she died—yas-tiddy. I'll fix him a pallet down to the basement, then I'll be right up."

For a second Mamie Lee's expression hovered back and forth. A dutiful cleaning woman... An anxious grandmother. When she came back from the basement it was neither.

"Yaas'm," she said. "Where do I gotta begin?" Talking to Mrs. Kleinman, she spoke gruffly, as she did when talking to her own children, annoyed at their demands but even more at her own habit of yielding.

By noon the first floor was clean even in Mrs. Kleinman's eyes. Every surface of wood in the rooms shone from polish; even the air shone with the odor of polish. The tan linen furniture covers had been washed and ironed by Mamie Lee and returned starched and scratchy to the chairs. Mrs. Kleinman pulled down the windows and the shades, blue ones to keep out the July sun, white ones to hide the blue.

She gave the children a quick lunch in the kitchen: meat lifted out of the soup kettle, tomatoes Marc brought in from the garden, and plenty of bread and butter; but she would not let them drag their pillows downstairs for their naps. The first floor had to be kept just so.

"We'll die of heat," Ruth protested.

"All right, Sarah Bernhardt, that's enough from you." Mama gave her a shove.

Bertha said timidly, "Upstairs is terrible, Mama. We really will die of heat."

"Better upstairs where dying won't show. Quick, Freddy, run back to the store. I forgot lemons."

When Freddy said he wouldn't go again, not when the sidewalks were so hot they couldn't be walked on, Mama seemed too tired to care much. She said, "Someday I won't have to ask you. Papa will buy me a telephone. I will stand here like this and tell Mr. Green over on the corner that I want him to send me a lemon. 'Hello, Mr. Green, hello. I want a lemon,'" she shouted, mimicking herself.

Then all the children laughed and Mama laughed and Mamie Lee at the door laughed too. Marc saw that Mama really was tired. Her eyes looked deep and rings were under them. Her hair was disorderly and her face had a simultaneous frown and smile. Only her creamy neck remained beautiful. Marc said to Freddy, "I'll get the lemons if you finish the grass."

By late afternoon all was in readiness. Mama again looked more pretty than tired. She had brushed her hair with a wet hairbrush. In front it stood up high in a neat pompadour and at the back was the tortoise-shell comb they called Mama's World's Fair comb. Hans had bought it, saying it would make them all remember the World's Fair forever.

While Mama was dressing, Mamie Lee shouted up the narrow back stairway, "Mrs. Kleinman, the children are picking. These victuals ain't gonna taste of nothing but fingers."

It wasn't like Mamie Lee to tattle, so Mama knew Mamie Lee was worried about the baby or its dead mother or living father, but all Mama said was that Mamie Lee should send the pickers out on the front porch and tell them not to dare get themselves dirty.

When the children ran down from the porch even for a moment Mrs. Kelley next door or Mrs. Edgewood on the other side would send them back. All the neighbors in the Yellow Row knew about the visitor but not why this was an important day for the Kleinmans.

The Row consisted of five houses three feet apart, each fronted with yellow brick, each a cube except for jutting front and back porches. The Yellow Row lived one life, looking down a little on the people in the just-completed flats across the street and up a little to the people in the Rock Row, houses faced with white rock and topped with slanted slate. If to the casual passerby these differences were not apparent, the whole block seeming just a half-built-up district of cheap new houses neither very pretty nor very ugly, the residents of the Row were less insensitive, the differences never forgotten.

The twins were the first to spy Mr. Kleinman and Mr. Cramer. Around the corner, up beyond the Rock Row, two little men walked in step with each other like busy toy soldiers. Though Papa was a short man, he was taller than Mr. Cramer. Everything Papa was, Mr. Cramer was more so, almost to the point of caricature. Each man wore a small black derby. Each wore a black suit with tight trouser legs. Each wore a gold watch chain crosswise of his potbelly. Each carried a cane. Though the evening was hot, they walked rapidly, their jackets flaring out behind. When they reached the Kleinman walk the short legs stiffened, wheeling the quarter turn.

Even before Mrs. Kleinman came out to greet her brother-in-law Mrs. Edgewood hurried lanky Charles and limping Monica into the house. Then Mrs. Kelley with a flat hand shoved the young Kelleys inside. Soon all the porches were empty. It was manners in the Yellow Row to let each family live its great moments unobserved.

Introducing Mama, Hans's voice was reverent, but he spoke in German; and the children, who had never before heard him speak German, found the sounds amusing. The twins began to giggle. Ruth's Alice-in-Wonderland comb fell from her hair. Bertha, reaching for hers, popped the hooks on her belt. Freddy, trying not to laugh, rattled a tune by scraping a stick against the ribs of the bench. Only Marc kept his laughter far within where it struggled with love for his father and wonder at the unimportant appearance of this important man, Gustav Cramer.

Naming his children, Papa touched each child on the head as if bestowing his blessing. "I have Marc. I have Freddy. I have Ruth. I have Bertha."

They were his treasures. He peered into his brother-in-law's face to see whether Gustav Cramer was a man capable of observing how extraordinary they were.

With Papa's help Uncle Gustav—as the children were told to call him—explained in halting English that he, too, had two sons and two daughters and, strangely enough, they were the ages of the Kleinman children, except that his twins were not really twins but a year apart. Instead of Marc the eleven-year-old was named Sholem after Uncle Gustav's father, dead of course, since a Jewish boy could not be named after a living grandfather.

Papa said Marc was named after Aurelia's father, Marcus, also dead. Then the stranger looked frightened. He shook his head. Surely this was not a possibility even in America. Surely the first child, the first son, was not named by the mother. Surely the first was named by the father.

Papa smiled, but then he saw Mama back of Uncle Gustav. Quickly Papa sobered his face and told Uncle Gustav that Freddy was named after Friedrich Schiller. He and Mama had hesitated between Goethe and Schiller. Of course, had they named him after Goethe they would have called him John, not Johann.

Uncle Gustav said that, too, was not possible.

Though Papa did not usually smoke before dinner, his hand now reached into his pocket and touched at his cigars. He said had he named his boy after Johann Goethe he would not have done so because Goethe was German, only because Goethe was a great artist; and since an artist belongs to the whole world it is as proper to call him John as Johann, more proper because John was an American name.

Uncle Gustav's lips drew together in a tight, gray cluster while his face grew redder and redder. His eyes looked down at the floor; he shook his head.

Gently Papa said, "Not important," but only as if he meant it was nothing to quarrel over.

He rose and opened the shining glass door of the bookcase, drawing from a long row a few narrow blue books brightly trimmed in gold and a red book from another row. Both rows were known to the children as Papa's German Books. They were the ones he meant when he said that he came to this country with two hundred books and two suits of underwear. Now he handed a volume to Uncle Gustav, who turned very happy and said, *"Gut! Gut!"*

Then Mama said that supper was ready. Gustav ate rapidly and much. The potato soup, the pot roast and noodles were things he understood. Mama, who could speak no German, was talking to him in a language he found beautiful, and he was replying in a way she approved. After he took his third portion of noodles she rushed out to the kitchen and fetched her noodle cutter. It was shaped like a toy piano with a crank-turned roller at one end. She showed him the bright pictures under the lid and then the sign on its back, "Made in Germany." After that he was happy and said things in German which made Papa proud; yet soon their voices rose angrily.

Mama asked, "Hans, what is wrong?"

"He goes back tomorrow—without seeing anything. He has visited only the German House and his own exhibit in the Varied Industries Building!"

"It is nothing to get angry about."

"You are as bad as he is." Papa, who rarely was cross, was now very cross and with Mama as well as with his brother-in-law. "This Fair is not a circus. It is the world come together in one place: the people of the world as well as their products. From China, from India, from Japan, from Russia, from Australia, from Africa. From lands we never heard of. It is a chance to understand the world, to make peace with other nations in our hearts. So he comes from Germany and sees nothing but a building which reminds him of Charlottenburg!"

"You will keep still," Mrs. Kleinman said.

Papa wiped his face and shifted his coat back a little from his hot body. His lips twitched with amusement as he mumbled, "You are very polite all of a sudden."

It was Papa's way of telling Mama she cared for nothing so much as hurrying Papa's family, which had not wanted him to marry an *Americanische*, back where it belonged, to Germany.

As soon as the *Schnecken* were praised and eaten, the coffee cups refilled and emptied, Uncle Gustav reached for a box which he had brought with him into the dining room.

Mama rang the bell, a little lady of brass, then steps could be heard hastily thumping up from the basement. The baby had not cried all day, but Mamie Lee had hurried downstairs many times. After the dishes were gone and the table crumbs brushed off into a tin crumb tray, Uncle Gustav opened the package. The first gift was for Papa, an ivory figurine, a man in knee breeches carrying a pair of geese under his arms. Papa told the children this was a replica of the famous fountain which stood in the market place in Nürnberg.

"Where your father had to wear the badge?" Marc asked.

"The fountain is—beautiful. The water makes a pretty sound."

"But, Papa——"

Choking, Marc had to stop. Surely a city which compelled Papa's father to wear a yellow badge because he was a Jew could contain nothing lovely, neither a fountain nor a copy of a fountain. In such a city water did not sound beautiful. Papa's eyes, unable to tell falsehoods, said Marc was right, entirely right, but his lips said to Gustav Cramer, "Very kind of you. Thank you. Very kind."

Mama's present was long and narrow and wrapped in numerous layers of tissue paper. Before he handed it to her Uncle Gustav made a speech which Papa carefully translated. It contained compliments for Mama, so again Papa looked proud. When all the tissue paper was taken away, Mama spread a black lace fan mounted upon sticks set with mother-of-pearl. Mama held it with the are just touching her chin. Papa said the children must see how pretty it made Mama look, prettier than ever.

She stood it on the mantel above the gas grate, just back of Uncle Gustav's chair. Then she stood Papa's goose-man in front of the fan. The ivory against the black lace was exciting, and everyone gasped. Papa said no home anywhere could contain anything handsomer.

But Marc and Freddy did not like their presents: mittens knit by Tante Martha. At that time no boys in America would wear mittens; mittens were for girls. Marc and Freddy tried not to laugh or to look at anyone while Mama kept saying the wool was very fine and the pattern lovely, and Aunt Martha was an excellent knitter and very kind to take so much trouble for Hans's boys.

The twins received needlecases they did not want, together with presentation speeches they could not understand. They tried on the thimbles, which were too large, and rearranged the bundles of threads, and then stacked the cases in front of Mama's place.

Although Papa's eyes kept looking at the goose-man and his lips kept saying, "Very pretty," something in his face showed that memories had been stirred which made him want to be free of debt to this brother-in-law from Germany. He put aside his cigar and went into the shadows of the front room. When he came back to the table his hands were filled with objects which the children saw at once had been intended as birthday surprises for them, meant to preserve their memory of the World's Fair, as Mama's comb was intended to preserve hers.

Marc's was a penwiper with enlarging pools of varicolored felt on which sat three carved monkeys, one hearing no evil, another seeing no evil, the third speaking no evil. Papa sent it to Sholem. Freddy's was an East Indian flute carved from the tusk of an elephant. Freddy could make music out of anything—even by thumping Mamie Lee's tubs and whanging the basement pipes. Now Freddy's fingers hungered for the flute, but it was sent to Uncle Gustav's younger son.

The gifts sent to his little girls, Gretchen and Rosa, were of gold. Papa's fingers tenderly unwrapped two medallions topped by little loops through which, Papa explained, either a gold chain or a black cord could be put. Uncle Gustav had seemed happy as he accepted each gift, but this time his finger pointed angrily to the fleur-de-lis on the back of the ornament. Then Papa explained to him that the Fair celebrated the purchase of the Louisiana Territory from France. He said it all over again in German and shouted into Uncle Gustav's purpling face. Uncle Gustav seemed proud to be a little man with so large an anger; he shouted louder and louder and Papa shouted louder and louder. At last Mr. Kleinman grabbed both medallions, without any tenderness in his fingers, and also snatched the flute from Freddy's lips and restored it to Uncle Gustav, who rose and said he had to leave.

Mrs. Kleinman spread her eyes at her husband, chiding him for his behavior, so in a little voice such as he might use to Mr. Kemper at the store, Papa said, "Well, well, come along, Gustav. I will walk with you as far as the streetcar." Earlier he had said he would take him downtown to his train.

When Papa returned Mama grumbled that all the work she had done ended only in quarreling, but it was easy to see she didn't care.

Papa cared. His head grieved between his spread hands, his elbows on his knees. He said, "Germans know how to eat. Not how to be friendly with the world. They think they are better than other people. The officers are better than the soldiers; the soldiers are better than the men without uniform; the men are better than the women———"

Mama, cheerful again, interrupted. She turned to the twins, halting the wicker rocker while she spoke. "Never marry a German! Your father is the only German in the world who's not a tyrant. *Never* marry a German. Don't ever bring one around here."

Then everybody laughed, even Papa a little, because it was like Aurelia Kleinman to interrupt in order to give advice on marriage to seven-year-olds. When an idea came into her mind she spoke. She never could wait until the proper time.

Papa said, "Mama forgets that all her ancestors came from Germany. Her parents lived in Arkansas, yes, but they were born in Germany."

"My ancestors are dead."

"It is not something that washes off like dirt on the hands .... Yes, it is!" Now Papa became excited and pleased. "That is what that kind of thinking is! Dirt! And America is clean water which washes it off."

They began to talk about Americans who had been washed clean and some who hadn't. Some who treated their wives as servants. Or as children.

Again Mama said to the twins, who were playing jacks on the top step in the light of the street lamp, "Never marry a German. Your father is the only decent German."

This time Marc reminded her that Papa was not a German at all. Didn't she remember his naturalization papers in the leather case in the locked drawer?

Mr. Kleinman took his boy on his knee. "I am glad you do not forget that your father is an American."

The boards of the back hall squeaked as Mamie Lee came for her money. It was the first Mr. Kleinman knew about the baby. He bowed a little from the waist and expressed his sympathy. His words were formal and polite.

They went into the hall where he could see the tiny boy under the gaslight. When Mamie Lee turned to go out the back way, Mr. Kleinman held open the front screen door. He put a large coin into the baby's curled-up fingers.

After Mamie Lee had walked through the light of the second lamppost Papa asked where she had kept the little one all day.

He shook his head. He bit at his cigar until it pointed upward toward the ceiling. Too unhappy to sit, he paced the small porch. "No," he kept saying in torment, breathing heavily. "No. That is not the way it should be in America. A baby belongs not in the basement."

"Do you want him in your bed?" Mrs. Kleinman demanded. Before he could answer her she added, "It is also my bed, remember!"

Marc saw that Mama knew how to live. She did what she wanted to do and was happy, while Papa never knew what he wanted to do because he not only wanted to be happy but he wanted everyone else in the world to be happy too.

The next week, on the day that Mamie Lee came, Mama got up early as always. Before going down to the kitchen she looked into the back bedrooms. In one Bertha and Ruth were still asleep, pink and white and beautiful because their toothlessness did not show. In the other Marc was awake and reading.

"Freddy, where is Freddy?"

Marc had not noticed that Freddy's bed was empty.

"You are a fool!" Mama shouted, and grabbed his book and threw it into a corner.

She called Papa out of the bathroom. "Where is Freddy?" she demanded.

Papa, looking out the window, waved his shaving brush toward the woodshed. Its door stood open.

"Freddy and his silly pigeons!" Mama sighed in relief. Then by way of apology to Marc she said, "Your brother, too, is a fool."

But no one called Freddy a fool when he wheeled the old baby buggy up the walk. He had restored a missing wheel and nailed a large box to the frame.

Later Marc turned the hose on it, and after it had dried Mama lined the inside with part of an old patchwork quilt. She showed Mamie Lee how she could roll the baby wherever she wanted him on the first floor, though the best place was back of the kitchen stove, safe from drafts.

Mamie Lee fetched the baby from the basement. When he was in the buggy she said, "Bless my boy child! He's fixed out like a king. I sure gotta name him Freddy. Reckon I better call him Freddy-boy so nobody gets mixed."

She was happy, but Papa was proud. "Freddy," he said, "you're all right."

Marc, certain he was more troubled in his heart about Mamie Lee and the baby than Freddy was, wished he had been the one to repair the baby carriage. Freddy was like Mama, caring only a little. That way he could easily think of something to do, but Marc, like Papa, was so deeply troubled and by so much that he could never think where or how to begin.

CHAPTER II

ON THE MORNING of the first day of school the yellow row was in a hubbub because rain was falling at an unrelenting angle, and by noon Kingshighway, the wide boulevard at the corner, would be impassable with mud. The children claimed they could get across Kingshighway if each carried an armload of bricks, dropping them at leaping distance, passing others forward to the foremost crosser. Bricks were plentiful enough in the growing neighborhood. But where would those bricks be when it was time for the children to come home again?

Mrs. Kelley called jovially to Mrs. Kleinman, "Mine want to take their lunch."

Mama frowned. Only neglected children took a lunch to school. She turned to Mrs. Edgewood, who was more genteel than Mrs. Kelley. "What are you going to do?"

Mrs. Edgewood pursed her lips.

Mama was a quick guesser. She said, "I have more bread than I can use."

When it was established that the Kelleys and Kleinmans and Edgewoods were going to take their lunch, the four Giovannis screamed Italian at their mother in the basement kitchen. Only Dr. Wollo's household was unaffected. It was the last of the Row and childless, though one girl after another who hung up wash or emptied garbage or cleaned the woodshed or washed down the steps was a girl swollen with child. The Wollo household was forbidden to the children.

Those who brought lunches were told to eat them in the basement, a dark, hollow room which screamed back multiple echoes of every shout thrown against its walls. The adjacent toilet room poured out odors in ugly rivalry with the fragrance of bananas, apples, and sausage.

Freddy ate, ran, and played, but Marc sat watching others run, trying not to hear the happy shouts, balancing the hunger of his stomach against its revolt. When at last he spread his sandwiches on the torn clean dish towel in which Mama had wrapped them, a large red-haired boy grabbed one from what he called Marc's "sheeny lunch." He was out the door and gone before Marc could get to his feet.

While anger, which was shame and helplessness as well, stifled Marc's breathing, another boy came to stare. Izzy Randowich whispered his fear and disdain. "It ain't kosher. You got pig sandwiches."

"Ham."

"Pig."

"It's a ham sandwich."

"Pig is ham. You———" The rest was a name Marc didn't understand. But he understood what he felt for Izzy Randowich.

They fought with no skill, only fury, knocking heads against the concrete floor. Fighting Izzy Randowich, Marc was also fighting the boy who had called his lunch a sheeny lunch. The word always maddened him. Because of it Marc pounded Izzy, since he was indeed in Marc's own thinking a sheeny; and because he was, Marc had to endure humiliation almost too great to be endured.

The next day Marc was sick. It was not an illness which had anything to do with the swelling of his lip or his discolored eye, only with the shrinkage of his throat and stomach. Nothing could be swallowed in comfort, and even without food his stomach was strangely heavy.

Mama looked at him angrily. "You are like your father." It was an accusation.

Marc replied, though he had to tilt his head to let the pain flow to one side so that he could look up at her, "Papa does not fight."

Mama mumbled, "I know what I know," and went away.

At noon she wakened him to read a note which Freddy had brought from Miss Pile. It was prim writing, in ink, and said: "Dear Marc, we miss you very much."

Holding it lightly lest it break from sheer loveliness, Marc read it aloud to Mama, who nodded happily. "You see, she is a lady. She knows you are Jewish, but in her head there is no sheeny. She couldn't think sheeny if she tried."

Mama was running down the stairs before Marc could ask how she knew his fight had to do with Jew and sheeny. He had told nothing, nothing at all; yet Mama knew. Leaning back against the big pillow, he remembered Miss Pile reading a story, her voice purring with fun, or Miss Pile teaching grammar, drawing a spider on the blackboard, its arms and legs for adjectives and adverbs. "Maybe we'd better not get into all that," she would say. "One thing I'm sure of—the *ly* on the end. That's always the adverb, but sometimes it isn't there when it ought to be."

Then she would have a large boy open one of the great windows. She would ask the children to stand up straight for her sake and take exercises for their own. She would take exercises, too, getting red in the face and out of breath, and finally she would have to stop and restore hairpins, laughing and looking very pretty. After that she would say, "Now we've done right by our bodies; let's do right by our souls."

She would open the big cupboard with the swishy silk curtains at their windows and give out little squares of paints. Someone would go outside for a pitcher of water and fill the small pans on the desks. Someone else would give out paper.

Whenever Miss Pile said they could paint anything they wanted, the little girls would paint flowers and the little boys hills with setting suns atop them. But Marc would paint something on Miss Pile's desk—her green shawl, a pair of Indian dolls, or the dancing girl on her inkwell. Once he tried to paint her tatting-edged handkerchief stuck into a book to keep the place. The other boys said Marc's painting looked like the Cascades at the World's Fair, but Miss Pile said it didn't matter what it looked like because Marc's colors were good.

Coming back into the room. Mama carried a tray with a bowl of chicken broth, some crackers, and a cup of cocoa. She said Marc was fine again, all well, his headache gone, his eyes and lip still large but not hurting, his stomach only hungry. It was the sleep that cured him, she said. So why not surprise Miss Pile and go back to school?

At first Marc thought his stomach wasn't well yet, but trying the broth as Mama commanded, a little at a time, he discovered it was; so he put Miss Pile's note away carefully and went back for the afternoon session.

One Friday as Marc was leaving school an old man with a long white beard and a skullcap stopped him. In broken English he asked whether Marc would like to earn some money, and in that moment Marc knew he longed to buy Miss Pile a present for Christmas.

He followed the man through the back door of a house on the other side of the wide avenue, in a neighborhood older and less clean than the one in which he lived. The man showed him candles and a well-laid grate and told Marc to come back at sundown to light them. On Saturday mornings he must come to lay the fire again, also one in the kitchen range. It seemed a job not worth even the little the old man offered, but, hoarded week after week, it would buy something for Miss Pile.

Later at home Marc watched the clock. The old man had said he must come promptly at six.

"It will wait until after supper, whatever it is," Mama said.

When he did not heed her command to stay, she said, "Hans, you are no father. You never correct the children!"

Mr. Kleinman looked up from his book. "Mama has worked hard to prepare the meal. It would not be polite to come to it late."

Marc, at the door, paused. "I'll be back. Papa, I'll be back soon. I promised."

Hans closed his book. "You gave someone your word? Is this—— Is it something of which you are ashamed?"

"No, it isn't like that at all."

Aurelia Kleinman had no patience with her husband's dillydallying with the children. She demanded, "Then what in heaven's name is it?"

Papa rose to his feet. "That we have no right to ask, Mama."

"No right to ask. With your own son? Eleven years old. A fine father you are!" she scoffed.

Marc slipped out the door and ran down the street.

The old man in the skullcap ordered Marc to hurry. The fires caught easily, as did the candles. Marc wondered how this could be called work and why someone was paid for doing it. As he rose to his feet he heard a boy's voice. Into the room came Izzy Randowich, his hair and eyes very black, his cheeks very white. Once more they were enemies, though this time not with their fists. From Izzy's mouth sputtered angry words spoken in a foreign tongue. The grandfather spoke angrily, too, to Izzy but about Marc. Aunts and uncles crowded into the room already crowded with a table set for dinner. All sputtered the strange tongue. One laughed.

At last Izzy rendered the verdict "You are no Jew," he shouted contemptuously.

Marc resorted to words of his father's: "To be a Jew is not an act of will. The important thing is to be a good American."

An aunt with thick glasses said she would explain it to Marc. She asked him a great many questions which he answered carefully. She said many things Marc did not understand. Then she shrugged her shoulders and mumbled under her breath, "He has been brought up a *goy*. We might well keep him for our *shabbas-goy*."

But the old man said Marc was no Jew and, because he ought to be a Jew but was not, he could not be their *shabbas-goy*.

Marc had expected the Fair to go on forever. He was surprised when Papa said this was the last week and he would take Marc along with him on Saturday.

In the streetcar Papa talked of Mr. Kemper, his boss. "To him the Fair is nothing. He went once. Now he says he has seen the Fair. He didn't want to let me off. The man is a dunce."

"Why aren't you the boss, Papa? You aren't a dunce."

"Every man is a dunce. One in one way, one in another."

"You could be a better boss."

"I could run the store better, yes. Then next thing I must run a larger store. In a larger city. And so and so .... A man must know how he wants to live."

"Uncle Oscar runs a big store. And Uncle Carl."

"Your mother's brothers are hard workers. I have not the courage for running a store. I am not fair to Mama .... " He began to argue with himself. "Mama is happy anyhow, without money. The only way a person can be happy. Happy by nature. When I come home at night I don't want to think of a store. I want to read my books and play with my children and have peace. I am not a brave man. I want only peace. *Sholem*——"

The Hebrew word gave Marc the chance to ask about being a Jew. Why was being a Jew something you were blamed for being and also for not being? He told about the red-haired boy who called his lunch a sheeny lunch and about the fires in Izzy Randowich's home.

Papa laughed until tears had to be wiped away. He brushed his mustache right and left as if he had just finished his coffee. "A *shabbas-goy!*"

"That's what she called me."

Papa said all that was such nonsense that he was ashamed to let his son know grown men could quarrel about it.

"Why is it a sin for them to light their own fires?"

"Why do the Kelleys go to Mass before the day is bright? Why do the pale Edgewood children spend beautiful mornings indoors at Sunday school?" Papa got angrier and angrier. "Didn't I tell you every man is a dunce, some one way, some another? ... Let us enjoy the Fair."

His hand tapped at his breast as it always did when he got excited, as if the tapping somehow comforted pain.

After they had passed inside the gate Papa said, "If you are interested in religion, then you must be interested in all religions."

"Orthodox too?"

"Orthodox is only stubbornness. Once men did not know how to cure pork so that the disease germs were killed. Now we do know how, but still the stubborn Orthodox refuse to eat pork. Worse still, they refuse to let you eat pork!"

Papa was so angry he had to sit down on a bench for a while. He was cross with Marc, telling him to look at the water flowing down the Cascade steps, not at his father. Marc could hear him cough and could hear his fist tapping at his breast. At last Papa said there was a great deal about religion he could not understand. He had tried. "Perhaps it has been spoiled for me by name-callers ... ." He shook his head unhappily.

Marc tried to help him. "Uncle Oscar says religion is what makes all the trouble in the world."

"And what does Uncle Oscar know about trouble? A rich man with a big house and a big store? Let him keep his mouth shut about trouble. ... He has never lived in Europe. When he and Aunt Clara go over there they live like king and queen. Ride in a carriage. Eat the best. Uncle Oscar hasn't seen children starving ...."

They stood now, a little man and his boy, alone with their thinking, while the crowds of people, laughing and talking, rushed past. The men were dressed much as Papa was and swung their canes as he did, gaily. The women wore white shirtwaists with pretty ruffles and long black skirts which swept the pebbled walk unless they held them up a bit, prettily, the way Mama often held hers. The children were dressed as Marc was, with a straw hat, a starched blouse, and tight dark pants. It was not their clothes which placed them apart from the others, only their way of visiting the Fair. The others seemed to dash in and out of buildings on impulse. Papa stood still, deciding where to go.

At last he stopped squinting his eyes and said they would try to see how men worshiped. Trying to admire, they looked at the red-and-gold peaks of an oriental temple, but, alas, it was locked and they could not go inside and feel it as Papa said they should. Instead they walked up and down the long aisles of another building where religions were kept within fenced areas. Most of what showed were books and statues. Marc thought the Buddhas, with their bare bellies, ugly. Soon, however, he was entranced by an ivory goddess, a graceful Chinese lady with a long swirling skirt, flared as if she were walking. Her hands were like Miss Pile's, and even though there were hundreds of reproductions for sale Marc found each lovely. He told Papa as soon as he had enough money he would buy one for a Christmas present.

Papa's hands tinkled coins in his pocket. "You want that for Mama?"

"I just want it," Marc answered.

Papa bowed a little. "You have the misfortune to have a father who is not rich."

After that for a few minutes they were strangers.

Papa tried to explain the six-pointed Jewish star to Marc. When he found things he did not understand he would mumble, "More nonsense." He was pale and perspiring. When Marc called out, "Look, Papa, the Kelleys have one of these," Papa's lips smiled while his brow frowned, and he told Marc not to speak so loudly about such things. It was the Virgin and Child. Papa shook his head. "It is a beautiful story, yet it has caused the Jews much trouble."

They sat on a bench, but it was not as it was other times when Marc was alone with Papa, laughing equally much at the ways of the world and Papa's ways, as if after all there was nothing to get excited about, life being so much fun. Now Papa did not joke. He kept crossing his knees, although his legs were too short for crossing, and breathing very loudly and at last speaking.

"Marc," he said, "a father should be a strong man. He should be able to teach wisdom to his children .... You have not such a father. You must try to be strong for yourself. Learn things for yourself. Your father, unfortunately, is not a man who can teach you anything." He twisted around and looked back at the building of religions. "Religion is not statues. It is not stars. It is something else. ..." To himself he mumbled, "It all seems the god-damnedest nonsense."

Then both of them were silent and ashamed, for Papa had never before sworn in the presence of his children. At last he began to chuckle. "The worst of it is that your silly papa can't understand it and yet he gets angry. He is not altogether silly, for one thing is clear—religion has always fought science."

Marc asked about electric lights.

Papa said the church invariably knew which side its bread was buttered on and how to get the butter; therefore, it of course used candles to enchant people and electricity to light the church. "It is a matter of faith. Uncle Oscar believes in electricity and machines in the same way the church believes in God. Both are wrong very likely." Papa was now a tired little man, weary of his own efforts. "I believe in my children. That is my faith. They will learn about electric lights and how to make life easier for people. My children will live after me. That is my eternal life. I have Marc. I have Freddy. I have Ruth. I have Bertha."

He felt better, ready for jokes again. He looked at his watch and whistled and said it was time for that surprise he had been hinting at all day.

The hands of the great floral clock which covered a hillside showed, as did the sun beyond it, that six o'clock was nearly here.

Of course it was Mama. She was smiling and waving, a lunch basket on one side of her and the twins and Freddy on the other. Mama said Papa should give his family a good time. Mr. Kelley had taken the Kelleys into everything on the Pike. And that Mr. Edgewood, who never had laughed in his life, had taken his children to something which made them laugh. Even his sad little Monica had laughed. And the Giovannis! The children as well as the parents had come home sleepy from wine.

"What have you been doing out here all day, Hans? What have you and your father been doing, Marc?"

Marc looked at Papa and Papa at Marc. Obviously it was impossible to tell Mama that they had been searching for the truth in religions and had failed. Mama would have searched for samples and found them.

She retaliated for their silence with more remarks about Papa's neglect of his family. "Hans, you have been here all day and haven't even thought how you could give your children a good time!"

What she wanted was a good time for herself. But Papa heard only what she said, not what she meant. "Come with me," he answered. "I know just the thing."

Even the twins could see that Papa was pretending to know something he didn't know, but Mama was also pretending—pretending she believed him; so they all hurried as if someone among them knew where they were going and what they would see when they got there.

Though it was not yet entirely dark, the Pike was already crowded with people blowing whistles and shaking feather ticklers into the ears of strangers. It was lively and Mama liked it, but Marc saw that Papa longed to get out of the crowd. A painted man in a peaked hat yelled, "Starting now! Starting now!"

Inside the tent the backless benches were nearly empty. The shrieks and shouting sounded far off, though they were just beyond the canvas.

"It is nice in here," Papa said.

"Roasting," Mama answered, though not as if she cared.

"See," Papa said proudly, "I do think of my children's pleasure."

It was a long wait and the twins begged to go outside again. Freddy, asking no one, rolled under the tent. He came back when the music started, a melody played very high on a flute like the one Papa had given to Uncle Gustav for his little boy. The melody went round and round, and all the time nothing happened except that some incense rose from a large kettle. After a while a woman came out, dancing, twisting, and dancing. Her face was painted too red and her eyebrows were too black. She wore pink tights and waved some varicolored veils, first showing one side of herself, then the other. Mama began to talk German under her breath to Papa.

"Wait," he said. "The next act is what I wanted the children to see."

Then it was over; the lights went on; there was no next act.

"You fraud, you!" Mama said to Papa. All of a sudden she laughed. "Wait until I tell the Edgewoods what you took your children to see!"

Papa laughed, too, and all the way home, while the children ate sea-foam taffy, Papa and Mama laughed at each other and themselves as if it didn't matter that Papa had failed again. But Marc did not laugh.

Because Hans had selected the wrong performance on the Pike, he bought tickets for a vaudeville show starring Presto the Magician. On Saturday afternoon the children, in Marc's charge, called for Papa at Mr. Kemper's shoe store. The twins wore new red challis dresses, partly basted because Mama could not finish in time. The boys wore blouses Mamie Lee had starched so much that they rattled. All four faces shone from soap.

As soon as Papa saw his boys and girls he became lively with pride. Holding the twins' hands, he introduced each child to the other salesmen and to Mr. Kemper. Even the customers made admiring remarks.

Twice Freddy had to be ordered down from the top of the tall ladders, but Marc stood still, trying to discern in Mr. Kemper's ways what there was that made him Papa's boss, saying "Hans," though Papa said "Mr. Kemper." Even now he was making Papa look unhappy. They were talking in low voices at the side of the store, Mr. Kemper, a slumped, nearly chinless man with wide spaces between his teeth, lacing a shoe, looking at it and lacing it and refusing to look at Papa.

At last Papa said in a voice no longer mumbling, "If that is the way it is, then so is it. I do not break a promise to my children."

He buttoned the top button on his jacket and, looking at no one, took the hands of the twins in his and left the store, a little man walking bravely. Marc remained to call Freddy down from the ladder.

"What is wrong, Papa?" Marc asked when they caught up.

"If we do not hurry we shall be late," Papa answered, and Marc knew the answer was like his own about the ivory figurine, telling only that he would not tell.

The show was so far below them that the actors seemed elves.

A family in red tights rode bicycles swiftly and at times upside down. Freddy kept saying he also could do it if only Mama would let him. In the second act a man juggled bottles while racing around on roller skates. He, too, was in tights, as was the next man, a musician who banged his tunes out of bottles. Now and then he would surprise his audience by hitting the note out of what looked like mere furniture. Soon Freddy, who had been beating his rolled-up program against the air in time with the melodies, struck Marc over the head and at the same time bonged the right note. People nearby were laughing and enjoying Freddy's excitement as much as the activity on the stage.

When the lights went on for the first intermission the manager came up the steps of the balcony and invited the children and Hans to sit in a box. Papa said no, these were the seats he had bought, but even while he was refusing, Freddy and the twins were following the man. On the way downstairs Papa said to Marc, "So now the Kleinmans are in the show business."

He smiled, proud that other people were admiring his children. Yet Marc could tell that the pride and pleasure were only a little way inside Papa. Farther within was something unhappy caused by Mr. Kemper. Marc resolved never to put himself within the power of a Mr. Kemper.

In the box they sat on gold chairs, the children next to the rounded barrier and Papa back against the dirty gold curtains. When the twins leaned far over the edge Papa would move forward and hold onto Bertha's or Ruthie's skirt.

Now there were large tawny moons and lavender sunsets and happy black-faced people singing gaily as they gathered pretty white cotton into fancy baskets. Beautiful ladies sang and danced. One singer, flirting, held her finger tip beneath her chin. After that Ruthie's finger tip would coyly prop Ruthie's chin, even when Papa asked her if she wanted a drink of water.

Marc liked the scenes about the Presidents of the United States. The actor, swiftly changing wigs and coats, became one great man after another. He recited parts of their speeches and bowed deeply and solemnly in response to the applause.

A big placard and a blare of noisy music finally proclaimed Presto, a dark man elegantly dressed in evening clothes. In the spotlight his satin lapels shone, as did his hair and his wand and his patent-leather pumps. Presto took large things out of small, cut a woman in two and put her together again, and with ornate gestures displayed his capacity to perform the impossible. Whenever he was about to execute an especially baffling miracle he would shout, "Abracadabra whoop-la!"

Even Papa enjoyed that act. He kept saying, "Mama will be sorry she didn't come instead of going to Aunt Mimi's party." Each kept trying to remember things to show Mama. Following the crowd out of the theater, they would pull imaginary rabbits out of imaginary hats and whisper "Abracadabra whoop-la!"

As soon as supper was over they acted out the show for Mama and Mamie Lee, holding Freddy-boy on her lap. Papa, too, was part of the audience and laughed and thought at the same time. When at last the children were ready for bed and Mamie Lee gone, Papa told what had happened.

He was seated when he said it. His round eyes were on a level with the children's. He looked into theirs, one after another, seeing nothing.

"I am no longer a man with a job," he said, shrinking into a very small man indeed. Then taking a deep breath and growing larger, "Neither am I a man who disappoints his children. I asked Mr. Kemper before I bought the tickets. Then because a few extra customers come in, he wants me to let my children go by themselves. This I cannot do, I tell him. I have promised to take them."

"He fired you?" Mama asked.

"He said either I stay for the busy Saturday afternoon or I go for good. So I said, 'If that is the way it is, then so is it.'"

Mama looked frightened in the same way she looked frightened when she had nothing left in the grocery-store purse.

"We could have gone alone, Papa," Marc said.

"In Canada once a theater burned down," Papa said. "Many children——"

Mama slapped Marc. "How you talk! You 'could have gone alone.' If you had gone by yourselves the theater would have burned down. Certainly. Hans, you did right."

She looked angrily at Marc.

Papa rose to his feet. "I am now a man without a job, but I need not therefore be a man whose wife slaps her son because he speaks up. It is well to speak up. ... I wish I could speak up to Mr. Kemper."

In his eyes were tears.

Aunt Mimi always brought her crocheting, so Aurelia sent Bertha and Ruth upstairs for the mending basket. One should carry the basket, the other the overflow.

The men sat near the front window of the little room, Uncle Carl in Papa's chair boasting about his successes, complaining occasionally about Uncle Oscar; Papa in a straight chair brought in from the dining room.

The women chose the upholstered rockers. Mama kept searching for her thimble or thread or scissors or needlecase or emery ball and losing them as soon as they were found. Mending, Mimi joked, Mama was a hen scratching for worms.

Bertha and Ruth and Fred dutifully kissed everyone good night and went upstairs, but Marc sat cross-legged on the floor. With his back to the men, he could still hear what they said and at the same time watch the row of little shells grow as Aunt Mimi crocheted.

Marc waited for Papa to say he was a man without a job so that Uncle Carl, who gave jobs to many men, would offer one. But Papa said nothing, and when Marc at last felt as if he had to say it for him, Mama heard the words not yet spoken and said crossly, "It is time for *Backfisch* to be in bed."

Backfisch was Papa's word for those too young to count. Marc looked at Papa for defense. Papa said, "Yes, Marc, it is time for bed."

Kissing Marc good night, Uncle Carl said with mock seriousness, "When you grow up, are you going to be like your father, scared to death you'll get ahead in the world, or like the rest of us, scared you won't?"

Glancing at Papa, Marc saw that Uncle Carl's fun hurt. He answered, "When I'm big I'll sit in my own good chair and brag about my own money and Freddy will have to sit in the dining-room chair." He spoke in defense of Papa, but it was Papa who objected the most. Mama laughed at her brother's discomfiture and said, "See, Carl!" Aunt Mimi stopped crocheting and went into a fit of giggles.

After a while Uncle Carl put his arm around Marc and said gently to the others, "It's all right. The boy's all right. He didn't mean a thing by it." Then to Marc: "I've got a Saturday job for you. Who can tell? Someday it may be Hursch and Kleinman."

Working at Hursch and Company, Marc observed that Uncle Carl was an honest man, yet adapted his honesty to the ways of the world. He would say, "Honesty is the best policy." Or, "To do the right thing in the long run pays dividends." Or again, "A Jew has to be more honest than anyone else."

At first Marc, dusting the samples of furniture, sharpening pencils, emptying wastebaskets, running errands, could not understand why it was that Uncle Carl, who was rich and successful, was constantly worried about the handicap of being a Jew, while Papa said only that a Jew was lucky to be born in America. Once Uncle Carl roared, "Of course Hans Kleinman doesn't have to worry. What does he care about getting ahead? He's satisfied to be a shoe clerk for the rest of his life. On one side of him lives a politician, on the other a carpenter. Hans Kleinman has no ambition."

Apparently a Jew in America was not punished for being a Jew if he did not want to get ahead; yet Uncle Carl was only agreeing with the habits of America when he said that it was Hans Kleinman's duty to be ambitious.

Certainly both Uncle Carl and Uncle Oscar were ambitious, but their ways of being Jews differed. Uncle Oscar was president of the company, which owned both the big store he managed and the smaller store Uncle Carl managed. Uncle Carl's store was halfway uptown; Uncle Oscar sent it all the merchandise he couldn't sell in his fine store downtown. "I have to market your mistakes," Uncle Carl would shout when Oscar would come to the Midtown and criticize the way Carl did things. If Uncle Carl shouted louder, he would then phone Aunt Mimi to invite Oscar and Clara for dinner soon. If Uncle Oscar shouted louder, Aunt Mimi would phone Carl that Clara had invited them for dinner. There were few phones in the city but already two systems: the

Bell and the Kinloch. All the Hursches and the Manns had the Kinloch system. "Who has the Bell?" they would ask.

Every once in a while Uncle Oscar would employ a man to work in Carl's store. Because Carl was supposed to employ his own men this always caused trouble. Oscar would tell Carl he should count himself lucky to have such an industrious man. Carl ought to be reasonable; could Oscar fill his nice downtown store with *matzos-ponims?* A *matzos-ponim,* Marc learned later by asking Papa, was a man who looked like a Jew; it was not a nice way of saying it. Oscar would add that Carl had to realize a man in business sometimes had to do favors. The new employee was the nephew of a lawyer who had been very helpful or of a wholesaler who had to be appeased. Whenever a man with a note in his hand would ask to see Mr. Hursch, Carl would howl, "Another nephew!"

But he would engage the man because he never could think of an adequate reply to Oscar's contention that the *Schwarzes* wouldn't care. Most of Carl's customers were Negroes, and Papa said *schwarz* meant black. And black men, though Christians, had no hatred of Jews.

CHAPTER III

LIKE A TOY balloon blown to a size and radiance inevitably temporary, St. Louis had been blown up by the World's Fair. Now the air was hissing out, the display buildings torn down, the people of distinction gone, the others walking the streets looking for more jobs than the shrunken city could offer. Papa did not join them. He stayed at home and wrote letters to shoe stores asking to be a salesman. Sometimes he said he could also keep books.

He wrote his letters in ink at the dining-room table. He would get all dressed up and be a shining little man, just as if he were going downtown to Mr. Kemper's store; then he would pull the shade far up and remove the table scarf which looked and felt like a rug. He would fold it neatly.

Mama would say, "Take care with that ink," as if spilling ink was all that troubled the Kleinmans. Even Marc was not allowed to watch.

After the letters were sealed Papa would walk to the neighborhood post office. When he came back late in the afternoon he would look very pale and say that of course he had eaten lunch.

During supper he would be quiet, but sitting back in his chair afterward, he would talk about Mr. Kemper: Papa had not just sold shoes; he had fitted feet and tried to make the customer know that in Mr. Kemper's store comfortable feet came first, selling shoes second. More than that, he had listened to Mr. Kemper's troubles, all that about his wife and the way she criticized everything he did. To think that Mr. Kemper could——

One night Mama said, "You act as if all chat's wrong is that Mr. Kemper doesn't love you any more. If he was a woman I'd be jealous."

Then all the children laughed and Papa, too, laughed a little. Marc saw that Mama was right. It was the hurt of Mr. Kemper's broken friendship which Papa thought of nearly as much as that without a job he could no longer support his family.

In the evenings now Papa did not read or invite Mama to go out. Saying he was going to step next door for a minute to call on Mr. Edgewood, he would stay all evening, and if Mr. Edgewood was not at home, then Papa went to see Mr. Kelley.

At the Kelleys everything was always jolly. The Kelleys laughed and played pinochle and drank beer. When Papa came he, too, played pinochle and drank beer and laughed. The Kelleys were fat and many of their friends were fat and had what they called City Hall jobs. Before the last election they had been very much frightened and had said the Dirty Crooks—which was the other party—might get in.

"Then what?" Papa asked.

"Then what?" they mocked at Papa. "We lose our jobs."

They did not know Papa had already lost his. Mrs. Kelley guessed it by seeing Papa walk past at the wrong hours for going to work, but Mr. Kleinman had said nothing. So Mrs. Kelley said nothing, not even to Mr. Kelley.

Mrs. Giovanni guessed it because the second Kleinman boy now brought her some of his pigeons twice a week. The Kleinmans were out of work, so the Giovannis had squabs for dinner. She offered to kill some for the Kleinmans, who were too soft to kill their own, but Freddy shook his head and set off with the money. In Italian, Mrs. Giovanni told her children the Kleinmans preferred to eat meat which had never been a pet animal. She wiped her eyes as she said it and looked at her canaries which she loved and would not have wanted to kill.

Mamie Lee lay in bed teasing herself: Today you're a retired cleaning woman. All you got to do is figure out a way to eat. You and Freddy-boy. She chuckled, and the baby, in his padded wooden box, rolled over.

Mamie Lee, you got smart children. Specially Orvell. He's a papa and a widower and a schoolboy. Up in Chicago, not eating. Just sitting still listening to white men talk.

It was a fact which made Orvell nearly a stranger. Long ago Mamie Lee had decided to work for white people, obey their commands, even to love them in the way she loved the Kleinmans, but never to heed when they began talking their thoughts. As soon as she learned of Orvell's intention to sit in the classrooms of white men she argued, "If they ain't gonna talk lies, what's it gonna be? I know the truth and you know the truth. You know it ain't gonna be that. Come they know the truth, let 'em quit talking and do something."

She quoted herself to herself now. It still sounded all right. Trouble with Orvell is, he's right much like that poor Mr. Kleinman. What's a little Jew man got to be surprised about when he gets fired? Leastways a colored man knows he gonna get fired, first chance they get. That Mr. Kleinman ain't ever believed the world gonna get tough. Too much like my Orvell, always fancying folks is good as he is. Bet right now Mr. Kleinman's worried about how I'm making out without my day.

Mostly, I'm gonna have to keep my Freddy-boy out from under them ice wagons. And away from the rats he thinks is puppies. If Orvell's teachers ain't no good, we sure doing a lot of bad living for nothing.

She wished Orvell could take white folks the way she did. Let them rule the roost if that was what they wanted, but never forget they were only a pack of spoiled kids with temper tantrums. She who had scrubbed their floors and washed their clothes and cooked their meals for many years had only been tending the helpless: kids with dollars in their fists. It was what a mother had to do for kids because they were kids and because she was a mother. But what Orvell did was just crazy, paying out his good money and hers to listen to the spoiled kids talk. She had replied to Orvell, "Call it lecturing or call it anything else, it's still said by spoiled brats."

Her thoughts wandered back to Mr. Kleinman. Mrs. Kleinman was just folks, wanting her own way, and sort of cute and, when she wasn't angry, sweet as sugar. Screamed at the kids the way everyone else did. It was Mr. Kleinman who was different. And his Marc was going to be just like him.

Freddy-boy fretted and she reached over and lifted him into her bed, pads and all.

She kissed him. In the mornings he was mighty pretty, his eyes big and bright and his lips easy with smiles. He'd be all over the bed now, crawling. Her rest was over, and she knew it.

"Freddy-boy," she said out loud, "we're going out to the Kleinmans, pay or no pay. Ain't no good staying around here, you playing with rats, me looking at Mr. Kleinman's baby eyes with all that hurt in them. Reckon a man ain't smart to let folks chase him out of the land where he was born."

As she dressed she told herself she was silly to work for nothing; mostly, she was going out there because she hated to try out a strange job. Some folks were kids and put on airs like they was grown up. Leastways the Kleinmans didn't do that. They acted like kids, looking for fun and laughing hard when they got it.

That afternoon Mr. Kleinman was still out for his walk and Mrs. Kleinman was doing her marketing, with the children at her heels, when Mr. Kemper rang the doorbell. Mamie Lee answered.

Mamie Lee said nobody was at home. She said it grumly, for she guessed who Mr. Kemper was and why he had come.

"I came to see Mr. Kleinman."

Without yielding the door an inch, Mamie Lee replied, "He ain't here."

Mr. Kemper leaned forward anxiously. "Has he taken a job?"

Then Mamie Lee was sure. She looked majestically past Mr. Kemper's shoulder. "He's been considering two places. One ain't offered enough money, but the other got more money in it, got lots. Seems like I heard Mrs. Kleinman say the mister he going down about it this morning." Frigidly her eyes scanned the stranger. "You know Mr. Kleinman?"

Mr. Kemper looked nervously at the other porches. Outdoors like this, he felt at a disadvantage. He had missed Hans Kleinman. Customers came in, asked for him, went out without buying. And the books were in a muddle from Mr. Kemper's failure to make daily entries. He didn't even have anyone he trusted to send to the bank with the money.

He cleared his throat and readjusted the umbrella handle hooked over his arm. "Tell Mr. Kleinman that Mr. Kemper called. Can you remember that? Tell him I want to see him at the store."

"You can come in and write it down," Mamie Lee conceded. While he wrote she decided upon further strategy.

"I reckon I can't say for sure he can come tomorrow. Not with this chance to make better money. But I'll tell him you come by to say hello." She opened the door.

Mr. Kemper peered at the Kleinman parlor with its books and its cleaning-day shininess. He couldn't observe that the prettiest things were birthday presents from the Hursches. "I'd be willing to pay—— Tell him I'll pay him the same the other job offers. He should come back to me. Tell him I said I want him to come tomorrow morning." The pale, lashless eyes blinked rapidly.

Mamie Lee knew that it would never do to leave this to Mr. Kleinman. Her voice soared to a high pitch. "Mrs. Kleinman, I think I heard her say Mr. Kleinman was going to get four dollars past what he's been getting."

Mr. Kemper frowned. "Tell Mr. Kleinman I'll pay him five. Tell him I'll expect him in the morning. At the usual time."

When Mr. Kleinman arrived home Mamie Lee hid her triumph. "Mr. Kemper says he gonna pay you more. I reckon he's right ashamed he ain't never paid you enough. Was I you, Mr. Kleinman, I wouldn't go to talking about it. Let that kind of boss alone. Less said, the better."

At the table she heard him tell the children. "I suppose Jo Kemper found out what I did. I suppose Jo Kemper missed me after all. We were always friends. Always were, so I thought."

Everybody was happy tonight: Papa because he had his job; Mamie Lee because she had taken care of Mr. Kleinman, who didn't know how to take care of himself; Freddy because he wouldn't have to sell more pigeons; Marc because Papa now would surely call Mr. Kemper Jo; and Mama because she would not have to give Hans the message from Carl.

Carl had told her to tell him: "Oscar and I will find a place for Hans in the business if he gets some ambition in him. We're not going to take in a brother-in-law who doesn't want to get ahead. We're not willing to be embarrassed. If Hans will just get ambition . . . ."

Now she wouldn't have to see the hurt in Hans's eyes as she told him that.

As the days passed Marc became more and more certain Miss Pile would like his Christmas present; soon he would have enough money for the Chinese figurine on sale now in a downtown store. Perhaps she would stand it on her desk across from the peasant doll. He foresaw how she would clasp her hands and gasp with rapture. Each week the waiting became more tedious. It seemed especially slow after Room 3 started making red paper chains and Santa Claus faces.

They made so many that Room 3 was well trimmed and still extras remained. Those were sent to another room, and thus the principal learned what they were doing. In the presence of the class she asked Miss Pile a lot of questions. Miss Pile's face and neck turned red, then too white, then red again. After the principal left the room Miss Pile said to put the paper and shears and paste away and get out their grammars and turn to "Adverbs" on page 84 and read that part aloud.

The next morning a substitute was there, an old woman with wrinkled skin and gray hair and a rumpled voice.

Marc's heart drummed at his ribs when he saw that Miss Pile's books were gone and her peasant girl and the pretty shawl.

As the file of boys came down the steps at noon, the principal, a wide woman heavy on her heels, stood flicking the blackboard pointer against her full skirt. Marc stepped out of line to ask where Miss Pile was. He had to say it twice because his voice squeaked and failed him.

When the principal understood, she straightened up quickly. She pulled her chin back against the hollow place in her neck. "Miss Pile has gone to her home in the country. No, I certainly do not know the address."

The pain of it was so great that Marc no longer enjoyed entering his secret world of daze and dreams. When he thought now, he wanted to think of something.

Uncle Carl reported that the boy was waking up. He was seeing things. He had a good head on him. He was all right. He worked hard. He was a real help. He earned his pay.

To himself Marc explained his new habits differently. He who was smarter than Freddy was no longer content only to be smarter; he would also act smarter. It was not enough to be wise as Papa was wise, infinitely and without purpose. It was better to be only somewhat wise but to use what wisdom a boy had with vast results.

Marc was fascinated by the Madonna on the wall of the Kelley dining room. Vaguely he realized it had something to do with going to Mass early on Sunday mornings.

Mrs. Kelley, standing in the doorway, said, "You believe Christ hasn't come yet. Don't you? That He's coming again."

"Me?"

"Jews believe the Messiah will appear on earth someday— don't they?"

"How do you know about the Messiah if he hasn't been here yet?"

Mrs. Kelley crossed herself and her children and said to Marc, "You poor thing, you. Come get some cookies. Boys, run outdoors to play."

She was a fat, jolly woman who swayed when she walked. Her eyes were blue and her hair black. Marc knew she cried easily when someone was hurt. Mrs. Kleinman always said Mrs. Kelley had a good heart. And now she was crying over Marc.

At home that night he asked Mama, "Do we believe Christ is going to come on this earth and save us?"

"That word 'Christ' has caused us lots of trouble. Say 'Jesus.'"

"Don't we believe in the coming of the Messiah?"

"How do I know what we believe with all the work I've got to do around here? Ask your father."

"If you're Jewish, then you believe it too."

"Of course. Ask your father what Jews believe."

"Don't you know?"

"Whatever it is, I believe it."

When he finally got Papa's attention, Papa put his book aside. "You have made me leave Faust in hell in order to answer your questions."

"Mama said Jews don't believe in hell."

"Only while reading Goethe."

Papa listened carefully to Marc's accumulation of what Jews believed. He lighted another cigar and puffed rings. Then he said, "To believe as Mama does is very fine because Mama does it. She wants to do what is right and so she believes what she is told to believe. Obedient. But thinking is something which must be free to go where it will. Like a bird which flies, not needing to arrive anywhere. Thinking must obey nothing and nobody.

It must look for the truth, freely. Men who can think like that are inventing electric lights and telephones and automobiles and a thousand other things to serve man, thus they are creating a new world for man to live in. The common man becomes a king. They are———"

"But, Papa, what has that to do with the Messiah? What can I tell Mrs. Kelley?"

"It makes no difference what you tell Mrs. Kelley. She will go on believing as her church tells her to, just as your mother will believe what Uncle Oscar says the Jew believes. Believing is obeying. Thinking is something else."

"I don't want to believe. I want to think."

After Papa was again reading, he lowered his book to say, "If you are going to think, I must try to send you to college."

"I am going to college, Papa. I'm going to be a lawyer."

Now Papa closed his book. "College takes money .... Hans Kleinman's son a lawyer.... Why, that would be—would be very fine, Marc." Then to himself: "In America anything can happen."

He looked far off and kept his book closed.

When the autumn holidays came the Kleinmans went to Temple. As they walked across Kingshighway, Freddy cake-walked ahead of them. The twins lagged far in the rear. The evening was sullen with heat and the little girls fretful because Mama made them wear hats. In protest they snapped the elastic under their chins, thus shifting their millinery to strange angles and making their necks sore as well as hot.

Marc walked beside Papa and asked questions. Papa said the Jews started and ended a day at sundown, thus tonight and tomorrow until six o'clock was *Rosh Hashana* but not tomorrow night, except for the Orthodox, who always observed a two-day holiday lest they make a mistake. Stubborn, Orthodox, and foolish. But reckoning a day from sunset to sunset was not so strange as Marc seemed to think. It was reckoned in that way because the Jews began reckoning their holy days centuries before mankind invented clocks.

This particular holiday was New Year's Day, and after the services were over all the men who had been trying to steal business from each other all year would wish each other a prosperous New Year, but day after tomorrow they would again seek to capture customers.

Whenever Papa said anything like that, chuckling little chuckles which did not halt his speech, only made it ripple, Mama told him to hush. She wanted to be part of the Temple and have her children part of the Temple because she wanted to have good times with people who wanted to have good times with the Kleinmans. Her only faith in the matter was that in the Sunday school the four little Kleinmans would surely be taught something which would make them good.

"They are good," Papa contended with a sudden last-minute hope of escape.

"You see nothing."

"Mama, they are very fine children. I can say that even with Marc hearing it. They are fine children."

"Hush."

Papa looked down at Marc carefully. "He is a child. Not a fool."

"If Oscar and Clara can send Alice and if Carl and Mimi can send their boys, then———"

"Because they buy the finest clothing for their children does not mean———"

Mama stopped to fan herself. She was tightly laced and short of breath. The evening was heavy. "Hans, when children grow up they must have friends. Will and Monica Edgewood, Art and Tom Kelley, they're all nice children, but when they are old enough to go to dances they won't remember to invite our children. By then the Kleinmans will only be Jews. Our children might just as well learn now that they are Jews."

After that Papa was silent and did not speak even when they reached the tall flight of wide steps leading up into the Temple. At the corner men and boys surrounded a new automobile parked in front of the building. It was long and red and shiny, with a few steps which folded up and down at the back. The chauffeur, in a long tan duster, a cap, and goggles, was showing how the steps worked.

"It's Oscar's," Mama whispered. "I knew he ordered it."

Even then Papa could not speak to answer the children's questions. His fist kept knocking lightly at his chest, trying to silence the pain. Aunt Mimi's friends paused to talk to Mama, and she was jolly with them. Their husbands looked at Papa, surprised not to know him. One man asked, "Are you Kleinman of Kleinman-Roth? No? Oh, you're in Oscar Hursch's organization. No?"

After the man left, Papa said softly, "I am nobody. I have the good fortune to be nobody."

At the top of the long flight they entered a lobby, and now all voices were whispers. Mama sat between the twins and Papa between the boys. Because that put Ruth and Freddy next to each other Mama rolled her eyes at them in condemnation to offset any ill behavior which might come. They were the lively ones. For a while the strange hushed mood and the solemn twilight awed the children. They looked up at the high ceiling and the huge chandeliers hanging by great metal chains.

When the organ started Freddy clapped his ear against the wood of the pew in front of him to feel the vibration. His movements always were swift, monkeylike movements, and now even Mama smiled, though she jerked him up and shook her head.

Chanting came from the choir loft. A side door on the platform opened and the rabbi walked out slowly and solemnly. He wore a full-dress suit such as Presto the Magician had worn. They were the only full-dress suits the Kleinman children had ever seen.

As the singing ceased the rabbi came to the front of the platform and prayed in Hebrew. Some in the audience mumbled along with him. The web of sound surprised Freddy. He stood up and Mama sat him down.

After a while the drone of the strange tongue made them sleepy. Then the rabbi's voice rose dramatically. He stood with his back to the audience, intoning loudly. With bowed head and folded hands he faced a pair of double doors steadily parting as if of their own will. While they moved slowly away from each other, a standing double scroll was revealed, its gold and satin cover glittering in the light.

When the rabbi at last ceased reading and praying he began the story of the escape of the Hebrews from Egypt and slavery. He described the sea and the men and women standing at the water's edge. Behind them were their masters seeking to capture and punish them. Then the waters parted. The Jews passed through. Now the masters were in sight! Armed and merciless and swift. Nearer, nearer. The waters closed. Pursuit was impossible. The

Jews were free! The rabbi raised his fist and shouted, "The waters closed!"

Marc asked Papa softly, "Tides?"

After a moment Papa nodded in affirmation.

As if the rabbi had heard them, he began to decry that idea. It was not tides but God's will. The pursuers were wicked, unjust men. Tyrants. The Jews were especially beloved of God. His chosen people. God was a just God and a zealous God. The sea was rolled back by the same Great Being who had once said, "Let there be light!"

The rabbi's voice hummed and shouted and whispered. At times it rang like a bell struck; at times it glided like a stream of honey; once or twice it roared great throaty roars, causing even the grownups to look frightened. Papa rose. Taking Marc by the hand, he walked out.

As they waited for Papa to be able to breathe, the night was soft around them. He coughed and his fingers clawed at his chest and his shoulders were bent. When he was able to stand straight again they walked slowly along the boulevard hand in hand. As soon as they came to some steps near a lamppost where Papa could see Marc's face they sat down.

"Some of what you heard tonight, Marc, was truth. That about not being ashamed of being a Jew. One tells the truth about oneself always. It is one thing to teach a boy that he is a Jew, something else to teach him that God is a kind of magician. Look in your schoolbooks to learn about tides. To a rabbi you do not go to learn about arithmetic, also not about tides. From him you hear stories with fine lessons attached. That is enough, God knows. Why does he have to pretend it is true?"

"But we are God's chosen people, aren't we, Papa?"

Now Papa became excited again. "Listen to that fellow in there and you would believe that God chose the Hebrews because they were the people in the greatest trouble, but if that were so, then today the Negroes would be His favorites. Obviously they are not His favorites. Marc, you must be careful not to believe such talk even when a rabbi says it. Can you tell me why?"

He made Marc explain what was truth and what was half-truth. A boy who wanted to be a lawyer must keep his mind ready for what was true. He must search in the chemistry book and in the laboratory and in history books written by men who knew how to search for the truth and were not trying to prove something they wanted to believe.

Voices of people coming from the Temple began to hammer at the dark.

"We will meet Mama. We will not make her feel bad by talking like this before her."

"Mama ought to know about tides too."

"Tides are not important to Mama. ... A boy understands, but not in order to make someone else feel that she does not understand enough."

After that, though he continued to hold Marc's hand, he talked as if to himself. "Even I, a nobody, could tell there was no truth in that tonight, yet all those big men——"

"They were not big, Papa."

"Big in business. But they sit there like stupid schoolboys, letting that man yell nonsense at them, thanking him for his half-truths and his scoldings." Papa shook his head in grief.

Marc said something he had long wanted to say. "Papa, you are not a nobody."

After a while Papa answered, "Yes, I am a nobody."

"It is a half-truth, Papa."

Papa chuckled. "You are right. Every man is important to himself.... And to be even a nobody in America, it is a great privilege, for a man can be nobody and yet be his own master. He need not take anything from anybody."

The great doors of the Temple stood open. People were saying, "Happy New Year," and shaking hands. They were jolly and laughing.

Papa said, "They feel better. Religion can make a man feel better.... But it is not science.... Nor the whole truth. Mama will scold us for leaving."

CHAPTER IV

BERTHA AND RUTH were on their way to uncle oscar's house to spend the night. Aunt Clara had said they were to bring nothing but their combs and toothbrushes. Mercy knew Alice had plenty of gowns, ones she and Oscar had ordered on their European trips.

Before the twins could say anything Mama told Aunt Clara they would love to come and, after Aunt Clara left, scolded down at them. "Just let me hear you haven't been nice to that poor Alice and you'll catch something you won't like."

As the older, brainier, and more successful of the Hursch brothers and as husband of one of the well-to-do Mann sisters, Uncle Oscar now lived in a huge newly built marble-fronted house with a double set of front doors and a terrace of gray granite steps. Like its neighbors, the house stood out near the sidewalk where its grandeur could be admired. It stood flatly, firmly, and honestly on the building line, neither losing an inch through carelessness or overcaution nor cheating a little by puffing forth a bay window.

The avenue ran out into the country and down into town. Nevertheless, the block Oscar Hursch and Ellinger Lake lived on was flanked at either end by high pillars. Though they had beseeched the city for gates, thus far they had had to be satisfied with the pillars.

Giving the twins final instructions, Mama ordered them to stop their giggling and playing tag and such nonsense as soon as they came to the pillars. At that point Bertha was to see that Ruth's hair was not down in her eyes and Ruth was to see that Bertha's shoes were not unbuttoned. Uncle Oscar's house was two miles away; they were to walk and not get lost. "Remember, no sass to anyone, Ruth. And, Bertha, speak up; don't act so scared."

She said nothing about the doorbell, so each rang a long ring. Because Bertha suspected Ruth's was longer, she rang again. Then Ruth. Then Bertha.

Ruth said, "When my little girls go to see Marc's or Freddy's they won't have to be so good. I'll tell them to do anything they want."

Bertha replied, "I'm going to have all boys and I hope they have all girls, and I'll tell my boys to tease their girls."

Elaborating on this theme, they sent themselves into wriggling and giggling so that when the inner door opened they were bouncing about in the vestibule like popcorn in a hopper.

Fräulein was very cross about all that ringing, but she kneeled to unbutton their coats and take off their bonnets, an inscrutable act which made Bertha happy and Ruth unhappy. To Bertha it was a foretaste of the luxury they were about to enjoy, and she tried to look like an idle queen, drooping her eyes and twisting her neck. Ruth took it as an insult to her ability to remove her own wraps and stood stiff with anger and embarrassment, causing Fräulein's nose to turn bright red and her pale lips to hiss: "Like a ssstick she ssstands, like a ssstick ... ."

Alice was waiting for them in the nursery on the third floor, Fräulein told them. They were impatient to go right up, but Fräulein cautioned them not to go up the elegant front stairway but to use the back way. Her words were roughened with accent, not softened by it like Papa's. When Papa said Ruth's name it was not quite Ruth but it was longly said. When Fräulein said it, "Root" was chopped off like a puppy's tail hit by an ax. Excitedly correcting the children, Fräulein would repeat, *"Aber nein, aber nein, aber nein."* When she spoke English the words seemed too bulky for her mouth.

Alice was waiting just inside the door of the nursery, a large room with dormer windows, linoleum floor covering, and shelves of handsome toys. She danced up and down with excitement, pausing now and then to peer through her thick glasses to make sure which was Ruth and which Bertha. Instead of greeting them she raced back to her toys, hopping about with grasshopper jerks and sudden springs.

Vaguely she knew it was not only the greenish cast to her skin and the stiff kinkiness of her dark hair and the thick lenses and the stutter at times possessing her tongue which gave her mother pain. It was not only that Clara Mann Hursch had wanted a pretty blond daughter like one of the twins, but she was also disappointed in what the stuttering tongue said, what the blinking eyes liked to look at, but most of all by Oscar's disdain for his wife's inability to transform their daughter into a picture-book child, sweet and pretty and charming. To alter all of Alice's habits, physical and mental, Fräulein had been employed.

Fräulein had been unhappy in Germany because of a love affair which came to nothing, the young man being so poor that her father shouted, "Do you want to sleep in a hut with cattle all your life?" After the young man looked elsewhere for a bride Fräulein went to Karlsbad, where she worked as a waitress and met the Hursches, rich and generous travelers from America. She asked to come to the new country with them, whereupon Aunt Clara had been almost frank about the Alice problem. For some years now Fräulein had been meeting it industriously. Zestfully she corrected Alice's speech, her manners, her appearance, her thoughts. Twice a week she took her to have the brass wires tightened on the protruding teeth and to have renewed the rubber bands which held the upper and lower jaws in painful alignment. When Alice would remove these Fräulein would hiss, "Do you like to be ugly, Alice? Answer me!"

Before the twins arrived Mrs. Hursch had said they were little girls who went to public school instead of to the Institute.

"But why?" asked Fräulein.

"Their father cannot afford—— Hans Kleinman is a shoe clerk. He is a nice man but without ambition. Mr. Hursch used to hope he would—grow.... Mr. Kleinman is still a shoe salesman."

"Ach!" Fräulein lamented. Pompously she put the more expensive toys into the closet. "No use having your best things ruined, Alice. *Aber nein, aber nein.*"

It was Mr. Hursch, in one of his most incomprehensible moments, who had insisted that the twins be invited. Observing his daughter's chronic discontent, he wondered why she who had the best of everything couldn't be a gay little thing like those twins of his sister's. It couldn't hurt to invite them over, since telling Alice that it was her duty to be happy had not worked.

His edict had sent first Clara and then Fräulein into flurries of preparation. Despite all the forewarnings to Alice, the afternoon was a great success. The hot chocolate Fräulein brought on a tray was lusciously topped with marshmallows and the cookies plentiful, as a commentary on the poverty of the twins.

Whenever Fräulein's back was turned Alice made a face at her. Suspecting the disloyalty, Fräulein's turnabouts were swift, whereupon Alice's face stiffened into boredom. The twins tumbled to the floor in giggles. To maintain her dignity Fräulein recalled first-floor duties and left, but only after ostentatiously locking the largest of the doll houses.

Alice had never before made faces at Fräulein even behind her back. It had been fun, but now, suddenly, Alice felt unhappy. She got out her sewing cards and held them up for the twins to see. The finished ones, stitched with bright wool, were discernible pictures. One was half stitched and some not yet begun. They were stamped "Made in Germany," but Fräulein had bought them here in St. Louis on her day off.

Working at them would teach Alice to use her eyes. Though Alice held them at the tip of her nose and turned her head this way and that in her effort to see, still she made mistakes. Fräulein would rip out the stitches, and then that card would not count toward the two-a-day stint. If Alice made a fuss, she had to do her own ripping, to teach her to be a lady.

"Tell on her!" Ruth urged. "Tell your mother!"

Breathing so deeply that knots came into the veins of her neck, Alice explained the conniving of which her mother and Fräulein were capable. The two were more than twice as bad as either one.

While Bertha and Alice talked Ruth stitched up four cards, her fingers quick and lithe and capable. Then Bertha stitched two. They hid them in the small desk which was Alice's, the sole place in the room Fräulein was not free to examine.

"She's honor-bound," Alice explained, but stuck the cards under the blotter and locked the roll top.

Ordinarily Alice ate early in the butler's pantry with Fräulein, but tonight, because Mr. Hursch had some sort of idea about his daughter and nieces which Mrs. Hursch said Fräulein was to be patient with, the children were to eat at the table and

Fräulein alone in the pantry. To be certain Fräulein would not have her feelings hurt, Clara sat with her while she ate. After all, if the woman got into a huff where would Clara be with Alice on her hands?

As soon as Uncle Oscar came home the house became lively. He rushed about, showing the twins the chandeliers which had both gas jets and electric bulbs. While the butler touched the taper to the gas, Uncle Oscar snapped on the bulbs one by one and, each time a light came, swung around to see the children's faces. "Watch," he kept commanding, though there was no need to say it. Hopping with excitement, Alice begged to have all the first-floor lights turned on at one time—all of them! Even Fräulein became a little enthusiastic. She turned on the twelve little lights on the black statue near the hatrack in the hall. It was a figure of a draped lady holding a bunch of flowers. Each flower was a light. Some of the bulbs were burned out, but most of them glowed and the children danced up and down with glee.

Uncle Oscar was wild with joy. Ever since he had built this house it had been admired; Clara was proud of it, but this was the first time he had been permitted to show the kind of pleasure he really felt, pleasure which was also pride in himself and pride in the marvels of an age of miracles when houses could be lighted not only by gas but also by electricity.

"Watch," he called as he touched a match to the gas logs in the parlor. Then he rushed to the other parlor where the logs were slow to catch but after a while they gulped loudly and then burned. Three logs, dotted with perforations, each a tiny blue-and-yellow flame.

Oscar Hursch rubbed his hands. His was a thin face with a fat mouth and fat nose and quick dark eyes. Now the wonder and ecstasy of a child brightened it. He looked at the gas logs and at the lights and at Clara. "Our grandfathers wouldn't believe it!" he said. Admiringly he watched the excitement of his nieces. Then he ran into the hall where a small door of brightly polished wood crouched beneath the stairway. Holding the handle, he said, "Guess! Guess what!"

Alice screamed with derision when Ruth guessed that it led to a great cave, and even louder when Bertha in a small voice which had to be coaxed louder guessed that it led to a dog house.

Uncle Oscar laughed at their faces when they saw it was a lavatory. In the back hall where he rushed next there was also a place to wash one's hands; they had seen that and their faces showed no wonder, not even at the tall swan's-neck faucet curved above the copper sink in the butler's pantry. They had seen the telephone and the stove which was part wood-burning and part gas. They opened the snap-back lid of the speaking tube and stared in and saw nothing, except Ruth, who was almost sure she saw a garden in the moonlight. Alice ran upstairs and talked into the tube, and then Bertha and Ruth took turns listening and answering until Alice commanded Bertha to put one ear tightly against it. Treacherously she made the tube shriek.

To brighten Bertha again Uncle Oscar said he would play the Victor box, and while the needle bobbed up and down he held first one twin, then the other, to look down the horn and see the little man who was singing.

No one heard the doorbell ring or the butler open the door, so that when he tiptoed in and whispered to Mr. Hursch that Mr. Ellinger Lake was here Uncle Oscar got excited and waved his hands, as if ashamed that he was boasting about his house to two little girls. He answered the butler in a cross voice and scowled at everybody, nearly dropping Bertha as he rushed to Ellinger Lake, but by the time he found him admiring the new painting over the mantel Oscar was jolly again as he shook hands with his tall neighbor.

Mr. Lake couldn't stay. He had brought the latest official letter in regard to the gates. But Uncle Oscar saw that this was not the purpose of the visit.

Oh yes, Mr. Lake suddenly remembered, something to be said very casually. Perhaps Mr. Hursch recalled that Mr. Lake had suggested the way to go at getting those gates was to talk to some of the men at the Merchants' Club? Mr. Lake, being a member of the Merchants', had invited Oscar Hursch, who could present the thing more forcibly than Ellinger Lake, to be his guest for luncheon at the next open meeting which would be a week from today; but Mr. Lake had been at the club that noon for the closed meeting and there was some difficulty ... Mr. Lake took a deep breath and looked at and then through the new painting, trying to find a way of saying, and yet not saying, that the difficulty was something entirely unimportant and not at all related to Mr. Hursch's being a Jew. Finding his lips unequal to the task, he wetted them a time or two and said that the difficulty was something which would not long remain a difficulty, not when it was really explained properly. In his opinion a man as successful in furniture as Mr. Hursch and a man who bought as much lumber from Lake and Lake and was so clever about having expensive furniture copied and marketed right here was a man who was not really ... A man like Mr. Hursch was an honor to any community, and he for one had found him an excellent neighbor and one of these days ... And so he bowed and blushed and, looking a little like an elongated pink shadow, went away.

By the time they sat down to dinner, which had been ready when Ellinger Lake came, Uncle Oscar, silent at the head of the table, began to be like the Uncle Oscar that Uncle Carl so often complained about in whispers to Papa. Cross and very busy. Why didn't the maid walk more rapidly when she passed the food? Why hadn't the butler carved the roast while they were having the soup? Why didn't the cook fry the potatoes? If Aunt Clara was afraid to tell her, he wasn't. Why couldn't Fräulein help in the kitchen? Why did Alice make so much noise eating? If it was those rubber bands, then why did she have to eat so many crackers? Why was Alice always in white? And always in summer dresses even in winter? Put her in wool and she'd get some color in her cheeks. No, Clara must be mistaken; he couldn't believe all the little girls at the Institute wore white wash dresses.

Aunt Clara tried to keep his voice down. Yes, he was right. She urged him to eat.

When he had finished he felt better and told Aunt Clara she looked fine in her black velvet dress. The rose-point collar they had bought in Florence was beautiful, an elegant touch to an elegant dress. Where were they going tonight? To the club?

"Whist at Mimi's and Carl's. Have you forgotten?"

Oscar scowled. He didn't like Mimi's sharp tongue. Not tonight. Not after Ellinger Lake's visit. He tried to want to go to Carl's.

Suddenly he looked and felt righteous. "I don't believe in cards on *shabbas*." He seemed to have forgotten the many games that he himself had played on Friday night.

Clara smiled a small smile. "Didn't you say something about the club?"

He ate the last bite of apple dumpling. His voice was stubborn. "It's Friday night and I think we ought to go to Temple."

"You know how Mimi is."

He strode up and down his long dining room. He was smoking a cigar, not the way Hans Kleinman smoked, slowly and with rings, but biting the end and now and then drawing his teeth back from the bite. Then he would pull at it hungrily and repetitively send up great masses of smoke.

"How can the Jews expect to be respected if they don't respect themselves? I don't care what Fräulein hears! If she doesn't know were Jews it's high time she found out. In business all day long a man is pushed into a corner because he is a Jew. If he wants to make money he has to sell cheaper, produce faster and better and cheaper. Make up for being a Jew. Well, if he's a Jew he's a Jew. He'd better be a Jew all the way. I will shout it! Why not be a Jew? It isn't as if you're asked to believe anything you can't. The Reformed Temple lets you believe or not believe. If half those fellows Carl likes to fill his house with would go to Temple instead of playing cards on Friday night they'd be better off. All they think of is money and cards and———"

Suddenly he turned upon the twins. "If your father would just take a little interest in the Temple. If he'd try to get ahead in the world. If he'd try to give your mother what she deserves. A house with electric lights."

"Let's go, Oscar," Aunt Clara said, "to Temple and then to Carl's."

Bertha turned pale. Ruth said, "Papa knows all about electric lights. He teaches Marc how they work. Mama doesn't want electric lights. My papa is polite at the table."

Fräulein hurried in. "It iss too late for little girls to be up. Too late to eat supper after dark. We will go to bed. Root, you are a bad girl. Bad. No more up late. Aliiiicccce. *Aber nein, aber nein, aber nein.*"

Putting Alice to bed was an intricate procedure which began with brushing her hair one hundred strokes on each side and another hundred in the back. It also necessitated taking manifold precautions lest she catch cold. Gas heaters were lighted, blankets and towels warmed, rugs laid against doorsills, towels along window ledges, screens unfolded and moved out and stood here and then there. Ointments were rubbed on her chest, alcohol on her legs. One cream was used for her hands, still another for her face. A glass of pink gargle and then another of colorless mouthwash to be sure food lingered neither around the brass brace nor the elastic bands.

All the while Fräulein kept asking the twins about their home. Did they have a furnace, *aber nein?* Yes? Well, then, did they have gas grates? *Aber nein, aber nein.* Lucky little girls to be able to visit Alice and warm themselves by her gas grates! Did they have a playroom on their third floor? In Alice's, one day, a ball would be given at which she would make her debut wearing a white satin dress with a train; she would dance with the handsomest, richest of men to the most beautiful music. *Aber nein,* not even a third floor? And of course Fräulein knew they had not a telephone. Not even a Victor box. Did everyone sleep in one room, in one bed? *Aber nein,* but only three bedrooms and of course small ones. And no Fräulein to care for them, not even a cook or a housemaid, though mercy knew Anna was not worth her salt. Spoiled girl, always getting angry and now claiming she had to go home to work on the farm. *Aber nein,* who wanted to work on a farm? Sissssssilly girl, that Anna. And very likely the Kleinmans had not enough to eat. See, Alice, how grateful you should be that your father is a ssssssmart man and therefore rich?

While Alice was in the tub the twins were to undress themselves and put on the gowns Fräulein had laid out. Heavily starched, the sleeves were flat, crackling as Fräulein pushed her hand through. The yokes of open-work embroidery were surrounded by ruffles.

Fräulein ordered the twins to stop shivering and be grateful, for of course these gowns were better than the cotton-flannel ones they had at home. Only peasants wore cotton-flannel gowns, she added.

She kept right on hurrying through the room. She and Alice had quarreled while Alice was in the tub, and now she left her alone to smear talcum on her hands while Fräulein tiptoed upstairs.

Soon she was back with her face very red and her eyes spread with rage, her lips curling out moistly. In her hands she held the sewing cards.

"So!" she shouted. "So you are little li-arss! Li-arss. You have made Alice do thisss thing. You! You!"

When Fräulein would not hush, Alice shrieked and turned stiff and did not relax until Fräulein poured cold water over her face. Then her gown had to be changed and her body rubbed warm. She was put into bed with a hot iron well wrapped. The twins were sent into the room across the hall. Fräulein would sleep as always in Alice's room.

In bed Ruth whispered, "I hate her! I hate Fräulein!"

The room was misty. Through the transom the hall light slanted a faint rhomboid across the ceiling; through the high windows moonlight entered. Grotesque shadows touched and left the chandelier.

Even when they heard Fräulein snoring they did not laugh and giggle as they were wont to do when they were in bed at home.

Bertha said, "I'll never come here again."

Ruth sat up. "We're going home!"

"Now? Mama won't like it if we come in the dark."

"Papa will say we did right."

Mama told the twins they were bad, but she told Aunt Clara and Uncle Oscar and Aunt Mimi and Uncle Carl that the twins had done the proper thing and she was proud of them. Fräulein was a horrid creature. Poor Alice! The argument lasted for a long time and involved several of Aunt Clara's relatives, members of the stylish Mann family.

Uncle Oscar was caught midway in the quarrel. Disliking Fräulein, he disliked even more the fright in Clara's eyes when she thought she might be without Fräulein, so he said Clara was so kind that her help walked all over her, a statement which made Clara a little proud. In the end they compromised by dismissing Anna, who intended to leave anyhow. After that Clara said Fräulein's faults were solely the result of overstrain in having to deal with Anna.

The twins heard and later in the basement mimicked Fräulein's "Sisssssssilly girl." They showed Mamie Lee how Fräulein twisted when she walked. They said, *"Aber nein, aber nein, aber nein,"* for her, and when Mamie Lee laughed they told about Alice and the sewing cards until Mamie Lee said it was sad enough to bring tears to the eyes of a dead man.

Just as Papa lived one life at home and another selling shoes, so Mama lived one life at home and another among the foibles and favors of the Hursches and Manns and their friends.

At the dinner table sometimes Papa would tell about a woman with a hole in her stocking who wanted high-heeled white satin, of another whose feet smelled like cabbage and who wanted red slippers, and the one who said her husband weighed

two hundred pounds and liked his sauerkraut cooked with tomatoes and did the store have anything in button shoes?

Then Mama would bring out her world to share. Unlike
Papa's brief episodes, Mama's stories were long and winding.

At times Papa would sigh and say, "Aury, come to the point."
Or, speaking up toward the ceiling, "It is like a tree. Everything
branches into something else."

One evening she began, "That reminds me, Hans, you will
have to buy yourself a full-dress suit. Also a shirt ...."

"Aury, it is not enough to talk. What are you saying?"

"Even the children can understand. It's because you don't
want to go to Oscar's party. Think how Clara would feel!"

"Have I ever before heard of Oscar's party?"

"There's no use telling a man who won't listen. But now
you have no time to waste. You must get your suit and be ready.
There will be lobster and champagne. Oscar plans to give everybody a fine time."

"Oscar will feed people who are not hungry. Does he know
there is a famine in——"

"Keep still with your famines!"

"I have no money for a full-dress suit."

Aurelia looked as if she would cry. Papa said there was something Mama must understand. "It is hard for a Hursch to understand anything she doesn't want to understand," Papa sighed.

He opened the drawer where the purses were kept in a
canyon between the napkins and the tablecloths. He lifted
the purses out one at a time, not opening them. "This for
food. This for clothing. This for rent and insurance. This for
pleasures."

Hans's fingers felt at the purse for clothing. Obviously it was
empty. "There is nothing for a full-dress suit."

"You were the one said Marc was growing too tall for his clothes." Mama's eyes flashed.

"Yes, but now there is no money. And nothing in the one for pleasures .... The insurance is paid and the rent, so that is gone and"—his hand weighed the food purse—"this is light. Mama."

Mama's eyes flickered. She was trapped. She said, "A package came for you today," and sent Freddy to get it, as if nothing had been decided or even discussed, nothing at all.

The package with strange stamps was from Uncle Gustav, who had at last complied with Papa's request to send pictures of his family.

The photographs were just the size of Papa's palm. He would hold an oblong of cardboard and guess who the person was. Then he would turn the picture over and see what Martha had written there. Often his guess was wrong and he would shake his head a little.

"The women are very pretty," Mama repeated, and then with a little American anger in her voice: "Look at them, they can't laugh. Too good to laugh."

Papa said surely they were happy now that life had become less difficult for them. Most of them were blonds—had she noticed?—like the twins. Then his fingers, being very careful of the cards, matched up the families into little groups. Gustav, Martha, and two sons, sober boys, and two daughters, good, solemn-eyed little girls.

Mama said she was surprised all the children seemed so— so—so unlike children.

Without looking at her Hans said, "You're surprised because you've never been a child in Europe. I never saw a lighthearted child until I came to this country. The way the children laughed and played and were free seemed more wonderful than Niagara Falls. Everything over there makes them serious. Everything they do at school or at home is completely important. They must study hard. They must become great men. They must respect their parents. They must do this and do that."

He didn't want to discuss it, but Aurelia kept going back to the subject. Wasn't it nice that both Martha's and Helena's sons were to be doctors? And weren't they remarkable, those youngsters, to know what they wanted to do?

Papa laughed at her. "They know," he scoffed. "They know nothing. Their parents know for them. Jews over there can't take life hit-and-miss. Those boys have to prove themselves. Most jobs are closed to Jews. They cannot enter this trade or that——"

"But lawyer and doctor are better," Marc said.

"Not being allowed is often a step up," Papa answered. "It is not nice to go up because one is not wanted down." His hand was tapping again at his chest, tapping and clawing a little. "In Germany a Jew must go up."

Mama said, "Well, they must have got over being poor. Look at them. No more famines for them."

Papa shook his head. "There are no pictures of the dead." Then he rattled off names quickly, as if he had thought of them often and so had them all ready to say. "Those died of consumption. Bad lungs. Too little food. ... These are the ones who made a little money. They spend it educating their sons. Then the son perhaps becomes *Herr Doktor* and the fathers of the rich girls will offer their daughters in marriage. A *Herr Doktor* over there is not just a man who takes care of you when you are sick; he *is* someone. It's that way for everybody, for the gentiles too. Well, they may have all that business! They may keep it."

Freddy, counting, said there were seventeen. "Seventeen Dutchmen." Mama laughed. "All related to my children, who also look like Dutchmen."

Papa was smoking now and happier. "We Jews take on the color of the land we live in. I have never met a Kleinman with dark eyes. No one in my family is dark, and there are some extreme blonds among us, yet we are Jews."

"The Randowiches!" Mama snorted. "Garlic and all that jabber."

Papa looked at Mama quietly. He knew what she meant. The neighbors tried to put the Randowiches, who had recently moved into the Yellow Row, and the Kleinmans together because both were Jews; but to Mama the Randowiches were not so much Jews as queer neighbors who lived in her country without speaking its language, who lived in a neighborhood without patronizing its meat market, who considered the Temple Mama had at last got Papa to join as worse heresy than the Catholic Church, which the Kelleys attended, or the Presbyterian Church, to which the Edgewoods belonged. In Randowich eyes looking at the Kleinmans, there was condemnation. In Mama's eyes looking at the Randowiches was contempt.

Papa bowed a little to Mama. He said, "In every family, in every people, there is good. Tonight I will call upon Mr. Randowich. I will welcome him to the neighborhood."

Mama began to stack the soiled supper dishes noisily. "When you come home you will take off your coat on the porch. And shake it."

Papa had scarcely gone to the Randowiches before he returned. He was pale and he coughed and he tapped.

"What is it, Hans?" Mama asked from the kitchen.

At first Papa did not want to talk. His face had grown dusky red as he stood looking out the window into the night

and coughing until at last he took one of the little pills
Mr. Stonecipher, the druggist, had told him might help.

Later, when the dishes were done and the children were in
their bathrobes and ready for good-night kisses, he looked from
one to the other as if he was seeing them from a hilltop, as if they
could not hear him mumble, "I have Marc. I have Freddy. I have
Ruth. I have Bertha."

"Stop that!" Mama shouted to his inattention. "What happened?" She was sewing now and rocking and chewing gum, no
part of herself quiet or unhappy.

"In that household many people live————"

"I knew that," Mama interrupted. "All ugly and dirty and
without manners."

"Though it is late now and dark, they are working. The children as well as the parents, the grandparents and all the others.
Mama, they are poor. We must be kind to them."

"Nonsense! They are poor! We have nothing left in the
purses and we are not poor. They have purses filled with money
and they are poor. You are easily fooled, Hans."

"Only one room has any furniture. The dining room
has a table and chairs, but even in the dining room there are
machines and people stitching. The front room is all machines.
Upstairs, machines. The children sit cross-legged on the floor
and rip. It is like in Europe .... No one smiles. Only works. It
is a sweatshop."

"Sweat, yes," Mama said, refusing to feel sorry for the
Randowiches.

One evening, shortly after Mama announced that they must
attend Uncle Oscar's party, Papa said he was going out, and
going without Mama.

"Where? What are you up to?" she demanded, as if she thought he might have a sweetheart somewhere.

"I will take Marc with me."

They rode three streetcars before they reached the Alps, a restaurant with a bar along one side and a range of cardboard mountains along the other. Between the peaks was a toy train coming around a curve. At another place a toy house half showed. At still another two dolls in peasant costumes were leading a flock of sheep along a path. They were larger than the train and too large for the house, but both Papa and Marc thought the effect pretty.

A waiter rushed up and, talking in German, showed Papa something about his shoes. Papa stooped down and felt at them and looked critical, then proud. In English the waiter said to Marc, "Nobody could cure my poor feet like Mr. Kleinman cured them."

Papa, very solemn, said, "This boy wishes to become a lawyer. Therefore, I must come here to ask of you a favor."

The waiter, who was really Herr Wagner, showed them to a table. Papa said he might bring a stein of draught and for Marc, soda water.

Herr Wagner had a red face and yellow hair which lay in large smooth ringlets all over his head. He was about Papa's size. He wiped off the table and washed it and wiped it again before he set the stein and glass down; then he told Marc to go over to the bar and pick out some sandwiches from those heaped on the big platter. They were free and the corned beef on rye was good, made with lots of butter.

When Marc came back Herr Wagner was saying but of course, of course, Mr. Kleinman was welcome to his suit. Of course, nonsense, he could not pay for it; well, a good cigar if he

wished. Everything would be in order. Ach! Mr. Kleinman better buy himself a tie, else he will look like a waiter. The correct
tie was white, likewise the vest of white piqué, and of course as a
waiter Herr Wagner wore black.

Papa, enjoying the beer, said, "All right, I will buy the tie
and vest. But I prefer to pay rent on the suit."

Then the man talked German again about his feet and his
shoes and how he could not have worked at all if Mr. Kleinman
had not ordered those shoes special for him.

Just before they left Herr Wagner said, "You are welcome to
it. What do you think I am to charge a man I owe so much? Do
you think I am a Jew?"

Outside Papa lamented, "If I tell him I am a Jew he will feel
ashamed. If I don't tell him I am ashamed. Oscar's party! It is
bad already."

The lace collar which Mimi Hursch gave Aurelia to wear to
Oscar's party refused to fit Aurelia's old black dress, no matter
how much it was tucked in or pulled over. Aurelia took the irrec-
oncilables to Mrs. Laurety, who lived in a little house embedded
in a row of small grown-together houses.

At first Mrs. Laurety kept her hands in the huge pockets of
her sewing apron. Then her fingers began to open and close the
scissors which hung from a braid of tape at her side. Then they
stuck pins in and out of the pincushion hanging several inches
above the scissors. At last Mrs. Laurety placed both spread hands
beneath the mound of abdomen as if to support it and thus rest
her back.

She shook her head. "It's old style," she said.

"It's good material," Aurelia countered. "Mrs. Edgewood
sent me."

"She's a saint, if you ask me. Jews for neighbors. Two sets."

Aurelia snatched her dress from Mrs. Laurety's hands. "I'll take my things, please!" she said.

Mrs. Laurety held on. If Mrs. Kleinman took that dress, Mrs. Laurety wouldn't be able to sew another stitch all day. She hadn't meant a thing against the Jews. Her own mother's sister had married a traveling salesman who was a Jew—both dead now, of course—but if it hadn't been for them, Mrs. Laurety wouldn't have had a shirt on her body when she was growing up. They had given her all the fun she ever had in her whole life. Wiping at her nose with a piece of the tissue paper out of Mrs. Kleinman's box, she said her husband gave her a pretty bad time of it with his drinking. Didn't Mrs. Kleinman know how a person said those things, not meaning them but because everybody else said them and so it was something to say when you wanted to keep your own troubles under lock and key? Mrs. Edgewood claimed one family of Jews was nice, the Kleinmans, of course. But the other——

For a moment Aurelia did not know what to say or do. No one could be expected to like the Randowiches.

"The other family is poor," Mama said. "They, too, would like to have furniture. Mr. Edgewood earns good money as a carpenter. I am surprised at Mrs. Edgewood. I don't know the Randowiches, but it is not for Mrs. Edgewood to call them Jews!"

Mrs. Laurety drew the tape tight around Aurelia's waistline and took some other measurements and said, "Leave it to me." She would make the black satin into a fine garment, fine enough for any party, even Uncle Oscar's.

While Aurelia was getting dressed she was glad she had let Mrs. Laurety make the alterations, but as soon as she and Hans entered the Regal Club, she knew that no dress would do if it lacked a train. All the other women, except a few aged great-grandmothers, wore trains. Walking, the women held them up out of harm; dancing, they let them wave by a loop over their little fingers; but standing, they let them swirl on the floor. Always the train was demanding attention and getting it.

In the dressing room the women touched their noses with feathery powder puffs and exclaimed over one another's appearance. Aurelia waited a long time for a chance to get to the mirror. One group would go out, and before she could catch a glimpse another group would be there, saying the same things the last group said. Several looked at her, uncertain whether to speak.

Hans, his sleeves only a little too long, was waiting for her where the steps fanned out into the large entrance hall. On this floor were the card rooms for the men's poker games. Beyond those were kitchen, dining room, and cloakrooms. The decorations were dark, trimmed in gilt, and handsome. The club looked like other clubs in the city which excluded Jews from membership; but the Regal was built by Jews, excluding only those who were Orthodox. The men who built the Regal and supported it were successful in business and German in origin. They were well-dressed men of good name. They and their wives and children went with one another, at times whispering angrily of gentiles who scorned them, and disdainfully of Jews such as the Randowiches whom they themselves scorned.

They saw Hans standing most of the evening at the edge of the foyer near the corner of the second-floor ballroom. His childlike short arms and large thoughtful eyes made him seem younger than he was. He stood very still, like a boy unaware that others might be thinking about him and looking at him. Occasionally his eyes would brighten with pleasure: a couple danced beautifully, the crystal chandeliers laid gleaming rivers across the ballroom floor, or the orchestra made a clever dash for a finale. Once when a waltz was played Hans sought out Aurelia and they bobbed among the dancers like whirling corks, interfering with the large circle glided by the others. Halfway around they stopped.

Aurelia went back to being jolly with the old ladies. Proudly they told about their grandchildren, though conceding that the way their parents lived spoiled them; the children these days got everything they wanted. *"Alle yiddishe kinder ..."* they would say, not finishing the sentence whose conclusion all knew, because to finish it would remind them that most Jews in the world were poor and suffered bad times. Surely a fine affair like this should not be saddened by prayers for less fortunate Jewish children.

Frequently during the evening Clara, her cheeks rosy with excitement, came to see how Aurelia and the old ladies were enjoying themselves. She would sit down for a while and quote bright bits said elsewhere in the hall and ask if she could send them punch or wine. When she left she always said she had to go to attend to someone. After a while they would see her dancing and they would agree that she was an excellent hostess.

Mimi came only once, but she stayed for four dances. She took off her satin pumps, hid them under the couch, and wrapped her stockinged feet in her train. She made Aurelia leave the old ladies and come with her to a long settee against the wall. She said Hans and Aurelia ought to take dancing lessons, that Hans might be a *Schlemihl* in business but he was all right in evening clothes.

Mimi told Aurelia not to care a snap about a train. Aurelia looked fine from the waist up, and the others looked fine only from the waist down. She would trade with her and quickly if she could. Dresses were temporary mistakes, but a long nose like her own and kinky hair, what on earth could be done about that? By the time Mimi left, Aurelia felt better, except when she recalled that Mimi had referred to Hans as a *Schlemihl* in business.

As soon as the orchestra played "Pomp and Circumstance" everyone went downstairs to supper. It was midnight and the dancers were hungry.

Aurelia ate the lobster, all of it, but Papa, across the table, could see that it was as if only Aurelia's body was having pleasure. His own Aury, the gay little chatterer who spoke her thoughts in turn as she thought them, was not there. The quick-eyed woman with the pretty comb and lace collar was a woman who said nothing because she sat, a stranger, at a family feast.

These others, the great jolly family, laughed a great deal, teasing one another about amusing episodes, needing only half a phrase. All would laugh because all were acquainted with the whole phrase and the whole episode. They knew everything, if not the rock which lay at the center of the character, at least the many habits which jutted from the rock.

This was the intimacy and the identity of family life, lived beneath a canopy of concern for the welfare of all and for each within the all. In Papa's eyes some of it seemed overintimate, leaving a man's life too naked; but the penalty paid earned something. No family in this group would ever be left jobless; no man or woman would hunger or, if bereaved, sit alone. No man need fear for the loneliness of his child, born into a clan, marrying there, never having to stand by himself against a tempest. Well, Hans Kleinman, is it more important to sit home and read Goethe?

Arguing it with himself, he argued also with Marc. Manhood was stirring within the boy, stretching out limbs, converting dreams into purpose.

"I am separating Mama from her brothers."

"Uncle Carl and Uncle Oscar come here lots."

"They are dutiful men. They will go outside their lives to perform a duty."

"They are more polite to you, Papa, than to each other."

"They envy me. I can see them asking themselves many times: 'Has a man the right to live his own life as he pleases?' "

"I have heard Uncle Carl shout at Uncle Oscar, 'A man *has* the right to live his own life.' I have heard him say those very words."

Hans's cigar pointed toward the ceiling. "That is what he shouts, but what he does is what he really believes. Carl lives neither his own life nor Mimi's, nor even Oscar's. He is trying to do what he believes America requires of every man—to become a success."

Marc had to wait for Papa's thoughts to come back.

"In America, what is needed? What is required of a man by his times? Science knows how to make life easy for every man, to satisfy his hunger, to give his wife a fine home, to permit him to drive his children across our wonderful land, tiring not even a horse. Someone must be the *Schadchen* between science and the people. *Schadchen* in the old country is the matchmaker, the marriage broker, who for a price brings about a marriage. The go-between. Well, businessmen must do that, men like Carl and Oscar———"

"Papa, it's money they're after."

"That is only the candy with which the times fool them. They are *Schadchens* between science and the people. I know it looks different, even to them. But that is what it is."

How like Papa, Marc thought, to see even that which hurts him in its noblest light! A man might be a lesser man, but he would have a better chance in the world if he saw that which hurt him as something hateful.

It was in that moment, that Marc thought, On Monday morning when I go to high school I must decide which course to take, the College if I am to study law, or the General if I am to work all my life for Uncle Oscar ....

Then Papa would see and choose and end this looking into nothingness. Papa would have to decide.

On the day of Hans's visit Oscar had begun the morning genially. Then all the jovial good humor disappeared in a flash of distaste. A letter written to him contained a phrase which implied more than it said.

The man who wrote the letter, of course, was a tactless fool, a spokesman for snobs who were Oscar's competitors and cursed his days with their preference for Christians. It went round and round in his head painfully.

In the next instant he was shrieking at an employee carrying boxes awkwardly and with every likelihood of dropping them. Oscar strode across the office through the swinging gate, leaping out with such abruptness that a box fell. He pulled the remaining ones from under the man's arms and angrily stacked them between the chin and hands.

"This way! This way!" he bellowed. "The customers of Hursch and Company want goods in perfect condition. This way you will hold them in the future. This way!"

Then he stooped and opened wide the box which had fallen. Not one of the glass Christmas-tree ornaments had survived. Oscar had never liked carrying these holiday specials which were not furniture. He threw the balls singly toward a nearby trash container. They smashed and scattered and he screamed a loud reproof at another employee who should have been calling the porter and his broom.

For a while Oscar was purple and then white, a short man puffed with rage. Hans Kleinman stood watching him. Oscar knew Hans had come at last for a place in Hursch and Company. The sad serenity in the round blue eyes added to Oscar's fury.

To have those eyes staring calmly at these outbursts ... With his feet still spread as they had been while he threw the glass balls, Oscar ran his hand down his face, wondering in the moment of blackness whether he would ever, ever be able to manage Hursch and Company without these sudden furies. There was a cycle to them: sudden anger, then shouting, sarcastic reprimands meant to terrorize employees into action; after that, a cellar-to-roof inspection, caustic with denunciations merited as well as unmerited. Later his shame would pretend to be pride, an era prolonged over several days during which he would brag to Clara how he had put life into this man or that, brought order out of the chaos of this department or that, initiated a change which he had indeed been pondering for some time. The hot fury of his flashes did melt problems which had before seemed fixed. They did indeed improve Hursch and Company.

The era of peacemaking came last. The man who dropped the boxes was father to a son who longed for a bicycle; the boy received the bicycle as a gift from Oscar Hursch. The man who should have called the porter had an invalid wife who received bottles of wine known to have tonic qualities. Reveling in his benevolence, Oscar glowed with good humor and gave again and again until in the eyes around him he saw forgiveness. Then he felt good and could accept the invitation of the Merchants' Club with conspicuous indifference to their intended honor and with equally conspicuous indifference to their implied insult. Since he had never observed the causal connection between the slight he sustained and the temper he displayed, he held only himself, not the Merchants' Club, accountable for the episode. By the time he went to the luncheon he went admiringly. Obviously these were superior men, and Oscar Hursch could go into their presence gratefully.

But in this moment of seeing Hans's serenity there was no gratitude in Oscar's heart, only the need to hurt. He shouted that he was busy and pointed to the chair upon which Hans could wait.

The office was an open one where Oscar's conferences and interviews and signings were clearly visible. Obvious also was Oscar's intention to keep Hans waiting for a long time. He moved to a chair nearer the window and, drawing a small volume from his pocket, settled down to read. He neither saw Oscar now nor heard his voice, hoarse with self-commiseration or shrill with castigation.

Oscar could not so easily shut out Hans Kleinman. That he sat there calmly reading, complacently sure of a job, was infuriating. That he changed from the chair designated for him was an affront.

Oscar ordered him in. He did not ask what Hans wanted, but as if in masked apology began to state his own troubles—the stupidities of his employees which had to be eradicated.

"They wonder why they don't get ahead. I rush from morning till night. I have no time for idle talk—and reading."

It was a rebuke.

Hans replied, "That I have seen. It is why I preferred to work less hard, but now the children are growing up. Marc wants to go to college."

"And very likely you have lost your job."

Hans was surprised. "No, I have resigned. Mr. Kemper offered me more. I preferred to see what you had to offer."

"A man shouldn't resign his job until he has another."

"Mr. Kemper thought it courteous. He said so."

Now Oscar felt rebuked. "What can you do?" he asked with a cynical smile.

Hans looked past Oscar's ear out into the shopping arena. Customers were still staring curiously at Oscar for his show of temper.

"I could make suggestions."

"Suggestions!"

"A wall around this office."

"How can I manage the store if I don't see what goes on?"

"You would look down at your desk at the report of sales. By that you would judge. Not by how a man stacked boxes."

"Hans, you have no right to speak to me like that! You should speak with respect———"

"I have respect for the way you feel inside, Oscar. A big man like Oscar Hursch should not bother about box stacking, only about sales."

They sat in silence, the fat features of Oscar's dark lean face contorted with feeling. He tossed his pencil onto his desk. "Anybody can see that what you say is true. Anybody. It is nothing. I have no wall because I am Oscar Hursch. It's the way I do things. But I've built the largest trade in the city." He smiled, again sure of himself, superior. "What else can you do? Besides make suggestions?"

He was already converting what Hans had said into a satirical story to tell Clara: " 'I could make suggestions.' 'Unfortunately we have no Suggestion Department.' *Hans Kleinman, Head of the Hursch and Company Suggestion Department* would look well on stationery! 'I could make suggestions!' But, Clara, think of it, my own brother-in-law talks such nonsense!"

"I can sell goods. I get along with my customers. They come back."

Now Oscar reached a short arm for a pencil. "Carl can use you. I'll give you a note."

Carl, showing Hans around the Midtown, lamented, "Most of the stuff is *meshofes*."

"Trash," Hans translated to Marc, who had followed them.

"It's what the *Schwarzes* want."

"They are poor," Hans said.

"The yokels go for *meshofes* too."

Carl resembled Oscar but was thinner and less angry. Now his eyes were clouded with discontent. "If I had Oscar's money—— If I was head of a firm, I'd sell only the finest merchandise. I wouldn't carry *meshofes*. Only the best." As he spoke he banged his fist down on a table. It shivered under the impact. "See what I mean, Hans?" With both hands he gripped the sides of the table and bore down on it until the legs leaned at crazy angles. "See? *Meshofes*." Looking contemptuously at the table, he was looking contemptuously at Oscar and Oscar's dominance over his life.

Hans coughed a little. He gazed out the window at the uneven roofs of the poor, united by the haze of smoke pouring from their flues. He watched a trolley car swaying and bouncing as it descended a hill.

"To go downtown costs five cents."

"That's the hell of it," Carl conceded. "Any yokel with a dime to spare goes downtown. We get only those who are hard up. And the kikes and the *Schwarzes*."

Carl rushed off to carry the broken table out of sight, Marc helping him.

A salesman came weaving his way through the aisles of furniture offered for sale. He was followed by a Negro boy. The salesman swung two rockers into position for sitting, naming the price of each. The costlier was a sturdy plain piece; the other had a meretricious prettiness. It was as flimsy as the table Carl had broken.

The boy kept looking at the sturdy rocker, sitting in it, and rocking with one foot as motive force, the other held high as if in imitation of a woman he had seen rock in such a manner.

"She sure would like it fine," he said.

The salesman asked, "How much you got?"

The boy handed him a paper sack filled with dulled coins: dimes, nickels, pennies, one half dollar, three quarters.

The salesman counted it. "That all you got?"

"Yes, sir."

"Then you gotta take this one." He teetered the red rocker.

"Is it—is it—right strong?"

The salesman frowned; then he patted the boy on the shoulder. "You buying this for your granny, you said?"

"Yes, sir."

"She'll like it. It's not as good as the other, this walnut wing, you understand, but she'll like it."

The boy surrendered his coins.

"Twenty-five cents extra to deliver."

"I'm aiming to carry it, sir." He leaned forward and, with the red rocker half on his head, half on his back, walked through the crowds of the Midtown.

When Carl and Marc returned they found Hans coughing, his face purpled, his fist at his chest. He motioned to them to go away. Out the window he was watching a red rocker weaving through the sidewalk crowds.

Explaining to Hans how to read the price tags, Carl said, "Each letter represents a number." Angrily he added, "It had to be in German, of course. So my salesmen have an excuse for making mistakes."

"That was Oscar," Hans said.

Carl nodded.

At times Hans was a good salesman; at other times he would say to customers, "We have nothing for you. Yes, this is a bed, but it will come apart."

If they were meek and disappointed and while fingering their money showed that they were really fingering hard work and dreams, Hans would stand very straight and say, "Nothing for you today. Nothing."

If they argued and turned angry he would show them everything, naming prices, offering no information, taking their orders without a thank you.

In the midst of such a day, bearded old Grandfather Randowich, wearing his skullcap and long coat, came to buy a rug.

Hans said, "How much have you?"

Mr. Randowich replied, "How much is it, so?"

Coughing, Hans led the old man to the stack of rugs. He sat down and told Mr. Randowich to sit down too.

"Rugs are pretty colors. They also are hard-wearing or flimsy. You must buy not only pretty colors but also a rug which will last . . . ."

Mr. Randowich shook his head and shrugged his shoulders, then he spread his fingers and hissed a speech at Hans. Hans was an American, not even a Jew, and therefore knew nothing. For what did a man work hard? For rugs? Did Hans think Yessel Randowich was a child? To work and make his children and grandchildren work late into the night in order to buy a rug which would live longer than they would?

Suddenly the face between the beard and skullcap became creases and wrinkles and smaller wrinkles. The dark eyes moistened with laughter. The stiff, righteous patriarch was a jolly, beautiful man.

Hans laughed, too, and stiffened his shoulder against its desire to shrug as Mr. Randowich's shoulder had shrugged.

"Perhaps you do not wish new things at all."

The hand tugged at the beard. The eyes now were deep, staring eyes. Yessel Randowich spoke rapidly, resorting to Yiddish now and then but always repeating in half English.

With his Jewish father's Jewish blessing on his head, he, Yessel Randowich, had left Russia where Jews were shot by the Czar's hirelings for nothing more than praying Jewish prayers and eating Jewish food. And here what did he find? He had come to America where Jews, though free at last to be Jews, neither prayed Jewish prayers nor ate Jewish food. Ate *trefa* and prayed not at all. Ach! Ach! He went on with his story....A pogrom. His father. His mother. One sister. Two brothers-in-law. Their children. All dead.

The survivors, one family at a time, Mr. Randowich had brought to the land of the free. The young first. He had just sent for the last Randowich. His brother and brother's wife, old like Mr. Randowich himself, and childless because in the attempted revolt of 1907 his brother's sons had lost their lives. Old, and sons dead. To leave dead sons in Russia and come to America was not easy, but better than staying in Russia.

Soon they would be here. Mr. Randowich would make them welcome. Mr. Randowich and wine and cakes—yes, and a rug.

"Ach! Ach!" he concluded. "Rug for welcome." He shrugged.

Hans stuck to his point. "With the last Randowich here, you will not have to send for more Randowiches. You can make your house nice, like an American house. A rug——"

The old man was talking rapidly, twisting and twitching and talking. After one had saved his own, did he not save others? Palestine was the Jewish homeland. Jews eating Jewish food, praying Jewish prayers, living like Jews....

"I am a Zionist," he said harshly.

"You are an—ist," Hans said angrily. "I will send you this rug." He laid his hand on the top one.

"Show what you have."

"I show nothing," Hans answered. "Either you want a nice rug or you don't. If you don't, the top one or any one will do."

They argued, and at last Hans turned back a few rugs to the red one Mr. Randowich wanted. As soon as he saw the color he said yes, this would do.

It was true that Mr. Randowich bought thinking only of Palestine.

Telling Marc about it, Papa tried to be fair. "Six points on a star, that is important to him. At least the man cares about something besides his own confort.... Marc, the American businessman, as I told you once, is playing *Schadchen* between science and the people. A good *Schadchen* rushes back and forth. He goes to the home of the girl, to the home of the young man. He knows both households well—but these *Schadchens*, these American businessmen, they rush back and forth, but they do not go inside. They are too comfortable for *Schadchens*. They sit in soft chairs and eat good food and——"

"What would you have them do, Papa?"

"Study science. Study the people too. Think of others, as Mr. Randowich thinks of others. He may be Orthodox, but he is not a bad man."

Papa reached into his pocket and drew out a small book with a shiny, stiff cover. In it were pressed flowers mounted above Hebrew writing. "He sells these for the benefit of Palestine. I do not want to go there. I do not believe in Zionism."

"Why did you buy it, Papa?"

"At least the man has faith. That is something. He may be right. Who can tell? Just because I don't need Palestine, being fortunate enough to be an American, others less fortunate may."

Coming from deep sleep to a misty daze, Marc did not open his eyes, only turned in his bed, remembering that his leg muscles were sore because he had worked all day and then danced nearly every dance at the high school prom. Pushing the covers away from his neck, he heard a sound and became aware that it was that which had awakened him. Papa still pacing the floor as he had been pacing when Marc came home!

He got out of bed, dragging a blanket around his shoulders, tiptoeing through the lightless house, and found Papa as he had supposed, with his fist tapping at his sternum.

"I was about to go up," Hans said guiltily, peering down at his watch; then he sighed and with his thumb clicked the lid closed. "Nearly three. Mama must be asleep."

Marc pretended not to see his father's worry. With a comic gesture he wrapped the blanket, Indian-wise, around his body. "Heap much cold."

Hans paced again. "To sell good shoes is one thing. To sell trash—*meshofes*—— It sticks here." He motioned toward his chest.

"Mamie Lee likes Uncle Carl's store. She can get what she wants at a price she can pay."

"She is throwing away her hard-earned money."

"Poor people have to buy things too."

"Correct."

"They can't pay high prices."

"Correct."

"If Uncle Carl doesn't sell trash, someone else will."

"Correct. Lots of others do." Hans sat on the edge of the chair, his hands on his knees, straight-armed, as if to push the knees away. "It is all correct.... Yet it is not right."

"You cannot change it."

"Correct also."

"People have always been poor——"

Now Hans leaped up. "That's it. It is no longer necessary for people to be poor."

"We, too, are poor."

"Not like that, Marc. We eat enough. We have a nice house. We are not really poor. We just have nothing to waste. Being poor is different. No one here is poor as peasants are poor in Europe. No one. Not even the Randowiches—not even Mamie Lee...."

"So?" Marc's eyes asked Hans if somehow now at this point he could not find peace.

Hans answered, "In this country even the Negroes know they have the right to live decently. That is a fine idea. Very fine. Rockers are not only for kings."

"Are you going back to Mr. Kemper?"

"What nonsense are you talking?"

"If you're going to work for Uncle Carl, then what is all this about, Papa?"

Hans looked around the dim room at the bookcase, at the mantel with Mama's fan, at the ebony screen. "It is not a rich man's room nor yet a pauper's. You are a good boy, Marc. You will be a kind man. You will have no one to help you, to give you a start. You have the misfortune to have a father who is—is———"

Marc, waiting to turn out the light until Papa had put a match to the gas in the bathroom, saw that Hans Kleinman walked up the stairs like an old man. Yet Papa was only forty, not eighty like old man Randowich.

On a Saturday afternoon Oscar made one of his surprise visits to the Midtown. He plunged in, well-dressed, well-groomed, red-cheeked with hurry. His dark eyes flickered everywhere, penetrated everything. He was like a hunter who stands in a meadow seeing neither the soft colors of the grasses nor the grace of the trees, so intent is he upon finding that which he has come to kill.

Oscar Hursch had come to seek out Carl's mistakes. Walking through the first-floor aisles, he angrily straightened chairs so that the row was precisely even, slapping them into position so that the salesmen heard and saw and trembled. In the elevator he showed the man how to pull the rope so that the landing would be more accurate.

On the second floor the crowds were smaller. Oscar spied little groups of customers not being served. They were looking at price tags, trying couches, waiting. At the edge of the department some salesmen stood looking for customers.

Oscar rushed up to one of the waiting groups. The customer he approached was a Negro who said he was waiting for

Mr. Kleinman, and only Mr. Kleinman would do. Oscar swung around to a Negro woman with a grown daughter at her side. They, too, were waiting for Mr. Kleinman. And the next. And the next. All were waiting for Mr. Kleinman. Hans, himself, could be seen showing a coal stove, intently examining the accuracy with which the tin pipe fitted into the oval iron opening. An entire family formed a semicircle, breathless for his verdict.

A curious feeling of weakness akin to extreme fatigue took possession of Oscar's body. He no longer was a hunter. His former anger urged him to berate the inept salesmen and ask: "Why don't they want you? Why do they prefer my brother-in-law, Hans Kleinman?" But he pushed his anger from him for the time being. This was an important business situation which had to be analyzed. On his capacity to analyze and then act, Oscar Hursch had built a successful business; his thinking became as sure-footed as a cat walking fence tops.

When he saw Hans writing down an order and saying good-by to the customers, Oscar, smiling genially, strolled with the slow pace of affability toward Hans, ready to congratulate him.

"Well ... Hans ..."

"Hello, Oscar," Hans replied in absent-minded tones. "Hello." He walked on toward the Negro woman and grown daughter. Obviously he was not awed by the visit of Oscar Hursch.

Turning on his heel, Oscar left the Midtown.

When Carl learned that Oscar had been in the store and had not looked him up he said, "Now what? Now what?"

Marc, whose Saturday duties included listening to Uncle Carl's complaints about Uncle Oscar, put down the column of figures he was checking and said, "He was here. Papa saw him."

Then Carl was angry at Hans, as Oscar so frequently was at Carl. "Why didn't your father say something? Is he too good to inform me what is happening in my own store?"

"Papa was busy."

Carl started to say something, but Hans Kleinman's remarkable sales could not be scoffed at, even in his absence. Certainly not to Marc, always abruptly defensive where his father was concerned.

Carl slumped down in his desk chair, idly tapping a pencil at his knee, wondering by what magic the Kleinman children were respectfully devoted to their parents while his own Emil and Charles and David were chronically impudent and untrusting.

CHAPTER V

CLARA'S DINNER HAD been a great success, and now everyone sat
back proclaiming delightful discomfort. They had eaten too
much, but the food, as always, had been delicious, the soup
thick and flavorful, the roast juicy and properly browned, the
Schnecken bursting with pecans and citron and raisins.

Oscar, at the head of the table, had played the good-natured
host with scarcely a trace of irritability intruding into his telling of jokes. Fräulein had brought Alice, charmingly dressed,
into the room for the properly brief appearance before her aunts
and uncles. The young girl had made her *knix* very gracefully,
with a dip neither too high nor too low, and with almost no
awkwardness.

The talk now was of Rabbi Schau. Oscar praised the rabbi as
an emissary of good will in the community. His Sunday-morning
lectures were attended by non-Jews as well as Jews. He spoke
only on issues of concern to the entire city, never narrowly, on so-
called Jewish problems, thus showing the Christian world that
the best Jews of the city were not clannish, except in so far as
the snobbishness of gentiles forced them back upon themselves.
Wisely Rabbi Schau never looked directly at the walls ghettoing
his congregation, but beyond them, at the sky and distant towers
against the sky.

"Thank God he no longer holds Friday-night services," Carl said jovially. He slapped Mimi on the back. "My *Frau* prays for me on Saturday morning——"

"Coming in at the last minute!" Clara laughed.

"How about you?" Mimi countered, and then the women agreed that it was impossible not to be late to Saturday services, what with the necessity to market first.

Oscar declared it was an insult to Rabbi Schau for them to come after the services started, an insult the rabbi had mentioned more than once; he was ashamed if his family, too, was guilty.

Mimi giggled and made eyes at Oscar, whose face betrayed that he both liked and disliked her. She was never properly respectful to him, yet her irreverence, when directed elsewhere, was amusing enough. Witty, gay, jet-eyed, Mimi was not the dignified lady his Clara was, but her coquetry was flattering, and Oscar saw clearly that he, as a burdened man, at times needed beguiling. Now Mimi teased, "And which of the Hursch men prefers Temple to chicken livers?"

Into the hearty laughter the women tossed their comments on the delicacies to be had at the Greenland Market only on Saturday mornings. Both Mrs. Hursches shopped there; all Mann sisters married to non-Hursches also shopped there. Of the ten women present, all but Aurelia Kleinman, who lived too far away, bought from Mr. Greenland and to keep peace gave to his Lutheran Church and put up with Gabby, his delivery boy, who never failed to leave his horse where it could nibble foliage, or to dump his baskets on the kitchen table, ruining tablecloths wherever he went.

Laughing with Mimi, Oscar knew but did not admit that he was among those who loved chicken livers more than services.

FANNIE COOK

Mischievously Mimi said, "Friday night is the proper time for Temple you know."

They agreed, however, that Friday-evening family dinners were too delightful to renounce; surely a fine family such as this had to come together, and Friday night was convenient for everyone.

Mimi declared, "Temple doesn't mean a thing to me, not a thing. I go for Carl's sake."

Then one after another of the Mann sisters declared that the Temple was as nothing in their lives except as a proof of their family loyalty, a place to go to say prayers for dead parents or grandparents, to meet cousins who otherwise, alas, would not be met for weeks at a time.

Old Mrs. Mann looked with indulgent, moist eyes at one after another of her daughters and at her sons, Milton and Henry. She straightened the ring her husband had given her fifty years ago and said, "To stick together is what counts. Stick together and you won't need strangers, not even the rabbi."

Oscar, trying to defend the Temple, said that Rabbi Schau was a scholar worthy of respect.

Mimi rose and imitated the rabbi reading prayers, nearsightedly holding his book against the end of his nose, peering above it, frowning at the tiptoeing late-comers.

"He can't possibly see who it is coming in late. Not possibly."

They laughed and rose, the women following Clara into the parlor for coffee, the men following Oscar into the den, where the butler would serve port and pass cigars. The front doorbell rang. A half-dozen laughing couples—cousins and near cousins—were arriving. Hursch-Mann dinner parties circulated week after week from one household to another, and extra relatives who could not be accommodated for dinner came for after-dinner coffee.

Offering a chair, Uncle Carl would say, "Here, have X25," which had been the Hursch and Company code number while it was still in stock. Sometimes the women, changing places in a room, would say, "I'm going to R41," smiling proudly as they proved that they, too, could participate in the rites of Hursch and Company.

The two dozen men in Oscar's study smoked cigars and listened as Oscar reported his trip. He had just returned from New York, where everyone was feeling better now that the depression of 1907 was well back of them and never again would a depression so devastating be permitted to occur. The talk in the East was of expansion, improved machinery, laws against sweatshops, and whether the public could be made to take a reasonable stand against something called Parcel Post. If the United States Post Office was to side with those anarchistic firms which called themselves mail-order houses, what would happen to honest, solid businesses where a customer could come in and see what he was buying?

Oscar leaned forward and began to whisper. "It makes a man ashamed to be a Jew. Of course it's the Polish Jews again, or the Russians, but all Jews will be blamed. Mail order. And time payments. And they won't listen to reason. I met one on the train. I told him it would be resented."

Henry Mann said, "Nonsense, Oscar. You're too sensitive. Gentiles are opening time-payment businesses and mail-order firms too."

Oscar looked up at Milton, who stood with his back to the gas-log fire. "The Jews will be the ones who get the blame," he said curtly.

Then Milton Mann spoke. He was elegantly made, as if Nature had created him in order to display her ability to combine strength and delicacy within the same human frame. He was slender and tall and graceful, his mannerisms those of a cynic. He chuckled before he spoke. "If they make only a little money they will be called Jews. If they make a great deal they will be called merchant princes."

In the parlor the women wove the threads of their housewifery into a firm family fabric. They told one another what they had bought and where. Clara, with her usual efficient kindness, wrote numerous copies of the addresses of the New York stores from which Oscar had brought presents: the lovely bronze reading lamp with green glass shade in their bedroom, delicious Nürnberg *Lebkuchen* and excellent cheese, Swiss naturally, and fine lengths of cloth for dresses Fräulein would smock for Alice.

Mimi agreed to write the letters, and if the others wanted to add their orders to hers she would order for them too. The women, except Aurelia, ordered lamps and cakes and cloth of the same kind. In each household the Hursch and Company furniture and bric-a-brac were so similar that a Mann or Hursch immediately felt at home. The men liked it, and the women frequently were permitted luxurious purchases by simply stating, "Clara bought one, and of course the others will be ordering."

That Aurelia did not order at this time was in its own way merely showing proper deference to the mores of The Clan. The Kleinmans had agreed to move into a new house now that Hans was earning more, and all the Hursches and Manns and Mann cousins and the cousins of cousins would be sending *Hausgeschenks,* presents like those to be found in their own homes, which had been presents, in turn, from other members of the family. It was part of the weaving back and forth of the shuttle of kinship.

Now they asked Aurelia about the new house and she said they had nearly decided on one.

"In a nicer neighborhood," Clara commented, "near all of us."

"The people in the Yellow Row are nice too," Aurelia said. "But the new neighborhood is—well, better."

Mimi laughed. "We can keep an eye on you Kleinmans. It's better for us too."

Meeting Mimi and Clara to look at the house, Aurelia was at first a giddy young girl. Loneliness had surrounded her ever since the twins entered school, for it was then that she began to notice that she had no card club, no Temple Club, no relatives close by to draw around her as others did, shawl-like, to warm their aging shoulders.

The Hursches had grown up in a small town which did not expect its young to remain. Midway in age between Oscar and Carl, Aurelia had come to the city as Hans's bride about the time her brothers were getting a start, assiduously relearning what their parents had forgotten of Jewish customs, and eventually marrying the wealthy, beautiful Clara Mann and the stylish, witty Mimi Meyer. Aurelia loved Clara and Mimi as much as she could. She learned that intimacy among married women began with the ability to shop in the same places for the same things, and that, of course, was determined by how much a woman had in her purse, by the way her husband wished to live.

But now, suddenly, Aurelia was being rushed by the sorority which was The Clan. Clara's enthusiasm was gracious acceptance of Oscar's desires in the matter; Mimi's expressed the mild fondness of a casual heart.

Flushed and pretty in a brown dress which made her eyes browner and her cheeks pinker, Aurelia was nearly as overcome with embarrassed joy in the presence of the new house as she had been when Hans proposed.

Daintily Mimi and Clara wrinkled their noses against the odor of new plaster and fresh varnish. To Aurelia those were smells as rich and lovely as the lilacs she would plant and the honeysuckle vine that she would try to transplant from the old house.

Her joyous heels tapped from room to room. Her mind fluttered plans all over the house.

Mimi teased, "If you move Hans's chair downstairs again I shall die of exhaustion."

Clara said yes, it really belonged upstairs in the sitting-room half of the bedroom. "The alcove for your bed, the chair there near the grate."

Aurelia loved the alcove. It was the feature of the house which made it different. Otherwise the house was like many others, not nearly so large as Mimi's, which in turn was much smaller than Clara's, but similar to some lived in by distant cousins.

In every detail of arrangement and trimming, too, the house made obeisance to its betters. Though it could not rival, it could and did extol. Clara said it really was right for the Kleinmans, ever so much better than that box they were in. If the third floor seemed hot even now in spring, the maid might not mind. Time enough to worry about that in midsummer. Aurelia should get rid of Mamie Lee and get a full-time girl, white, of course, since she would sleep on the place. Clara would ask Eileen, though Eileen, nice as she was otherwise, was horrid about recommending. Never yet had she recommended a friend, though there must be other girls in her home town who wanted work.

The house had a pantry; hereafter for birthdays Aurelia would receive parts of a set of decent china. A nice pantry and a closet in each bedroom. She would need a girl to stay with the twins at night, because from now on Hans and Aurelia would be going wherever The Clan went, and giving dinners too.

"The rent may be too high," Aurelia said. "I'll ask Hans——"

Clara spoke up quickly. "Let Oscar see about it."

Both Mimi and Aurelia could tell by Clara's tone that she thought Oscar would be better able to handle a landlord, and besides, if the rent was too high for Hans's salary, something could be arranged. Clara was integrating the Kleinmans into The Clan with energetic attention to details.

As they were about to leave, while fitting the key into the lock, Clara's regular features tightened irregularly and she said, "Of course, Hans's sales have fallen off. Getting a new house may put ambition—— Well, he'll try harder, doubtless. Not do such strange things——"

"Strange?" Aurelia asked. "How strange?"

Mimi slipped her arm through Aurelia's. She mimicked Carl's voice. " 'Hans forgets a man is in business to make money.' "

"What does Oscar claim he did?"

Mimi shoved in first. "Brought your carpenter neighbor down one Sunday and had him put braces under all the shaky tables and chairs. Sweet, I thought it was, but to a man in business such things sometimes taste sour."

Clara shook her head. "It wasn't businesslike. He didn't even ask permission."

Aurelia defended Hans. "Hans doesn't like people to be disappointed. He paid Mr. Edgewood himself."

"With your spring bonnet, eh, Aurelia?" Mimi teased.

Aurelia straightened her hat. "I like this one," she said.

Mimi laughed. "It's your last chance to choose one you like."

Clara spoke with sober benevolence. "I know a woman who makes over hats. As soon as you're settled we'll see what she can do for that—though the straw——"

Aurelia looked at Clara, at Mimi, even at all the Hursch-Mann women who were not present. She saw that in spring they wore dark blue suits and dark blue hats trimmed in lighter blue.

"Blue isn't becoming to me," she said.

"It's the—the nicest—the most refined color," Clara answered.

Mimi laughed. "You'll learn to like it, Aurelia. You're on the family necklace now. You'll have to match. You can't get off the string. Not now you can't."

"Why should she want to?" Clara demanded.

"This is a lovely house," Aurelia said, walking back to it. "A pretty place for children."

Clara agreed. "When the twins begin to have callers you won't have to be ashamed."

They were down the walk before Aurelia said, "I've never been ashamed of my house."

"It's all right," Mimi said. "Sweet."

"But this is more what you should have." Clara spoke with finality. Then she smiled and took Aurelia's hand in hers. "You're to come home with me for lunch. Eileen promises us something good. Mimi, you're welcome too." Even Aurelia could see that Mimi wasn't and that Aurelia was rapidly becoming Clara's favorite non-Mann female relative.

Although Hursch and Company had no Suggestion Department for Hans to head, Oscar quietly adopted Hans's suggestions.

He would judge Carl's work by his ledgers. Carl, hurt by Oscar's requests to bring his books, sent them one Saturday by Hans and Marc and not to Oscar's store but to his home. He would show that Oscar.

Marc, now a tall boy nearly seventeen, carried the huge books, all but one, which Hans carried to prove he could.

They came after a long day's work at the store and arrived unfortunately when the Hursch household was in a convulsion of pre-guest activity. Mr. and Mrs. Ellinger Lake were coming for dinner.

As if the books were shameful objects, Oscar told Marc to put them quickly out of sight, upstairs. Alice laughed from her throat and said, "Beneath the eaves, Marc. I'll show you. Come."

Marc's presence had performed the miracle of converting a gray-green wraith into an exotically charming coquette. Oscar was amazed at his daughter and annoyed at all Kleinmans.

To be a Kleinman was to be without respect for riches and the rich, without ambition, beyond predictability. This Marc, only a poor boy, only little Hans's son—yet able to set Oscar Hursch's daughter aflame.

Slow anger began to possess Oscar. Anger at people who upset the plans of those above them. With gigantic effort he decided to alter his plans.

"Come," he said to Marc when, with Alice at his side, he reached the landing. "Come. I want to talk to you."

He led the way into the small room called his den. It contained three chairs set at talking angles.

"Marc," he said stiffly, neither seating himself nor inviting Marc to sit, "Carl tells me you work hard. The question is are you like—— The question is—have you ambition? Hursch and Company can use energetic, dependable young men with ambition. You made a good record in high school. That isn't important, but it doesn't hurt. If you want to learn my business, climb the ladder—I can make it a lot easier for you than it was for me. The question is, have you ambition?"

Through the words Marc heard Oscar Hursch's disdain for Hans. The boy bowed an American version of Hans Kleinman's bow of formality.

"I've made my plans. To study law."

"That takes money."

"I've worked Saturdays and vacations and———"

"How much have you? ... Absurd! That is not enough even for one year." The tinkle of Alice's laughter, reaching, reaching for happiness, came to his ears. "I might be willing to lend you———"

The bow again. "You're very kind. If the need arises———"

"If! It has arisen. You talk like your father." The accusation was not lovingly said, as when spoken by Mama.

Oscar demanded that he speak up. What was wrong? Wasn't Oscar Hursch, creator and president of Hursch and Company, good enough to give assistance to a Kleinman?

Marc's feet shuffled against the carpet. He sighed and, effortfully, spoke out at last.

"It might hurt Papa's feelings."

Then Oscar was silent, squeezed mercilessly by iron tongs of jealousy. Dazed, he stared at Marc. At his loyalty. He, Oscar Hursch, a successful man, would give his right arm, or so he mumbled to himself, his right arm for a son who felt toward him as this boy felt toward Hans Kleinman. What was it? Carl's three boys, too, were without respect for their father.

Anger flowed back.

Oscar held in his anger, held it in even later in the hall when Ellinger Lake, arriving early with his wife, was visibly charmed by the Kleinmans, father and son, conspicuously pleased by the very qualities Oscar found infuriating.

It was Mama who decided the Kleinmans should not move out of the Yellow Row. The dishes were in baskets, the furniture wrapped in old bedspreads, the new house scrubbed from attic to basement when she changed her mind.

While Marc was packing Papa's books he told her, "Uncle Oscar hasn't read these.... Yet the other day he spoke of Papa as——" Then he told her what had happened.

Mama dropped the wastebasket of kitchenware she was carrying. "Oscar Hursch said that—to Papa's own son!"

She turned away and began to cry softly. She wiped at her nose with the corner of her apron. "It will be like that. Papa was right. He said everything would be changed. In the new house we will have to live like The Clan. I am a Hursch, not a Mann. Oscar has become a Mann. I am a Kleinman. Not a German Kleinman." She swayed and struggled with the difference between German and American Kleinmans. "I am Hans's kind of a Kleinman. I am not going to be a Mann. Marc, wouldn't it be better if Papa worked for Mr. Kemper?"

"He earns twice as much now."

"And Mamie Lee gets twice as much. And Freddy has a piano. That's all. The purses are still empty. No matter how much Papa earns, they'll be empty. It's the way I am. Marc, don't stand there like a dunce! Would it not be better if Papa worked for Mr. Kemper?"

"Papa was happier there."

"Then why didn't you say so? Stop mussing up Papa's bookcase!" She was already carrying the kitchenware back to the kitchen.

Marc followed her. He was laughing inside as Papa sometimes laughed, trying not to let her see. "The vans are coming in the morning early———"

"You were the smarty who told them to come. You can just tell them not to come."

"Mama, you rented the other house. You paid for a month."

"Go live in it if you want. By yourself."

She had entirely forgotten the new house near the Hursches. She was moving back into the Yellow Row, joyously. All Mama wanted now was activity, any kind, lots of it.

"What is a new house," she demanded of Marc, "if you don't want to live in it?"

When Papa came home, a tired, little man, determined to be patient with the necessary disorder, Mama refused to let him see that it was for his sake that she was renouncing life as part of The Clan.

She scolded at him: "The least you can do is get out of my way. Take a nap before supper—so I can get this place in order again."

"What has happened, Mama? Has the new landlord———"

"What new landlord? I never did like his looks, that stuck-up man. In the Yellow Row we have nice neighbors and a nice landlord. Freddy, quick, hang these pictures. Ruth, bring the ladder. Bertha———"

Papa sat down in the chair Mama was unwrapping and became a taller man but still very tired with white crescents under his eyes. "Mama, you are leaping again," he sighed. "In the morning we are moving and——"

"Some men take no interest in their homes. Why should we move?" She confronted him with dramatic silence, drawing in her mouth, halting the roving of her eyes, her hands straightening the towel turban on her head.

Papa's gaze stared beyond her at what a home means to a man and a man to a home and why Mama, about to move, pretended she was not moving. At last he repeated her question. "Why should we move? The Kleimnans are moving into a new world. It is therefore necessary to move into a new house."

"All right, all right," Mama mocked at him in angry tones. "You can move over with your high-toned Manns. Maybe you can find yourself a high-toned wife over there. The children and I like the Yellow Row. And I like Mr. Kemper's shoe clerk. As soon as this house is in order I'll go down there looking for a husband. 'Mr. Kemper,' I'll say, have you a clerk who would like to be my husband? A clerk who would be a nice papa to my children? Four children, all bad.' "

Then Hans understood. He turned very pale. His hands trembled. And his lips quivered. When tears came to his eyes Mama slapped Marc, who was too big for slapping.

"Hurry," she said. "Carry this stuff back. Freddy, run downstairs and put Mamie Lee's tubs where they belong. You girls, get that table set for supper. Quick!"

Papa's tears need not be seen by his children.

PART II

1911–1917

... one to another with brotherly love ...

ROMANS

CHAPTER I

BECAUSE HANS SAID the day would never be forgotten by any of them, Aurelia wore her best hat and commended Hans for buttoning the white piqué edging into his vest. Marc in a new dark blue serge suit, much too heavy for the steamy September day, saw that to his parents this moment was not only important but also sad.

Though Hans had talked pridefully all these years of Marc's plans for going to the university where he would become an educated man and therefore an American of importance, now under the glassed roof of the shed of Union Station, he seemed only astounded to discern that the dream also contained the anguish of parting. Again and again he murmured, "This is the first night a child sleeps in another city."

Weeks ago Aurelia had cried in dread of the separation, but now she was caught up by the elation of the young men and women who were leaving and became a giggling little woman, her busy eyes enviously watching the fun.

Observing Hans's sorrow, she began to scold Marc. "Don't wait until every shirt is dirty before you send your wash home. And stop all that silly reading———"

Hans interrupted, "Mama, at a university a man reads. He———"

Papa was still explaining when the "A-a-all a-booard" freed Marc.

As the train began the lurching and jerking which would ultimately deliver its passengers to the transfer junction, hot air rushed at Marc's cheeks; cinders sought and found his eyes; soot settled in his ears and in the folds of his neck. From the fields rose in rapid alternation the odor of cabbage gardens, freshly cut wheat, decaying cornstalks.

When the tracks began to follow the Missouri River handsome bluffs rose on the opposite side of the stream, their white draped with greenery trailing from crevices; at the top, trees and bushes; at the base, an inverse repetition upon the water seeming only more bluff.

Marc was completely captivated. Hans had consulted with someone at the public library in order to appraise the scenic advantages of the two routes to Columbia. Freddy, laughing at Papa, had said either train would get Marc where he was going.

Hans answered, "A man does not travel one hundred and fifty miles without trying to see something."

Now Marc felt that he was seeing a great deal and let his mind shape phrases to be put into a letter for Hans so that he, too, might experience the journey.

Marc's seat mate shared his admiration for the landscape. Passing forests, he, too, exclaimed at the beauty of their shadowy depths. At times he compared the scene with the Severn Valley, again with southern France.

Byrn Darrow was the motherless son of a Navy officer. Since babyhood he had been shifted from one school to another—in the Orient, in Switzerland, in Germany, Italy, England—always in order to permit him to spend time with his father, the whole ironically totaling only a few holidays and an occasional week end. "I was suckled at the breast of the multiplication table," he said with airy nonchalance.

Remembering that the younger Manns hurried East to colleges they considered superior to the state university, Marc asked Darrow why he chose Missouri.

"Dad wanted me to know my own country. Said the coast was never the place to learn the ways of a nation. 'Go to the interior,' he wrote, so I took the map."

He sketched one now, showing Marc that Missouri was the middle of the country and the country itself was a vast central slice across the continent. Darrow's stubby fingers placidly tapped a pencil at all this middleness and seemed delighted that it was intensified by the central location within the state of the university town itself.

"Moreover," he said, "at that point exactly, northern plains meet southern hills, becoming neither plain nor hill." He nodded toward the undulating, opulent countryside beyond the window.

Darrow's admiration stirred pride in Marc, making him announce that he was a native of the state, though, alas, he had seen only the city until now.

Rural freshmen crowding into the aisles drawled words oddly elided. The day was "s'hot." Greeting each other, they said, "Hi, there!" or "How ya doin'?" They scrutinized Darrow's tweeds skeptically. Their talk was of weather and crops, pie suppers and quilting bees, of what their fathers did and in what they believed.

Pretending unawareness of their recurring glances, Darrow said to Marc, "The best of school is that a fellow learns to stand on his own feet and let the other fellow stand on his, as if born of no one, bred of no one. Gives everybody an even start."

He let Marc see that what he said summarized a long experience.

Evening had come by the time they reached Columbia. Marc stood alone in the noisy confusion. Only while he was on the train had he learned that it was customary to reserve rooms in advance. His omission did not trouble him; after years of longing and earning he was finally here, that free and glamorous being: a student away from home.

His face was lively with anticipation. Marc was neither homely nor handsome, neither dark nor fair, neither conspicuously tall nor short. His manner was shy; his head was lean and delicately molded; his eyes were hazel in color, large and eager, as if expecting to like what life might offer. When disappointed his surprise showed at once. Then his eyes would cease to be Aurelia's fun-seeking eyes and turn as gently sad as Hans's. People who saw that they had hurt Marc were likely to be irritated by the swiftness of his perception.

With raucous rhythm a circle of brown men shouted, "Cab! Cab! Get your cab! Haul your trunk! Cab! Cab! Cab!"

Other brown men wearing white coats were scattered through the crowd, each a little withdrawn from the fraternity or sorority group he served. Now and then, in response to a gesture or a whistle or his first name commandingly spoken, one would step forward to take charge of a suitcase.

Weaving through the press of people, calling out names of certain freshmen, fraternity men from competing chapters would occasionally converge upon the same newcomer. Then the speed with which the suitcase was seized would win or lose the contest. By jesting side play the colored men made a game of it among themselves, but only surreptitiously, since the fraternities exacted awed fidelity as well as obedience. Sometimes a newcomer had several pieces of hand baggage which disappeared in as many directions, and his own departure would resemble a jolly sort of kidnaping.

Soon the shouting ceased; the train meeters and their captives disappeared; horses could be heard dragging cabs away from the bricked area in front of the station.

Remaining on the platform were solitary young men and solitary young girls frowning at baggage checks, peering anxiously toward trunks pitched from the train and stacked like blocks into a high, uncertain edifice.

Among the last to leave with a fraternity group was Byrn Darrow. Captain Darrow's rank and affiliations made his son a starred prospect on several lists, but Byrn himself had been eyed with only qualified approval by some who regarded his clothes, his accent, his luggage, his short stature as needlessly unlike their own.

As Byrn turned to wave to Marc, the cordial gesture and friendly smile were observed by Bob Reid, a sophomore disgruntled at the moment because he had failed to capture Darrow for the Deltas.

Remembering the Rush Week adage: To get a man, get his friend, he now approached Marc. A room? Well, the way to get a room was to come with him. "Some of the fellows at the house have a list."

This show of friendship was the fellowship which Marc had expected from the campus. He was pleased by it. He would one day extend it to other freshmen. Miraculously a cab was waiting for them.

In the semidarkness Reid surveyed the substitute he was offering Delta and was satisfied. Not bad-looking. Neatly dressed. Good manners. Pocket money, very likely. He planned a phone call to an alumnus in St. Louis, just to find out the usual things. Were this fellow's people prominent or rich? Did they live in a nice neighborhood? What could his family's position do for Delta? Was the guy himself all right? Would a pin on his vest hurt or help the chapter?

The cab was passing houses jovial with song:

"Old Missour-rah
Dear Missour-rah
Dear old Var-si-ty
Ours are hearts that fondly love thee ..."

Marc's fingers drummed on the cab door. "I'd like to try that," he said.

"You play the piano?" Reid asked alertly. He was quick in his movements and in his speech.

"Only that sort of stuff. And dance music."

Reid canceled the call to St. Louis. A pianist was as vital to a chapter as checks from home. Delta's sole musician had graduated last June. If this guy played with a good strong steady beat, his folks could live on the levee in a tent—well, almost. Kleinman was the pearl in the freshman oyster. Reid as a rusher was all right. First-class!

The cab groaned around the curve of the Delta driveway before Marc realized he was being taken to a fraternity house. In his panic he wanted to run away without explanations or good-bys, but energetic, debonair strangers had already seized his mandolin, Papa's gladstone, Mama's box of *Schnecken*, hurrying them between tall, veranda pillars into the massive house.

Marc's fury was at himself. Hatred of himself as a trusting fool. He had been through all this before. He had vowed they would never have another chance at him, and here he was playing the target again.

The other time had been during the first weeks of high school. Those, too, had been lively, fun-loving fellows, the kind Marc himself was, the kind he liked. They had been fine boys with what Mama called nice American manners. They had seemed to adore Marc. He must eat at their table in the lunchroom, sit with them at football games, bring his girl to the dance at the country club. Discovering Marc liked amusing stories, they brought him hilarious bits of their experiences. Then one morning they had hurried past him, raced self-consciously around corners, sat at a different table in the lunchroom . . . .

Hans had said Marc must ask what was wrong, for surely someone had told them an untruth about him. "Marc, you will never own anything more valuable than your good name. You must ask. Only by asking can you clear your name." Trying to believe in Papa's wisdom, Marc had forced himself to ask; his voice had betrayed him with an unforeseen squeak. In return he had been asked a question: "Why don't you eat with the Jewish boys?"

After that he couldn't eat with Izzy Randowich or with any Jewish boys, even those named Stein and Marx and Fox; couldn't listen to their talk of *rishus,* a word meaning hatred of Jews.

It was better to be alone. To go home and pound out tunes on Freddy's piano. Or to read long novels about heroes wanted wherever they went.

After a while Marc began to read anything. Articles. Advertisements. Lists of figures. Anything. Mama would stand and look at him. "You can't fool me," she would say. "You're sitting there doing nothing."

"I'm reading, Mama."

"There's reading and reading."

A terrible race would begin in his mind. He would turn a page, and against his will his sight would scurry wildly around and around, halting only, and then in frozen terror, when it found a *J*. Each *J*-word had to be examined cautiously before the page could be read, lest it be the word *Jew,* waiting to spring its attack. *Just ... January ... June ... Jolly ...* If the *J* was indeed *Jew,* the page was hastily turned.

He had fought the habit and that frantic whirring fear which went with it. In painful battle he had triumphed, but even now when he was tired, it returned. He wasn't going to bare his back again to the dagger of prejudice hidden beneath the cloak of nice American manners.

"Reid," he said, and his voice came to his own ears as a stranger's voice, "I didn't know we were headed for a fraternity house. I——"

"Come—on—in!" Reid's voice was exultant and loud and masterful, his face as eager with anticipation as Marc's had been on the platform. He wouldn't like it if Marc said he knew how fraternities felt about Jews. That would be destroying the cloak.

"You see——" Marc began once more. "I—I—I'll be earning my way—— I ——"

But Reid only pulled him forward. Walking up the steps, Marc thought of Papa. Hans Kleinman had a phrase for this, a way of reminding himself that the current distress was only temporary. A sigh and a phrase: "After all, it isn't a marriage."

The Deltas were able hosts. Even Marc, rigid with resolve not to be ingratiated, gradually eased into the fun. It was witty fun, teasing one another, laughing at last year's pranks; a way of saying: "We were freshmen once, as green as you feel now, as unsure of what to do; and you, one day, will be as we are, and brothers, perhaps, to us and to each other. Lords of the campus. Deltas."

Because the evening was cool for September, they called Zip, the houseboy, to build a fire in the deep hearth. While the leather chairs were being drawn into a wide semicircle Marc spoke to Reid. "I'm leaving now. Thanks a lot. If you'll tell me where my things are———"

Reid's friendly voice silenced the group. His hands had managerial habits, and now they indicated that plans were not to be altered; everyone was to remain.

"Listen, fellows. Don't anyone worry about not having a room. Delta has plenty engaged for you all." With swift thumbings he indicated directions. "Some right on this block. Some on College. Some on Hitt. We engage them every spring in blind names and then turn them over during Rush Week to—to—well, to certain freshmen." He paused, letting them observe that he wouldn't dent Pan-Hellenic rules even by describing those present as rushees. "So don't anyone worry about leaving. We'll look after you. Fact is, there's no way of getting a decent room except through us. And you, buddy"—he turned affectionately to Marc—"you sit right here next to Bob Reid."

The other Deltas stretched on the floor or in the window seat, except a genial, handsome, pipe-smoking senior named Hart Bromage, who stood at the mantel corner relating Delta triumphs. The mantel against which he leaned was crowded with trophies. He reminisced amusingly about them. His riant talk sketched an amiable picture of campus life: Delta supreme in athletics, in good times, in campus politics, above all, in honor. The other fraternities might break rush rules: secretly pledge in advance, see their rushees oftener than allowed, coax freshmen to break dates with other chapters. Well, anyone who wanted to go in for that sort of infamy wasn't a Delta at heart; Delta didn't want him; Delta wanted men of honor; only men of honor could maintain Delta tradition. Delta brotherhood was sacred. Bromage's voice was devout; the faces turned toward his, awed.

The mystic moment was sustained just long enough. Then Bromage, abruptly leaving the mantel, crisply suggested that Gordon and Brooks show the house, especially the freshman rooms, empty of course, until after Pledge Day.

Determined not to go, Marc sat down at the piano and let his fingers find "Old Missour-rah, Dear Missour-rah ..." He played softly. Then with embarrassment he realized that Bromage's suggestion had been made in order to get the freshmen out of the way. There were sounds on the gravel of the side driveway, and now, at the moment when he might have been escaping, there were whispered orders to Zip to help unload the stuff and get it into the Chapter Room closet, and fast. Bromage's voice and Reid's could be heard counting.

Marc kept his head down and played louder. His back was toward the driveway door. He didn't want to know what was going on. When it was over he would insist upon having his things.

Coming back, dusting off his hands, Bromage was amiably triumphant. Now the liquor for the Pledge Banquet—one week from tonight—was in the house and safely locked away. Frowning, he explained to Marc that the town was dry, legally and actually. To have some shipped in was impossible. The trains wouldn't handle it. What a chapter had to do was hire a wagon and drive twenty miles each way, besides paying many times the proper price. But what would a pledge banquet be like without a few toasts?

He lowered his good-humored voice confidentially. "This Zip—damn his black hide—refused to go for it. Some crazy superstition turned him pale...." They laughed at that. "Rush Week isn't the time to fire a houseboy, but let him dare refuse just once more"—Bromage narrowed his eyes and jerked his thumb over his shoulder—"and out he'll go!"

The room was filling again. Reid said, "We owe it to our younger men not to let Zip get by with that sort of thing. Our fellows have got to learn how to give an order and make it stick!"

By way of apology for the unmanliness of accepting Zip's refusal, Bromage belauded his services as a houseboy. Waited table right. Neat—he'd better be. Always there. Hardly ever left the place. Down in the basement sleeping, very likely.

By chance Marc's fingers, toying at old tunes, found one which caused the Deltas to converge upon him, singing, "Delta Brothers Are the Best." Another familiar melody evoked, "Cheer for Delta, Brothers, Cheer!" Another song. And yet another.

Now they were a bunch of fellows with a bunch of gay tunes; and Marc, banging out melodies, was having a good time too. They patted his shoulders praisefully and said he was a great musician. At their insistence he played more Delta songs, then "Old Missour-rah," "For He's a Jolly Good Fellow," and "I've Been Working on the Railroad."

Marc's playing had taken the starch out of the evening, and the Deltas were wild with gratitude. At first Marc had been assigned to Hitt Street, then to College, which was nearer. Now he would be right across the street.

In reply Marc asked, "When a fellow hasn't anybody to help him—how's he supposed to get a room?"

Reid, overhearing, shouted, "What the hell do you care?"

They laughed Marc into a kind of brotherhood.

Thumping out chords, Marc estimated that the pledges would be moving into fraternity houses a week hence. Plenty of empty places after that. If he could just get out of here now without their room, without——

They were greeting someone, a Delta arriving tardily.

Marc remembered Cliff Harkness from high school, a senior when Marc was in his first year. Both had been in the Glee Club, Marc as accompanist.

At first Harkness shook hands with Marc heartily. Then his hand turned limp. His smile frayed into a frown. He looked about in stern bewilderment, searching out Delta eyes, silently asking: Since when does Delta rush a Jew?

In the next instant Harkness's arm was linked through Bromage's. With a plausible excuse on their lips they sauntered toward the back hall. In response to a signal, Gordon left. Then Brooks.

Then Reid, too, disappeared. He came back almost immediately: a fat-faced, scowling, blushing youth, no dance steps in his walk, no pride in his eyes. His voice was thick. He breathed heavily. He told Marc he had been mistaken about the room across the street. But a Hitt Street one was available, though only for the night. He'd walk over with him now, introduce him to the landlady.

The others said again and again that Marc's playing had been swell. Simply swell. He'd have to come again sometime. Perhaps for their Christmas party. Swell of him to help out tonight. Simply swell. Here was his suitcase and his box and his mandolin. Was there anything more? Should they——

The dagger and the cloak. The elegant cloak. Even while wincing under the impact of the dagger, Marc admired the cloak. Yes, Mama, these are nice American manners.

He bowed a little, his father's bow, which was always in a way a bow to himself. Gentle, formal, cold. "Thanks, Reid. I won't need that room. No, I don't want it. Don't come, Reid. I'd rather you wouldn't."

Reid wanted to come. His shoulders twisted; he bit at his fingernails.

Saying good night to the others, Marc called Gordon "Brooks" and Brooks "Gordon," and even he was not sure whether he had done so on purpose, so confusing was the turbulent swirling smashing about within his ears.

The night was cloudy, moonless. When he passed a house he could see, then darkness again. Mostly it was feeling for the narrow sidewalk between the weeds tangling out to snare his feet. An abrupt drop scuffed his shin against his suitcase and nearly threw him on his face, tearing open his anger, pouring out its curses.

Back of him he heard heavy breathing, then saw a white coat. "You're headed wrong. This is the Farm. I have a room for you down at the hotel."

It was the Delta houseboy, and he tried to take the suitcase.

Marc jerked it away, his pride rearing wildly. If this hireling of the Deltas dared ... "Tell them———"

"They didn't send me. I slipped out the back. They don't even know I came." He gave Marc time. "That glow down there, that's Broadway, where the hotel is. This reservation I got on my own. Just as they pick up student rooms, I pick up hotel rooms.

This one I was holding for an alumnus due in on that midnight train. But it's not promised. You can't get anything else at this time of night. Maybe you don't remember me. I'm Orvell Sultan, Mamie Lee's son."

Marc could recall having seen him only once, briefly, years ago. "They called you Zip."

"They're not going to know anything about Orvell Sultan if I can help it. Up in Chicago I ran out of money. I have to have a reserve before I enter law school. Can't get time for reading law any other way. Right now I'm only ten credits short for my A.B. Living in Chicago is high. This isn't anything but a wet old basement room, but it's regular meals and tips, and once the semester gets started, I'll have morning time for studying. My P.O. box is in the name of Orvell Sultan, but at the Delta House I'm Zip."

The voice was different. Back there it had been "Yes, suh, I is," and "No, suh, I ain't." It was still softly Southern, but it spoke grammatically and with the intonation of a college student.

He was telling now about his refusal to fetch the liquor. "Seems to me I can't afford to go against the law. Not if I'm going to practice someday. The law is the reasonableness of a country, the place a man can turn for justice, the thing a man can count on. Way I figure it, when the Deltas have law-breaking to do, that they can do for themselves. I'll black the boots and scrub the floors and pass the platters, but that's all."

Marc heard it and lost it and heard it again. Those last moments at the Delta House kept returning. Marc Kleinman was a throbbing throat, a great weariness in the thighs, his will distant, trying to bring the parts of himself together again.

Nearing the lofty, street-corner lamps of Broadway, Orvell whispered, "You got to let me carry that suitcase. This is the South. We can't walk together like this. And you can't go alone.

Night clerk's crooked. He'll charge you double unless you're with someone who knows the rates."

Marc tried to ask what sort of hotel it was, what the cost of a room was, but the pieces of himself were still strewn about. His question came out: "Ever stopped there?" He was aware of its absurdity before it was fully said.

Orvell wheezed a long laugh. "Reckon you don't know Columbia. Reckon you don't know St. Louis. Reckon you don't know Chicago. That hotel's only a dump. A tenth-rate dump. But they don't want Orvell Sultan there, not any more than the university does."

The dim lobby was empty except for two salesmen comparing notebooks. Orvell moved to the desk quickly, tapped the bell for the night clerk, looked around at Marc, and motioned toward a chair. Then he retreated to the back wall, stood with his hands folded, a dark V against the white coat.

The night clerk arrived, buttoning his collar, tightening his tie. His eyes were red and his hair mussed. Coming swiftly, Orvell leaned far across the counter. Marc caught the word Delta.

When the clerk went away to consult his lists Orvell whispered, "I have to make these reservations in Delta's name, but you're not beholden. They never heard of this one. Say, don't go letting those Deltas hurt you. They're only a lot of pretty boys spoiled from home, trying to find out how to be men. Swinging around acting big."

Returning, the clerk lifted the big register and turned it toward Marc for his signature. By the time Marc put the pen down Orvell was disappearing out the exit. In the distance the Katy wailed its approach.

Not finding the key, the clerk again went away. Marc was still waiting when Zip appeared outside, carrying several suitcases. Following him were a pair of fine-looking, well-dressed alumni, the Delta type, listening to Bromage's yarns. Back to help with Rush Week, brothers come home again. Bromage's cab was waiting. Zip loaded the suitcases next to the driver.

Pacing the mildewed hotel room, fingering the Gideon Bible, grappling for a firmer hold upon his pride, Marc weighed what there was of Jewishness within his feelings and his faiths and found it mostly love for his father. Although within Hans Kleinman there was as little Jewishness, Hans would be stricken if Marc should say he was no Jew or join a Christian church to prove it.

He looked out the window, down at the Townsmen's Club, boisterous tonight with alcoholic laughter. Drunk or sober, those unseen men wanted to know whether Marc was a Jew.

His resentment was hot metal beneath his feet. Vaguely he felt the penalty should be balanced by some asset of value to himself, but, pacing, he spoke aloud. "It doesn't mean a damn thing to me."

If it meant so much to the others, well, it was their problem, not his. He would not go about apologizing or explaining or justifying or declaring. Let them find out for themselves. Or see it on his person if it was there to be seen. Or not see it. The problem was theirs; let them deal with it.

Byrn Darrow had said a fellow would be on his own here, as if born of no one, bred of no one, accepted for what he himself was and did. Well, Darrow didn't know everything.

But that was the way Marc was going to assume it was. If in their insolence they asked the direct question, Marc would talk about the weather. They would learn to mind their own business. He wanted neither their fraternities nor their insults. This was his university as well as theirs. Born of no one, bred of no one, judged by what you were and did.

CHAPTER II

THE NEXT MORNING, in the confusion and clatter of the tiled corridor, Marc registered for classes. The instructors behind the tables were young, quick, keen-eyed, shabbily dressed. The man who took care of K-N gave clear-cut instructions as he handed Marc the cards.

In search of a place to write, Marc made his way through the crowd, out from beneath the high central well, and at last found a quiet clearing. His resolution, solid within his will at dawn, suddenly was not solid at all, for the blanks inquired about his father's religion, his mother's, his own. A man could talk about the weather to another man, but to his university to which he had come in warm fealty, trusting the urbanity of its science, of all its attitudes which grew from science like sturdy crops from rich soil ... No, he could not predict rain .... He could only lie or tell the truth.

Yet what was the truth? Father's nationality? German-American, yes, but where was the space for telling of Hans's naturalization papers and his pride in them? And was it accurate to say of Hans, who had never joined the Temple, though he had let Mama do it for him, that he was a Jew? If Izzy Randowich's father, with his long beard and his chronic praying, his *shabbas-goy* and his sweatshop home, his son who worshiped kosher, was a Jew, then was Jew the proper word with which to describe Hans?

And Mama, with no interest in creeds and her admiration of nice American manners, was she, too, Jewish? And Marc, who had shunned the Temple as a source of enlightenment ever since its rabbi had spoken foolishly of tides?

Turning the yellow card around and around, Marc knew exactly what they wanted. Whoever designed these questions was not inquiring about Hans's state of religious wonder.

He paced the corridor, pausing once to let the toe of his shoe play at a loose tile. What was it to be a Jew? What his parents' parents believed or were? The shape of the nose, though Marc's had missed the traditional curve? Or was it only the willingness to put a chip on your shoulder for a cause about which a fellow didn't care? Should it be put there as tribute to Hans? Or in defense of his own self-respect? Proof of a fellow's ability to carry any load those about him considered his?

He finally wrote that his father's nationality was American; his father's religion, Jewish; his mother, born in Arkansas, Jewish; and that he himself was a member of no church or other religious organization.

Looking for a room, Marc thought of Mama. This was what she scornfully called "American housekeeping," a phrase she had acquired from German-Americans: split shades, torn curtains, ragged rugs, unmended bedspreads, floors without varnish, spotted wallpaper, balls of dust beneath the beds, windowless bathrooms.

By contrast the dormer room on Miss Ophelia Spell's third floor seemed the best of all possible homes, for it was clean without being austere. The gingham-trimmed window couch invited; the matching curtains were cordial; the oval rug was gay. From the desk chair Marc could see both the sunset and the university dome.

In his letters home Marc wrote nothing about the evening at the Delta House but in detail about his room, drawing its floor plan and sketches of each wall. Subsequently he described rocks found along the Hinkson Ridge, converted now into a pair of book ends. He described a wastebasket bought at the local variety store.

Mama replied: "Freddy falls in love with every girl he sees. You fall in love with a room."

Papa's reply was a long, carefully worded, impersonal essay. "Lucky the man whose room is also his companion, his fine friend, his good workshop. Should the world turn unkind—which, God forbid, I hope it never will for you, Marc—then a man's home is his palace. It is like his family, always glad to see him. I am rejoiced you have such a nice room, though in America where all is friendly—in the schools, I mean—a room is not everything. Go out also with your many friends."

It was Papa's way of asking whether Marc had any friends in Columbia.

Marc himself did not know the answer. He was never lonely. When he chanced to meet Darrow they stood and talked. The other roomers at Miss Spell's were pleasant. Except for them, his acquaintances were men whose names began with *K* and therefore sat beside him in classrooms. Leaving Logic, Keller; leaving German, Kerber. Going to classrooms, he walked alone.

Yet had a stranger searched the campus for a happy face, he might have selected Marc's, for in his eyes glowed worship for his university and fond faith in its power to make of Marc Kleinman a useful man, completely American. The footworn hollows of the stone steps into Academic Hall were venerable in his sight. The dome, which by its eminence served the countryside as compass and by its bell served Columbia as clock, was a symbol of all that was high-minded and true. The Columns, a row of ivy-grown Corinthian pillars topping a smoothly grassed mound, were hallowed sacred ruins, not merely the remnants of a fire but symbols of Missouri's steadfast faith in education. Often a pair of students could be seen lounging beside them, talking in low voices of hopes and dreams and plans. When Marc came he dreamed of a world that was wide and of how Marc Kleinman might serve it by learning to live within the spaciousness of the United States of America, neither walled in by the ways of his ancestors nor walled out for any reason.

Marc pushed away the memory of his first evening. Twice, meeting Reid on the campus, he observed that Reid blushed and broke into a jerky jog trot. Once a greeting from a passer-by puzzled him, and it was only minutes later that he recalled the man as Hart Bromage. Another day Hart paused to give Marc news of a concert. In his friendly manner was the implication that the Delta proscription was not of his making.

The Deltas dimmed from Marc's life. Because the fraternities and sororities mingled mainly with themselves and one another, there were few encounters of any kind.

Marc's first invitation came through Miss Ophelia. One evening as her roomers returned from supper, she turned from the telephone to say, "Professor Parkhurst wants you boys to come over to his house tonight. He's the one they call Uncle Sed."

Her pale cheeks crinkled mischievously. She was a dainty, thin woman, always hugging herself, as if cold. Her costumes invariably had romantic overtones. Tonight a blue silk rose nodded coyly from the belt of a pink dress. During her sixty years or more on the edge of campus life, at first as the daughter of a professor, later renting out rooms, she had become expert at giving amiable, panoramic descriptions of local events and personalities.

Now her withered cheeks glowed with fun over Uncle Sed. "Go on. Go on over to Uncle Sed's. I'll be waiting to hear about it."

When they returned she told them Sedley Parkhurst's campus history. "Used to be in English. Kept giving Dr. Woodfield—he's Chaucer, you know—heart attacks. Woodfield was wild when he found out Sed was reading Robert Service to his poetry class. While the others were writing articles on the semicolon, Sed was writing sentimental sayings for love magazines. He'd show everybody his checks. To a man, the English Department frothed! But of course Prexy can't fire him. Sed's the only one on campus the Legislature likes. Speaks for nearly every high school graduation in the state. Anyhow, he's Uncle Sed now, the man who's supposed to be Big Brother to you fellows. That was a way of jockeying him out of English ... ."

The scorched marshmallows were not alone in being overdone that evening. Uncle Sed, bustling about, was overbusy. His welcome was too affectionate, his great soft hands too caressing. When he talked of good habits his voice was too arcane, his lips too moist. When he prayed in farewell his eyes were squeezed too hard, his intimacy with God too similar to his good-pal attitude toward the fellows. The big, pink, heavy-shouldered, tawdry man captivated some of the freshmen crowded into his home, amused others.

Marc's attention was fixed upon his own unfamiliarity with what to all the others seemed completely familiar. Their talk was in an idiom unknown to him. "He is a Christian man," turning out to mean only that he was a good man. "Vespers" were something—what?—which all but Marc had attended. A Presbyterian said he had transferred his letter from his church at home, and only Marc did not understand. They spoke of the Galilean. The Last Supper. An apostle. The Philistines. The necessity to bear one's cross.

Marc was nettled by this blank within himself singling him out from the majority. In some lapels shone Epworth League buttons.

"How many Methodists present?" Uncle Sed shouted. "Raise your hands." Marc was astounded to learn that dancing was a sin to a number of his classmates and to more of their parents. Fraternities were bad, not because of their snobbish insularity, but because they gave dances. Fleetingly Marc felt himself on the side of the fraternities.

Sitting cross-legged on the floor, Uncle Sed's adorers looked up worshipfully, as if they who had never met this preceptor until tonight had known others so like him that they had in a way known him too. When he paused they urged him to speak again.

He brought out cards. Those who signed would be automatically registered for Sunday schools. No compulsion, of course. They were to sign for the church of their choice. But they were to go to some church and take their friends.

"Here's a favor Uncle Sed is asking." His eyes explored the young faces. "This is confidential. I understand Jew boys are beginning to come to our university. I'll have all the facts in a day or so." He held up the yellow registration card. "Thing is, we ought to offer them Christ. If you know of a Jew boy on the campus, bring him to Sunday school."

After that the talk was of Jews. Most of the farm boys said they had never seen a Jew. Small-town boys told about the Jew who ran a store on their Main Street. They imitated his foreign accent. Uncle Sed roared.

As soon as Marc posted a notice on the student-employment bulletin board announcing himself as a pianist available for small dances at a modest fee, the phone calls began to be for him. Miss Ophelia would summon him, or sometimes, if he was out, she would make the engagement, later handing him a card with the time and address. Then she would tell him who the people were or why a sorority was giving an afternoon dance. When he returned she would ask him to join her for a cup of something hot, or on Sunday evenings to share a wisp of chicken salad and the beaten biscuit whose excellence proved to all Columbia that the aristocratic tradition of the South was its own, and good, and that Miss Ophelia whom they loved was its worthy disciple.

Marc began to read the Bible. The beginning stirred him with its drama and impressed him by its literary magnitude. When he reached the story of Noah and his daughters he was shocked. He began to skip, omitting the cruelties and sex sins, the genealogies, the threats of the Lord, and the confessions of the sinners.

Reading the battles, he accepted them as history. A few characters became people who had lived. In Isaiah he found poetry. Byrn agreed; those passages were handsome but unfortunately reminded him of a Swiss schoolmaster's habit of reading the Psalms on the mornings the porridge was burned.

One afternoon Marc found three letters for him on the hand-painted china platter Miss Ophelia used as a card tray. One was from Hans, a long commentary on a letter he had received from Gustav Cramer. "His son—Sholem—your age, Marc, has just finished his year in the German Army. Now the one Freddy's age enters. The father, like a fool, writes, "They have the honor to enter the Army.' Fine honor! Gustav Cramer writes as if he believes Germany will soon have war. He claims 'the Fatherland' is surrounded by enemies. My brother Albert has lived these many years in France. He writes that France can hear Germany rattling her sword. It is true, Marc, those German officers think war is something splendid. I thank God every day that my sons are Americans and need not think of war."

Aurelia's letter, as usual, was short: "Dear Marc, It is hard to have you away from us. Hope it turns out to be worth it. If you aren't earning enough to eat right, come home. Books aren't everything. Try to be noble. I want you to turn out to be a noble man. Love from Mama. Want some cookies?"

The third letter was signed, Nettie Harris. "Dear Mr. Kleinman: Mr. Harris and I would like you to be our guest for supper Friday. Mr. Harris knows some of your St. Louis relatives. Sincerely, Nettie Harris."

Miss Ophelia pursed her mouth. Her arms hugged at each other more tightly than usual. She nodded her head. "Mr. Harris runs that lovely store on Broadway. I always buy my dress materials from Mr. Harris himself. Go, by all means."

Her pallid eyes blinked their astonishment. Marc could see she knew something she wouldn't say. When he went to Uncle Sed's she had waited until he returned.

"Go, by all means," she kept repeating now.

Marc phoned his acceptance; he would try to be on time, but he was playing for a dance that afternoon and if he was a little late——

Mrs. Harris laughed. "My husband is usually late. Come when you can."

Arriving ten minutes past the hour, Marc found the Harris home to be a large brick house, stately with columns, set far back from the street. Nettie Harris rose from a lawn chair to meet him. Her face was pink, her eyes moist from trying to suppress her laughter. Periodically she lost the contest and her giggles would burst out, ending in an up-scale gasp. Her spread hands held her plump sides as if to ease their pain.

She led Marc to some chairs under an elm. "Listen to that," she said, indicating by a nod the cause of her amusement. From within the house men's voices droned or spoke in unison.

"Poor Sol," she kept saying. "I'll bet he's in stitches."

At length she was calm enough to explain: The Harrises had lived in this town for years. Lived like their neighbors, though of course they didn't belong to a church. "So, naturally, I didn't belong to the auxiliaries and clubs. Oh, they always invite me to the bazaars. We go to things like that. I didn't really care, not after I began helping Sol in the store. Too busy to care. Anyhow, we don't know a thing about Jewish prayers and all that. I never even allowed Sol to say Jewish words around the children."

A swell of chanting from indoors stopped her. Sol appeared on the porch, shaking his head and mopping his brow. He was a short man, not unlike Hans Kleinman in build, but stouter. The chanting ceased abruptly. Someone spoke to Sol through the screen. Still shaking his head, he went inside.

"Poor Sol. That Randall boy is a regular ox." Through her laughter she told about Randall, a student invited as were all Jewish students on campus. Professor Parkhurst had phoned Sol on one of the busiest days. Asked him to invite the Jewish boys for their holidays. Poor Sol wasn't even sure when the holidays came. Wrote down to St. Louis to find out. To Marc's uncle, Oscar Hursch. Well, the minute the boys got here, this Randall ox began to give orders. A little table. Candles. A tablecloth. Not this one. That one. Even the number of guests didn't suit him. Nor the way the chairs stood. Sol told him to take off his hat. Instead he made Sol put his on! That was when she left.

"I never heard the like! I thought we had let all that die out generations ago. Do your parents—— Of course not! I could tell the minute I saw you," she said approvingly. "You're not that kind. Well, we're not either, I can promise you that!"

When at last they went into the house, they found everyone shaking hands and saying, "Happy New Year!"

Ira Randall turned out to be Izzy Randowich, scowling his scathing disapproval of Harris household ways. He inquired about Marc's father. The Randowiches were no longer living in the Yellow Row. They had moved to larger quarters.

The dinner might have been cooked by Aurelia, so similar was it to her style of cooking. The soup was thick with vegetables finely cut. The bones of the roast were sawed and tightly wrapped around the beef. The gravy was dark brown, the potatoes tinged deep tan from baking near the roast. The red cabbage was finely cut and contained apple. The bread was rye and the butter sweet. At the end of the meal there were *Schnecken* with citron, raisins, and pecans thick within the brown-sugar mixture.

All but Randall ate heartily and said this was like home. Randall sat very tall with arms folded, touching nothing. He mumbled about meat and milk and not kosher. Mrs. Harris, frowning, offered to have her cook boil an egg. "It will be kosher. I'll serve it in the shell."

"Nothing," he answered.

Sol Harris kept his eyes averted from Ira Randall, as if he dared not trust himself to look. All these years Nettie Harris had lived uninvited, and now this whippersnapper repudiated the validity of her Jewishness!

With an impatient gesture he leaned forward. "What was your name, young man, before it was Randall? And if you are such a good Jew, why did you change it?"

Randall shrugged mournfully. "A man changes a name because he must. To get along."

Sol Harris's face reddened angrily. "Since when must a man change his name to get along? Everyone in this town knows I'm a Jew. I get along."

Again Randall shrugged. "Harris is not a name like Randowich. It might be——"

"It might be, nothing! They know I'm a Jew. Everyone knows it."

Again the shrug. "It is no sin to fool the others."

"The others!" Sol Harris spluttered. "My neighbors are not the others!" In his anger he upset his cup of coffee.

"Papa," Nettie Harris said, "in this house we do not raise voices." There was no laughter in her now.

Randall stood up, his lips a scornful arch; from habit his fingers groped on the doorpost for the *mezuza* which was not there. After he was gone they were silent for a time. Sol Harris looked worn out. "Mama," he said, "your dinner was very good. After all, what is there to Judaism but good cooking? That is the best of all .... Nettie Harris is a good cook, eh, boys?" He was apologizing to his wife because her work had brought her no pleasure.

On the way home Marc walked with Clarence Weiss, a tall, heavy-set, lumbering-gaited youth with curly red hair. They agreed, too, about the Harrises. Nice people. And what a dinner! But a fellow went to a university to live in America, not in Jewish America. To live as everyone else lived. That play Zangwill wrote, *The Melting Pot*. That was the way it should be. America melting away the differences.

"Unmeltable Randall," Marc said, and Weiss, acquiescing, repeated the phrase.

They looked at each other with liking, but because each meant to be melted, here where the pot was warm, they made no plans to meet again.

"Good-by, Weiss."

"Good-by, Kleinman."

They turned at the same moment to wave.

Miss Ophelia was waiting, the alcohol flame freshly lighted beneath the lofted teapot. Marc said his supper had been so large that he could not drink tea. He did not say there had been *Schnecken* and thick soup, nor did he tell about Randall and the services.

He sat with Miss Ophelia as she sipped and smiled, but she revealed nothing about the Harrises. The secret look in her eyes which Marc had observed earlier, he now understood: She had not realized Marc was a Jew until he told her he was invited to the Harris home.

Now she knew and saw that he would not discuss it. She was very courteous, a demure hostess not fully at home at her own party. Her thin, knobby-jointed fingers plucked at the tea cloth, at imaginary crumbs, at the black velvet ribbon around her neck, at the cameo upon it.

And Marc, very quiet, sat waiting for her to decide about the unspoken fact between them. He did not fidget or help her. He let her see that his Jewishness was a problem not of his making.

She peered into the empty teapot, stacked the small bowl of wet tea leaves within her cup, and just before she turned to carry them to the kitchen she said, "Every year I tell myself it's wrong to have a favorite and then I always do have one boy in my house I like the best. Don't tell the others, Marc, they might turn jealous." Her laughter floated back to him. "Jealous of Spinster Spell. Good night, dear."

Marc had noticed her many times. A tan-haired girl, hurrying. Usually she wore something blue to match a pair of azure eyes. They were handsome honest eyes, widely spaced, and friendly; the lashes were long and thick.

At the change of semesters the new schedule of classes sent Marc and the girl home at the same hour and in the same direction. She walked with graceful, easy rhythm, as if she might be humming a march and keeping step.

One icy day she slipped and went down laughing. Marc helped her up and slapped the snow from her books and papers. Thanking him, she blushed and said, "Well, anyhow, now we've met," as if the disaster had reached a remarkably happy conclusion. A dimple high in her left cheek flickered as he added, "I've seen you going by."

She was Hallie Wade, daughter of Professor Langley Wade of Sociology, and lived only a few doors from Miss Ophelia's house.

Before they had walked many paces she said, "My father was dismissed from a college in the East for standing by his principles." She turned to look fully at Marc. "Daddy's a wonderful man. He was the youngest associate professor on that campus."

When she saw that Marc accepted Langley Wade's superiority she talked gaily of campus doings, as if only that fundamental needed settling as prelude to their friendship.

Miss Ophelia, of course, saw them together and greeted Marc with little chirps of praise for Hallie Wade. The very nicest girl, and how that delightful ray of sunshine ever grew up in that dungeon of a home with a grieving father and mother afraid of her own shadow would remain forever as the very greatest of mysteries.

During high school years Hallie had never belonged fully to Gown or Town, and a girl had to belong to one or the other to have a set of her own. But Langley and Vera Wade scarcely ever set foot in Westmount, so Westmount young folks, naturally, forgot to invite Hallie, very likely assuming she went with Town, and Town, of course, knowing she was a professor's daughter, hesitated to ... Well, hesitated. So the poor kid had to make her own fun and—Miss Ophelia nodded approvingly—apparently Hallie had learned how. "She's a freshman this year and I do hope she'll have a good time. Did you ever see a sweeter, jollier face? I do adore Hallie."

Before many weeks had passed, Marc, too, adored her.

CHAPTER III

PROFESSOR LARCUM TRANSFERRED will Shakespeare from the seventeenth to the twentieth century and gave him to Marc as a friend. With Byrn Darrow sitting cross-legged on the window seat Marc read aloud passages which proved that the playmaker concurred in their belief that a man was in a sense born of no one, bred of no one, and that what he was within himself and what he did with what was there would determine his fate. Too much jealousy, a wife killer. Too much ambition, a murderer. Too much indecision, murder and suicide both. True, his usurer was a Jew, but Marc was not planning to read *The Merchant of Venice.*

Marc was planning to be, as Mama urged, noble, and Shakespeare's belief in character as fate made that possible. "Look to your character" was better than "Look to your religion," and different. Different as hell, Marc assured himself again and again.

At afternoon parties Miss Ophelia and her friends weighed campus personalities upon the scales of their joint opinion, each adding what she could, all accepting the total verdict.

Marc's name evoked lively talk, for nearly every woman present knew something about that terribly nice Jewish boy who stayed at Miss Ophelia's. The Delta house mother said he played the piano well, but then all Jews were good musicians, weren't they? Mrs. Bittner, blushing, said she mustn't be quoted, of course, but President George Bittner had been ever so much amused by the story of Kleinman's hours and hours of conscientious guarding of the bag on the snipe hunt. Mrs. Mooren, a thin, timorous woman, said "Professor History," as she called her husband, thought Kleinman asked good questions and that was a sign of a good mind.

Miss Ophelia had the most to tell. She was wearing a billowy black dress with a red rosebud belt and matching hair cluster, and she tugged more than usual at the cameo on her velvet neckband. She said Kleinman was the sweetest boy she had ever had in her house, and they could just stop their tittering because she hadn't forgotten the procession of other sweet ones. This was different. It wasn't just bringing in her newspaper or making his bed before his 8 o'clock or washing out the ring around the bathtub. It wasn't those autumn leaves for her Indian basket. It was the way he acted as if he were her son.

When that lazy darky who was supposed to fire the furnace didn't show up during a whole week of zero weather, claiming he was sick—though funny it had to be during the freeze—well, anyhow, the other boys just complained about the chilly house, but Kleinman went down and kept the furnace going.

Nor was that just what she meant. It was mostly the way he loved the campus and was so proud of the fine things it stood for and angry about the wrong things, for that was the way she felt too: proud when the Minneapolis Symphony played, angry when Uncle Sed spread his Parkhurstism about for everyone to see. The remark about Uncle Sed stimulated "Chaucer" Woodfield's wife to observe that Kleinman was doubtless a fine fellow.

Throughout the discussion there had been furtive glances at Vera Wade's pale face. It was, in fact, partly in order to draw from her an expression of how she felt about Hallie and Marc that they had been repetitive in their praise. When she broke her silence it was to say, "Langley thinks Marc's very intelligent, and I always believe brains are the most important, don't you?"

Professor Larcum had never been successful in dissuading his wife, the former Minerva Bates, from giving teas. Periodically she would happen upon a Limoges basket which had been her mother's, hold it aloft on two fingers, look at it dotingly, and say, "Lark, we ought to give a tea. This is darling with cookies in it."

While the guests were there the professor would sit silently in the corner, drinking cup after cup until his nose was brightly reddened and his eyes moist. Enhazed with horror by his wife's remarks, he would listen, wincing now and then, drink, and bounce up with cheerful alacrity at the first mention of departure.

Most of Mrs. Larcum's comments were watered-down quotations from the professor's own breakfast-table witticisms, for the Larcums were agreed about everything except the policy of sharing their quips with the campus.

Lark's only defense against his wife, whom he adored when they were alone, was to haggle about the invitations until the list excluded all men of campus influence.

Stowing away the professor's woolen gloves that spring, Mrs. Larcum came upon the Limoges basket. "Lark," she said, when they had agreed that a week from Sunday would do, "we haven't had the president. Do you want to invite them or shall I?"

Lark peered through his reading spectacles, thereby transforming his wife into a blur. "It won't do to have the president at the same tea with freshmen. There's a talented fellow—needs encouraging—I want him to come."

Having lived with the professor for thirty years, Mrs. Larcum knew he simply did not want the president, but no one could really want the president with all those bleak silences of his and that fear of the Legislature in his eyes.

"Lark," she said, "you're cute but not clever. Invite twelve. I might put popcorn in this time."

"Mrs. Lark," he answered, "you were born in the fall of the year."

Whenever Lark lacked an explanation he would comment in grandiloquent classroom tones upon the time or place of his wife's birth, implying that these irrelevancies explained everything. It was an old sweet joke between them.

Obliged now to invite a promising freshman, Dr. Larcum sent for Mr. Aynley, who graded papers for him and doubtless was aware that his chief did not know one student from another. To Larcum students were not individuals but rows. "I have fifteen in my course this year" meant fifteen rows. As persons, students were tops of heads lowered over rushing fountain pens; as rows, they were a delightful reason for musing aloud about the great mind Dr. Larcum privately called W. S.

This morning Mr. Aynley looked deplorably shabby and red-eyed. Dr. Larcum came to the point at once. "Who is my most promising student? Freshman."

Incapable of brevity, Mr. Aynley weighed and explained and qualified. This one could write, but his style was—— Well, that one could grasp things. Another had a remarkable memory. Still another handed in excellent papers and——

Dr. Larcum sighed his boredom. "Not a thinker in the lot, very likely."

"Kleinman's a thinker, sort of a thinker. Some of the stuff he writes doesn't sound like what you said at all. He sort of figures things out for himself. I tell him it's what leads him into error. A man's grades suffer needlessly——"

"Does he write sense?"

"It's sense, but that's not what he's here for. I tell him the way to get grades——"

Dr. Larcum shuddered. "Brilliant mind, has he?"

"I guess it's what could be called brilliant."

"Tell him I want to see him. What's that name again?"

"Kleinman, Marc Kleinman. Jewish." It was almost a question.

Dr. Larcum answered, "Jews are likely to be brilliant." He felt sprightly this morning. He began to write. "Might as well put down that name on our Honors List. Save going over the ground again later."

"There's another Jewish boy. Weiss. Clarence Weiss."

"Brilliant too?"

"Weiss is weak. Grammar. He's from Joplin. The mines, you know. Always have trouble with grammar from the mines."

Dr. Larcum's eyes were seeing the tea. All faculty and the freshman boy who was going to make Honors because Aynley, who was without a spark himself, scented brilliance. That and being a Jew. "Maybe those boys would like to come together."

"Come?"

"Send them to me, Mr. Aynley."

Dr. Larcum walked briskly toward his lecture room.

Had the tradespeople settled in Westmount, doubtless the region would have had a scheduled system of cab service, but the professors, thinking of the fares they would have to surrender, said walking and bicycling were healthful sports. Arriving guests would enter, reporting the hardships of the climb.

On the day of the tea Lark began by sympathizing; then, as the afternoon advanced, became taciturn. He listened in anguished silence to Minerva's stories about his varicose veins, his long underwear, the sequence in which he performed his toilet, and her comments thereon. "I always tell Lark he's an old maid at heart. Else why must he always brush his hair first and shave afterward?"

A pink balloon of a woman turned to Marc, who sat beside that nice Hallie Wade. "Mr. Weiss," she said, "I hear you're aiming to study law."

Marc answered, "My name is Kleinman."

"Then that one's Weiss." The woman, unembarrassed, nodded past a half-dozen other students toward Weiss, whose cheeks flushed until they matched his hair.

It was a mistake which had been made before, drying Marc's mouth and warming his forehead, for the two were dissimilar; but with Randall living away from the campus, Weiss and Kleinman were the only two known as Jews. The confusion of their names was the confusion of those to whom the fact of their Jewishness outweighed their manifold differences.

When the rotund guest called Marc "Mr. Weiss" for the third time, Professor Larcum rushed into his study and remained there.

A man from the Physics Department began to talk of great discoveries, and then someone discussed the difference between the inductive and deductive method and the limitations upon each. The plump pink woman drowsed, but when she awakened she again called Marc "Mr. Weiss."

Hallie had just returned from carrying empty cups to the tea table. She slipped her arm through Marc's and, dimpling, whispered, "Why don't you put her in her place?" But she said it as if the whole thing was completely amusing, the woman so fantastic that she might at any moment ascend as did other balloons, that she was indeed as likely to pop into nothingness.

While her guests were at the door saying their farewells, Minerva Larcum squinted into the twilight. "That little darky's still on the curb." She turned to her husband, who was just returning. "Lark, what did he say when you asked him what he wanted?"

"That he was waiting for someone."

The plump woman could not figure out whose dishes the mother was washing. "If they have to bring their children along, they ought to make them stay in the back. That boy's old enough to be left at home. He must be at least eight."

They stared at the human salient on their street. "He hasn't moved all afternoon."

Outdoors the small brown boy came forward shyly. "Your name Mr. Kleinman?" he asked. He looked from Marc to Hallie, until she sauntered beyond their voices.

"Mr. Zip, he says please will you come to see him? Tomorrow morning. Visiting hours is 10 to 11."

"Visiting hours?"

"Mr. Zip, he's in jail."

A butterfly lighted momentarily on Marc's coat, then winged away, its color brilliant in the twilight. The boy pursued the swooping yellow, lost it, pretended to be still pursuing it, ran through the corner lot and down the steep hill toward the part of town where dark boys were too numerous to be noteworthy.

CHAPTER IV

IN JAIL ORVELL was a helpless, aghast man with quivering lips. At first Marc did not observe the others in the cell—several colored men in the dark—not until their quarreling voices rose and their scuffing caused him to turn his head.

Through the bars, his hands holding lightly to them, the prisoner whispered hoarsely. He explained what his rights were. The fellows at the front desk simply did not know the law or they wouldn't have held him for more than two weeks without preferring charges. All Kleinman had to do was call this to the attention of the prosecuting attorney's office.

His heavy lips thinned to hardness as he talked. "They haven't even questioned me." He looked weary; his eyes drooped as if they had been staring overlong at that reasonableness which was the law of the land, searching for flaws or, failing that, for patience with its tardiness.

The prosecuting attorney was in a hurry. A speech to make. Young. Dapper. A flower in his buttonhole. Swift eyes and a shapely chin. A good-looking man.

At first he was breezy: The business of the prosecuting attorney was to prosecute .... Then he became fatherly, advising Marc to stay out of this; a fellow never got any thanks from niggers, no matter how much he did for them. Marc waited quietly through the anecdotes. Finally the prosecuting attorney, tapping his fingers on his straw hat, became evasive and lordly. "Just leave this to me."

By good luck Marc found the head of the Law Department in his office, though hurrying to get out of the heat, up to his cottage in Minnesota where there would be no stacks of papers, only fishing by day and articles for law journals in the evenings.

His manner to Marc was genial, though he had never seen him before. "What is it, son?" Listening, the austere man lazed back in the swing-about chair, twirling a pencil, watching it twirl. His eyes left the pencil and lingered for a while on the Columns.

Then he brought his attention within the room again, sat forward, arms folded far across the desk, a tall man hunched over, looking up earnestly from under bushy eyebrows. "You expect me to set this right?" He talked about the lag between the way the law of the land was supposed to work and the way it did work. He told how much had piled up because he lacked a secretary; he was overburdened now; he hinted darkly that town men threw in monkey wrenches. "You expect me to set this right? Years ago I used to get involved. Can't do that and have time for my academie duties. The day I decided to shut my eyes and ears to events and stick to law theory I began to be useful to my university."

He took Marc to the outer door and patted his shoulder and looked deep into his eyes. "Good-by, son."

Langley Wade turned white with fury. "Two weeks in jail and no charges!"

His tugging loosened the eyeshade. Hallie fastened it again, fondly smoothing her hands over his hair, over his cheeks, and finally cupping the quivering chin within her gentle palm. She shook her head at Marc and by a wink warned him that this was one of the subjects not to be discussed with Langley Wade.

Her father tried to think of someone who would see that justice and a Negro were jointly defended, but gradually his rumbling voice talked less of Orvell and more of the American Constitution and of the episode some years ago which had ejected Langley Wade from a professorship.

As he finished Hallie returned to the room with a tray of tall glasses. They agreed with her comment that the mint afloat in the lemonade looked very pretty.

Sol Harris led Marc out of his office where his secretary was writing bills, out into the yard-goods department where bolts of percales barricaded one side, bolts of gingham the other.

He was so short that he had to tilt his head far back to look into Marc's eyes. His suit was well pressed; a lodge pin was in his lapel.

He whispered, "Marc, I've lived a long time in this town .... A Jew has to know when to keep still. Some things he mustn't see or hear. I say to you what I would say to my own son: Let this alone. Nobody's forgotten .... Ach!"

"You mean he's done something I don't know about?"

"You're too young. You'll make trouble. The poor *Schwarze* has done nothing. That won't help him any .... The kindest thing you can do is to let him be forgotten. That way he'll get out sooner."

"Mr. Harris, the law of this country——"

"Don't say you've been here. Maybe I can drop a hint." He was talking to himself now. "You'd be better off if you prefer charges! I could advise that. No need to wait until——" Then he squinted his eyes at Marc. "And what could you do? What difference?"

"The law requires——"

Sol Harris shrugged. "Yes, it requires."

"This way they can change the charges around to suit themselves."

"You talk like a child. You're a nice boy, Marc. I know your uncles.... Upright men.... Let this alone."

"It isn't fair."

"No, it isn't fair. I can't make it fair. You can't either. Sol Harris has lived in this town a long time. I've got along with my gentile neighbors. It's good to know when to keep your mouth shut.... Remember you are a Jew."

Remember you are a Jew.... Remember you are a Jew.... Remember you are ... It was a mad dance within his head. The world was a room acutely tilted.

He did not stop at the campus, nor at Miss Ophelia's, nor at Hallie's. Crossing the Farm, he headed toward the Hinkson Ridge. He picked his way to the cave where he could lie full length and look out upon the countryside.

He tried to think it through. He tried to ridicule "poor Sol." Remember you are a Jew.... To that he retorted that he would remember he was a man and an American. He lost his thoughts again and again, as if the rope of reasoning had been jerked away. He would go back.... Remember you are a Jew....

He slept heavily. When he drowsed into wakefulness he saw that to remember he was a Jew would only be claiming less right than other men to being an American.

Never that. Never. I will not remember I am a Jew. I will remember only that Orvell Sultan is unjustly jailed.

He told Miss Ophelia all of it except about remembering he was a Jew. She shook her head at him. Dr. Larcum was the man to see.

When it was explained, Dr. Larcum said with forthright vigor that of course something must be done for a man falsely accused. By phone he consulted several faculty men who agreed Prexy was the only one on campus who knew how Gown could deal with Town.

President Bittner said, "Inform the head of the Businessmen's League. He's a responsible man."

When Marc returned to Miss Ophelia's she said she had run over to the Delta House. The Deltas had left for the summer, of course, but she had had a long talk with the house mother about Zip. Did Marc know he stole?

"They're going to charge that he brought in liquor."

Miss Ophelia spoke gently. "Marc, boy, you can't judge them like other people. That's silly, dear."

Several minutes later she added, "You're a dear boy, but you don't understand niggers and you don't understand Columbia. You'd better just let Columbia take care of its little spats the way it wants to. This town knows how it's got to do with its own niggers. Have a fine summer, Marc, and forget all this foolishness. Good-by, dear." She drew his head down and kissed him.

But Marc did not go home. At the last minute he decided to stay. He remained in town long after classes ended, waiting for the hearing to which he had managed to get himself summoned as a witness.

Searching for Justice of the Peace Clagger's courtroom, Marc found a shabby building around the corner from Main Street. A pool hall, then the lunch counter known as the Greasy Spoon, then a vacant store. Up narrow, tall, sighing steps. A dark hall. A door: *C. Arnold Clagger, Justice of the Peace.*

Mr. Clagger sat in a rounded armchair, his back to the tall, grimy windows. Next to him was a table where a man was taking notes. A half-dozen silent, furrow-faced men, hats far back, teetering chairs, chewed tobacco.

Marc was motioned to the chair for witnesses. It faced the window and the chewing men. The brass spittoon was next to Marc's chair.

He sat with his legs away from it.

Clagger ordered him to raise his right hand. Clagger, muttering through saliva. "... S'help me, God .... Say, 'I do.'"

A long full stream, another, another, and Marc rising to avoid them, saying "I do" as he arose.

The oath had to be readministered. The witness had to be seated in the chair, his hand raised while he swore. Clagger was a particular man.

The questions: "How long have you known the accused, this hyere nigger houseboy, known as Zip, alias Orvell Sultan, nigger houseboy claiming to be thirty years old?" A dozen questions about the "aliases." What other names were used by the accused? *Orvell Sultan, stooodent.* Laughter. Contemptuous laughter. In Marc's heart fear for the hunted throbbed within his scorn for the hunters.

Triumphantly they asked the question expected to fell him. Did he know where the nigger houseboy was on the evening of September 6, 1911?

The question, a surprise ... Then Marc did know. His first evening in Columbia. At the Delta House. Marc's hands were cold. Anger was gathering. He tried to remain calm, respectful, to these men, who could make the jail key turn either way.

Yes, he knew where the man was from 8 P.M. until after midnight.

Are you a Delta? You were rushed and not taken? ... A guest for one evening? ... Only for one evening, but on the night mentioned Zip was within sight from——

Spitting with poor aim, they could not shake his testimony. A dozen others, they claimed, knew that on that night this hyere nigger houseboy had hauled hard liquor from beyond the county line to Fraternity Row, peddled it up and down, thus corrupting students.

Not waiting for a question, Marc said he could get some Deltas to testify that Zip had refused to haul their liquor. Marc's eyes glowed; the truth would clear up everything.

Clagger banged his gavel and ordered him just to answer questions. Clagger and the others were less jovial now. A spitter got up and moved the spittoon. Two, whispering, took some papers from the table and went into an inner room.

Clagger asked and asked again about the aliases. They laughed when Marc told about correspondence courses. Wheezing into silence, one man muttered, "Them niggers! What next! Correspondence courses! Likely the buck can't even read."

The two came back, whispered to Clagger, compared legal document with legal document. Clagger turned on his secretary. Why the hell couldn't he be more careful?

To the witness, Marc Kleinman: "Do you know where the nigger houseboy was on the evening of September 7, 1911, the evening after September 6 previously mentioned?"

"Other men brought in the liquor."

"The witness will answer the question."

"I don't know where he was on the seventh."

"Witness dismissed." Clagger, scolding the secretary, who apologized loudly, mockingly. Everyone leaving. Marc protesting to Clagger. Clagger waddling speedily to the inner room. The door locked.

During dinner that first evening at home Marc's eyes kept fleeing, returning, fleeing from Mamie Lee's. Hers were mournful, bulging black marbles in a gray-brown mask.

Afterward in the kitchen her great lips wept; her great hands twisted a dish towel into a rope, twisted, straightened, twisted.

"Marc, you don't need to be in no guess why they done it. They done it because Orvell's black. That's why they done it."

On the front porch, whispering, Marc assured Hans there was something else. Other colored men in Columbia walked the streets freely. Why had Orvell been snapped up?

"Did he sell liquor, Marc, or didn't he?"

"The fellows get their own. Sometimes they take a houseboy along to help. Papa, nobody really belives Orvell dealt in liquor. If the case had opened up before the fellows left town—— I believe Hart Bromage would have testified. The point is, it couldn't have been proved on Orvell, simply couldn't."

Papa said, "When a man is on the ground, he can be stepped on." He coughed and tapped and went inside to write Orvell a letter.

Aurelia began to scold the twins. Did they have to sit there doing nothing? "Bertha, get that hat of mine, the one Mamie Lee likes. Give it to her. Ruth, quick, run, before she leaves—that scarf Freddy sent me. Quick, you girls, give them to her. Give them to the poor thing."

In two successive letters Hallie wrote that her father had something to tell Marc he wouldn't even tell his wife and daughter, something very mysterious which had made him swallow his huge pride and pay a call on Uncle Sed, whom he had always described as a man-eating shark in a pinafore, whatever that meant. Of course she knew Marc was working and couldn't get away, but Miss Ophelia sent word that she had not rented his room to any of those messy summer students, and Hallie herself would be glad to see him if he decided to come. It might as well be next week end, when there was to be a hay ride and wiener roast.

Though the morning was so hot that the house had to be kept closed and darkened, Langley Wade wore his eyeshade. He motioned Marc to a chair, shut the door of his study, and began by swearing Marc to secrecy. "You must protect me," he kept saying. "I speak to you in confidence." He approached his news only gradually, for his story began with the campus episode known as the Holy Hogs. He spoke with angry gestures and with angry words.

"The money for this fine academic institution comes from the State Legislature, and the State Legislature is made up mostly of farmers or lawyers for farmers. Seems they care more about hogs than history. According to them, what we teach on the old red-brick-and-ivy campus is frills, nonsense. Look at the fine new buildings on the farm campus and you'll see what those fellows really care about. Some aren't even keen about that. They laugh at labels on corn. But the most skeptical knew that hog serum had the power to save the lives of sick hogs. One year the hogs of one of the legislators were ailing, so he wrote up here in a hurry. He addressed his letter to an instructor he had taken a fancy to during Farm Week. Marked it *Personal.* The letter was forwarded to Michigan. Before the serum arrived the hogs were dead. He vowed this university would never get another cent of the taxpayers' money. We nearly didn't. President Bittner went on his knees. Pleaded. Begged. Lost twenty pounds. Aged ten years. We laugh about the Holy Hogs now. Nobody laughed then." He pulled the eraser out of the pencil he had been toying with. He ceased pacing.

"When little men get power, look out! They've held a stick over Bittner's head. And now this is where the liquor charge comes in...." He sat down heavily and looked around, as if assuring and reassuring himself that no one listened; his voice sank to a thick whisper.

"Last fall three legislators came to Bittner. Wife of one of them had heard something about liquor served at those pledge banquets the fraternities give. No doubt she was making mountains out of molehills. Parkhurst says the drinking wasn't heavy, but nobody could deny there was some. Bittner tried to make light of it, but he had tried that with the hogs. He saw that he was getting into trouble again. He sent for Parkhurst. Parkhurst called the fraternities together and asked the town boys to take it up with their fathers. Their fathers gave the boys hell but told the legislators it was only one glass of light wine, and boys will be boys, and wild oats have always been sowed. After three hours of talking those fathers came back looking pretty down in the mouth. The Holy Hogs were to have a sequel: the Unholy Bottle. Again the legislators made it clear to Bittner that someone had to go to jail or the university appropriation would be drastically cut. Again Bittner sent for Parkhurst. Sed sent for the fraternities; the boys went to their fathers. The fathers understood what would happen to their stores if the university shrank in size. At this point I lose the trail a little. Apparently they took it up with a local politician who said it had to be someone from Fraternity Row. Obviously no one wanted to send his son or his son's friends behind bars. Very likely they didn't even want their boys to know what was going on. It was all kept very quiet. Certainly Bittner doesn't know the whole story. At that point a Negro houseboy was in a risky spot. ... He was the fellow who could be sent away with the least fuss."

Marc said, "Some houseboys did help fetch liquor. Orvell didn't."

Langley Wade pulled his eyeshade lower. "He was unlucky. When they found out he used one name at the post office and another at the Delta House, that made their case."

A distant lawn mower droned and paused and droned again. A child laughed. The sounds were muffled by the closed shutters and windows. Inside the house water spattered in the kitchen sink. Someone was chopping ice.

Marc's mind staggered. Later he was to hate injustice and ache with pity for Orvell and surge with anger, but in this moment he was only grappling for footing, struggling to restore steadiness to a universe in which he had moved about and lived all his life and now found did not exist.

His reverence for learning had been reverence for this university and for President Bittner; yet President Bittner was helpless. His mind lurched toward his old esteem for those who governed and now turned out to be only little men. Toward the practice of law which could be a profession but apparently also could be only a way of——

Across the room the gray-faced angry man became a professor again. He analyzed and argued and demonstrated that nothing now could be gained for Orvell by opening the case; it would only put the spotlight on a man whose chance for release lay in being forgotten. Some student might go behind bars, some lad better off getting an education. And Bittner, that gentle, poetic soul who ought to have been reading Virgil aloud to his classes and explaining Horace, would merely be forced into another controversy with the hog lovers.

CHAPTER V

WHEN THE SUMMER was nearly gone fred came home. he had sold his band instruments. Last winter the Fred Kleinman band had been booked throughout the season. Hans would not let Aurelia ask questions. The boy must not be embarrassed. A poor boy did not give up a nice income like that for no reason. Something must have happened. The least they could do was talk of something else.

Fred, however, looked remarkably well. His skin was tanned, his cheeks red, his forehead peeling. His hair was newly trimmed. His suit was flashy. His dark, deep-set eyes moved quickly; his walk was swift. He looked victorious.

They warned him about Mamie Lee. When he heard about Orvell his mouth fell open, then closed rigidly. He pulled out his purse, fat with ten-dollar bills. Two of them. Four of them. "Get him something, Mamie Lee."

When she went into the kitchen again Hans said across the dinner table, "Money, yes. She can send him something to eat. That was nice, Freddy, but that doesn't get the poor man out."

"I can't get him out, Papa." His manner implied that he did not intend to try. "I'm going into business. We played at the best resorts along the lakes. A week at this hotel. A week at that. Places where champagne was nothing at all. Businessmen and their families."

Hans put down his spoon. "You think it's easy." He snapped his fingers. "Like that."

"Can't be hard. They aren't smart men. Not really smart. A man's either down or up." His thumb pointed down; pointed up.

Papa said, "Now look, Freddy. Don't act too big for your britches. Look right here in the Yellow Row. Mr. Edgewood's a brainy fellow. He———"

Fred was very sure. "Papa, getting rich is a game with rules. Most fellows balk at one rule or another. The guy who gets there is the guy who follows all the rules. Never quarrel with the rules. A banker in"—Fred squinted—"a banker in Charlevoix told me that."

Aurelia sniffed. "Does your uncle Oscar know you are coming into his business?"

"I'm not. Thing to do———" He squinted again. "Patent-medicine manufacturer in Petoskey told me the thing to do is to go after something new. Get in on the ground floor, he told me, or, better still, dig the basement yourself. Give the customers something they haven't found out they want. Something they haven't heard of."

"Fortunetelling," Ruth said, looking into his palm.

Fred laughed. He slapped the twins on the back and told them they were as pretty now as the prettiest debs he saw up North. His laugh showed that he didn't need anyone's approval. He was sure of himself. "Moving pictures. Opened quick. One after another. I've got five piano pounders lined up."

"You'll lose your money," Aurelia said. "Five new picture shows in St. Louis! Who will go to them? Easy come, easy go."

"Every businessman takes chances. Business is a gambling game. I met a guy that made and lost four fortunes before he made the one he lives on now."

Aurelia was staring at Fred's neat hair, neat nails, bragging shoulders, excited eyes.

"What's her name?" she demanded. "Why will she need so much money? Is she a Jewish girl?"

Fred blushed. "Yes, she's Jewish. From Chicago."

Aurelia kept at him. "What's wrong with her? Why will she need so much?

"I'm the one, Mama. I've watched those rich men all summer. For some, making a big success was easier than a little success. Depends on the kind of guy you are. When I get going it won't be any harder to go 'way up———"

Ruth and Bertha giggled.

"Laugh—but honestly, for some a big success is easier than making a little success like Uncle Oscar's."

"So now Uncle Oscar is only a little success!" Aurelia enjoyed the joke. "When you lose all that money we'll feed you."

Hans stood up, went around the table, offered his hand to Fred, and bowed a little. "I wish you luck," he said. It sounded like good-by.

Aurelia scolded. "Shame on you, Hans! Instead of keeping the boy from making a fool of himself. Moving pictures for a dime and so he'll be a millionaire washing his face in champagne. Oscar and Carl will laugh."

Marc spoke thoughtfully. "This is what Fred believes he can do. What he wants to try. Let Uncle Oscar laugh. And Uncle Carl."

Fred said, "Marc, you're going back to the university. I want you to———"

Aurelia broke in: "If you want so much, why don't you try to learn something?" She was angry now.

"Mama, I'm not Marc. What I'm doing is O.K. for me. I wouldn't be any good at a university." He smiled at Marc. "But my brother. My big good-looking brother. My brainy brother——"

Happily Hans said, "You see, Mama? You see! No man can be expected to do more than his best."

Aurelia began to stack the dishes. "You don't have to encourage my children to be money-chasers. You always did think what they did was right. You spoil them and—— Wh-wh-whaat! Mamie Lee's gone?" She turned on Fred. "You and your forty dollars! So now, Fred Kleinman, millionaire, you can just come right on out to the kitchen and dry the dishes!"

The next week Mamie Lee said she was sorry about the way she rushed off. The man she had to see was leaving town.

That was all she would tell. She had given Fred's forty dollars to a Negro politician who promised to get Orvell out. Mr. Lew Cherry delivered brown votes to white men in exchange for small mercies for his people, money sticking to his fingers both ways.

Mamie Lee made him earn hers. She sat in his office twice a week, waiting for news. It was always the same: "This has got to sleep till the senators make their inspection trip. The senators have got to see Orvell there."

It was December before the Senate Eleemosynary Committee went to Jefferson City. The members stared approvingly at the massive-jawed bloodhounds chained near the gate, at the reassuring thickness of the rock walls, at the men in stripes being marched across the courtyard. The senators stood briefly in the noise of the workshop which brought all those complaints from commercial broom makers. They watched the steam from the kitchen vats. They saw the thousand tin plates, each with a raw onion ready for the men's dinners. Walking down corridors, they talked about the new tiers built for white men and argued over sun and cleanliness and money spent on the wicked. They followed a swaying lantern down the corridor of the old cells, forcing their sight to penetrate the dark to Orvell, whose presence behind bars proved that the campus would be dry next year and forever after.

Orvell was in the Kleinman kitchen on Christmas Day. He said to Marc, "During my unwilling sojourn in Jeff City, I made plans. I don't know why I went to the pen. Evil men put me there."

Mamie Lee's wide hands clutched at each other. "Evil man got you out too. Ain't no man more evil than Mr. Lew Cherry. Mr. Cherry's got evil too—only he uses it for good."

Orvell waited for her to finish. Then he continued talking to Marc: "You tried to help me. Nobody else believed it made much difference. One more Negro in jail, or one less." He shrugged. "All those little laws I once thought so important." He laughed at himself back there, the innocent he had been. His voice rose. "Well, if the laws aren't important to the men on top, they're not going to be important to me." Then of a sudden tears flooded his eyes.

Mamie Lee had been cutting up vegetables for soup. She dumped them in with a splash. "Never yet knew a man wasn't rotted by going to jail."

When she turned and saw Orvell's tears she nodded. Her voice was gentle. "You never meant what you said. You gonna do right 'cause you're made that way. Keep on doing right and you'll believe in it again. You're gonna do right for Freddy-boy's sake."

"Lew Cherry, the grasping, dirty——" Again the laugh. "I won't report to Lew Cherry! I'm going away. I'm going to graduate in law and I'm not going to graduate under a jail name."

Hallie's father and Marc became close friends. Their talks sometimes lasted until the night contained neither the grind of wagon wheels nor the click of footsteps. Langley Wade would slip farther and farther down upon his spine, his large feet extending farther and farther into the room, his face becoming ashen with sage-green shadows. By day and by night he wore his eyeshade. Student rumor said he was nearly blind, but Marc often saw him read fine print swiftly. The eyeshade was to keep Langley Wade from seeing too much of the world which had hurt him and to prevent the world from observing his humiliation.

After a long evening of piano playing Marc often drowsed in the misty room while the man beneath the eyeshade nervously puffed his pipe and told what he had read that day and what he thought of it. His voice was frequently high with indignation.

A thin, restless man, he would twitch himself from side to side within the wide Morris chair. Its pad was covered with dull green because Mrs. Wade believed green might help her husband's eyes. Everything within the room was either dull brown or dull green, giving the room the effect of a lichenaceous cavern.

The walls were lined with open bookshelves sparsely interspersed with doors and windows. The only ornament was a handsomely mounted barometer. At eye level, thumb tacks fastened charts to a shelf. On them Professor Wade kept records of weather, of temperatures, of his schedule of classes, of the number of papers submitted daily, of the number graded, evidences of Langley Wade's effort to cling upon the captious sea of daily living to what he could of rational methods and scientific observations.

To avoid further campus conflict he never spoke extemporaneously in the classroom. Chapter by chapter, sentence by sentence, word for word, precisely, he recited his textbook. But to Marc, awake or drowsing, he poured out opinions.

Mrs. Wade told other faculty wives at tea that "Mr. Wade can converse with Marc Kleinman by the hour, and you know how particular Mr. Wade is."

After that Marc began to be invited to Westmount, where Langley Wade had refused to live. He was asked frequently and went frequently. He admired the mannerly way of life and liked his hosts and hostesses. Because Miss Ophelia had told everyone about that terribly nice Jewish boy living at her house, Marc no longer had to choose between replying to anti-Semitic remarks or by his silence accepting a friendship on a false postulate. In Westmount it was assumed that every guest was worthy of respect.

In Marc's mind an absence of prejudice became vaguely associated with age and education. He tried to understand the sweetness of these lives. Most of the faculty people were as genial and as free of restlessness as Miss Ophelia. They were urbanely unmoved by questions which tormented Langley Wade.

Books which brought angry clouds of smoke from the Wade pipe here were discussed calmly. Men from the English Department would analyze the style; men from Sociology, the effect on the public; men from History, earlier books of a similar kind. Nobody became excited even over books which had sent Langley Wade into a three-month digestive upset.

Marc discerned that a man of education and culture had a field in which he was an expert and stuck to it with equanimity.

The summons was mysteriously worded: "Your name was given by an honored member of the faculty. We invite you because you are a man of high ideals. Our distinguished guest believes in good times for all young people. We need your help."

Entering the designated classroom on the Saturday evening specified, Marc saw at once that he had been invited because he was a Jew. Weiss was there. Randall. A dozen others newly come this year. Some he had never seen. Some he had not known to be Jewish.

Uncle Sed finished his introduction of Samuel Baumfield, who had come all the way from New York to organize a new fraternity. When Uncle Sed left the room Mr. Baumfield ceased reading his speech, put his eyeglasses away, and said since the fraternities would not take in Jews—well, since they were so unfriendly, the thing for the Jewish boys to do was to organize their own fraternity. Better to stick to your own, anyhow. Have your own fun. That didn't mean all Jewish boys would be asked. Only the best. Not even every young man in this room would be invited. The situation was being carefully studied.

He whisked some pledge ribbons from his pocket. A pledge button. He mentioned Greek letters. He pulled back his vest to show the pin.

Weiss whispered to Marc, his thumb indicating Randall. "He'll be dropped. A couple of others. It'll be a good bunch."

Clarence Weiss seemed to have forgotten his earlier faith in the melting pot. And unmeltable Randall seemed to be longing for this particular warmth. He looked expectant and eager.

Marc left the room. On the porch facing the Columns, he paused. A fat, caressing arm encompassed his shoulders.

Uncle Sed had been near the window, listening. He whispered, "Baumfield is going to make you Regal Master. To start it off right. It's a fine honor. We went down the list and we agreed."

Freeing his shoulders, Marc said he would not join.

"They'll have grand times. A house as fine as any on the campus. I've been worried about you Hebrew boys." The warm hand was tight on Marc's arm. "That Randall fellow won't be asked. This is for the elite."

As Marc moved toward the steps Uncle Sed demanded, "Why not join?"

"I'd miss Randall. I couldn't get along without Randall."

Uncle Sed stared at that, recognizing it for the truth and untruth of irony which he never understood and of which he always disapproved.

Joy and torment pounded through Marc's head like twin rivers. He tried to understand the turbulence so that he might understand himself. Who am I? thudded constantly at his mind. And why is it this way for me?

His walk, always erect, became overerect. He had grown taller and thinner. When he was happy his unhappiness was back of his joy, shoving it on to hilarity. On such a night he accepted a last-minute appeal from Hallie to escort her to her sorority dance. They tried the latest steps, with Marc's delight whirling Hallie into the music so that their grace and precision and ecstasy were watched and enjoyed. Some Deltas were among the guests, but even Hart Bromage, back for a visit, shaking Marc's hand, seeking him out again and again, did not penetrate Marc's pleasure to the pain immediately behind it.

The next day, however, Marc saw his high spirits of the evening before as crass nonsense and saw himself as the half-welcome guest too much at home.

Hallie teased him about the nicety with which he drew lines past which he would not go. He would call upon her at her home but not at the chapter house. He would escort her to the All-Student Annual, a motley function, and once a semester to the lovely formal given by her chapter, but he would not come to her sorority house as guest at their dinners. He would play for their small dances, as he did for any small dances employing him, but while playing he did not want Hallie idling by the piano. He would press her hand swiftly and tell her to run along to her party. Because she was likely to appear at any campus dance where he was playing, he ceased playing and became a photographer. At football games he would snap pictures and have hundreds of copies ready to sell as the crowds left the stadium.

Weiss and the others were bustling about the campus in various stages of initiation. They had rented a house and were furnishing it, entertaining parental visitors, pausing at first to coax Marc, then to accuse him of anti-Semitism, finally to ignore him conspicuously.

They had excluded Ira Randall. Shortly after Randall was sure, he left Columbia. Marc saw him going, weighted with bundles and suitcases, staggering toward the depot. Helping, Marc talked of inconsequential campus events.

Ira was silent until his baggage was settled in the train. Then he said, "I didn't want to leave before the year was over. Guess I just don't get the hang of it. Thanks for carrying my things."

He sat down and stared out the window, pretending to peer at a distant object of compelling interest.

Because the university grade system gave students quantitative rewards for qualitative successes, both Byrn and Marc made many extra credits. They now devised ways of adding to this surplus by taking advanced courses and thus arranged to have sufficient credits for graduation by the end of their third year. Byrn was in haste to begin working for a graduate degree; Marc was only eager to get on with living.

In a fond moment when love for Hallie also seemed the necessity to explore his own past, Marc told her about Orvell. In reply she looked at him as she was wont to look at her father.

At first her feeling for Marc had been mostly infatuation, then affection for a good playmate. In them both was an extraordinary energy, a gay rushing about, a chattering, a give-and-take of wit.

Marc had no rivals. Hallie went with him so much that she was thought of as Marc's girl. She thought of herself as his girl and was content, for Marc offered happy escape from the dour ways of the Wade household.

Yet it was only when he told her about Orvell that she began to fall deeply in love with him.

Marc would lament, "I should have gone into every office on the campus to tell them about Clagger and his kind of justice. Someone somewhere——"

"And be known forever as a complete nut?" she would counter. "Marc, you did everything you could. More than anyone else would do. A fellow can't go around acting queer."

She sought to draw him back to the usual. It was what her mother was constantly trying to do for her father. That Marc needed to be drawn back flooded her with tenderness for him.

Spring came to Columbia fondly. Blossoms trimmed the trees, the tall locust, the squat fruit trees, the winsome red-bud, the exquisite dogwood shy within the groves. Long rows of bridal-wreath bushes turned white, hugging the huge build-ings, making the vast structures seem to rest upon great mounds of tossed lace. Bedecked, the entire countryside celebrated the season. The air was perfume; the sunshine, a caress; the breeze whispered that to be alive was good.

Marc and Hallie rushed into each other's arms. They prom-ised nothing, saying only that they loved with all their hearts.

On a visit home Marc saw Orvell Sultan, now Otto Street. Had he violated his parole he would have caused Mr. Lew Cherry to forfeit his bond and to collect for it week by week from Mamie Lee.

"I'm at Illinois U," he said. "Couldn't go East and be here to report. It won't be long now before I get my degree."

Otto Street was thin. He wore a frayed suit too large by several sizes.

Marc said, "You've gone hungry for it."

"Some folks go hungry and don't get anything in exchange." The smile was genial-bitter.

Achieving the top of the long hill, Marc and Hallie would glance back across the valley toward the university which they loved more heartily because they loved each other. Westmount was a plateau high enough to look directly into the great

Cyclopean eye of the university, the golden dome topping Academic Hall.

From the crest they did not have far to walk to reach the Larcum home, prettily average in size and style of architecture, as were the other homes in the faculty district. Between the houses was space sufficient to symbolize the peace and respect and neighborliness between families.

Hallie and Marc were frequent guests at the Larcum home, enjoying the talk about the new wonders of science and the prediction that the world would soon be an easier place for living, permitting men and women to give their attention to the good life instead of to the grim necessities of mere existence.

Into this paean of hope Hans's letters, with their worry about war, struck discordantly. Gustav Cramer in Germany and Albert Kleinman in France again were expecting trouble. Aunt Martha mentioned scarcities created for the housewife by the Army's need for this and that. Each time he wrote Hans would conclude: "It is not good. I am glad my sons are Americans."

Embattled behind his thick glasses, Dr. Mooren replied to Marc's questions with facts: Wars and enmities had always existed between France and Germany. But he would not predict. "As a historian I think back, not forward." He laughed.

Only ashen Langley Wade, cowering beneath his eyeshade in his drab study in his drab house, agreed with Hans. He went to his shelf where magazines were stacked in neat piles. He slapped the dust from the journals and showed Marc articles, some a year old, which he had marked "War."

"Of course there will be war," he said.

"But no one in Westmount has————"

The hand which pushed the eyeshade back was trembling. The eyes were glazed. "No, no one in Westmount." he said.

By Commencement Week the idyl of spring had been routed by the insolence of summer. Many among the graduates felt the final ceremonies to be funereal within their lives, marking the end of their freedom from the rotund parental pair come to view the awarding of diplomas, the end of being born of no one, bred of no one. Soon they would become embedded in farms and households not their own.

There were tears and promises of reunions and presents and dances and a commencement address which suggested that a new and grander world was on its way, the direct result of the splendid web of roads and bridges being thrown across the country. The most important graduate today, the speaker said, was the one receiving a degree in engineering.

Byrn and Marc, by a bit of trading, managed to walk as a pair in the commencement procession. Byrn said his father had written something about the importance of roads, but it was after having lunched with an Army man, and Army men loved roads almost as much as Navy men loved ships.

When Marc told Miss Ophelia good-by, she said that whenever he wanted to come back to visit she would have his room for him, and of course he would be coming back to see Hallie.

CHAPTER VI

Aurelia agreed with uncle oscar and uncle carl that if hans were not ill with something more ominous than a cough he would not brood because a little archduke somewhere off in Europe had been shot. Though the evenings were warm Hans sat indoors searching the newspaper with a magnifying glass for more news, now and then putting the paper aside to continue his search on the globe he had given to Marc as a present on his tenth birthday.

Marc tried to divert him with talk of what went on in Uncle Oscar's store. Hans listened, sighed, and said, "You are kind, Marc. You pretend you do not care that you must work for Uncle Oscar. In a few weeks my cough will be better. Mr. Kemper will take me back full time."

A few months ago, when Fred had started more shows than he could finance, he rushed home saying he was broke. Too broke to go on. Marc would be back soon, he assured Aurelia. Marc would look after everything. Freddy paced the floor and pondered and suddenly said, "I'm too broke to do anything but get married. No, Mama, I'm not taking Celia's father's dough. I'll start over again in Chicago, or maybe California. I'm too broke. I got to get married. We'll elope. I haven't a dime for the trimmings."

So Marc had no choice. The twins had to be kept in high school; next year they would be seniors. Marc went to Uncle Carl, who narrowed his eyes as if Marc were a piece of fine furniture and he the appraiser. At last he turned to his desk. "This time it's Carl who's writing the note. You look good, Marc. You're an able boy. A gentleman. The kind Oscar would give his right hand to be. If that brother of mine tells you you need to learn the business from the bottom up, remind him I have already taught you the business."

After the sealed note was in Marc's hand Carl walked with his nephew to the door. His ruddy face glowed with enthusiasm. "You're the answer to the maiden's prayer. Oscar doesn't want long noses about the place and doesn't want strangers. If you can learn to get along with Oscar you're set for life, boy. Set pretty."

When Hans's pain became too great he would go to Dr. Armstrong's office for more of the little pills he chose to call his indigestion pills.

On the day the Kaiser's army slashed into Belgium, Marc came home to find Hans breathing badly and asking for the night edition of the paper. Marc shared his campus faith with his father. "It can't last. The world is too civilized. There won't be a long war. Not in this day and age."

"Over there war is an old story."

"This is the twentieth century. Don't forget that."

"Germany has always been in the war business. *Deutschland über alles.* It is her trade."

Dr. Armstrong came to the house now. When Hans inquired about half days at Mr. Kemper's store, Dr. Armstrong's bushy gray eyebrows would loft into the wrinkles of his forehead. He would look down through his glasses, his head tilted back. After a pause he would ask, "How did you feel today?" as if the question also answered Hans's question. He seemed to under-stand that Hans did not really want to go downtown.

Hans would sit in the large armchair, looking too small for it, his folded newspaper across the knees of his blue bathrobe. Mama would come in and fluff his pillow, scold if there was a spot or, more frequently, praise him if there was none. She liked to fix his hair and would change his things needlessly, as if he were a doll and she a little girl playing games. He sat quietly and let her do as she wished. They did not speak except that at times he would murmur: "I have Marc. I have Freddy. I have Ruth. I have Bertha."

Then she would tiptoe out, knowing she had heard his report of himself to eternity.

When the war was well started, people would ask each other: "Are you pro-German or pro-Ally?" Their voices sounded as if they might have been inquiring about baseball: Are you rooting for the Cardinals or for the Browns?

Uncle Oscar spent a great deal of time telling people he was pro-German. He would mix into the declaration a lot of stories of the handsome entertainment he and Mrs. Hursch had received on their trips. "Munich is the prettiest city in the world. No, Dresden is. You see, it is a beautiful country. And culture—the best medicine, the best universities, the finest art ... ." He would look around as if to ask whether he had not proved that it was impossible for a man who valued the best in civilization to be other than pro-German.

Dr. Armstrong, pausing as he wrote out a prescription, asked Hans one evening which side he wanted to win.

Hans answered: "My sisters live in Germany. My brothers were not welcome. Like myself, most of them left. One went to India. Three brothers are Allies now. It is not pleasant to think that their children are"—his lips trembled—"at each other's throats."

The next time Dr. Armstrong came Hans said, "Where the whole thing is wrong, how can either side be right? How can a man——" He could not continue.

In the dim hall downstairs Dr. Armstrong spoke in calm, hushed tones. "I'm sure you realize that Mr. Kleinman's heart will not improve."

Marc wet his lips. "Is there anything ... ?"

"Just keep him quiet."

"He is quiet."

Aurelia shook her head. "He is not quiet. He's trying to stop that war over there. He sits, yes. In his nightgown there are no wrinkles. And in his sheets. But he is not quiet."

They began to choose the bits of news to take into the bedroom which now for the first time seemed more Hans's than Aurelia's. Formerly the room had seemed hers; now nothing of Aurelia's was visible. At night she slept on a cot next to the large bed, and in the morning the cot was folded and put out of sight. On the dresser stood Hans's new brush and comb sent by Celia and Freddy out of empty pockets. Before the Large mirror was a mounted and shellacked map Mr. Edgewood had made. In Mama's best hand-painted vase were flowers. When those sent by Aunt Clara and Aunt Mimi would wilt, Ruth would bring fresh ones and watch while Bertha fiddled them into position. Between the marble book ends were the books Hans liked to read: *Coriolanus* in German, and Goethe.

It was fully his world. Into it Marc did not take Uncle Oscar's news of Fräulein. She had remained even after Alice had gone East to college, managing the household, arranging the great dinners, flattering her employers, and obsequiously rubbing her hands until the last moment. When she left she said she was leaving to help a friend. Soon they learned she was in charge of the dining room of the recently expanded Alps.

Uncle Oscar's own preference for Germany over France was not of the kind to make him feel at ease when he and Clara went to the Alps to see Fräulein. On the way home he said, "There is something strange about that place. It's more than a restaurant. The German counsel at that table in the corner was too serious. Looked as if it was business hours for him."

"You never have understood Fräulein," Clara answered.

Oscar cleared his throat. "I am no longer pro-German."

During the election campaign Hans was happier. When Marc came home one day wearing a Wilson button, Hans asked for it and had Aurelia pin it on his bathrobe. Marc told him about the first election of Woodrow Wilson and how the entire university had been for him because everyone believed putting a college president in the White House would bring the intelligent ways of a campus to the direction of the country. It would be a major triumph for civilization.

Hans nodded. "When Woodrow Wilson is dying he will be able to say to himself that he kept a nation out of war. He is a lucky man."

On the day war was declared Marc rushed home to find Hans staring at the headlines with tears in his eyes. A yellow-red flush suffused his face; his fist crushed at his bosom. Aurelia was removing the map and the globe.

Hans spoke through his cough. "It is too late—to love a country after you have left her. That war business over there is why I left. German men have always believed in war the way other men believe in God. Now they drag us into it." He became a little delirious. He would open his eyes and say, "It is too late to love a mother after she is dead."

Dr. Armstrong said it was nearly over. Except for leaving Aurelia, Hans was glad. Fred and Celia came, holding hands and kissing and snuggling. They tried to be cheerful in Hans's bedroom and outside they tried not to be.

Fred said, "I'm too damned married to want to go. I don't want to be a soldier boy."

Marc answered, "I'd like to put an end to German bullying forever." That reason could be given to Freddy because it was a reason many were giving. Nearer Marc's heart was the feeling that trouble had come to this country, and because it was his country and the land which more than any other was the land of the free, it was also his trouble.

Fred's fingers rattled at some coins in his pocket. His eyes wandered over Marc's face. They searched and found, and searched. When he left, he handed Aurelia an envelope filled with bills. "There'll be another every month," he said.

That afternoon Marc enlisted.

Marc wired Hallie. Their only meeting was in a clattering corner of the sprawling railway station. They sat in the second-floor waiting room a few paces away from others who waited. No one they knew was on the opposite bench, and this they accepted for privacy.

Marc's satchel was at their feet and his orders to report in his pocket. He told Hallie all he had not been able to say to Fred.

"But, Marc, you have always told me you did not believe in war."

"I'm not willing to have this country defeated. It all comes down to that."

Their hands were interlocked, their fingers stiff with the anguish of parting.

"I love you, Marc. Sometimes I wish I didn't love you so much."

As if the train bells were not clanging their parting, Marc began to tell Hallie of his life. No longer content to be born of no one, bred of no one, he told about growing up in the Yellow Row and how it had been in high school, at one with neither the fraternity boys nor with the Jewish boys, only at one with the Glee Club. He told her about the Deltas on that first evening, but most of all he spoke of Orvell and that he had failed him and so had failed himself.

"Marc darling, you must use common sense. Look at Father."

She detailed Langley Wade's fall: the promotion of which he was proud; the wires from New York for articles; the students who came to him as to a well in an oasis; the meetings in his study. He had rushed in and out and about their home and the campus, an exultantly happy man, believing in himself and in his power over his times. And then, the day he was summoned by the president of the college, who had for years been or seemed to be his friend and now was only an employer dismissing an unsatisfactory employee for having written articles which the trustees found offensive. Langley Wade's anger and his applications for other teaching posts. On the next campus Langley Wade again was busy and a well for students, but only for a few months. The dismissal came before the semester was half over. On this occasion he was less angry and more frightened. They remained on that campus and were stared at. Vera Wade went to bed with a heavy cold and huddled indoors until they moved. Her nose ceased running, but she said she felt ill.

Finally, Missouri and the eyeshade and recited lectures from the book written during the exultant days and the avoidance of Westmount, because confreres had become in Langley Wade's eyes only men who had not stuck by their principles. No wires for articles. No students except Marc. No joy in anything.

Marc watched Hallie's lips and the sweetness of their movements, the way they thinned and turned as she talked. His eyes fondled the texture of her skin and hair. A slow blush would deepen upon her cheek. She was softly beautiful this morning, a grave and gentle girl.

When traintime had nearly come he said, "Hallie, go out to the house. I want you to meet Papa before he dies. Mama will be glad to see you. I want you to know them and I want them to know you. Hallie darling, I shall miss you terribly."

Later, as they hurried down the stairs, he said suddenly, "It's hard to believe the world is a sensible, good world moving toward perfection and then to find that it has gone mad. Spattering blood over all of us. It's hard to wake up from university days and find that true. My darling, I'm sorry."

"We were not meant for war, Marc, you and I."

"I am going."

Hallie smiled as if amused by the whimsical ways of someone at a great distance who happened to be herself. "Then I'm going too. I'll join up somehow. If this is your war, Marc, it's also mine."

PART III
1918–1935

The captive exile hasteneth that he may be loosed, and that he should not die in the pit, nor that his bread should fail.

—ISAIAH

CHAPTER I

THE GIANT OF war had spent itself. the kaiser had fled. American soldiers stationed some miles from Trier looked at their picture-book village and longed for home. Marc Kleinman, billeting officer, was returning to headquarters along the curving, cobblestoned street. Behind him could be heard the hoarse shouts of sergeants carrying out his orders. By packing in three soldiers where there was space for only one, by evacuating a few more Germans, he had made room for several dozen legless men en route to the States. Unexpected, they had appeared a few hours ago, together with M.D.s and soldier nurses, all of whom had to be kept for the night.

For Marc, war had been learning to work eighteen hours a day; to stay awake when weary; to run when his arches ached. He was tired now, but only with the habit of being tired.

As he entered the building he was met by a messenger announcing that a visitor awaited him. She stood in the half-light of late afternoon, erect, short, shapeless, old. Beneath the round black hat with its wilted feather was a replica of Hans Kleinman's face wearing an expression his had never worn. She seemed to brace herself against an inner ramrod of resolve. In a rigid hand she held a limp white handkerchief. She was watching an American soldier as he distributed among the legless some yellow flowers she had brought for Marc.

That she was an old woman at first was more important than that she was his father's sister. Her shapeless figure in its black dress reminded Marc of Aurelia as she had looked at Hans's funeral.

He moved closer and peered down into her eyes. His palms cupped her elbows. Gently he turned her toward the light. Through the chill appraisal of her look he saw Hans's features feminized. Her eyes glazed with tears; her left cheek twitched; she murmured, *"Gott in Himmel! Gerade wie Hans!* It iss Hans I see.

To Marc's German she replied in English. "I am Martha. Your Aunt Martha."

The *th* was more accurate on her lips than it had ever been on Hans's.

"You were his favorite," Marc said.

Her throat seemed to be swallowing tears. Lowering her head, she opened her handbag to bring out a home-sewed case of black fabric. The decorative stitches were the same as those on a muffler she had sent Hans, the one Aurelia tacked to the collar of his robe so that in those final weeks it would be there for him to stroke.

Martha's fingers, short like Hans's, fumbled as she opened the case. Marc looked down at two young men in the enemy's uniform.

"Thiss one iss dead now—since two years. Sholem would be *fünf-und-zwanzig.* Thiss one——" She shrugged and shook her head. "I do not hear. *Drei-und-zwanzig.* Dead, perhaps, or in captivity." Like Hans, she spoke her numerals in German. She looked at the legless boys. "Gretchen iss singer in Berlin. Married to Fritz Alsberg. Also in captivity. My other daughter iss widow. He lies dead in Belgium. How iss your father? Gretchen hass good voice."

Only then did Marc recall that no one had written to Hans's sisters of his death now that it was possible for letters to go through. No one had thought of them.

She took the news calmly, only a slight frown appearing between her eyes. Her pallor and her white hair made her look aged, yet her ways were energetic. Very rapidly she began to inquire who was yet living. Freddy? Ruth? Bertha? All alive! How happy Aurelia, how lucky! "You in America had not so many years as we."

She spoke of the war as of a devastation performed by Nature. Her eyes watched the legless boys greedily. Marc observed her desire. Instead of the dead Sholem ...

He turned her so that she would not see them. As his hands touched the roundness of her arms he knew that he would write Hallie and tell her it was all nonsense to wait until they returned to the States. They must be married over here, a little away from the stench of war, in London perhaps. And soon.

During all the rest of his aunt Martha's visit Marc's attention was partly truant, making plans. Could Hallie manage to be married in something blue? In a blue dress with a white lace collar?

Meanwhile the old German voice was rattling off the chronicle of the families of her sisters and brothers. When she said a date it was the date of a war death. Letters had begun to come through from France and England. She spoke those deaths with the same intonation as the German deaths. "It iss like Fate, *nicht?* It comes. No one wants war. Like Fate it comes."

In a letter from France she had learned about Marc. "You saw Albert in Paris."

"Once. Uncle Albert looks like my father. Yet he also looks French, speaks French, thinks French, eats French. Heloise is pretty. Looks like her French mother. It was before I could speak the language."

"But Albert—his name used to be Aaron—Albert surely speaks English. Why not?"

"A little. His wife and daughter speak only French. His son was home on leave."

Again she mentioned a date, quickly. It must have been the boy's last leave. Albert's son had fallen in battle.

With great effort she kept her face unweeping. She even tried to be a little jolly. "Albert eats French! What does that mean?" she demanded, a comic tone lying lightly on her question.

"It was a typically French meal. From the bouillon to the fruit, French. Fruit for dessert."

She drew herself up with mock hauteur. "My husband when he lived ate *Schnecken, Strudel, Torten, Kaffee-kuchen.* Not fr-r-r-ruit."

Then Marc recalled that Martha's husband had been Gustav Cramer, whose visit to the World's Fair had brought him to the Yellow Row.

"In England iss Carolina's son, Kleinman Wolff. He iss chemist. He wins honor now for some discovery. Something perhaps to stop war?" She had tried many times to get permission to see Hans's son. "Ach, now Hans, such a dear, gentle boy—Hans always wass. Hans iss dead."

Marc stooped and kissed the flabby cheek. He tried to ask her to come again, when the legless soldiers would be gone. Instead he said, "I'll call on Kleinman Wolff in London."

Her face brightened. "*Gut, gut!* You go to London?"

"Later. To be married."

She opened her bag again and moistened a stub of pencil. She wanted to record the name of the girl and the date in the

Bible at home where she had recorded all the others. Freddy's and Celia's too.

Marc laughed. The bride would have to be told first. And his mother.

"You Americans," she teased. "It iss joke."

He assured her it was not a joke. She shook her head and smiled upon him. Desire again was in her eyes. Marc did not like to look at it. So he kissed her and patted her shoulder and assured her that as soon as his mother knew, she would write to Martha and the letter would contain the girl's name and the date of the marriage.

In leaving she asked the question all Aurelia's friends and relatives would ask. "Iss she a Jewish girl?"

When he said no, the old woman stood very still for a long moment. Her expression softened and now she looked like Hans's sister. "Anyhow," she said, "I wish you good luck. A long, happy life. Many babies .... And no war .... No war for your children."

London was a lavender-gray mist with buildings only a little more gray. On the wide sidewalk before St. Paul's a carpet of pigeons, lavender-gray too, rippled as the birds pecked and strutted. When the young American officer and the girl in a blue dress with a white collar approached, the pigeons scolded and waddled in quicker tempo, then at the last moment rose, disappearing into a cloud which was also the stately dome of the cathedral. Watching them, Hallie's eyes were brilliantly blue. Marc thought he would never forget them as they looked in that moment. An hour hence, in a civil ceremony, they would be declared man and wife. In the meanwhile they would visit St. Paul's.

Inside the great doors they stood within a majesty which suited their mood. The cathedral was nearly dark; footsteps were distant, shuffling. Distant, too, was the rumble and whine of an organ. Whispering, they extolled the joy of being together. Hallie said she could not have stood the separation another day.

"Marc, you'll never know———" Then abruptly she brightened and said the war was not to be mentioned again. "Let's vow, Marc, always to be happy."

Holding her head high, she said being happy was mostly wanting to be happy. She gave him a fond glance and he looked at her with adoration.

As they were about to leave the cathedral Marc looked down the twilight of the nave and asked, "Isn't your mother an Episcopalian?"

"Marc, what are we going to do about religion and church and all that?"

"You must do what you prefer. I shall join nothing."

"It's time to go," she said.

At luncheon, after the ceremony, trying not to hold hands across the table, trying not to show even to each other the great turmoil of joy and exultation within their hearts, Hallie kept saying, "We're going to be happy together. Very happy."

The last day of their honeymoon had come. It was Sunday and the morning began with the jangled tolling of bells. Churches seemed to be on all sides of the Bloomsbury bedroom where Marc and Hallie lay in a mist of half sleep. The incessant ringing was so loud that the bells themselves seemed only inches from their ears.

When they ceased Hallie whispered, "Keep your eyes closed, so we can see the long path down the garden. A lemon tree is flattened against the wall of the great house, and tiny flowers———"

Marc laughed. "Too much sight-seeing. Wake up and observe the liver-colored spots on the ceiling, also the view—a sooty wall three feet distant from our window. Darling, you deserved elegance for your honeymoon."

"I'm in the garden . . . ."

He told her to come out and make up her mind whether she would like to pay a call upon Kleinman Wolff. "There's a wife too. And I believe some children. We'd phone first."

"Sir, I cannot refuse shelter from this English rain. Besides, I've never been inside an English house." She sat up and rubbed her eyes. "I'll find out how your family will take me. I've been wondering."

"You haven't really?"

"No, I haven't. I have the craziest feeling that everything will be all right. That everything all our lives will be all right. That once we're thoroughly out of this hideous war we'll never again have any troubles of any kind."

Marc kissed her into silence. He said, "We agreed not to mention the war. We'll soon be home."

"I do feel cleansed of it somehow. These three days have——But, Marc, I had never believed——"

"I know, dear, I know."

"—people could be happy and then they do that to each other!" She was shivering and in her eyes was a look Marc had never seen there before. It was fear of some sinister human quality which might get off the leash. It was a fear which parted her lips and turned them white.

Comforting her, Marc said, "We'll have to try to see that it never happens again. There'll be millions of young people everywhere——"

With a sharp gasp she said, "We'll do all we can, but we'll also be happy."

They walked through Hyde Park to a street where the houses were tall and thin and as stiff as an unused stage-set.

Waiting in the hall with the umbrellas and hatrack and gleaming brass, Hallie whispered, "Tell me about him, Marc."

"His mother was my father's oldest sister."

They were led up an etching-hung stairway of soft carpeting and shiny stair rods and into a study where Kleinman Wolff sat at a desk writing. He rose at once to greet them in a manner which was cordial in an embarrassed British way. He was much taller than any Kleinman Marc had ever met, yet he, too, had a torso which seemed overlong for his legs. His eyes wore a studious expression even when merely estimating the need for more coal in the grate. His face was as gray as London itself, and his voice seemed entirely British. The man might have been recognized anywhere in the world as a Londoner.

Mr. Wolff had little idea who Marc was. At first he assumed Hallie was the relative. When Marc explained, the pipe was lifted toward an oval oil which hung above the fireplace. It was a tender depiction of wistful eyes and soft hair and a lovely pair of shoulders.

"That was Carolina Kleinman Wolff. My mother died when I was born. I was her only child. Wasn't she lovely? My father always said she was. I've rather thought the picture proved it. My father was on the silent side, you know. Somewhat stern, I suppose. He told me little about her except that she was very beautiful and very good."

Then Marc realized that he knew more of this man's mother than did Kleinman Wolff himself. He hurried to say, "My father

spoke of her with affection. Aunt Martha tells me you have discovered a new chemical. Something, she said, which will perhaps
put an end to war."

Mr. Wolff turned serious. It was an easy, philosophical kind
of seriousness in which there was nothing of personal concern. "I
was on the trail of an anesthetic. Stumbled on poison gas instead.
I'm not so childish as to believe that poison gas will cause wars
to cease. The catalyst is in the way we trade, I presume. Some
believe the very danger involved will deter declarations. I don't
accept that either. I want you to meet Elizabeth."

She had slipped in quietly and stood there now, closing the
door behind her. She was tall, very thin, almost a caricature con-
firmation of the American idea of a London woman. She wore a
tweed skirt, flat shoes, and a sweater that was heather in tone.
Her voice was high-pitched and she seemed amazed at Hallie's
way of sitting in a chair. It was a cretonne-covered lounge chair
and Hallie snuggled into it with her feet tucked beneath her,
appearing more at ease than Elizabeth could ever have appeared
within her own home or any other.

Elizabeth's talk raced off at tangents, returning again and
again to apologize for inconsequential household slips. Did they
know, she asked, that London protected its art treasures from
bombs by hiding them in the subway? Did America have subways
too? And wasn't America wonderful? Who could have believed
troop ships could be brought across! Did America always wait
too long to make a decision and then rush to carry things out?
The British Tommy was the finest man on earth. Had Americans
learned anything during the war about how Negroes should be
treated? Fairly, you know. The French seemed to understand
it, but then the Frenchman had a talent for friendliness. Surely
one should not speak ill of one's allies. Was the British coffee

really so bad compared with what was served in the States? Why didn't people drink tea? Tea, at least, was good for trade. She had worked with disabled veterans until her husband forbade it. Thought it too depressing for her.

She rose to light a fresh cigarette from her last, and suddenly her lips quivered and her eyes blinked back tears.

Mr. Wolff took the talk away from her, returning it to chemistry. When Marc twitted him about the parallelism between his career and that of Dr. Chaim Weizmann a wry smile lifted the brows and twinkled his eyes. "But I shall not ask for Palestine."

"How much of that was a political move?" Marc asked. "It came at a time when the nations were delicately balanced in their national sympathies."

"Doubtless the Crown believed it worth trying."

"It?"

"An appeal over the heads of governments to the Jews of the world."

"I don't like that," Marc said, "though I feel Britain was on the side of decency."

"Decency must be implemented," Mr. Wolff replied. "America has many Zionists?"

"Among the Orthodox poor."

"Those who can remember what it means to need a refuge. I'm not speaking of myself." He squinted momentarily through the smoke. "Nor of you. We seem to be assimilated. Dr. Weizmann was born in Russia. I assume he worried about pogroms. Would you care to meet our children?"

Their Nanny was plump and gently stern. Albert was dark like his mother; Victoria, five, looked like her father; Edward, three, was the extreme blond Hans had taught Marc to expect in every Kleinman household.

Saying their good-bys, the women lingered to compare household ways. The men were alone when Marc said, "Aunt Martha is completely German, of course. In France, Albert is completely French. You seem completely English, and we, I suppose, completely American. Is the human being a chameleon?"

Kleinman Wolff sucked at his pipe for a moment. "To survive, a Jew must be adaptable. Darwin called it protective adaptation. The Jew who can't adapt himself is lost to the line. When times are out of joint, you know." Again his tone was philosophical. "Once in a while times do get out of joint."

It seemed to Marc an understatement of the carnage he had witnessed.

Later he said to Hallie, "I like that fellow. You know, I think he does it just right. The way he handles being a Jew. He lives as an Englishman but with no fooling himself or anyone else as to his origin."

Hallie slipped her hand into the crook of Marc's arm. "I wonder if it isn't silly not to forget the origin too. I wonder if it wouldn't be happier for his children. Marc, I hear people speak the word, Jew, in the ugliest kind of way. Without knowing why or even what it is to be a Jew."

"Does anyone know? Sometimes I think it's only having too much pride to deny it."

She nodded. "I think that's all right, Marc. For you. And for our children. It's the way we'll live it."

CHAPTER 11

FOR MARC, COMING back to St. louis was a bad dream in which paralysis battled with a frantic need to run. He was trying to come home, and without Hans there was no home.

Aurelia and Ruth still lived in the Yellow Row, and Hans's German books still stood behind the glassed doors of the bookcase, but there was no one to whom Marc could describe Germany's arrogant anti-Semitism even in her moment of defeat, no one whose mind would linger on *Tante* Martha's joke about Uncle Albert's fruit for dessert and her own husband's masculine preference for *Torte*.

Even before Hallie hurried to Columbia to see her parents Marc prowled up and down stairs in the little house, trying to enlarge it to its remembered size, trying to invest the ebony screen and the ivory goose-man with their former fascination.

Impatiently Aurelia said, "I've waited all this time for you to come back so I could get out of here and now you're back and you're no help."

"Where do you want to go, Mama? To visit Freddy?"

Aurelia looked over her glasses and put down her crocheting. "I don't want to run around in restaurants with movie stars until three in the morning. There was a picture of Freddy and Celia in the paper."

"Mama, that was one evening."

She tried to be fair. "No, I don't expect them to take Freddy's picture in bed in his nightshirt." Her chin crinkled. "I don't want to go all the way to California without Papa."

"Where do you want to go? You and Ruth?"

She was crocheting again, pausing now and then to wipe her eyes. "Ruth has her heart set on New York. She wants to ride around in tunnels and live in a room with three beds and no windows."

"She is a journalist, Mama. She wants a job."

"She's got a job."

"On the woman's page!"

"She can't boil water and she give recipes .... It's not recipes which drive her away. She tells me nothing. Bertha grabs the first man who ever looked at her and Clarence Weiss turns out to be a good husband. Ruth always had sweethearts. She won't go out with them any more."

"Ruth wouldn't be happy with Clarence."

Marc got up and prowled again.

Something had also died within the city. Once it had believed in itself: that its bad days were far in the past when fur traders who were husbands of white women came home from their expeditions bringing children who were half Indian; when lights were shot out in saloons; when politicians carried canes and used them on their rivals. Now the city again was unsure of its virtue. Men looked at returning veterans and tried to assuage their uneasiness by proclaiming that every home would soon have a radio. A man could sit in his parlor and hear great music and fine talks. These gifts would be for all people, not just for those who could afford concert tickets. And automobiles would be for every family. And homes would be built with garages, two-car garages.

Some of this was in Uncle Carl's eyes when Marc met him by chance in Union Station. Marc had put Ruth on the train for New York and Uncle Carl had come home from a buying trip.

Carl said, "Boy, you look fine. I heard you were back. Let's go in and have some coffee and we'll talk about where we'll put you down at the store. You look fine. I wish my boy was home." He turned unhappy and sighed. "David will be going to New York most likely. All those kids want is to get away from themselves. They want to live on excitement. Maybe they want to get away from us. Greenwich Village and poetry and—— Just wait until they get hungry! They'll see how much New York cares. What's wrong with St. Louis, anyway? Why don't they stay where their families amount to something? The other two are doing O.K. Both at Hursch and Company. But now about you, Marc ...."

As Marc talked Uncle Carl's eyebrows went higher and higher; his mouth puffed at an invisible cigar; his pudgy hands twiddled. At last he said, "You mean you want to wake up every morning feeling it's important for the world that you go to the office? You want to be doing something which would be important even if no one earned anything from it, like when a doctor sets a broken arm?"

Those had not been Marc's words, but he said, "Yes, Uncle Carl, that's what I want."

"Marc, boy, don't be an idealist. I thought you had more sense. Only a child—or a bum—thinks life can be like that. Believe me, every morning when I wake up for the last thirty years I think: Now I have to go down and have my *Tzores* again. *Tzores* mean troubles, nasty little troubles. At first I did it to support my family. I made a success. Hursch and Company is something in this town. We are a respected firm. After a while a man still loves his wife, of course, but he's not rushing around to hang diamonds on her. And then when I saw that my David didn't give a damn I began to ask myself why I didn't retire. Let the other boys take over. In the long run I find out that managing a good business is what I have to be proud of in life. I've got enough money. St. Louis still needs Hursch and Company. Furniture at decent prices. Better quality each year. I still like to meet my competitors and have them bow with respect, just as I bow to them with respect. Who am I in this town if I don't run a good business?"

Marc tried not to let his face show that he could not answer Uncle Carl's questions in a way he would like. He said, "Over there, with all the work and hardships of war, I was happy because I belonged to something big which I believed in. It made a lot of difference whether I got quarters for my men or not."

"Only loafers stay in the Army when a war is over."

"I'm not staying in, but I want to be part of something——"

"Hursch and Company."

"Something bigger than all the people in it."

Uncle Carl leaned back, outraged. Did Marc realize how many hundreds of employees Hursch and Company had? Did he know that figure would be tripled if they followed through on their plan for opening a chain of stores? Oscar could yell all he wanted—he still yelled, of course—but when he went to a board of directors' meeting these days the young men could and did outvote him. Again and again. Look at the fellows who were living well off Hursch and Company! All the Mann second generation, eight of them, and two of Carl's sons. Hursch and Company treated its young men right. Took one after another as they came back from the Army. Good boys. Nice to work with. A month ago they had taken Clarence Weiss, Bertha's husband.

"He said he was a friend of yours at the university, Marc. You'll be happy down there .... Good God, you don't look like a boy any more."

He acted as if it was all settled, as if Marc's refusal was only an aberration caused by bombs and battles. He rose to go. "What other job is there?" he asked to the denial in Marc's face. "You did want to study law, didn't you? I guess maybe we ought to have helped you out. But we thought you'd get over it."

Marc ran for a streetcar and made it and, panting, wondered why it had been necessary to run. It was necessary. He did not have to be anywhere at any time, yet he had to hurry. He had belonged to the United States Army and now he belonged to himself and to Hallie and to the unborn child she carried, and that was not enough. Within himself he was restive.

Looking at some old men bench-sitting in a public park, Marc knew that he wanted to serve men like Hans Kleinman but in need of sons. At the Social Work Building a woman who kept smoothing her hands and grimacing asked whether he wanted to work for a Catholic, Protestant, or a Jewish agency. If it was Jewish, of course, he would have to be able to speak Yiddish. If he couldn't, then, yes, there was still lots of "neutral" work to be done, since they hoped one day to bring all the agencies together, but he would have to have a degree in social work. She could tell by talking with him that he would be infinitely valuable to them because she could see that he had vision, the kind of imagination which they needed around there, but the accepted theory was that you had that only if you had the degree, though the grind for it drove all vision out of you. Suddenly she looked at him as if he were a luscious nectarine. "What you would mean to us as a board member!"

Then she spoke of the board members they had and how narrow they were and stubborn and, not meaning to, she let slip Uncle Carl's name; and, sitting there watching the tall comely woman smooth her hands, Marc saw that even here he would be working for the Hursches.

That evening Hallie read aloud. They were midway through Hardy's *The Return of the Native.* Marc, half listening, would let his thoughts roam when they wanted to, reaching out into America, searching for the place Marc Kleinman belonged. Yes, Hardy knew that for a native to return was bad business. A native remains or leaves. When Marc went overseas he had gone with a Missouri outfit so that in a way he had not gone at all. He had stayed among men who believed in remaining in Missouri. Remaining in Missouri was not just staying in a place. It was living a respectable life, a steady life, among friends. It was being sensible, mulishly sensible, even when to do so was disastrous. It was, as Byrn always said, being middle and being proud that what you did was going to retain ways already tasted. Byrn was right; it meant faith in middleness. Without that the wider are would fly centrifugally into nothingness. A man who wanted to pull for progress should not shun the center and become a mosquito attacking the granite shaft of society. He should enter and remain true to the faith that a businessman was the marriage broker between the people and science, the go-between who would give the one to the other.

So he took Uncle Carl's job. Before he went to work he made some sketches of furniture he thought suited to this era of action.

Uncle Carl said, "I want you to make good and you come with ideas! This is what Alice Hursch would like." Uncle Carl had never been fond of Alice.

Daylight was softening into evening. Tick ... tick ... tick ... Even the clock across the shadowy room seemed to drowse. And the baby. And Hallie.

Jill was a dawdling nurser, unlike her brother, who had come to the breast demandingly, his hunger so urgent that he was soon exhausted and would fall asleep half fed.

Engulfing Jill's tiny hand within her own, Hallie tried to want her to hurry, for the books declared a baby should not be permitted to dawdle. Jill would nurse for a moment; then the round blue eyes would discover the ceiling and the rosy lips would part in wonder, so that Hallie would have to tap the little cheek as a reminder. Jill never seemed to be single-minded about her feedings.

Very likely she would be scatterbrained, Hallie decided. Yes, surely. Pretty and scatterbrained and, of course, flirtatious, since even her baby smiles were coy. When Herbert first laughed it was because he was amused, but this infant laughed in order to make the face above her laugh. Perhaps it was only that Jill, being infinitely feminine, already lived only in relation to the life of another, smiling to woo smiles, nursing to please her mother.

Through the closed door Hallie could hear Herbert and Marc talking. Aurelia was there too. As usual, Marc was trying to convert one of Herbert's disasters into delight and, by the sound of their talk, having fine success. This disaster, like so many of Herbert's, was mostly his own protest at the perishability of something he had expected to be imperishable. A dandelion, picked for Marc and saved in Herbert's pocket, had traitorously turned into a yellow-green mess. When Marc saw the disappointed quiver of Herbert's lower lip he reached for paper and crayons.

Listening, she knew the drawing was almost finished. The dandelion must be at least a sunflower by now, for Herbert's voice shrilled with triumph. He was still as urgent about life as when he was a nursing baby, an affectionate little boy, yet, alas, something of a scrapper too. A few days ago, when a neighbor's child had been rough with Jill's buggy, Herbert had pounded and kicked and scratched his adversary. Hallie, sighing, did some equations. Love equals loyalty. Loyalty equals defense of that to which we are loyal. Defense equals violence—and thus, absurdly, love turns out to equal violence. And violence in a way was war, and Hallie had seen too much of war.

The baby stirred; she was falling asleep as reluctantly as a drop of honey drips from a spoon. The eyelids were nearly together, the flush in the cheeks dulled to waxy pink. The mouth still sucked, but without hunger.

Rising, Hallie held the baby to her and kissed the soft neck. An ecstasy of pleasure suffused her body and her mood. Being a mother, she decided, gratified all there was just now of Hallie Kleinman. It was like entering a new land, a wide, wonderful land—but not too wide.

She wondered whether Marc's world was too wide. For happiness. He kept reading it wider. Caring as much about strangers in far countries as about the neighbors next door. Caring absurdly much about science.... Yes, she had told him, Einstein was a great Jew.... No, Hallie, a great physicist, and physics soon may transform the world.... What world, Marc? Ours?... Ours, Hallie, but even as he said it she knew he had to make an effort to shrink his to match the one in which she lived, where the kingdom was this house; the potentates, Herbert and Jill.

Buttoning her dress, smoothing Jill's covers once more, she glanced across the room at the clock standing in the glow shed by the night lamp. She really must hurry. Tick ... tick ... tick ... The seconds seemed shorter now. Herbert had to be calmed and put to bed and somehow induced to stay there while she and Marc ate dinner tonight with Marc's mother, who spoiled them both outrageously, talking about Jill's charm and Herbert's sturdy affections.

Hallie had wanted to be happy, and this, yes, this was happiness.

The Regal Club, which had only Jewish members, was brilliantly lighted. Oscar and Clara Hursch were celebrating their wedding anniversary. The Ellinger Lakes were there, old and fragile and thin, and also Oscar's lawyer and his wife, the Andrew Goffs.

Most of the several hundred guests, however, were Hursches and Manns and the men and women they had married. With a few exceptions, and those only among the peripheral in-laws, all before the war had called themselves German Jews. They now called themselves American Jews but, when among themselves, still scornfully used the term Russian Jew, the word *kike* having been abandoned as bad-mannered, the word *Polacken* being whispered only by lips dry with age.

Among the guests were many good citizens who had strengthened the commercial or professional or philanthropic buttresses of their city. Tonight as they danced they commented that the Oscar Hursches carried their age well and that, for all his jumping from temper to generosity, old Oscar Hursch was an honorable gentleman and his wife a kindly woman. They were throwing a very handsome party, even if it was exactly like every other club party.

Clara was too timid, or perhaps too wise, to venture into new ways, so on the table was the standard club array of platters covered with huge mock flowers whose petals were shrimp, caviar, lobster, and other delights. The fruit holders were tall and gracefully arranged, with spears of bananas up-pointed above drooping bunches of grapes. The cakes were numerous and elaborately iced in white. Waiters ladled food, passed plates, set and reset tables.

The lounge in which Oscar and Clara received their guests was separated only by wide open archways from the dance floor. Among the dancers was Bertha, who now came hurrying hand in hand with her pink-cheeked Clarence. They told Marc and Hallie where Mama was and to lose no time in finding her because she had news.

Bertha and Clarence were known as a sweet couple, for they had cheerful faces and solicitous ways. Clarence was one of the youngest buyers in the city and Bertha one of the youngest matriarchs. It was Bertha, not Aurelia, who reminded Marc and Hallie of the approach of birthdays and anniversaries and indicated the degree of obligation the event merited. She would say: "It's not an *important* anniversary; it's only their eighth; a phone call will do." To Bertha anniversaries were important only if multiples of five.

On their way to find Aurelia, Marc and Hallie met Alice Hursch just home from New York, a circumstance her black dinner gown, her walk, her hairdress, her entire manner proclaimed conspicuously. She was as stylized as a mannequin and as expressionless until she saw Marc. Though she had never before met Hallie, she held them both to her, gripping Marc's right arm and Hallie's left with her long fingers, handsomely manicured, handsomely ringed.

"Ah, Marc," she murmured, "if we only hadn't been cousins! Hallie, you won't mind my adoring your husband? He's the only Hursch I ever met with a soul. And now that he's handsome too! Promise me you'll come to see me tomorrow night. I have a surprise. You are the only ones I want to see."

Her sweetness had always been like that, bitterly aimed at someone; her father, who was also a Hursch and therefore had no soul; her mother, who had insisted that she come for this event, but whom she did not really wish to see. Marc recalled how she had flung herself at him in her girlhood. He had pitied and almost liked Alice.

Aurelia was watching the dancers from a recess lined with plump old ladies dressed in black. "Well," she said to Marc and Hallie, "Clara has a good-looking daughter at last. Stylish. She's going with someone here. Clara won't say who it is. First she divorces a husband—that rich one—for a musician. Now she divorces the musician for someone else. *Übergespaant.*"

Speaking the foreign word, Aurelia dimpled proudly. Since living in her new modern apartment, where she had moved shortly after Marc's return, many of her neighbors were widowed and Jewish, and she had learned a few phrases. People who didn't like Jews were *rishus;* people who were high-strung and happy about it were *übergespaant;* people who were poor and begged were *Schnorers.* She offered the words as proof that she had been accepted into an amorphous family now that her own was scattered. Her best friends she referred to as The Girls.

Her news was of Ruth. Ruth would be here tomorrow. For a moment Aurelia glowed with anticipation—Ruth curled up reading on Mama's couch, Ruth nibbling out of Mama's icebox, Ruth giggling when Mama clattered pans in the kitchenette.

Ruth, who was Bertha's twin, never told Mama what she ought to do. Ruth was tousle-headed and amber-eyed, a beauty who wore sweaters and low-heeled shoes and looked like an adolescent on her way to a gym class, yet never walked a block she could manage to ride. Ruth was lovable and impetuous and brave.

Aurelia hesitated because she didn't know how to take pride in the rest and she wanted to tell it pridefully. Alice Hursch had come up and was standing arm in arm with Marc. Aurelia spoke quickly. "Ruth was married Sunday."

Marc asked his brother-in-law's last name, and when Aurelia said Ricardo, Alice shrieked herself even flatter and taller. If it was Lou Ricardo he was one of the greatest painters in this country. He knew what it was all about; his work simply knocked you for a loop; he could paint a potbellied capitalist—she glanced toward potbellied Oscar Hursch—so realistically that—— Yes, he was really good, Lou Ricardo was.

Aurelia looked happier. She said, "Well, she'll be here. That's something. I like weddings. Four children and only Bertha invited me to the wedding." She laughed at herself. And because Alice had praised Ruth's husband she smiled at Alice, who was half closing her eyes in delighted memory of the right guy, the guy with guts....

"Will he be good to my Ruth?" Aurelia inquired, leaning forward. "Will he be a kind father?"

At that Alice pretended to swoon against Marc's shoulder. "If Ruth ever hangs a diaper in Ricardo's studio he will kill her. But verrry politely. Lou Ricardo has manners."

Aurelia answered proudly, "Nobody ever bossed my Ruth. Not even Bertha. If Ruth wants to hang up diapers——"

"That's it, darling Aunt Aurelia. Ruth will want nothing Ricardo does not want. He'll bewitch her."

"Bewitched," Aurelia answered, "it's easy for a woman to be happy. It's all right if she is bewitched. I am satisfied that she marry this Ricardo. But when I meet him I'll tell him it's his duty to keep her bewitched."

Alice laughed, shrilled, and mumbled that Aunt Aurelia was wonderful and, by the way, there was a man now in Alice's life, a man with a soul. Looking up with a shy blush on her mannequin cheeks, the glitter of her eyes softened to a glow. Alice let them see that she was in love.

"He will be here—soon," she whispered, and after she had rushed off Aurelia said, "She wants us to believe he is a little Jesus."

And then through the halls ran a murmur and a hush, alternating as if waves of surprise and consternation were crossing the great hall, piling up before Clara and Oscar Hursch, arm in arm, looking brave, smiling narrow, dismal smiles.

Alice's smile was exultant and became throaty laughter, and her sleek black dress shivered with delight. Her eyes turned in adulation as she walked forward to meet Ira Randall.

Alice phoned the next day to say that Aurelia must bring Lou Ricardo and Ruth that very evening. Marc and Hallie were coming. Who would have dreamed a trip to St. Louis could have turned out so truly wonderful!

Because Ricardo was Spanish he looked more Jewish than the Kleinmans or the Hursches, who looked like Germans, round of head, pink of skin, stubby of figure, and blond, or if dark, dark of hair and not of skin.

Ricardo walked past Oscar Hursch to his paintings, and after moving rapidly from one to another he turned to Ruth and with surprise in his voice said, "There are two good ones."

In reply to Oscar's expostulations he said no, the others were not forgeries or anything like that, just sentimentalized and therefore bad, bad for the soul—well, just bad. Two good ones out of twenty; that was a fair percentage for a rich man. Most rich men ... He shrugged his shoulders and looked more Jewish than ever.

Ruth put her arm through his fondly. Her features were less regular than Bertha's, her expression piquant with a mixture of merriment and defiance. Though she wore tailored clothes, her appearance was shaggy, for her hair was short and worn flyaway, and frequently her blouse hung out in the back or her stockings were twisted and her flat-heeled shoes scuffed. Yet even to the Manns she was a vastly attractive girl.

Before the twins reached their teens they had been ardent ice skaters, Bertha always repeating the same figures accurately on a small area thoroughly tested by other skaters, while Ruth skated ecstatically, scarcely seeing the ice, so absorbed would she become in the delicious gliding and whirling of her improvisations. She was still meeting life that way, and those who condemned it as dangerous were nevertheless likely to be charmed by her abandon and grace.

Now Alice, with one arm around Ruth's waist and her hand in Ira's, said the young people were going into the library. They wanted to talk. "We'll be all right, Mother, you needn't come in to look after us."

Ira had become a man of compelling appearance. His eyes were penetrating and sad, pleading for the privilege of retaining what he had left of his faith. Step by step, after struggle and sorrow, he had yielded to the demands of American living— working on the Sabbath, eating unconsecrated foods, moving too swiftly for household prayers, following the money he had earned into places said to be Jewish, but in his eyes utterly un-Jewish. At first his retreats had been made in anger and a part of a self-discipline sternly imposed.

Ira hungered frantically for love and approval. As a boy he had won the adulation of his grandfather's household by unrelenting and showy devotion to the old ways. When he left the university he left determined to learn how to win new affection, for those who had loved him in his boyhood were dead. Soon he discovered success made generosity possible and that by coupling generosity with fair play and courtesy he could gain admiration. His serious eyes, his immaculate grooming, his precisely correct clothes showed that he wanted people to like him.

But he was an austere figure. Alice realized at once that he would not bow low in the presence of Hursches or Manns; and she, who all her life had been bowing low under protest, was at once entranced. Their affection for each other had a disdain for those from whom they fled. Marc sensed this and was swept by a wry loyalty to them both.

At first there was a confusion of talk about new music, modern art, and two lecturers recently in town, one picturing the Russian Revolution as the return of the Dark Ages, the other picturing it as heaven. Ricardo, listening in silence, amused himself by assigning each of these strangers to the part they played in society. Except Marc. He could not make him fit anywhere.

Was Marc more than a businessman deeply in love with his wife? That sudden flashing laugh; those gentle eyes. Everyone spoke fondly of Marc—Ruth and all these others too—but said only that he was a darling.

He turned to Marc. "What kind of a businessman are you?"

Marc looked first at Hallie, who, with a quick snapping together of her graceful hands, seemed to be begging Ricardo not to do this. Then Marc said, "I'm a businessman who obeys the rules, but not all the rules. ... I have a brother who believes a businessman must obey all the rules. Not only the rules of business, which, of course, I obey, but the rules of success which give orders to a man's entire life, commanding him what to think, whom to marry, where to live, what his children must think, and to what schools they must be sent to learn what to think——"

Ricardo interrupted: "I can see you're not that kind of businessman, but I can't see what kind you are."

"Have you ever seen a Missouri hound-dog in a field of high wheat? He goes far into the field. He can't see out. He turns around and around and around and thus makes for himself a cozy place to lie down and be content. The wheat field is large and he doesn't know where it ends or where he is within it, but he is comfortable."

"You are bewildered?"

"To be bewildered, a man must try to think. I try not to think. I pass the homes of the poor and I try not to wonder whether the man in there is a lesser man than I. I try to believe he is so that I may feel I deserve my better home. But I don't believe it, so when I'm asked to serve on a welfare board I agree and I go to meetings and sign letters and make decisions and vote. On the way home I pass homes without screens or even windows and I still don't believe I'm better than the people who live in those houses. I'm a very lucky man and should be grateful that luck is so important in business, where all is orderly and ledgers are kept and luck seems not to count."

"You were their nephew——"

"A relative of necessity has luck. Impossible to escape luck. Had I gone into real estate, they would have bought their houses from me. Had I gone into insurance, their policies. I've done better, however, than other nephews and yet I'm not better than the man in the house without screens."

"You're a business philosopher."

"I have merely observed a few facts."

After that Ricardo did not speak to Marc, but his eyes constantly were with him as if they were asking questions and finding answers. Ricardo was, in fact, painting Marc. The hands were the most important area of the canvas. It was a tall narrow canvas with Marc along its right edge, seeming even taller and thinner than he actually was. Those gentle hazel eyes were peering out the window, and Marc's face would not have its flashing smile or its kindly attentiveness but would be just features as it was when Marc had said, "I have merely observed a few facts." The hands, however, would have expression. They would be ready to act strongly, but what they would do no one could see though everyone would try.

Since Alice had made it impossible for Clara to come into the library, Clara sent Eileen with a tray of drinks. Eileen reported the presence of sandwiches on the dining-room table. "Little sandwiches, Miss Alice." She had lived in this household for nearly a quarter of a century now.

As Clara surmised, the sandwiches lured the young people. They strolled toward the dining room just when Carl and Oscar in the parlor were arguing about the philanthropy of young Rockefeller and Julius Rosenwald.

Oscar shouted that Rosenwald's half million given to the Hebrew Union College would do wonders for the Jews of this country. What they needed was religion, respect for the faith of their fathers, and manners; now that the country had gone mad on a spending spree it was more important than ever, and rabbis were the natural leaders of their people, and therefore———

"Therefore nothing," Carl shouted back. "A Jew, of course, couldn't do it, but I'm damned glad Rockefeller did. Russia has always given the Jews a bad time. The Czar wants his people to forgive him for his crimes, so he lets them enjoy a few pogroms. These revolutionists over there, these new cutthroats—give the devil his due—they're sending fellows who lead pogroms to prison. Trying to give the Jews a new start. You don't want more Russian Jews in this country, do you? Of course not. Rockefeller doesn't either, so he gives his money for Jewish colonization in Russia where it belongs. We ought to thank him for it, but has any Jew done anything but run him down? I know about his father and the oil and the dimes. I know all that. I'll tell you one thing——"

Whenever Carl began to tell Oscar one thing, Oscar would shout back and tell Carl another, so now their wives tried to quiet them, their eyebrows lifting high to remind their husbands that someone who was not Jewish was present.

Worse than that, Carl had forgotten that Ira Randall was present. Both Carl and Oscar had forgotten that they could no longer shout about Russian Jews. The things they had been saying to each other all these years must never be said again. The brothers looked bent and frightened, as if they knew they were too old to find new things to shout; if a man could not speak against some Jews, then he must share and share alike with all Jews as if he approved of them all, as if he himself were no better than the worst of them, the kind they agreed deserved to be refused at summer resorts.

Ricardo wanted Uncle Carl to go on talking about the Russian Revolution. It really was a great gain for the people of the world, wasn't it, Mr. Hursch? The Jews, of course, must have been very glad to see the Czar dethroned, yet revolution? were they giving to Biro-Bidjan?

Abruptly the talk within the room ceased as if an orchestra were obeying a command; all the eyes were wide with surprise; the lips were agape and ready to speak in protest. Even the cynical Manns and their stylish wives looked rebuffed. Only Aurelia did not, just went on with her crocheting, not pretending that she cared about any of it.

With one voice, almost, Carl and Oscar said, "I am not in sympathy with revolution and violence. I believe in——"

Alice finished their sentence for them. "They believe in Hursch and Company."

"Of course we do." They blushed embarrassed smiles.

Carl added, "And the United States of America. Let's drink a toast to our country."

While the glasses were being filled Ricardo reminded them that the United States of America would be nothing but a set of agricultural colonies if there had not once been a revolution.

Alice's pretty lips curved with suppressed laughter. "That was a nice revolution. Conducted by gentlemen."

Ricardo turned to Marc. "My God, isn't anybody here grateful to Russia for what she is doing for the Jews?"

At that moment Clara called for the toast, but after it was acclaimed and the glasses restored to the table, Ricardo again put his question and there was a taut silence which indicated the family willingness to let Marc be their spokesman.

"Most of us here hold to the melting-pot ideal. Not only for this country. For all the world. We think Jews should live of a country as well as in it. I believe those in this room would like it better if the Russians and Mr. Rockefeller were not planning to put the Jews off in a colony by themselves——"

"My God," Ricardo answered, "it's the Jews with their dietary laws and all that who want to be put off by themselves."

Aurelia nodded at Marc, her eyes reminding him of what Hans had always said.

"There are many types of Jews. We of this group do not abide by dietary laws. I myself gave to Biro-Bidjan, but I'm a liberal and you mustn't hold these good people responsible for my ways. They didn't give to Biro-Bidjan. They are, however, generous to American charities."

Now Marc had said what they wanted and the room came to life, with everyone trying to explain to Ricardo that Russia had little to do with the Americans in this room unless the bloodthirsty Bolsheviks were to try to spread their revolution. If they did they'd better watch out, because then they'd learn what red-blooded Americans were like. They shook their heads and showed that the red-blooded Americans were themselves and others like themselves.

Ricardo said, "I was in Europe last fall. In October I saw Jewish students beaten up on the steps of a Hungarian university. In November I saw Jewish boys beaten on the steps of a university in Budapest ...."

Donald Mann flourished his cigarette holder toward Ricardo. It seemed to pause as it chanced to point toward the filigree brass lampshade, the Lalique vase, the satin damask draperies, the Italian cut-velvet cushions, and the high-backed carved rosewood chair. "Hungary and Russia are not America," he said.

Ricardo's face flushed and he looked as if he was about to speak angrily.

Hallie was standing in the doorway with her arm around Ruth. Her clear voice rose musically above the others. She said, "Wasn't it fine that Henri Bergson won the Nobel prize?" She pronounced the French name accurately.

Now everyone was happy, talking about Henri Bergson, who was a great man, a philosopher, and, though a Jew, a man who lived widely and so no one ever thought of him as a Jew.

Mimi had been trying to read *Matter and Memory* and wittily announced that in so doing she had reduced her memory to something which didn't matter.

While the others were saying good-by Ricardo drew Marc aside. He said, "You're attempting the impossible. Art and business are different. An artist must obey truth as he sees truth. After that he is free. But a businessman must obey a rule which has nothing to do with truth. He must make money. You can't live a business life as an artist lives, by an inner truth. It's that you are trying and it's impossible."

Marc explained Hans's idea of a merchant: a go-between who brought the fruits of science to the people. He laughed genially at Ricardo. "You paint pictures people don't want or even understand. I am nearer to the people. I know what they want and I try to give it to them. The people———"

"You eat their food."

"Yes, that's bad. But it's they who permit others to eat their food. In exchange for the products of science."

"Nevertheless ... Nevertheless ..." Swiftly Ricardo looked from Marc's hands to his eyes, for he was still painting him. "A man's heart is more comfortable today if he is an artist ...."

Marc bowed slightly. "I'm glad you are comfortable."

"I am not comfortable."

"No?"

"Marc, not even an artist—no one today is comfortable."

"I know that. I'll get the car. It's raining. Bring Mama and Hallie to the side door. Ruth will show you where it is."

CHAPTER III

WHEN THE GREAT crash came, mimi, who had been doing a little Stock Exchange gambling, went to bed with a three-month headache; but mostly it was the men who suffered. Milton Mann jumped from a tenth-floor window. Oscar told Clara that she would have to dismiss all the servants except Eileen, who would have to work for less. Homes were sold for a third of their cost. Some families lived in mansions without heat or light. Businesses declared bankruptcy. The shock and the frenzied human reactions to it prepared the depression which everyone now knew would come.

A letter from Fred written on imposing stationery announced that he was once more wiped out. It would not take him long to come back, but unfortunately Celia's father and all the Chicago bunch were wiped out too; could Marc see that Mama got her monthly check?

Bertha asked everyone the same question: "What happened to all that money? Where did it go? When stocks were up they cost a lot. Now they're down, but the money must be somewhere. Who could be the one hiding it?" Clarence could not persuade her to stop asking.

From New York, Ruth reported that the magnificent murals Ricardo was finishing were not wanted since the building was not to be erected at this time. For a while she would work as a waitress, her newspaper job having gone under with the passing of good times.

Bertha and Clarence received appeals from Clarence's family. Bertha stored away her best clothes and appeared everywhere in her marketing outfit and new cotton gloves. She looked older and very brave and said they were not worried, not a bit.

Mama said, "When we lived in the Yellow Row every one of the neighbors was a little afraid because we weren't sure where next month's meals were coming from. The Kleinmans and the Edgewoods and the Kelleys and the Giovannis, though I'm not sure Italians know how to worry." It was a question.

"Yes, Italians worry," Marc answered.

"I used to envy Clara and Mimi because they didn't have to wonder how they were going to feed their families next month. But now they worry. All the rich worry. They worry about next year, but it's the same. Marc, I think the poor are nicer people. Even the Randowiches. Because when the rich are worried about meals they get angry. Not at each other, but at the poor. At a man who stands on the street selling apples. Also at the man at the Charities because he wants money for the poor."

"You forget, Mama. The poor get angry too. Mr. Edgewood was often angry. Mr. Kelley. The Giovannis. It's only that when the rich get angry everyone listens to them. They write their anger in the papers. They speak it over the radio. And you listen."

Mama put down her knitting. It was a sweater for Jill. Her lips silently counted off the stitches. Then she looked around her little apartment, crowded with things from the house in the Yellow Row: Hans's books, the ebony screen, the ivory goose-man, the black marble clock which did not run and could not be fixed.

Her eyes at last came back to Marc's. "You are the brightest.
Fred is only quick. Ruth doesn't know what she wants. When she
married Lou it was like joining the church. Whatever he says is
right." Aurelia did not mention Bertha. "I used to ask you to be
noble.... I think maybe you've tried."

Marc laughed and told her it was time to come with him
to dinner. Hallie was waiting. Hallie was a wonderful cook, but
even Hallie got cross if dinner was not on time. And the children were like starved bears. Herbert, by the way, was getting
excellent results with his photography. He had an eye for the
dramatic. Bold, interesting stuff. They were going to develop
pictures together right after dinner today. The boy thought he
had some good shots.

Aurelia rolled the half sweater around the needles. She
picked the bits of wool from her dress. "You'll be thirty-five on
your next birthday. I want to give you something nice. What do
you want, Marc?"

Marc was rattling his automobile keys and walking toward
the door. He was pretending to be thinking only of dinner, but
he said, "I want you to tell me again that you think I've tried to
be noble—because I've done nothing noble and I haven't tried
very hard. I wish I had."

Aurelia looked at him as she used to look when he was a
small boy and she thought he might be getting chicken pox or
measles or mumps. Crossly she said, "Last year in the tornado,
did anyone else go into the buildings and carry out the people?
Did anyone else use his car as an ambulance? Back and forth
all night and all the next day without sleep? And give all that
money to the Red Cross and all those blankets and hire a carpenter to put in windows for the poor and——"

"There are few tornadoes, but in a tornado I am noble."
Marc's eyes were not merry, yet they were laughing at Aurelia.
And at Marc too.

The city was becalmed in the depression which had spread
over the whole country. Mercilessly the blaze of human hunger alternated with the chill of despair. They made their own
night and day, the days without dreams; the nights without
peace.

Becalmed, the city was like other cities, as those who moved
from one to another soon found out. The winds of trade stood
still. Even those who felt no hunger, no thirst, were afraid. At
times the great fear within them broke into small bits which
seemed like anger. Quarrels flared in families where the jobless
had crowded into a house which had been another family's home
and now was no one's home.

Maids who lived in great houses, or couples who lived above
garages in suburban estates, sometimes remained without pay
in order to have a place to stay. Those who did not live in—the
colored help—were dismissed. Factories shut down. Those business houses which plugged on, risking a loss, plugged on with as
few employees as possible.

The only flourishing business was relief. Social service
workers remained at their desks late into the evening. More
clerks were taken on. When the statistics were laid before
Marc's committee, a man with white hair agreed with a
woman in spectacles that the poor never saved a penny against
a rainy day.

Marc said, "This is not a rainy day. It's a torrential downpour."

They laughed, glad Marc Kleinman could make even the
relief situation something to smile about. The man with white

hair said, "Anyhow, we have to give them relief. We don't want-trouble."

Marc said, "I move we approve the budget as submitted." Glancing up, he saw that the woman with whom he had talked about a job years ago had tiptoed into the room. She was an executive, higher than the worker in charge of this meeting. She had come in only because she was too nervous to stay out. She had to know what they would do. She looked at Marc with a smile which said, See? You are invaluable as a board member. She smiled upon Marc and waved a little when the others were not looking.

In the blighted district midway between the business section and the midtown region of movie theaters and office buildings stood a large old church. When it was built it was an Episcopalian church for the aristocrats of the city. After they moved west it became a temple for a Jewish congregation. When the Hursches and Manns and all the cousins moved west, too, the synagogue again became Episcopalian, but for Negro Episcopalians, aristocrats like the builders of the church, though recognized as such only by the colored populace.

One evening its pastor permitted the church to be used for a meeting, but with the understanding that his name was not to be dragged into this, since it was not a meeting of his congregation, nor even for religious purposes.

The crowd, mostly women, almost filled the pews. Though they were dark, near dark and brown, tan, light as white, and even white with red hair, nevertheless they were Negro women, since they had some Negro blood. Tonight their anger spoke out against white women who paid less than last year and demanded more work.

In the back row Otto Street, Mamie Lee's son, sat, his hair neat, his dark blue suit, though worn along the pockets, well pressed, his gray eyes alert and anxious.

While the crowd was gathering Marc Kleinman and Hart Bromage were walking past the church, though they did not know about the meeting. Both Hart and Marc had had to do some forgetting before they could be at ease in each other's presence, but it had been done now and they were comfortable, or nearly so.

Usually Hart voted with Marc. He told everyone he could sec that Marc was a smart man who knew his way around, so why should Hart Bromage bother to do any thinking? He would come to meetings, sign any appeals they wanted signed, and lead a team which raised big money. Once a year he invited the board members, plus the staff, to the lawn which surrounded his large home and gave them a barbecue which was a barbecue: rotisserie chicken and rotisserie ribs and gallons of Ann Bromage's fanciest salads, some of which Hallie helped her make, for Ann and Hallie were now friends.

As they were approaching the church, Mamie Lee sat rubbing her arthritic fingers, her eyes on Frederick, who had turned out to be a social worker, a good man trying to help washwomen get carfare and lunch and something better than two dollars a day. Unlike his father, he did not look anxious. He looked angry.

Marc and Hart had been walking uphill for some distance. They said nothing about being tired or short of breath, but they did mention that turtle soup was too heavy and pancakes, good as they tasted, unsuitable food for walking men. They looked in as they went by.

Hart whispered to Marc, "By God, I think it's a nigger church. What do you think they're up to?"

"I know someone might be in there. I'll ask him one of these days."

"Somebody's chauffeur?"

"A lawyer."

"How'd you meet him?"

Marc looked at Hart's good-humored handsome features and the unawareness upon them and their unawareness of being unaware. He decided not to mention that Zip was practicing law as Otto Street, nor that Otto Street's name had recently been proposed for membership on their Welfare Board. Instead Marc answered, "Son of a woman used to work for us. Came to my mother when I was a little boy. Still comes once in a while."

Bromage was satisfied. He said, "Those old ones are grand. Loyal. It's the young ones get uppity."

Marc and Otto Street sat in Marc's office with the door closed. The walls ceased in mid-air; Otto's gaze traveled cautiously along the edge of the ceilingless room. The roar of the operation of Hursch and Company was only partially muffled.

The gray eyes in the dark, thoughtful face returned to Marc. In them were appraisal and caution. They were small eyes with few lashes. Otto Street was thin, extremely neat, his body and his left hand as relaxed as if he sat in a library reading, his right hand restless, touching his fountain pen, his notebook, the buttons on his vest, the case of his reading glasses, the crease in his trousers.

Quietly he said, "It's been a long time since we met. I hear of you."

"Yes, my mother tells your mother. And yours tells mine. You have saved many innocent people from jail. I congratulate you."

Otto sighed. "I've worked hard on my cases. Very likely you can guess why."

For a moment there was silence within the room while Otto Street became an aghast man, jailed, then himself again.

Otto said, "For a while I was bitter. Angry all the time, but I had nothing I wanted to do with my anger. I still had faith in the law. Seemed to me it just had to be made to function as it was meant to function. ... So I went back and studied harder than ever before: history, philosophy, and public speaking. Whenever I got the time I visited courtrooms, listening to the way the most able men did it. I got my degree. I've been Otto Street for a long time. ... I thought you were going into law."

It was not quite a question. Marc frowned. His shoes, pushing at the floor, floated his swivel chair around toward the window and back around again. Well, why hadn't he become a lawyer? Was it only that he had been obliged to support a household during those years when—— Or had the futility of his efforts in Zip's behalf become cogent in his life, though he had not been aware of it at the time? Perhaps it was that law had not been the sole worthy goal, just one desirable way of life among many.

Otto did not give him time to answer. He was talking about Hart Bromage, saying, "He's a friendly-mannered man. It's not so much friendliness to people as it's friendliness to retain the status quo. The way things are has suited Hart Bromage."

Marc sat fingering a folder containing papers he should have been working on, but only his fingers were thinking of them. His mind was exclaiming, By God, that's Bromage. Bromage to a T.... That was what he had been trying to put into words for himself for years. "How'd you find that out, Otto Street?"

"Have you forgotten that I knew Bromage at the Delta House? I've watched Hart Bromage ever since. I've seen him in the papers year after year. Hart Bromage, head of Bromage and Company, moves into a new office, or under a picture that Hart Bromage has gone on a board. I see him there, smiling, Hart Bromage, head of his lodge, gives dolls to orphans, or at the Veiled Prophet's Ball with Mrs. Bromage, and they're both smiling. I read where Hart Bromage laid the cornerstone for the big new church out in the swell neighborhood where he lives. Looks as if the whole world's set up to please Hart Bromage. Why shouldn't he smile?" And then in a different voice he was talking about the meeting. "Those women were wild last night. Hundreds of angry women. They want to make themselves into a union. They want Frederick to do their striking for them. Fred's employment office gets the phone calls asking for laundresses. They want him to refuse to send them except for more pay."

"Frederick looks able to manage his own job. You'd better let him."

Otto stood up. His hand fumbled at his buttons. "I'm scared these days. All this unemployment and my people so helpless. That meeting last night—— It won't come to anything. The most it can do is lose Fred his job. I can't be objective about Fred. I've put a lot of hope in that boy. I don't want them to—— I've always hated a scared nigger, and sometimes I think that's all I am—a scared nigger with some loose change in my pocket."

Then Marc saw that even now there were two Otto Streets, the brave, proud, battling lawyer who roared in the courtroom, and this one, tired, fearful, self-hating.

Marc said, "When I read my newspaper, time after time I see Otto Street. Otto Street doesn't get his picture printed, but I see him just the same. A man was falsely accused of murder and Otto Street has gone into court for him. Without pay ... At times I envy Otto Street."

They rose and Marc came around his desk; they shook hands, then Marc walked to the door with him.

CHAPTER IV

AURELIA SAT AMONG her sins, grieving. she told herself she was not a good woman, never had been, or she wouldn't be in this fix. Surely a good woman, knowing her Marc was going to have a fortieth birthday, would have saved her money and bought him a present.

She dried her eyes, dragged the folded ladder from kitchenette to dressing room, steadied it as best she could, and climbed to the top, thence precariously to the top of a chest of drawers. There, on tiptoe, she grappled at the air until her fingers ensnared a string which dangled from a round shiny black hatbox. Pulling, she brought hatbox, together with other boxes and bundles, down on her head in a noisy closet landslide.

The return was even more precarious, but now an expectant smile tugged at Aurelia's lips. She had twice paid the janitor to put the box out of her reach because she knew she ought not to wear her new hat before Marc's birthday, but even that much virtue was not in her, for she had in fact worn it to a luncheon with The Girls last week and they had given her the compliments she needed to make her feel the hat was right.

It had been bought only after hours of trying on and taking off other hats which mockingly accused her of being an ugly old woman. At last this black velvet one settled around her head in a nearly poke-bonnet manner, and before she knew it she was flirting at herself as if she would be wearing it for Hans.

"Take the others away!" she commanded, suddenly a woman who could give commands, for the reflection in the mirror did indeed confirm the saleswoman's flattering words. But she had also named a price several times what Aurelia had planned to pay. She was on the streetcar hugging the shiny black hatbox upon her lap before she realized she had spent all the money she had, thus making a present for Marc's birthday impossible. For years there had always been a way out of such predicaments. She would call Marc at his office and say, "Marc, the next time you come, bring me some of my capital." He would ask, "How much, Mama?" and bring twice the sum named.

Until this morning she had never let herself look too closely at the fact that she very likely had no capital. Hans had left insurance, a thousand dollars, and after he had been properly buried Ruth had taken care of the money which remained, until she left for New York, when she had turned it over to Marc. At first he had brought her small sums and said they were her interest. Later on, when she needed money, he said no more interest was coming but she should tell him how much she needed. When he brought it she asked, "Where did you get all this?"

For a second he hesitated and then said quite cheerfully, "It's your capital, Mama."

"The Girls say we shouldn't touch our capital," she countered.

Marc nodded, "It's all right for you, Mama, to touch your capital."

Now for the first time, on this rainy morning, she saw that there had not been any capital, and for years she had merely been taking money from Marc without even saying thank you. Well, what was a useless old woman to do? But for his birthday, no. No, not for his birthday.

The hat was disappointing atop her morning hair-twist and blue gingham dress. Nevertheless, it was beginning to cheer her when the phone rang and Hallie was asking if perhaps Aurelia would lend her some teaspoons.

Inspired, Aurelia said how strange that Hallie should ask for them! She was planning to give those very spoons to Marc for his birthday. Quite firmly Hallie replied she wouldn't permit it, not those lovely spoons which all the children and grandchildren enjoyed so much when they came to Aurelia's apartment. Besides, weren't those spoons a gift from all the Kleinman children to Hans and Aurelia on their twentieth wedding anniversary?

"What are you thinking of, Mother Kleinman?"

Aurelia's smallest voice answered, "I bought a new hat for Marc's party."

Before Hallie discerned the relevance of the statement she blurted out, "No one will be wearing hats, not in the evening."

During the ensuing silence Hallie suffered and beat her head with her fist and, thus stirred to activity, her mind produced a wonderful idea. She presented it as if she were ashamed to ask such a great favor of Aurelia and very fearful that Aurelia would not be willing to grant this very generous gift to Marc—for it was not only a favor but the sole gift Marc wanted. Just last night he said he would not open any package Aurelia might bring since all he wanted was for her to teach Hallie how to make those marvelous *Schnecken*, and that of course was a gift which would last as long as Hallie lived, and even Jill, one day, learning, would——

Aurelia became a wildly happy woman. No other gift could be as right for Marc as this. Neither Bertha nor Ruth had learned to make Mama's *Schnecken,* Ruth having only a kitchen which was a hot plate and jars of soaking paintbrushes, and Bertha always being burdened with cooks who were liable to get hurt feelings. Celia very likely didn't cook or even eat, only smoked and drank so that she would photograph as thin as the actresses.

Hallie could hear Aurelia's excitement and pleasure. She promised to call for her in the car, since Aurelia would have to bring the earthen bowl, the granite pans, and the stubby knife for cutting up citron, and, yes, it might be a good idea to bring the cheese tin, and then Hallie could learn how to make cheese-cake too.

Before Hallie left the house she phoned Marc to inform him about his birthday wishes and warn him not to put on too much of a show because Aurelia really was happy and Jill was pleased that Gramma would be spending the night there. It had some-thing to do with setting the yeast and letting the dough raise until exactly six in the morning, when something had to be done to it before it raised once more.

Marc answered, "She'll bring a red wool shawl to keep the dough warm. I know all about it. I could teach you myself."

The next day being Sunday, Marc did in fact hang around the kitchen making jests designed to flatter Aurelia. When Hallie rolled the floury mound into a monster pancake he scoffed because she touched the rolling pin to the dough. Couldn't she see that Mama just threatened the dough with those quick little approaches of the rolling pin? When Mama did it the rolling pin didn't actually touch anything. The dough flattened in meek obedience. And when the great pancake was buttered, again Mama touched nothing. Her bits of butter, all those raisins, the *tiny* squares of citron, the pecans and brown sugar were placed in mid-air exactly a half inch above the dough; then when Mama

rolled the goodies into the pancake and cut the roll into seg-
ments, neither the rolling up nor the cutting were done by tool or
by human fingers. Mama just thought about rolling the dough
and made little chasing movements with her fingers, but she
touched nothing, and when she cut the roll the knife really never
touched the dough at all.

Jill was permitted to butter the granite pans and Mama
said she did it very well, but Marc said no, that brush business
wouldn't work. The way to butter *Schnecken* pans was to have hot
fingers—warm from boxing a child's ears—and then melt the
butter into place that way.

It was all very jolly until Marc spied something in a newspaper wrapped around Aurelia's cheesecake tin. He took the paper
out of the kitchen, spread it upon the dining-room table, and
read it from one end to the other.

Mama said, "That's nothing, Marc. It's a paper a week old.
It's the paper Mamie Lee had around some washing she brought
back. My blankets. It's nothing."

"It's something," Marc said. Then, without explaining, he
folded the paper, gripped it beneath his upper arm, left the
house, and drove away.

Again Marc spread the paper upon a table. This time his
fingers held a pencil instead of a cigarette, and as he checked
off paragraphs he talked with Otto and Frederick. They were in
Otto Street's dining room.

Marc drummed the back of his fingers against the news
sheet. "This attack on the Welfare Board——"

Otto said, "Frederick wasn't aiming it at Marc Kleinman."

Marc continued: "What he said is true. We've caused the
trouble we try to relieve. We don't expect to cure it...."

They waited.

Frederick said, "If the businessmen would hire us—decent jobs, I mean—they wouldn't have to give us relief."

"But what you wrote in that paper is not said to the board. It's what you believe, but you don't say it."

Frederick answered, "We're invited to work on the board because we can be trusted not to say it."

Otto added, "For small gains we sacrifice the right to say what we think."

Quickly Frederick said, "It's necessary, but it isn't honest."

Otto asked a question: "Is it honest for Mr. Hart Bromage, who fired his typist the day he found out she was colored, to come to meetings and worry about Negro unemployment?" His forehead drew together in mimicry of the frown of a completely happy man.

Marc said, "I've not yet tried to change the employment policy of Hursch and Company. I will try. And I'll fail. Then what?"

They could not answer that. Their lips sagged with unhappiness.

Marc said, "What you wrote in that article is true. I'll say it at board meetings. I'll say it for you."

Gradually the things Marc said at board meetings were also said for himself. At first he did not fully mean them, for he could not renounce his consciousness of color. When a dark man would wander out of the caste in which society placed him, into the lobby of a good hotel, at the wrong ticket window of a theater, into the line of applicants for white jobs, or into a white man's hospital, Marc, too, was ill at ease, and later at meetings this continued in his memory. Until he became accustomed to these displacements, it was for Marc as it was when his pencil and pen were in his right instead of his left pocket. He suffered discomfort greater than reason could justify.

Trying to equalize his reason and his feelings, he walked about his city as if he were a man from a distant land seeing sights never before visible. He reported filthy alleys and was appointed to a City Beautiful Committee. He reported rat-ridden, decaying tenements, and the City Beautiful Committee shrugged its collective shoulders and said it had enough to do without getting involved with the Real Estate Association.

Then Marc walked again, taking down no names of streets since he did not intend to report anything. He saw that in the richest valley in the richest country in the world there was poverty, lamented by everyone, but everyone waited for Fate to arrange a cure. Sometimes Marc felt as if he were in a city of somnambulists, wandering aimlessly about within a miasma which would never clear and from which no one would ever escape.

On the night of Marc's birthday Herbert divided the evening into two disparate parts, for himself, for Marc, for Hallie, for those among the guests who sensed the change in their host and hostess.

At first everything was jolly, with Marc's surprised laugh greeting each newcomer, for he had not known who was coming nor that the group was to be large.

Hallie always meandered into a party, impulsively inviting this one and that, with no basis of selection besides her sudden, flashing conviction that the person she had just thought of would add to the pleasure of the evening. In this unpremeditated fashion she had gradually invited for tonight all who had in some measure won Marc's affection—their close friends, The Clan, but also several men from the Kodak Klub with their wives, several from the Welfare Board, the principal of Jill's school, two teachers from Herbert's, and Hart and Ann.

Though all were accustomed to coming to the Kleinman home, many had not met one another. Tonight they were lively with good-humored talk, as if eager to discern whatever it was in themselves and each other that Marc and Hallie seemed to like.

They were in fact pointing out their favorite corners in the rambling old house. Marc had bought this home years ago at a bargain because it was old and rambling, with several bedrooms on the first floor and evidences everywhere of the architectural vagaries of its builder. Most of these the Kleinmans had made to serve their numerous hobbies. The cavernous closet off the back hall became Marc's darkroom for developing films. On the rack midway of the dining-room walls Herbert displayed part of his collection of cartoons. On the bookshelves beneath the stairway Jill arrayed her costume dolls.

It was a comfortable house, book-lined and magazine-cluttered and unembarrassed about its activities. Bicycles and ice skates and overshoes and photographic equipment were not treated as shameful objects to be hidden away, since to Hallie they merely connoted the presence of her husband and her children.

Tonight Jill raced about gaily, fetching ash trays and drinks of water. She had housewifely ways reminiscent of Aurelia's. Though only eleven, she was pretty and pert and eager to look after everyone's comfort.

Aurelia, together with several younger women, hurried from kitchen to dining room, replenishing the *Schnecken* plate, cutting more slices from the enormous birthday cake, refilling the coffee-pot. Hallie never did more than set a party in motion. She would spend her time making the table alluring with candles and lace tablecloth, cakes and candies, and then be a little surprised that the sandwiches remained unmade. She was only distantly aware that fond and energetic friends or relatives were carrying the party forward, thus making it their party, and so in the end everyone would feel at home and have a good time, surely what a party was for. Aurelia enjoyed bustling about until Bertha insisted she go out and stand by Marc's side.

Bertha shared the Mann-Hursch disapproval of Marc's house, so baffling to their traditional system of gift-giving that even now after all these years some of the older Manns would meet Hallie with the remark that, alas, they still owed her a *Hausgeschenk*.

As guests continued to arrive, Marc, embarrassed by this great fuss over his birthday, remarked, "Hallie has forgotten birth is a universal phenomenon." And then, glancing up, he saw Hallie smiling beseechingly as if begging him to like his party, begging him to forget the black mood of the streets, the depression, the unemployment, begging him please to let her make this evening completely joyful. After that Marc began to tell some of his stories, keeping those nearest him in laughter.

The cleavage came without warning. Alice and Ira, arriving late, jestingly said Marc was to have no gift from them, nothing at all, but where was Herbert? They had brought Herbert an original for his collection of cartoons.

And then, because everyone knew collecting cartoons had been Marc's idea and that most of the assembling, mounting, and typing of the historic background annotating each item had been done by father and son together, they watched Marc's pleasure as Herbert unwrapped the package.

The gangling fourteen-year-old boy, so like his father but without Marc's gentle ways, stood his gift on the mantel. It was a bold depiction of the Reichstag fire, the flames licking not only the rafters of the venerable building but also the body of a phantom, falling figure labeled "The Republic."

At first there were little commendatory remarks about the powerful pull of the lines, the excellence of the composition, and the fine, simple legibility of the artist's meaning; and then Herbert, excited and pleased, examining the wrappings, found a printed sheet and everyone said he must read it aloud.

Before beginning he wisecracked in embarrassment, shifting his feet around, blushing for a moment toward Marc, then toward Hallie standing now arm In arm with Marc, her new blue dress and her present happiness deepening the azure of her eyes.

As he read, the hush, begun in politeness, became rigid, and glances meeting glances across the room dropped toward the floor. The statement was the cartoonist's long, laconic account of the treachery, the lawlessness, the Jew-baiting of those who set the fire.

The muscles of Herbert's jaws knotted and the knots jerked forward and backward. Looking up, standing very erect, seeing only his father, he said, "And now they're in power." It was only a statement of a fact, but in the boy's eyes burned contempt beyond his years.

A moment later everyone was murmuring again, only Marc speaking directly to the boy, but in all the faces was a thoughtfulness, a looking about in perplexity, a pondering of the purity and impurity of the human heart.

Then little pieces of talk everywhere in the room were saying the same thing: that this sort of gathering was good, with Jews and non-Jews learning to know one another, and wasn't it odd that even here in America there wasn't more of it because here tonight there was only warmth and friendliness and fun.

Soon people began to go home, for inexplicably in the same moment they remembered that they were tired; they remembered the dreary animosities of the day and the problems they would meet tomorrow, and that no matter how perfectly they met them, the air of America still would remain imperfect because of the cartoon of the Reichstag fire.

In the autumn of 1933 Marc returned home one evening to find Hallie at the door, cigarette in hand, and in her eyes a troubled look contending with the smile of welcome also there. She said, "Marc, my darling, here's a letter for you."

It wore the stamp of the Third Reich. The paper was pale lavender and very thin. The address, typewritten, had the name of the city underlined in the German manner.

"The rest of your mail is on your desk, but this—this might be important."

For a moment Hallie's fingers interlocked with Marc's and they smiled at each other as if secretly renewing their resolve to keep theirs a happy world; then they kissed with the restraint which seemed proper with the children there on the steps. Herbert was taller than Marc now and resembled him as completely as Jill resembled Hallie. They took Marc's hat and coat, hanging them up with competitive speed. Jill fetched his slippers and fresh socks.

"Pretending I'm an old man," he grumbled, and tousled her hair.

"Marc," Hallie said, and in her voice was a quality which came when she was talking about petition signatures on peace resolutions. "Marc, I do believe——"

"You want to know what's in it," Marc teased. He slashed the envelope with his penknife after glancing at the sender's address. "From Gretchen Cramer Alsberg, Nürnberg," he read, then opened the letter.

"Gustav and Martha's daughter.... There are two letters. The first is short—handwriting fairly clear—from Gretchen .... Says she writes only to introduce her husband, Fritz Alsberg, who until recently was an attorney .... 'I hope you will be so good as to consider with kindness his request. My mother, your Tante Martha, sends greetings. She is past seventy, but thank God she is well.'"

Marc handed the note to Hallie. He sat down in the stiff hall chair in which no one ever sat except to put on rubbers. He sat heavily. He read snatches of the other letter.

"...He laments the necessity to ask a favor of strangers.... Has never before been forced to ask help from others.... Has supported his family...that is no longer possible in Germany...forty-two years old, his wife, thirty-six...could begin again...a son...a daughter...desire immigration affidavits...would not bother us after reaching this land where it is possible for a man to support his family.... Has been in correspondence with members of his university brotherhood now in America and from them has learned it will not be possible to go into the legal occupation———"

"Legal occupation. What English!" Jill laughed.

Marc's eyes searched the floor and the walls and the ceiling and at last found his daughter.

"If your father had to write to Germany for a favor———"

"Go on, Marc," Hallie said. She was pounding out her cigarette.

"To give up his profession of all these years is a sorrow, but it will not leave him helpless .... Hard worker and can surely earn a livelihood. Gretchen is a singer and also can earn. Regrets he has no relatives of his own in America. Then he need not trouble a stranger. Gretchen has begged him to do this thing. She is very desirous of coming for the sake of their children. Eric is twelve; Marianna, ten .... He is sorry for the endeavoring——" He paused while they laughed. "For the endeavoring he is causing me .... I should reply in English since both he and his wife have knowledges of English."

"Knowledges of English" sent all four into laughter.

"I bet they smell of sauerkraut," Jill said. It was a phrase borrowed from Gramma.

Marc, looking back in his memory, saw Gretchen's father with Hans, giving the mittens, rebuking Hans for the naming of his children, going away less gaily than he came.

He fingered the lavender paper. "This seems to be the letter of a decent man."

Hallie said, "You must attend to it at once."

"I'll get my lawyer on the phone the first thing in the morning."

"Doesn't he write funny, Daddy?" Jill exclaimed as they went into the dining room hand in hand.

"He does," Marc said. "He does write funny ...." He held Hallie's chair out for her. He looked at Hallie, whose eyes were steady though frowning. "But I'm afraid all this isn't funny."

Hallie said, "He seems so embarrassed, so proud, poor man. I'm sure we'll like him. I feel as if I've known him for a long time."

"So," Marc joked, "he isn't to be pitied after all ...."

When the meal was nearly over and the talk had not been of the Alsbergs for a long time, Marc surprised them by saying, "Martha Cramer, Gretchen's mother, sent some pictures years ago. I wonder whether Mama still has them."

Jill said, "Gramma showed them to me. Gramma hasn't thrown away anything that belonged to Grandfather."

"And if Gramma has it, you've seen it," Herbert added. "You walk all over Gramma. You act as if her room is your playhouse." He said it, watching his father. This was the sort of jesting which usually pleased Marc, for he enjoyed the implications of intimacy between his daughter and his mother, but even this didn't seem to amuse him tonight.

An hour later he spoke again. "All the articles try to pretend that little paperhanger with the big mustache is only a silly sort of clown. Maybe so. Maybe he is. Even if he is a clown with a lust for power ... Very likely Fritz Alsberg has never seen the man. I keep thinking of the neighbors of the Alsbergs. What about them? They have lived near this family for years. The attorney whose wife is a singer. Two people who have learned a little English. And now they can't support themselves. And must leave the country. What about our neighbors? How would we like it if———"

Herbert laughed. In his chuckles was all the assurance of a boy who had passed his term exams with distinction. He put his arm across his father's shoulders. "You can't compare this country with those European ones, Dad. It couldn't happen over here."

PART IV
1936–1946

And a man shall be as an hiding place from the wind ... as rivers of water in a dry place, as the shadow of a great rock in a weary land.

—ISAIAH

CHAPTER I

HALLIE STOOD IN the arched entrance of the woman's world Tea Room. Ann Bromage usually arrived early enough to secure a small table against the wall, and yes, there she was, as sensibly dressed as a governess, not at all like the wife of Hart, one of the most dapper of men.

As Hallie twisted her way between the closely set tables she was greeted fondly by many, for she shared with these women the belief that by their endeavors the city would become less smoke-stained, less graft-manipulated, and less complacent than it was. In a way they were the conscience of the city, and now, during the lunch hour, the conscience was having a brief but merry holiday.

The Woman's World was around the corner, or down the block, or up the block from organizations for the proper care of the needy, the crippled, the tubercular; neighbored, too, by groups seeking to outwit the political machines to the end that government might promote the welfare of the people.

During the noon hour volunteers in these offices would hurry to the Woman's World to keep luncheon appointments with friends who for themselves preferred comfort to crusading yet enjoyed the lively talk of campaigns and civic conflicts. Some of the transients, like Ann Bromage, gave large contributions.

The Veiled Prophet Ball, Hallie surmised, was the occasion for Ann's appearance today. Ann could never feel entitled to the downy areas of her life until she had denounced them to someone. For that purpose she often chose Hallie Kleinman; Hallie could always convince Ann that those whose lives were heavily embroidered with pleasures need not apologize to the less privileged since everyone who had any wits at all accepted pleasures whenever possible.

"It was a horrid ball," Ann said now. "Never was there a worse Veiled Prophet Ball in all the years I've been going. Too many people, and such ordinary people! My dress turned out all right. Even Hart approved. There were lots of lovely dresses. Why we consent to wear them to that huge barn I'll never know."

"Everything is covered——"

"Yes, white tarpaulins. The place is large enough for a circus. And the Queen so young she might prefer one. But she looked lovely."

Everyone knew Big Business was the Veiled Prophet, that masked and bearded monarch who returned each October wearing a gold-stitched purple satin robe. On the first night of his visit he was drawn about the streets heading a procession of handsome floats and bowed graciously to the masses, black, white, and tan, banked and cheering along the route. The next day the school children would draw pictures of the Prophet and hear their teachers explain the legend depicted by the floats.

Rumor said that the man who bowed was only a double for the monarch who the next night placed the jeweled crown upon the head of the Queen, thus pronouncing her the leader of the ensuing social season, privately enjoyed, publicly described upon the society pages of the newspapers. The Queen always was the debutante daughter of the man who named the largest sum in bidding which was high, secret, and crisscrossed with paternal love and pride and something which was neither.

When Alice joined Hallie and Ann she reported that the talk at all the tables today was of the ball, many claiming to have guessed in advance who would be Queen. One woman who had estimated costs announced that the money spent on the ball might have brought the city's unemployed relief allotment up to the level paid by other large cities.

"Stupid talk." Ann pouted. "If no one spent for the ball we'd have far more unemployment than we have."

Without conviction in her voice Hallie agreed that the ball did give work to lots of people.

Then Alice, her eyes inattentively upon the wallpaper, asked, "How is Marc?"

So Hallie knew Alice had observed that Marc was eating his heart out, as Mother Kleinman said it, over the '30s.

"He's having fun with his camera." Hallie's pretty chin upped a notch and she dimpled through the smoke of her cigarette. "Marc spends hours on hours in his darkroom. Pictures of old men foraging In alley garbage pails; studies of Mamie Lee and her family. His light effects are good."

Alice's gaunt, olive face ceased twitching. Nearing forty, her mannequin beauty was exotic, intricate, and sultry. Her hair was neatly stretched about her well-shaped skull. Her earrings were large silver tassels, her lips moist red and full. Her thinned brows swooped like arching wires. At the moment her heavy lashes were lowered to conceal the glint of tears.

"Marc in his darkroom ... Ann in gold cloth ... Hallie playing peace ... Alice racing across town to see the Queen's bouquet of orchids ... Nothing we do is a sensible answer to the '30s."

It was an unmannerly truth to speak with such vehemence in the Woman's World on the day after the Veiled Prophet celebration. In belated apology Alice laughed and surreptitiously dashed the tears into a sheer green kerchief meant only for matching her hat and purse. She began to describe how Clara Hursch used to take hours to dress for the ball.

Alice refrained from saying that in those days a few carefully selected Jews were permitted to bid their wives or daughters into the procession of Matrons and Maids, that the Ellinger Lakes and Oscar Hursches went in the same carriage and later sat at the same table for the after-the-ball hotel supper. She just told about corsets drawn tight and lace-edged undies and powder secretly applied to Clara's back by Fräulein, who of course adored the ball and considered the Prophet kin to Wotan.

After that Ann and Hallie also told stories of their childhood, and so the luncheon ended in amiable laughter long after most of the other tables were deserted. Ann and Alice went shopping together for antiques. The hard times were squeezing handsome old silver and china and furniture into local shops, and those in the know could pick up really lovely things for next to nothing. With these heirlooms as substitutes, Alice was ridding her house of everything which had come from Hursch and Company.

One evening Marc and Hallie went to see a movie about Nazi Germany, shown at an obscure theater in a workers' section of the city unfamiliar to the Kleinmans. They drove past twice because no glittering lights proclaimed it as a place of amusement. The house was one of the many closed by the depression, and they soon learned that it smelled musty.

By the time they were seated their hands held an assortment of fliers thrust into them by excited men near the entrance. One sheet referred to the film as a Jew film and warned that it was lies. The man who gave it to them had bitter blue eyes in a marble face. Another handbill acclaimed the literary greatness of the author of the play upon which the film was based and solicited contributions for the benefit of German liberals, intellectuals, labor leaders, and others who fought against Hitler. These were handed out by Clinton Randall, Ira's and Alice's son.

"Did you see?" Hallie whispered once they were seated. "Clinton ought to be at the Fortnightly learning to dance. Oh dear, it seems as though Alice and Ira were married only a little while ago and here's their son nearly grown and involved in——"

Reading the sheet, Marc said, "This seems all right."

"Marc dear, I wonder whether you ought to buy tickets from Clinton. He's a lovely, precocious boy, but—isn't it a little like keeping up your old fight with Ira?"

The lights went out and in the interval before the film began Marc wondered about Ira and Alice and this boy. To Hallie he whispered, "I have no fight with Ira. What made you think of that?"

"Surely Ira and Alice couldn't want—— Marc, a boy of fifteen should be having fun."

He shook his head. "It's no longer so, Hallie, not in this world."

The story of the film was the story of a German professor, a specialist who conceived it his duty to remain a specialist. The professor refused to leave his laboratory to take part in politics until he learned that politics was about to destroy all laboratories, including his.

The tempo intensified from the andante of professorial peace to a crescendo of intrigue and torture and murder. Though the picture claimed to be only fictionalized reportage, it seemed melodrama. One of the liberal journals to which Marc subscribed had endorsed the unbelievable facts, but Marc's emotions were less credulous than his intellect. The brutality stifled him.

Hallie, always set a-tremble by suffering, slipped her hand into his and several times closed her eyes. When the lights went on again she said slowly, thoughtfully, "I wonder if it does any good."

Some around them were saying the photography was fine, but some called the film straight propaganda. There were a few couples present whom Marc and Hallie knew. They, too, were talking about the photography and the propaganda.

Marc said, "There is another question. Is it true?"

Then the talk became so animated that they forgot to leave and were asked please to step outside since the theater was about to be locked. On the sidewalk money was being collected and there were efforts to interfere. The man with the bitter blue eyes would follow people to their cars and with a detaining foot on the running board, whisper. His helpers stood beside other cars, whispering. They called back from across the street, *"Jude! Jude!"*

"They do not yet know the language," someone remarked, "but they are already shouting Jew!"

Hallie kept murmuring, "Marc, this is horrible. It's uncivilized. Why doesn't the policeman stop them?"

Those who had been talking together inside remained together. Most of the others in the audience were workingmen in leather jackets and their wives who wore no hats.

The sinister mood oppressed everyone. A man said to Marc, "So it's leaped over here to us. Tck-tck."

Hallie remembered that the Alps was just a few blocks away. When it was agreed that they would go there Marc invited

Clinton. No, he would not leave, he said, not now when there might be trouble. He was keyed up and restless. "Let them start something! Our boys are ready for them. Some fellows from the unions," he explained, and hurried away.

The Alps had changed little since Marc was a boy. The electric train still pursued its serpentine route along a papier-mâché mountain range. The iron sheep were newly painted, and the peasant costumes on the dolls were fresh.

The walls were as always; above the bar, mirrors alternated with oil paintings of florid, naked women posturing languidly. The flooring was of small white tiles; the tables round, where talkers could lean nearly across. The air was fragrant with the odor of freshly drawn beer. A man with a German accent briskly showed Marc and his party to a table in the center of the long room.

Near the kitchen door someone talked to attentive listeners who now and again pounded out a group laugh derisive in quality. Men and women from other tables formed a standing circle in back of their table. Now the standers melted abruptly into groups seated nearby.

Marc had the disquieting feeling that their going somehow was the result of his having lifted his head. He had never been able to get over his habit of trying to make sure restaurant noise-makers were not Jews. It was like the searching ahead on a page for J-words. Well, these were not Jews. He had seen enough to be sure of that.

Marc did not glance toward the table again, not even when he saw the young man with the hard blue eyes survey the room swiftly and stride toward that corner. Chairs, shifting to make room, screeched against the tiled floor. He noted suddenly that

Fräulein was at the table, and she looked at him insolently, her face scornful.

The blood was pounding at the base of Marc's neck, turning him a little sick at the stomach. He walked after the others, toward the electric train, trying to recapture the innocence with which he and Hans had watched the tiny cars enter and emerge from tunnels: the innocence and the wonder and the delight. Now he could not look innocently and his wonder had nothing to do with toy trains and there was no delight. Hallie's eyes were pretty with laughter. Masking her matronly adoration only a little, she said, "You look cold, Marc. You're not getting a cold, are you?"

He sat down beside her at the table. "At the Alps one must order noodles," he said. "No, I'm not cold." Like many others, Hans had always said, "At the Alps one must order noodles." The memory of his father was suddenly poignant within him.

Everyone at the table decided upon noodles in one form or another. The waiter stood very straight saying, "Noooodles? Noooodles? With butter. With vegetables. With cheese. With brisket. *Und* also in soup." He made a song of it. All the waiters at the Alps made a song of it. The second verse was about beer. "Light. Dark. *Oder* bock. Draught *und* bottled peer. Draught. Light, dark, bock, which iss it?"

The beer was brought in tall glass steins with large handles. On the night Hans had come to borrow a suit someone had started singing, *"Ach du Lieber Augustin,"* and then everyone sang at all the tables, plunking out the *"Ach's"* with their heavy steins. Hans, reaching over to an uncleared table, had given Marc an empty stein, but he himself had used a nearly full stein, and without spilling any. The picture of Hans plunking his full stein and blushing with the happiness of *"Ach du Lieber Augustin"* came nostalgically back into Marc's mind.

Tonight everyone seemed restless. They ate quickly, spoke in low voices about the movie, saying the beginning of the story was good, the ending overdrawn, but agreeing with one another that the main idea was that such things could not happen in America. The film was needlessly unpleasant.

Andrew Goff, Uncle Oscar's lawyer, asked Marc, "Do you think it really is happening even over there?"

Marc's eyes sought those about the table. Next to Andrew Goff was his jolly wife, Madge; then Barney Murphy, who reputedly could sell anything to anybody but who also couldn't refuse to buy anything, even tickets for a dumb foreign movie, and his wife Lorna, who couldn't bear to waste anything, even tickets, and so they had come to the show too; and Harry Dunn, a lawyer and liberal, a thin man with hay fever, and his wife Hortense.

Marc said, "Because I signed affidavits for a cousin I have received other inquiries." His hand arranged envelopes in stacks on the table. "These six are from lawyers. These three from doctors. This one from a journalist. Six and three and one—ten." Marc's hand gathered the letters. "The men who wrote these are no longer allowed to practice their professions. It is forbidden by law for Jews to practice their professions."

Again they ate noodles and then everyone spoke little polite phrases. Marc knew it had been as unpleasant for them to hear him say the word "Jew" as it had been for him to speak it. Because Marc had whispered across the letters his party was leaning as far across the table as were those at other tables.

Barney Murphy was the first to lean back. He elbowed his wife's ribs. "See, Mrs. Murphy, I wasn't such a fool when I passed up law school. Nobody ever says a guy can't sell automobiles. Come what may, Barney Murphy goes on selling automobiles. Trotting to Mass and selling automobiles."

For a moment everyone pretended that sort of thing was likely to happen to anyone, Jew or Catholic or Protestant. While they were declaring that an unjust government was bound to be overthrown, Hortense Dunn began an impromptu and intricate Freudian explanation of why little men like Hitler were also sure to be bachelors and want to run the world.

Andrew Goff covertly gave Marc advice. "Be careful about signing affidavits. The government can hold you liable for the bills those people run up. You might be called upon to support them for the rest of your life." Mr. Goff for a moment watched the sweet solemnity in Hallie's eyes and, with a swift glance back and forth between her and Marc, added, "I've looked after your uncle Oscar's things for a long time, you know. He and I agree. You have to be careful about arousing feeling." He didn't say what kind of feeling, but he paused long enough to let Marc realize he was talking about feeling against the Jews. "With the widespread unemployment situation in this country, to bring in men who would take away jobs might invite trouble."

Marc had insisted upon going back for Clinton, and now the boy was in the rear seat, tired and silent. Hallie swung around so that she could put her hand on his knee. "Clint darling, you know how much your cousin Hallie and cousin Marc have always loved you. But really, Clint, I do think your parents ought to know what you're doing and where you're going. After all, you're only fifteen . . . .

Quickly Clint answered, "I'm not ashamed of what I do, but you—— The Alps isn't a decent place to go. It's where the anti-Semites hang out."

Marc said, "I saw Fräulein at the back table."

"I'm glad you told me that, Cousin Marc. It's as I thought."

Hallie became excited. "Surely Fräulein has the right to go where she wishes. She worked at the Alps for years."

"Cousin Hallie, a worker who isn't loyal to other workers … The Alps isn't funny, not for workers, not for Jews, not for anybody."

They were now in the Randall driveway, a concrete serpent winding through a luxurious lawn. They waited until Clint waved from the opened door.

When they had backed out and regained the highway Hallie said, "I don't know, really I don't know why we should bother about the Alps."

Marc said, "I suppose we can't report a place for serving people who like Germany's anti-Semitism."

She slipped her hand into his. "Darling, you mustn't. That whole setup is despicable and ill-mannered and—— But it has nothing to do with you, Marc. Surely you can see that; Marc darling, you have always had a sense of humor."

He stopped the car so that she could get out under the portico.

CHAPTER 11

WHEN THE ALSBERGS came for dinner they had been in the city for a week, in the United States for six months. They were neatly dressed in clothes unmistakably German. Fritz Alsberg's smile was the overpowering fact of the evening. It was a gray smile of the lips only. The stretch back into the cheeks came unexpectedly or, when expected, tardily. It was abrupt as a mechanism is abrupt, and mirthless.

Fritz was tall and once had been heavy. His thick features seemed too large for his shrunken face. Had his eyebrows been emphatic they might have drawn attention to his eyes. As it was, there was nothing to look at but the mouth which, smiling, showed a quivering tongue.

Gretchen was a little taller than her husband or perhaps only looked so because she stood very straight, her shoulders back, her hands clasped.

"Ach, it iss a home," she said as soon as she entered. "A beautiful home. Piano. Books. Pictures. Ach, a home! Mother will be rejoiced to hear." She turned to Marc. "Your *Tante* Martha sends greetings."

At the table it was the women who spoke.

"Tomorrow," Hallie announced cheerfully, as if this family reunion were only a lark, "tomorrow we'll look for a place to live. What time shall I call for you?"

"Please"—Fritz seemed startled—"a man makes no debts until he hass job." His head snapped a quick bow.

"But you must live somewhere," Hallie protested. "That boardinghouse——" She halted herself and moved the silver-tailed salt-and-pepper birds two inches to the left.

Again the abrupt smile came and left Fritz's face. "When one iss uprooted, a home becomes very important. Naturally. But all-so I must not have debts. I must not give me that worry." His voice rose excitedly.

Marc said, "We'll talk about it after dinner."

The smile tried to come. Instead Fritz's mouth made swallowing noises. His pale lips gathered into a knot. His flickering eyes sought Gretchen's. A glow which might have been tenderness and might have been hope shone in them momentarily before they again became flat, dull hollows.

Gretchen laughed an opera singer's laugh. "See, Fritz? See?" She flirted her eyes at him. Then she said, "Come, Fritz, it will amuse them. Tell about job in New York." She addressed herself to the others. "Fritz Alsberg had job in New York. Tell them."

Marc thought, To tell an amusing story, or at least to try to tell an amusing story, even when you are thrown out of your native land, that is surely a Jewish trait. But Gretchen did not look Jewish. That red frizzy hair looked Irish. Yet this need to tell a funny story to maintain faith in herself, that was Jewish.

Since Fritz, smiling suddenly, made it clear he could not tell the story, Gretchen began. She was trying to put the tall, gaunt man at ease. She was also trying to convince her cousins that her husband had once been a man of standing and would be again if he were permitted to regain his self-confidence.

Her story was a sequence of ridiculous episodes resulting from Fritz's failure to understand New York slang, he who had received his English from the works of Shakespeare. Everyone laughed, Fritz blushing, Eric fascinated by his mother's histrionics, little Marianna's pallor becoming a deep scarlet flush.

Hallie asked, "You have brought furniture?" She was still determined to move them from the boardinghouse.

"Ah, really beautiful new furniture," Gretchen answered. "Lovely new piano, Steinway. Fritz buys fine new encyclopedia. We have new notes—I believe you call it music. One cannot take out money. Only things. We have for three rooms."

"I spend my old-age money," Fritz said, his voice rising. In a man's shrill, frantic soprano he shouted to Marc, "I do not want to buy new furniture."

Hallie said, "But you will also need money to———"

Gretchen blushed and did not look at Fritz. "Everybody who leaves Germany now iss interested in photography. I bring camera. Fine Leica. Fritz also. Also Eric. Also Marianna. They can be sold. One Leica has already bought tickets to this city."

Fritz's forehead knotted into deep furrows. "When one hass lived a lifetime without these indirections it iss not nice to be forced to———" He shrugged. "One is helpless."

Hallie spoke soothingly. "I hope you brought enough clothes. After all, that is what Germany wants. For you to spend your money before you leave." She sat up straighter. "I hope you brought plenty. I hope you bought things you had been wanting all your lives." In her face was good, honest American fight.

Fritz's lips swallowed themselves for a moment. Then his voice again climbed to soprano. "Ya, we bought clothes for Marianna—a box for next year and one for the next and the next and the next. All-so for Eric from now to '42. That iss what you call O.K. for Alsbergs. But how iss for Germany? How can a country grow strong by letting goods go *out? Out,* for God's sake? By smashing windows? By breaking furniture? It iss crazy. Altogether crazy! Please!" he said, and his upraised hands pleaded for other talk.

Hallie leaned toward Marianna, who shrank down into her chair. "Don't you like mashed potatoes, dear?" The child's pale, gracile cheeks tried to smile; the startled, glistening eyes stared, but at nothing.

Offhandedly Gretchen answered Hallie. "You have right supper for her. She iss tired. Always now she eats not enough."

"There'll be ice cream," Jill whispered across the table in mimic delight.

When the ice cream came Marianna only tasted and shivered and appeared more startled than ever. Marc carried her to the divan in the other room and covered her with the afghan Aurelia had knit for them. He stooped and looked at her carefully. In her features he thought he could see the little boy who had been Hans Kleinman. There was the same wide forehead and long chin and neat mouth which Hans had regained when he became old and ill.

Returning to the table, Marc brought the tin box of pictures and asked Gretchen to tell about them, but first she must give him news of Aunt Martha, whom he had met after the last war.

"Mother iss past seventy and deaf. It was not easy for her to say good-by. She talks of coming over, too, but of course her roots are there. Once while we were in New York in a letter she mentioned the possibility. She wrote that if she was not deaf——"

Fritz smiled. "I answered that. I wrote to her, saying that since she cannot hear does it make so much difference that what she does not hear iss English, not German? She will laugh. It iss not often one has privilege to laugh now in Germany." He sighed, and as if he remembered he ought now to smile, he smiled.

That is it, Marc thought, a Jew always wants the privilege at least to laugh at his troubles. It is that perhaps which makes a man a Jew.

Gretchen's fingers moved swiftly among the pictures. Over one picture she paused. "This iss my brother. Married to pianist. She was to play important concert." Again the pause was overlong. "It was announced and then something else was announced. Nazi government said a Jew could play in public only Mendelssohn. Anna could not accept it. After she was dead my brother went to Ecuador. Mother received a card. Only one card."

"Your sister?" Marc asked.

"Her husband, too, was in captivity after last war. Now they take their family to Palestine. They live on collective farm. He was attorney. Mother iss alone."

She put the pictures in little groups. "These dead. These emigrated. This one, your father's sister, was in Munich home for old persons. Nazis came in night and turned them out. We never heard again from *Tante* Anna. Nearly eighty. It iss to be hoped she iss not alive."

Before she had finished, Fritz, flickering quick smiles, said it was not right to keep the children out so late. Tomorrow Fritz Alsberg had a very important appointment. Really they must go home at once. No, they would take streetcar. They had tickets for the streetcar. And a map of the city. He pulled out a leather folder neatly engulfing these important treasures.

He bowed several shy bows and made a final speech. Gretchen, as if reluctant to leave, was humming to herself, looking again at the books on the long shelves. She ran her hands up and down their piano in full, rich arpeggios, and at last aroused Marianna.

Jill rushed upstairs and returned with a doll, one of several she had saved. She offered it to Marianna. It was an infant doll with bent knees and a long lace-trimmed dress.

Marianna did not raise her arms to take it, only hung her head in embarrassment, then looked at her mother, who spoke to the child swiftly in German. Suddenly Marianna seemed over-joyed. She hugged the doll, swaying her body from side to side as if to comfort the infant and herself too.

In the other room, whispering to Marc and Hallie, Gretchen explained, "For years Marianna had Annala—a doll she loved very much. All day Annala was in her arms. I hid Annala after the Nazis... Marianna has not played with doll now for long time. She will very much joy have."

"But why not?" Hallie asked, her handsome eyes deep with bewilderment.

"In these years in Germany very few Jewish babies are being born. I felt Marianna must not think like a mother. The disap-pointment would be too great."

Fritz bowed once, twice, again and again. "I am very happy you have the great joy of this beautiful home."

And then they were gone and Hallie was emptying ash trays as if nothing special had happened. Jill looked up at Marc and asked to be allowed to defer going to bed. When he did not answer or even hear, she climbed on his lap and kissed him.

Herbert was snapping his fingers nervously. When Hallie shook her head he stopped and began to straighten a stack of magazines, but not as if he cared either about magazines or order. His loyalty to Marc was intense and aggressive. For many years he had been defending his father. On the grade-school play-ground when a derisive remark was made against Jews or one which was not derisive, only conventionally derogatory, Herbert's fist had swung hard and without hesitation. Now he came to Marc's side and said, "Dad, it will cost a hell of a lot of money to go to Harvard next year. I know a swell bunch of guys will be pushing off for Mizzou. I'm going with them."

"Why on earth?" Hallie asked, and stood frozen, as if she believed the least movement of her body would shatter her world. After a long silence she spoke in a dulled voice. "Harvard is a wonderful college. Herbert, if you go to Missouri you would have to stay with your grandparents. You would miss out on college fun. All my life I've wanted my son to go to Harvard."

Then she moved swiftly to Marc's side and sat on the arm of his chair and spoke down to him, fondly, about the Alsbergs. "They're nice people. Very nice. And bright and talented. They're nice people, Marc."

"Yes, they're nice people," he answered.

Later to Hallie, Jill whispered, "But, Mother, did they do something wrong? What——"

"Sh-sh," Hallie answered, nuzzling her face into the curls near Jill's ear. "Of course not. We'll buy one of their cameras for Daddy. A Leica is a very fine camera. Won't that be nice? Daddy will love having a Leica."

By estimating the guests Uncle Oscar had chosen to be present, Marc knew that the dinner party was for the purpose of bringing Marc Kleinman to his senses. Whenever an official of Hursch and Company thought in a way which seemed unprofitable for the firm, the discrepancy was averaged off at a dinner party. This one had been summoned on short notice, and Hallie had been the first consulted about available evenings.

Aunt Clara whispered to Eileen to pass the silver tray with the canapes again, and finally crossed the room herself to Marc with a caviar-and-egg tidbit held daintily on a cocktail napkin.

"Marc darling," she said, "this is a new kind. I want you to try it." And then she returned with another shaped like a heart. "This one is very good."

Dear old Aunt Clara was getting more nearsighted and fatter each year but also becoming kinder. She suffered for every irascible word Uncle Oscar said to her guests, insisting after each explosion that the victim get the best piece of duck or a third helping of dessert, and before he left the house she would fumble about in the drawer of the hall chest where she kept little gifts. Because her eyesight was bad she sometimes confused the boxes so that Clarence Weiss once went home with a powder puff topped by a doll's head and Mimi with a cigar holder.

When Alice was in her teens and ignored by the dancing schoolboys, Marc had been Aunt Clara's stand-by. It was then he began taking Alice to dances and plays and movies, arriving in high spirits, as if his coming had nothing whatever to do with Clara's having confided to Aurelia about her daughter's loneliness and tears. Aunt Clara remained grateful, so that tonight, with Uncle Oscar in this mood, her persistent attentions confirmed Marc's surmise of trouble to come.

Bertha and Clarence were there, Bertha relating bits of news she had heard and talking rapidly, as if she were talking only to hide her dread, folding her handkerchief, unfolding it, folding it again, always precisely on its creases. Clarence, his hair seeming more flamelike than usual, was making a great fuss over Hallie. All were being conspicuously cordial to Marc.

Only Uncle Carl behaved as he always did; he ate and drank and laughed at Mimi's barbed jests. Uncle Carl and Marc understood each other; anything either one had to say to the other was not going to be said with caviar sandwiches, back-patting, or flattery of Hallie. Carl Hursch just sat there, a bald, pink-faced kewpie doll of a man in a gray business suit and red tie, kidding Mimi under his breath.

It was the omitted ones who made the plan legible. Aurelia was not there, nor Alice, since Alice always found ten-syllable words to prove Marc's simplest points. Nor was Ira, who was always raising money for Palestine as if Hursches and Manns were Zionists. Clinton, though he was old enough now to come, was not invited either, for then Herbert would have to be invited, too, and a son should not witness the disciplining of his father.

Beginning with soup in consommé cups above green-and-gold service plates, the dinner proceeded to baked chicken, avocado-and-grapefruit salad, and finally dessert, chocolate icebox cake, Marc's favorite. Aunt Clara proclaimed special affection for him as her reason for serving it tonight, adding that the entire menu was planned to please the young people, with due regard to the wishes of the women who were dieting.

Then the maid passed around the table with the *repoussé* silver coffeepot for extra coffee, the crystal goblets were refilled, the cigarettes and candy were passed again, and Aunt Clara said they should be put down on the table, and that was all. She whispered to the maid that she hoped the girls in the kitchen would enjoy their dinner.

Now they were ready to talk. Uncle Oscar dragged in the subject by holding up a Bohemian glass candy dish. "Clara, didn't we get this from Helena and Max?"

Aunt Clara, trying to look as if she really could see what was at the end of the table beyond the centerpiece of white gladioli, pretended that this was only chance conversation and she had had no forewarning.

"Yes, when we were with Helena and Max at Carlsbad, Oscar. We had given the Thalheimers something with which to remember the trip, and this was what they gave us. Helena was dear Hans's sister. I remember how pleased your father was, Marc, when we came back and told him about the good times we had together. Of course, like all Germans, they thought everyone from America was rich."

Oscar cleared his throat. "On my many trips I never met this cousin-in-law of yours, Marc. This tall one who walks like a German soldier and is now in our Rug Department. How is he doing, Clarence?"

Clarence, blushing, fitted one large hand carefully inside the other and said that Fritz Alsberg was doing only moderately well. His sales were not too bad, but there had been some objection, by other salesmen, to having him there at all. He looked so foreign, so German; his ways were excitable; he would learn, of course, in time he would learn.

They made it clear that this man, Fritz Alsberg, was not going to be fired. No, he would be kept—for Marc's sake—though it would be nice if Marc would teach him American habits. It was those others Marc was talking about bringing. They would cause trouble.

"We have to consider——" Oscar said, and the man who was always sure of what Hursch and Company should do now looked unsure and frowned toward Clarence, as if asking him to say it.

After a furtive glance toward the pantry door Clarence said, "We Jews in America have to consider our own position." He spoke overquietly in suave tones, to mask the avidity of his ambition to be a successful man.

Marc said, "Hereafter I shall not ask you to sign visas, Clarence."

"It doesn't matter who signs. The question is, ought anybody to be signing those visas?"

"If there weren't any unemployment problem in this country," Bertha put in, but anxiously, as if she were only begging Clarence to love Marc and Marc to love Clarence.

Bertha had a kindly face nearly moon-round, though her body was sleek as a mastiff's, narrow-hipped and easy of movement. The years had darkened her hair, but its brown glinted with lighter streaks. Her zeal for neatness extended to her own person. Even in company she was frequently peering into a mirror to see whether a hair was out of place. Her dressing table was arrayed with scissors, tweezers, and little brushes, grouped according to sizes and brightly clean, precisely placed. Her habitual preening annoyed Aurelia, who once told Marc, "Even if Hitler was coming, Bertha would worry whether her eyebrows looked right."

Now Mimi supported Bertha's premise. "One man can't save all the German Jews."

Then, because Mimi could never say anything which didn't irritate Oscar, even when she was agreeing with him, he shouted, "We must avoid prejudice. That's the long and the short of it."

"Those people have no place to go———" Marc began.

They didn't let him finish. Scoffing at his innocence, they told him this was a big world; there was South America, which really needed settlers.

"Let some of those Jews learn how to farm. It won't hurt them."

Marc had figures on quotas, and they knew that they had to believe Marc when he had looked up the facts.

Clarence said, "The gentiles resent it. Just because a fellow's a relative——"

Uncle Oscar said, "We have to learn to get along with our neighbors."

"What's the matter with Palestine?" Bertha asked.

Finally Aunt Mimi said, "Let them stay over there and fight the Nazis!"

Oscar flayed her for that until Aunt Clara pleaded, "Mimi was joking, Oscar. I think maybe we ought to send them checks to go to South America. I'll get wool tomorrow and knit mufflers for the ocean trip. On shipboard it gets cold. Do you ever hear from your *Tante* Helena, Marc?"

She asked it only because the argument seemed to be getting out of hand.

Marc answered by reading a letter from Helena's and Max's only son. It had been received by Fritz Alsberg, though it began "Dear Cousin Marc." Fritz had translated it into English, and now Marc read the letter just as it was written. The only interruption came at the very beginning, when Aunt Clara sighed, "I remember that boy. He had just been weaned and he cried a lot. Helena and Marx. What a sweet home they had."

After that there was no talk, no shifting in their chairs, no here and there with cigarettes and ashes.

The letter began with a request for affidavits: for himself and his wife, his two little girls, but also one for his son, twelve years old, formerly at school in Italy, now in England, where a family had offered adoption. Unfortunately Ilsa, Heinrich's mother, cried very much and did not wish to sign the papers. If they could come to America they could keep their son. Rudolph feared for the safety of many members of his family still in Germany. Near the end he mentioned a dozen others who ought not remain there without hope, but if necessary he himself could remain.

Marc said, "I'll not ask anyone here to sign affidavits again. In the East there's an organization———"

"Who is in it?" Oscar asked.

When Marc named the leaders Carl said, "They are big men."

Everyone seemed impressed.

Clarence jumped up. "But what right have you to sign, Marc? You're not earning a fortune. You couldn't support all those people. That's a contract between you and your govern- ment. You would have to———"

Aunt Clara turned. "Hush," she said. "Those people are almost in our family. If they had come a generation ago they would be here for dinner tonight, and now they are being forced to give up their own children———"

Clarence laughed scornfully. "That guy writes that. How do we know?"

Aunt Clara turned her face so that it was toward Clarence, whom she could discern only faintly. She shook her head. "There's nothing worse than to give up your own flesh and blood. Nothing. Marc, I'll get you some signatures. My broth- ers—though I believe they, too, have had letters."

Oscar pounded his fist on the arm of his thronelike chair. "It's not a question of signatures. I'll sign and sign again. If those prominent men on that letterhead can sign, Oscar Hursch can sign too. I met one of those men once. He's a fine gentleman. Sign, yes; give money to that organization to do the job, yes;

but bring in a lot of German accents to work at Hursch and Company? No! I won't have it!"

That night Marc said to Hallie, "I'm pulling out soon. I'm getting out of Hursch and Company."

She was brushing her hair and finished counting out the strokes before she asked, "What will you do? It's such a bad time. The depression isn't really over."

"It's a bad time only because I should have done it years ago."

CHAPTER III

EVEN AFTER HITLER'S inhumanity became clear the word "jew" was rarely spoken at the family dinner parties. The talk now was of world politics. Was that magazine article correct in claiming Mussolini's attack upon Ethiopia to be only the prelude to an attack ultimately upon the British Empire? And what could Britain say for herself in India? When board meetings were mentioned it was to report what some good Christian had said against Hitler or Mussolini.

After a while leaders came from New York, men like the Mann family, but wealthier and more important and more powerful. Because they lived in New York they looked not toward New York, as the Hursches and Manns did, but toward London and Paris and Berlin. They came to tell what they had seen or been told by trustworthy non-Jews. This attack in Germany was not going to blow over. It was not a temporary aberration. It was not just a problem for Jews.

The visitors did not mask their belief that Hursches and Manns, who had always been good givers, would have to learn to give on a vaster scale then they had ever imagined, unless they wanted refugee Jews to come here and be a burden upon gentiles and an embarrassment to everybody.

Uncle Carl said, "Jews have always looked after their own poor."

Uncle Oscar, seeming very old, said, "These are not poor Jews. I refer to the ones I met in Germany. They lived well. They had plenty. They were prominent people. They were nice people." He meant that they were nice in the same way the Hursches and Manns were nice.

The visitor answered, "They are poor now. Poor and persecuted and Jews." Then angrily, "Even those who were christened or who married gentiles, they too are now Jews. Their assimilation——"

One of the younger Manns said, "To get a university appointment they had to be christened. That was true over there for years. Everyone understood that. It was a formality."

Ira Randall was triumphant. "Their assimilation did not work."

It was a remark which grieved the others. Alice suddenly added, "Clinton wants to get into the fight in Spain."

The family took that to be just some of Alice's nonsense. They were thinking of the refugees who knew even more about art and music than the Manns and now were coming into the city, phoning Marc Kleinman and asking only for peace, that no one knock at their doors at midnight and drag them off to headquarters.

For once Oscar Hursch agreed with the labor unions. They were protesting that the refugees might take jobs away from American workmen, and Uncle Oscar said that this must not happen. Uncle Carl said he didn't blame them for kicking. It would be terrible.

But Aunt Mimi suddenly was entirely happy. She no longer had her headaches. She no longer had to decide whether to get up for lunch or not. She was up for breakfast. With some of her friends she was running a telephone-exchange business for the refugees. She would take orders for cakes or cookies or rich desserts, and refugee women who knew how to bake *Schnecken* and *Torten* would fill the orders. Those who knew how to make candies made candies. Those who knew how to sew or knit or crochet filled sewing orders. Overnight it became a large business. Mimi herself found a store to serve as a central shop. Earnest and efficient volunteers were in charge, some driving their cars to fetch or deliver orders. Buy-Now was a lively success. Beginning there, many of the refugee women got jobs or established businesses.

"Why is it," Mimi asked Gretchen Alsberg, "that you German women are braver than your men? We always thought women everywhere were the spoiled ones."

Gretchen trilled her opera laugh. "We cook over there; we cook also here. We clean our house over there; we clean our house also here. For us there is not so big change as for the men, who were important over there and over here are not important."

Mimi twiddled at the handsome button on her handsome coat. "I wouldn't know how to bake *Schnecken*."

"We took lessons. At night our cook—the new laws made it not possible for a gentile maid to work in Jewish household—but at night she came back and with the curtains together she shows me how to bake. Some of us took sewing lessons. We knew big changes were coming .... Whatever changes, a woman needs to know how to cook and keep her house."

Gretchen called upon Marc at his office. She said she came only to make an appointment, a quite secret appointment. She was trembling, trying to stand like an opera singer, a whispering pale woman whose eyes would abruptly bulge as she stared at the invisible over her shoulder.

"No," she pleaded when he said she must speak freely. "It iss not possible. I cannot here——" She motioned toward the people and voices beyond his office.

"They're not listening."

She stood in the exact center of the room, equally far from all walls, and moved her mouth with silent words which now and again became whispers.

"I have done something illegal. Fritz must not be told. He would worry, naturally; his mother, everyone left to us in Germany would be in danger.... They would kill.... Ach, I cannot sleep."

"Tell me," Marc ordered.

She breathed deeply and silently sobbed, then stood with her shoulders far back and her hands folded.

"When all this began over there we were allowed to take only a little money from the country.... I had some earned as singer. Fritz says I must give to government. He gives his. He gives also mine. But in here"—she touched at her breast—"I cannot give Hitler everything. I cannot! I can—not.... I keep out many marks—it would be about two thousand American dollars. Those marks are songs I sang. I cannot give to Hitler for guns. At night I lie awake. I beg myself to confess before it iss too late. It iss already too late. They will kill Fritz, who does not know I did this illegal thing.... I ask to go to Switzerland. I have cousin there very sick. She desires me to come. She and her husband are well-established people, Swiss people. I hide money on my body. I tell no one. I give money to my cousin's husband to save for me...." She could not continue.

Marc smiled. "At last someone who outwitted Hitler!"

"Now I cannot sleep. If they find out——"

"Where is the money?"

"When we leave Germany for good, I make excuse. I must see my dying cousin. Yes, she was dying, poor girl. I get the money again. French money this time. Now I must always hide it from Fritz. If he learns I have done something illegal he will——He, too, will not sleep . . . ."

Marc said, "Give it to me. I will have it exchanged for you."

"I will not get you in trouble."

He laughed at that.

"You Americans," she said, "you live like children. You do not know. You cannot know. Fear, you cannot understand. Fear under Hitler."

Marc left the office, and when he came back she had in her hands several tight, flat little bundles of white cloth held shut with safety pins.

"Keep it, Marc," she whispered. "To pay steamship fares. Hitler will no longer let them take their money to pay for journey. Buy tickets for those who otherwise might not get away."

She stood tall again, and though now there were tears floating in her eyes she looked proud. "I was brave—*nicht?*"

"Very brave, Gretchen."

"Ach, to be brave turns one old."

Heinrich Thalheimer and his parents—Rudolph, who would remain in Germany if necessary, and Ilsa, who could not give away her son, became Hallie's favorites among all the cousins in Europe.

"The boy is not far from Herbert's age. We could take him into our home. It would help. Yes, he will go to the university here in St. Louis and live with us."

Fritz Alsberg's mouth became a small white circle; his eyes, deep black hollows. "It would very much help, Cousin

Hallie, I can assure you. This cable which has come from Rudi. He iss very fine fellow. Rudi. In the old days he spoke out for that man you call the underdog. Today of course no one in Germany can speak out. Rudi, I hope, has learned to be silent. I hope he has. Well, this cable. It iss that there iss some delay. The American counsel in Italy makes very fine points. He cannot give student visa to boy who cannot go back to homeland. Student visa expires and Italy will not take Heinrich again since he iss not Italian resident. Germany also will not take him. In England he cannot reunite with his parents. It iss bad."

Hallie frowned. "I'll write to the counsel myself. The boy must go somewhere. Can't they see that?"

Fritz Alsberg's mouth again was a white circle, even smaller than before. "It iss that which Europe no longer sees."

All winter Hallie made plans for Heinrich. She bought single beds for Herbert's room, a pair of matching chests, and two desks. She hired a carpenter to add hooks and another rod to Herbert's closet, and when visitors came to the house she would show them where Heinrich was going to sleep.

"You can't call him Heinrich Thalheimer," Mimi said. "Why give him that burden? Heinie is worse. The boy should be told to sign up at school as Henry."

Uncle Carl said, "Let him make it Henry Thal from the start. Henry Thal isn't a bad name."

Mimi thought it wasn't good either. "Henry Thall is better. Everyone will know Thal is something cut off. Give him a chance. Let the students at least meet him before they make up their minds."

Hallie demurred. "Maybe his parents———"

Uncle Carl shouted, "If those guys don't want to be Americanized they'd better stay where they are."

As the months passed it became increasingly evident that they could stay where they were only with the greatest danger to themselves. A letter from Ilsa said Rudi had been taken away but surely he would come home soon, so could they hurry the visa? Hallie and Marc were very kind to invite Heinrich, and they would have from him much pleasures. He was a good boy, she wrote, and it would be a sorrow to have him cross the ocean without once more seeing him. A year and a half had passed since last she had seen her boy, but to go to Italy was not allowed. Nor to England. Hallie was a very fortunate woman to have the great joy of Heinrich in the house. He was a boy who brought pleasures to all those around him.

"She congratulates you instead of thanking you," Mimi said. "A German is a German. Even a Jewish German is a German."

"She sent me this." It was a pink hand-embroidered silk slip for a small pillow.

"Dutchy," Mimi said.

"She must have made it herself, poor thing," Hallie answered. "I'll put it on our bed."

At the end of eight months Rudolph came home, Ilsa wrote, and now they were without money to live in Germany and it was urgent that they leave promptly. Unfortunately the affidavits signed by Marc had now been declared insufficient, because he had signed for so many. Once the Thalheimers were in America they would ask nothing of anybody. They would work and they would not be in need, surely. Could Marc please get someone else to sign new affidavits? Please, if he could be so good as to ask one of his brothers or sisters ... It must be signed by someone as close as a cousin. A friend would not do.

Unfortunately again they had to ask yet another kindness of Marc Kleinman.

In that letter Aunt Martha wrote a note. The handwriting was thin and tremulous. She stated that she had now decided not to leave, since it was more important for the young to leave. She had never expected to leave Germany anyway. But it was now very necessary that her nephews and nieces leave soon. If the son of my favorite brother, Hans *selig,* could help Rudi, she would be very grateful. Rudi had always looked after everyone.

Marc wrote to Fred, who replied, "Same thing there, is it? I was signed to the hilt six months ago. We've adopted a half-dozen kids. Just financial. They are being taken care of in France. Celia is having a big time buying clothes for them."

Hursch and Company did not want Marc to resign. Oscar and Carl for once agreed fully.

"Marc's a good boy."

"He's done good work. No better sales-promotion man in the city. His ads are nice, gentlemanly ads."

"If he leaves, people will talk about us. They'll say we don't hire refugees."

"It's ridiculous."

"You talk to him."

"I have."

"Talk to him again."

But it came to nothing. Marc was not angry. He was just not to be moved. He sat through a long lunch with Uncle Oscar, listened to news of Ellinger Lake's cough, and heard about the projected luncheon to be given by an exclusive club of retailers to which Oscar Hursch now belonged. When Uncle Oscar finally said, "Marc, we shall not let you go," Marc answered, "You are very kind," in tones which implied Marc Kleinman would be gone on the date already set; it was beyond discussion.

Uncle Carl did not indulge in adroit preliminaries. He said to the waitress, "Bring this fellow the best plate lunch you've got and two desserts. Something good enough to make him change his mind."

Marc laughed, winked at the waitress, thus indicating he would have his usual lunch of corned beef on rye, apple dumpling, and coffee.

"Don't be a fool, Marc. You're a successful businessman. We've got something better for you, much better."

Marc reached into his pocket and brought out some photographs taken with the new Leica. His pictures had achieved a little fame. Once in a while a photograph by Marc Kleinman appeared in a local newspaper or in a local show.

Carl put on his glasses. Marc handed them to him one by one. The first was of their home taken from an angle which made the house and its shrubbery look manorial. Then he showed one of their cabin in the country, framed with native evergreens.

"Chiggers," Uncle Carl said sarcastically; then, "It's a safe place to wait out a war, but we are not at war."

"That's not my reason for moving, though I know, of course, that war will come."

"I hope to God not! I'd rather Hitler would wipe out every Jew in Europe!"

"He will. When he begins with the others, then there will be war."

Uncle Carl sucked in his cheeks and worked his lips in and out. "I have sons and grandsons," he said.

His nephew continued, "The trouble with Hursch and Company is that you don't believe Hitler means what he says——"

"Last time Oscar was over there he met a big industrialist, a very, very big man, mind you, a baron or something, a Jew. He says Hitler will do good. He says the eastern Jews over there are a bad lot."

"You'd like to believe Hitler will perform only little insults. Last year all Jews had to give their children Jewish names. This year Jewish automobiles must be registered. Insult by insult, he gets the upper hand——"

Carl's face turned red. "Do you think this big Jewish industrialist who backs Hitler is a fool?"

Marc answered, "Yes, a complete ass and a traitor." He put his pictures away and said, "Uncle Carl, you must bring Aunt Mimi out to see us. Hallie is making the cabin look nice. We can watch the sunset across an Ozark range."

"I'll wait for Mimi in the car," Uncle Carl answered. He was pensive. He pulled himself together. "I'll buy her a bottle of chigger killer." The salt-and-pepper set slipped from his hands. "I never would have expected this of you, Marc.... You're a disappointment to me."

He stood up and put on his overcoat, and Marc saw that Marc Kleinman no longer was like Uncle Carl's son.

All that winter Hallie continued to have good times, choosing them as deliberately as a child chooses ice cream in a restaurant, planning her pleasure in advance, trying to savor each instant. Seeking gaiety, she would invite company for dinner as a final fling before moving out of the house, not foreseeing that the talk would be of Hitlerian assaults upon the helpless. She would go to the movies and the newsreel would be of Nazi splendor. She would go to lunch with Ann Bromage and the talk would be of their sons and whether a war was coming.

One morning Hallie's mail contained a familiar long gray envelope from Peace, Inc. She put down the keys to her car. She had already delayed too long with the newspaper, reading and rereading pronouncements by last night's speaker. He had voiced the isolationist creed for a group called America First. What he said was a tangle of true, less true, and not at all true which sounded true, the sort of thing Hallie always found disturbing.

The enclosure this morning was a petition for peace and a denunciation of President Roosevelt for talking about Italy's stab in the back, for calling Hitler the names he obviously needed to be called, and for meddling in Europe's private affairs.

The latter, Hallie knew, meant taking up for the Jews; and Hallie, who was on her way to the hospital where Marianna's legs were to be operated upon in order to counteract the work done by punitive starvation under Hitler, saw that her life was at variance and she was no longer a woman sure of herself.

She sat down for a moment to still her trembling, but she continued to tremble. She told herself she was too old to begin to be the sort of person who did not know what she was doing in public work. She tried to bring Peace, Inc., and Marianna's legs and the ideas of last night's speakers and the petition together into a single image, but it was as if her eyes would not focus and she continued to see four images.

Moving about the room restlessly, she caught a glimpse of a mirrored woman whose handsome suit, tailored blouse, becoming hat, and serious face belonged to someone who was well able to know her own mind. Scrutinizing that earnest friendly-eyed woman, Hallie came to an agreement with her, namely that the one thing she was sure of was that Marianna had to be taken to the hospital now, this morning, and it was absurd for a woman who looked so matronly to be staring at herself in the mirror instead of fulfilling her promise to the Alsbergs.

She hurried and learned that in hurry she could not also be trying to think things through. She continued to hurry day after day, month after month. She became thinner and people said it was very becoming, and now and then she would overhear someone saying in surprised tones, "Have you noticed how pretty Hallie is these days?"

Her lean cheeks modified the squareness of her face into more intriguing lines. Formerly her large eyes seemed to fill the circle of her lashes. She would turn her head to see someone at her side, thus always looking directly forward. Now her eyes frequently slanted thoughtfully and were only dimly visible through the heavy lashes. Her mouth, which had been a smiling, talkative mouth, drew in upon itself a little, or, relaxing, would droop as if wearied.

Hallie was learning that even the most fun-loving people, the Kleinmans and the Manns and the Hursches, no longer had faith in fun. Like herself, they saw that to be without malice fun had to be an echo of freedom. If Hallie herself could not have fun, then she wanted to give it to others. If she could not give them fun, then she would give them peace. If that, too, was denied, she would give them love. It became compassion. Some was for herself. She had not foreseen, nor could she have believed, that she would have so little control over her own life. She had never envisaged a world of which she would have to beg spiritual alms. ... Please, World, give me a little of whatever there is ....

Marc felt more tenderly toward her than ever before, but it was as if she were far off, someone who would remain at a distance no matter what he might do. He knew she was suffering, that he was failing her as she was failing him. It was an inevitable failure, since for each the happiness of the other had become of modified importance in a world where so many others had greater cause for unhappiness.

They talked to each other less, and when they did it was to comment on the time of day, or the temperature outdoors, or what the butcher said, or the higher price of newspapers. They spoke not to initiate a conversation nor to continue one, only in order to break the stillness each wanted and needed, yet apologized for establishing.

The world had engulfed them as if they were a pair of beached shells snugly curved within each other, and now the waves had pounded them loose and sucked them from the shore so that they became two entities needing each other but separate and helpless. And knowing they were helpless, they no longer tried to find each other.

CHAPTER IV

ONE MORNING AURELIA woke up crying. she hadn't thought OF anything or dreamed, but she knew why she was crying and that she had to stop. She was crying because Hans was dead. Dead for more than twenty years and still moving around in Aurelia's heart. She turned, and the leg of the let-down bed which had been a few inches up in the air tapped the floor. Her life had become like that, something which didn't set right when it was down and was in the way when it was up. She watched her fingers make little pleats into the edge of the pillow slip. Knobby and bent with arthritis. Thick, ugly fingers. She tried to recall how they had been in the days when Hans used to hold her hand up to the light and say that they were the prettiest fingers he ever saw.

A chill ran down her back. How would she appear in Hans's eyes if he were to see her now? She jerked to a sitting position and looked across the room into the little mirror with Dresden cupids on it, the first present Hans had ever bought for their home and the last he could ever afford. She waited for her sight to clear. She saw a strange woman, one Hans never saw, with a frowning forehead and tan skin and hair dulled with gray, rings under the eyes and a bag under the chin. She dropped back and felt for her ribs and hipbones which had disappeared under fat. She didn't tell herself she looked all right, only that Hans would think of something to say to make her feel better about the way she looked.

She sighed wistfully. If she could have Hans, she would give up.... Dreaming of that, she bartered off one after another of her relatives and friends. She didn't address God directly, but she spoke so that He could hear it: Take Oscar and Clara and let me have Hans.... Take Mimi and Carl, too, though I'll miss them.... She bartered off one after another until she had no one left except her children and grandchildren and she could not bring herself to barter them, for they, too, were Hans.

She would have to bear it. Being without him ought to have grown easier, but it grew harder. When Hans was alive if she said things about people, he knew how much and how little she meant. Now if she told Clara that Mimi had come to see her—in like a whirlwind and out like a whirlwind—the next time she met Mimi her sister-in-law would raise her pretty brows and tell her that she was sorry to have been in such a filthy hurry last week. Nothing became something big. She wished she could be like other women who either didn't think about what people did or had tight lips. When Aurelia tightened her lips she nearly choked.

She tried to pray. *Now I lay me...* was what she said every night before she went to sleep, but it wouldn't do for morning. She had heard prayers at Temple: *Let Thy countenance shine upon...* To Aurelia that kept on being only a picture of the sun with rays springing from it. The Girls went to Temple and Oscar liked it when she did, so she had got into the habit of going every Saturday morning. It gave her something worthy to do. While there she felt solemn and good inside, as if that nice young rabbi were Marc because he said the same things in nearly the same words about what was going on in Germany. After Temple she and one of The Girls went downtown for lunch and sometimes to a picture show.

She tried to remember a prayer which would help her now. There was the *Shema* which soldiers lying on battlefields were reputed to mutter with their dying breath: *Shema, Yisroel, Adonoi, Elohenu, Adonoi Echod* [Hear, O Israel, the Lord, Our God, the Lord is One]. It wasn't the kind of prayer she needed. She tried another: *Boruch Shem Kavod Malchuso Laolam Voed* [Hallowed be the Name of the Lord, Our God, forever and ever]. That wasn't what she wanted either. She wanted to talk about herself in her prayers and she couldn't think of a Jewish prayer for that. They were all in praise of Him and she knew that was what she should have been wanting to say, but it wasn't. She needed help and comfort and to feel less alone.

It was Sunday morning, and on Sundays her children came to see her and brought her grandchildren. She was an ungrateful woman to lie here complaining.

She got up, dressed, folded away her bed, had coffee, washed breakfast dishes, and made her bathroom polished and tidy. Then the first knock came on the door.

Bertha and Clarence and their four children looked as though they had walked out of an advertisement for English tweed. The children were on their way to Sunday school, all but Lorraine, who would go with them to visit Clarence's mother, since Lorraine was too grown up even for the postgraduate class. Bertha was always fair. Next week they would reverse it; she and Clarence would take the four children to Clarence's mother first and come to Mama afterward with Lorraine only.

Junior and Monroe made straight for Aurelia's cooky jar and stood in the kitchen, stuffing themselves, so that they would have a good start before Bertha caught on and ordered them to stop. Melissa read Gramma's funnies until Lorraine crowded her off the stool. Before the girls ceased their bickering Clarence announced the hour and the six Weisses ran down the hall because both Bertha and Clarence detested tardiness.

Watching from her doorway, Aurelia knew they were waking up several of her neighbors, but she also felt proud of the children. Fine, healthy children, grand youngsters, the girls lucky enough to have hair like Clarence's, and Bertha an attentive mother and fervid housekeeper, not spoiled because her husband was doing well.

When Marc's son and daughter came, they were dressed for ice skating. Herbert was very tall now and beginning to look both like Langley Wade in his youth and Hans in his old age; a thoughtful face cocky with amused protest. He ate one after another of the sandwiches Gramma had ready. Jill said that was horrid but ate nearly as many. She was a restless girl, knitting at Gramma's sweater one minute, climbing up for the stereopticon the next, whispering teasing little secrets in Gramma's ears, tousling Marc's hair. When Jill and Herbert left for the skating rink Marc remained with his mother.

It was then he told her he had resigned from Hursch and Company.

She asked, "What's the real reason, Marc?"

"Couldn't stay in a job where I was getting along well yet not able to give those fellows a start. Mama, I can't kick off people who have some sort of right to expect me to help them when they're in trouble . . . ."

Aurelia answered, "They're Papa's relatives."

"They're human beings. Papa's family, yes. Papa's family is a very large family; it's all people, everywhere . . . ."

One Sunday morning on a day when the air was clear and the sunshine only pleasantly warm, Clinton came to say good-by to Marc. He was off to fight with the International Brigade in Spain and looked too young for blood and dying.

It was Marc who was frightened. The boy's smooth, narrow face was calm, as if the turmoil of feeling which impelled his decision had long since subsided. His eyes were the steady, unrelenting eyes of his father's; his lips were Alice's. Like his ways, his features were precise.

Marc had been washing his car and they stood beside it in the driveway far back of the house and nearly hidden by a willow; yet their voices were hushed. He remembered that Clinton's poems won commencement prizes at the private progressive school Alice had selected.

"I thought you wanted to be a writer, Clint," Marc said, meaning only that he wished even in this final instant to find a reason for dissuading him as valid as his reason for going.

And then because the boy stood rigidly unhearing, Marc at last said what he meant. "It's not pleasant for those of us who see that the fight's on and that it's our fight, a fight for all the gains civilization has made, to let the battles be fought by those who are so young."

Then Clinton seemed happy, as if certain now that he could tell Marc what he had come to say. "You remember the Alps? I went several times after you were there. Fräulein was always at the important table. She's a Bund member, of course. I can't tell you how I know, but I do know. You must watch, and if the day comes when she can do harm you must remember what I've said."

"I'm not a conspirator, Clint."

"Hitler wants to find the anti-Semites."

"I'll remember," Marc promised. His stomach felt weak, as if it had been hungry for too long. Though he had not moved, his muscles were exhausted. "Clint, I didn't think when we saw that film about the professor——"

"At least you understand it's the same fight."

"What do your parents say about this?" Part of Marc's mind had been fumbling back through the years, searching for the trail which had led Clinton to Spain.

"Dad knows a fellow must do what he believes is right. Mother knows it's right—but sees no reason for my doing it."

Marc patted him on the shoulder. "I'll be thinking of you, hoping our side's lucky."

The boy's frown made him for a moment into a man. "If the people lose in Spain, hell will break loose in Europe."

"Hell has already broken loose in Europe."

"And The Clan sits here——"

"They don't see that the hell over there is our affair here," Marc lamented. "They aren't alone in that."

Suddenly Clint was gay, letting Marc observe that he was also going to have fun out of this and that Marc need not look apologetic because he, too, wasn't going. With the zest of a confident man off to a thrilling adventure, Clint said, "This is the only chance I've ever had to kick a dictator in the pants. Hitler's out of my reach and so is Mussolini, but Franco's bent over. I can't wait to take a swing at him."

Then he was hurrying toward his red roadster, turning only momentarily to wave.

Marc watched as the car droned backward into the street, turned the necessary arc, scrabbled for quick purchase, and shot forward out of sight.

At the time Marc had built The Shack, some years ago, sawing and hammering Sunday after Sunday, with Herbert helping and Jill off in the woods gathering flowers, the big question had been whether Marc, who had never before built anything, could build a one-room structure which would stand. When it stood he wanted to see whether he could make it rainproof, and by the time that had been done Hallie herself was enthusiastic. She hung Mexican gourds and placed gay pottery on a rustic table. She covered one cot with an Early American coverlet and another with an Indian rug her mother sent.

Marc and Hallie were pleased that their friends liked to come out on Sundays. Jill's friends came too, as did Herbert's, to climb the hills and pitch horseshoes and loudly proclaim their perpetual hunger. Hallie continued to bring her brief case and book, but she rarely glanced at them because she was too busy being a hostess. Later, on the drive home, Hallie would say in a pleased voice, "Well, The Shack gave sixteen people a good time today."

She assigned certain guests to certain Sundays, and still there were too many.

Marc began to build another room. For a while a few of the men helped. Others just stood and teased him, but all agreed it was marvelous the way he was teaching himself to build a house.

One day Marc met Byrn Darrow, now an assistant professor at a local university, and learned that Byrn, too, was building. The two of them would often go out on Saturday afternoons and go first to one half-finished place and then to the other, comparing what they were doing, teaching each other little skills. They exchanged books on carpentry and went shopping together for tools. They were friends again as they had been in university days, just two men who liked to do the same things and liked to talk together, to feel trust and good will and affection running through all they said. Sometimes Herbert went along, and Byrn, who had not married, fell into the habit of calling him "son."

When Marc was preparing to leave Hursch and Company it was Hallie who suggested that they sell their house and live in The Shack. Herbert had gone to Missouri after all, claiming that he wanted to because the Mizzou School of Journalism was tops. He would be in Columbia for another two years, Jill for another four, and the house was too large. The change would be diverting, and selling would give Marc a little capital to start a business of his own.

As soon as the telephone was installed Hallie realized this was just city living on inefficient terms. She told Marc it was a betrayal of their loyalty to progress. The country was fun only on a holiday when there was a crowd. She hated being out on these hills alone or waiting in the city for Marc and then having to drive out in two cars because they had come into town separately. She hated worst of all to have Marc spend the day at The Shack reading articles about Hitler.

Her antipathy for the place grew steadily stronger. Alice gave the resentment form and directed it toward Marc on the day she came out to give the place the once-over. Walking out to the car with Alice, Hallie praised the green moss on the tree trunks and the violets beneath the leaves. Alice began to talk to herself. She said, "Marc's got everything lined up exactly the way he wants. But exactly."

Hallie saw that it was true. She had made the suggestion on impulse, with the vague idea that living in the Ozark foot-hills would be romantic and she would like it. It was Marc who liked it. For days bitterness gnawed at her. Marc was risking everything for his father's family. His position. Her home. Her happiness. The children's future.

She repeated Alice's words to him. She expected him to see what they implied: that this was not Hallie's life and that Marc was being selfish. Like so much that was said these days, it did not penetrate to the part of Marc that cared. When Hallie kissed him and said that he must listen, repeating all of it again, then his eyes glowed and he answered, "Yes, this is all right. This is better than the furniture business and life in town."

So Hallie tried to believe it was right for her too. She tried to be soothed by the gliding lines of the hills. Watching the sunset and the sunrise, she petitioned them to still her anger.

The situation splintered beneath a weight of trifles. One morning rain turned the spur road into a bog with Hallie's car stuck there. She could not shove it the few feet to the rock ledge; Marc had gone into town before the downpour; there was no one within miles who might help her. She phoned to say she could not attend the meeting of her committee, and the office secretary inadvertently disclosed that they had foreseen her absence and had arranged for someone else to preside.

A storm swept the hills that day, tearing down posts and wires so that Hallie had no light. Marc had failed to replenish the log pile near the grate. To keep warm she went to bed. A bird wailed near her window. Squirrels made abrupt, clattering leaps at the roof. She sobbed into the pillow. "Marc, you can't—Marc, we mustn't—Marc, this can't go on."

He didn't seem to notice that her eyes were red, but when she told him she was going to Columbia to visit her parents and the children he answered, "Yes, Hallie, you must think it out."

Then she knew he was aware of her loneliness and confusion and despair and did not intend to help her.

"You act as if it has nothing to do with you, Marc."

"I'll miss you."

"Marc, you've deserted me. You've taken your life away from mine."

When her sobs had quieted Marc gravely gave her an aspirin and a drink of water and held her hand. "I have in a way gone from you. I want you to be happy; yet it's not in me now to give my life to making you happy. You'll learn to do that for yourself. You miss the children. But in these times——"

"Hush, Marc, I don't want to hear another word about these times. I hate these times!"

He left the room, and the next day Hallie, without saying good-by, went to Columbia.

CHAPTER V

RUSHING EAST, ALICE obtained the agency for lines of Distinctively beautiful extravagances. Her father warned her against antagonizing their friends in the department-store business. Laughing at him, she said she would be careful. Her salesmen were not even forced to endure door-to-door soliciting. She herself made the appointments, imperiously.

She taught one refugee to redesign closets, another to decorate kitchen cupboards, another to modernize attics. The changes extended to the Ellinger Lake household and the Bromage household and the Goff household, as well as to the homes of the Manns and Hursches. All the house numbers glittering on the lawns now were alike, so that even before entering, the visitor was aware of the sympathies of those who lived behind the doors.

Oscar Hursch was not pleased by these evidences of Semitism to offset anti-Semitism, but other Hursches and Manns, going out to dinner at Hart's or Mr. Goff's or Mr. Lake's home, felt comforted by the symbols of allegiance.

When Alice, knowing she was not wanted, invaded Marc's Shack one evening at twilight and spread upon the table an epicure's picnic for two, explaining that Ira had gone East and she had come to twit Marc because he did not buy from her salesmen, he said, "I don't want to surfeit myself with luxuries in order to help the needy."

"How nasty of you, Marc darling, to say something horrid which is also conspicuously true."

"Alice, this is no place to pretend you're acting in a Noel Coward comedy."

"I—miss you, Marc."

They ate in silence except for a word now and then about the hooting of an owl or the call of a night hawk.

Later, pulling deeply on her cigarette, Alice said, "I have some money rolling around loose."

"Ira can advise you on investments."

She sat very still. Marc sensed her disappointment. She had not even found out whether he had sufficient reserves to support this jobless vacation. She had learned only that he would not accept her money.

As she left he noticed that she had dressed simply, in order to please him. She wore a gray sports suit with hat to match. Her scarf was scarlet, a color he had admired on her years ago. In the moonlight she looked like a stylish ghost. She had always been a little overfond of him, her catering to his tastes a shade more than cousinly. It was Alice's bitter retort to her family for waiting until she was grown to offer her affection. Now they demanded of her love, and she yielded love, but not to The Clan, only to her cousin Marc, knowing one must not love a cousin too much.

At times Marc's desire for Hallie struck like the moment in a storm when lightning and thunder come together; yet this need for Hallie was, like the lightning and thunder, something outside himself, assaulting his emotions but not of them. He wanted Hallie. He wanted her when he nested his head in his arms ready for sleep. He wanted her during the thoughtful hours of night. He wanted her when he awoke; when he saw the glow of dawn and the lavender dusk upon the hills; but he wanted even more to be alone. To feel the texture of the estrangement between peoples was urgent with him now. He wanted to learn of what it was made and remember how the parts came to be, and to discover what there was within himself which was of all men, and what was of some only, and what was of himself alone.

He grew very thin and appeared even taller than he was.

Fritz Alsberg subscribed to *Aufbau* published in New York. When Marc dropped in Fritz would read aloud: news items about the refugee world. Sometimes Marc would learn of the murder or suicide of German artists and scientists before the facts were reported in the daily press. He would discern new Hitlerian policies months before the radio commentators analyzed them. Often he would hear in the sorrow of a commentator's voice news not yet spoken.

Marc thought the sorrowing voices grieved as much for the unbelief of the ears to which they talked as for the barbarity of the deeds reported.

Hallie rushed back to the city once to express this very idea to Marc. She, too, had thought it. She knew which commentators he listened to and now she listened to them, coming to conclusions Herbert assured her were also Marc's conclusions.

She looked up at Marc with tears in her eyes. "If one is to believe these things," she said, "and I know they are true—then what on earth can be done? Are we to—to—— What can be done except go to war?"

"Yes, war."

"But you and I, Marc, we've seen war. We vowed after the last war———"

"There is no peace, Hallie. War or no war, there is no peace."

"There are still pacifists." She lofted her chin.

"They either do not see that there is no peace or, seeing it, they believe it makes no difference which side wins."

"No, Marc, don't say that! Don't say that! Please, Marc."

An hour later she boarded the train for Columbia.

Aurelia heard the slatted door squeak and then the key which could only be Marc's. She was already in bed. The door yielded, and for an instant the room was less dark.

"You should get yourself a home."

"I'll be all right on the couch."

"There on the chair. I put out Papa's robe for you. Last night you slept in your clothes."

"You saved Papa's robe?"

Crossly she retorted, "Why not save Papa's robe?"

Gasoline rationing made it impossible for Marc to go to The Shack as often as he wished, and the scarcity of hotel rooms transformed him into a vagrant. He was working in a factory now. War had come to Europe; production for England was of first importance.

Aurelia could hear him in the bathroom getting ready for bed. He would drop down on the couch, fall asleep at once, and get up in the morning gay and singing, but thinking of things he did not talk to her about. Oscar and Carl said Marc was making the mistake of his life.

Even when Aurelia heard Marc's breathing deepen she could not sleep. She kept telling Hans about it, Hans who would be happy to know Marc was trying to be a good man. Hans had

never doubted Marc and would not have doubted him had he
lived. Aurelia regained a little of the anger she had always felt
about that: Hans was no father at all; he took no responsibility
with the children, always telling them they were good. Before
she remembered she was talking only to a memory, she fell
asleep.

Walking through the older section of the business district
one day, Marc saw Clarence, Uncle Carl, and two of the younger
Manns going in the direction of the restaurant where the heads
of Hursch and Company had always eaten, except Uncle Oscar,
who disapproved of bare tables and waitresses in assorted gingham dresses. It was only six months since Marc had gone to
lunch with Uncle Carl. That the others were still going, still
telling jokes as they went, was to Marc as if a danger siren were
wailing and they had not heard. And unless they heard, Marc,
too, would be trapped, and so instead of pitying their deafness
he was angered.

Within the vast bank the air was many degrees cooler than
on the street; the sounds were metallic; the white marble of the
floors and walls a sharp contrast with the black of the iron bars
and gates. Downstairs in the safe-deposit vault Marc looked at
the monster wheels and cogs within the huge round door. At
closing time these would seal the room lined with locked metal
boxes containing proof of ownership of wealth.

When Marc had given his key and spoken his password the
bent old man who had become overparticular about fulfilling
every detail of his duty asked Marc to prove his identity by giving his father's name.

Marc wondered whether Hans, who had never rented a box,
had ever been in this place or in one like it, and what he would

have thought of men who, because they possessed so much, were in turn possessed by fear and the need to protect their fear.

Carrying his box to a booth, he opened it carefully. It contained insurance policies made out to Hallie and some government bonds which were negotiable, the proceeds from the sale of the house. It was for them he came now. He wanted to use them to develop plans for the factory he hoped to open. They were not there.

Instead there was a note in Hallie's rounded writing: "Dear Marc, I cannot let you ruin yourself completely. Apparently I shall need these to live on and for the children's education. I'll not come until you send for me, but I'll be hoping each day to hear. Hallie."

The note bore a date six months old.

The Hursches and Manns were not going to be refugees who had to run out of their country. They were simply running out of earshot of Hitler. He was saying things which made them unhappy with one another, confirming what each had been before Hitler spoke, making him less patient with those who did not share his opinions. They abandoned their weekly gatherings.

On Aurelia's birthday, however, Mimi gave a dinner party in celebration. When Marc quoted Fritz's news of deaths in gas chambers everyone was unbelieving and resentful.

Oscar scolded: "Marc, you must not say such things. You have no proof."

After Marc produced proof they sighed and even Uncle Carl turned cross. "Marc," he said, "forget it!"

Oscar Hursch told of the necessity for Jews to get along with their neighbors. Hoarsely he told long stories of how he had got along all these years with Ellinger Lake and his friends and now with Ellinger Lake's son, head of the bank. Uncle Carl said it was much simpler than that. He laughed at Uncle Oscar and his gentiles. All that was needed was a little kindness in this world, kindness to one's own. Hire the long-nosed nephew yourself. Don't send him where he can't be seen.

The younger generation, now in their forties, tried to make their elders understand that these problems were not important. The important thing, Clarence said, was to be an honest and respected man in business, someone who could be trusted. Do that and keep the country steady. He had no patience with people who thought this New Deal nonsense was going to save the world. O.K., Roosevelt was speaking up for the Jews in Europe. Very nice of him, but over here the Jews would be better off if he would shut his mouth and run the country as an efficient business. Efficiency and steadiness were what was needed.

Aunt Mimi, with a hidden laugh in her voice, said, "Clarence is more of a Hursch than the Hursches themselves."

At that Bertha looked proud and added her ideas: "I think we should work in our own organizations and not try to push ourselves. If they want us they'll ask us."

They did not bother to reply to Bertha because everyone knew that Bertha's zeal for putting things into boxes had at last induced her to put herself into a box. It was a Jewish box, and once she had placed herself where she decided she belonged, she never again looked out over the edge of her compartment, only set about making the interior tidy. They recalled the summer her Melissa was denied admission to the private school Lorraine had attended since, as it turned out, there was a quota of which Bertha had been unaware. Clarence had said she needed a vacation-brooding and anger were silly—so they motored East to the seaside. When they presented the resort's letter acknowledging their reservations they were told that the clientele was restricted and unfortunately Weiss was a name nearly anyone might have. The clerk himself was sorry about the error, but though they had driven five hundred miles that day and the two youngest, not understanding, kept asking when they could go into the ocean, the apologizing clerk was unable to offer any suggestion.

Bertha was a sweet thing but stupid; those who were on boards were certain that being on boards helped; if they never worked with a Jew how could they have any friendship for Jews?

"Let them keep their friendship," one of the Manns said.

No one ever mentioned Clint and his Communists, but everyone now was kind to Alice. Without explanation they sent her flowers. To one another they remarked that flowers might liven up a house overcluttered with antiques.

All winter they tried to come together without disagreements. There was always a quarrel and sometimes shouting, and the Randalls announced that the others could do as they pleased but they would not be there any more. Clinton had not been heard from for some time, and Alice was growing thinner and older and her looking like a skeleton now was not fashion but the assault of despair upon the human body.

Aurelia said to Marc, "I don't understand it. Every one of the younger Manns is marrying a Russian."

"They're good people, and charming. Even Ira, who is not always pleasant to be with, is nevertheless a man of principle."

"Why is it that the Manns didn't see that they were charming until the Randowiches had already made friends with that Ellinger Lake crowd? After that everyone intermarries."

"Mama, there's no important difference between Russian Jews and German Jews when they've lived in America for a while. The difference was in how much they'd been abused and how long they had been oppressed. Now the young people meet in school and because they're less narrow-minded than their elders they become friends. The difference today is between the Jews who work in factories and those who own the factories."

Aurelia looked up to see whether Marc, too, was in this quarrel. She said disparagingly, "Jews always must have something to fight about." She began to count her stitches and then, with the needles unmoving, she asked, "Why doesn't Hallie come home?"

"We have no home right now."

"Marc, it's your duty to have a home."

"Over there thousands and thousands have no home. They——"

"You're not over there, Marc."

"Hallie's father is ill."

For many years Langley Wade had been neither well nor sick. In a letter just received Hallie wrote, "Daddy looks very old."

Within a few weeks he was a dying man and Marc hurried to Columbia.

After the funeral Hallie came with Marc to see Aurelia. They were living in a hotel room and they sat, hand in hand, like newlyweds.

It was Sunday morning, a bright, sunny day; yet a wall light burned in the dinette.

"Why, Mama?" Marc asked.

Aurelia blushed. "I wanted to do something. For Hallie's father." Aurelia sighed; she did not tell them that she had lacked money for flowers, having overspent again for a hat. "It's what The Girls do when they have lost a dear one. They burn a light. It's for mourning."

Though Marc's lips twitched, he refused to let them smile.

Later he said to Hallie, "Poor Mama! Still trying to find out how to be Jewish."

"But it's so funny, Marc!" Hallie wiped the tears of laughter from her eyes. "Daddy who was a freethinker and born a Baptist. To burn a Jewish mourning light! Mama is wonderful. Bless her, she wanted to do something. Oh, Marc darling, I'm so glad to be home!"

In November of 1938, while the fate of Heinrich and Rudolph and Ilsa and their other children was still entangled with papers in Marc's pocket, pink ones made out to a steamship company and white ones made out to the United States Government, the newspapers were suddenly filled with stories of Nazi assaults upon Jewish stores and Jewish homes. A telephoto of an aged Jew, hatless, without a tie and with his Adam's apple bulging through his unbuttoned shirt, was by-lined by the announcement that, the telephoto process having been recently improved, telephoto pictures would henceforth be widely used. The man was perched high upon his household goods while jolly blond German citizens threw rotted eggs, stones, and offal at their amusing human target. Thanks to the new process, details were remarkably clear.

Marc became the persecuted man. "He should fight back!"

"No, Marc, no," Hallie said. "It's not what the other person does which destroys your self-respect. It's what you do."

Marc's fingers clung to the picture. "Turn the other cheek. Hallie, if the Jew continues to turn the other cheek, he'll be beheaded."

Looking across his arm, Hallie said, "The only one in that picture with any dignity is the Jew."

"No one in that picture has any dignity. A man who respects himself must fight for his life."

"You wouldn't do it, Marc."

"I hope Clinton is wrong when he says I'm unfit for combat."

Uncle Oscar wrote a letter of protest to the paper. Such a picture was embarrassing to good American citizens.

Yet the Jew with offal clinging to his cheek convinced all the Manns and the Hursches that something was going on over there which required them to give their money to that organization for which Ira Randall had been demanding money all the time. Little as they liked Ira's haughty ways of soliciting, they gave. When he replied with letters thanking them and added that from the size of the check he took it to be a monthly contribution, they consulted with one another and wrote Ira that it was quarterly. They were so much moved that they began to give to Zionist causes, not the socialist one to which Marc gave but to the university and to the hospital. In apology for relenting, Oscar said that learning was always important. Carl agreed and added that health was too.

Later, in February of 1939, a newspaper article caused them to question the necessity for their generous pledges. The director of American refugee work, Mr. George S. Rublee, had come to an agreement with the German government on the matter of German Jews. A field marshal second only to Hitler himself, a high Nazi named Goering who wore handsome medals on his plump chest, permitted his representative to make promises in the name of his government. Although all Jews must leave Germany, while waiting to go they would not be abused as formerly. They could take no money or possessions, of course, and only the able-bodied would be permitted to leave. Since the

United States and other highly developed countries could not accept 150,000 to 200,000 able-bodied men and women, some would be sent as prisoners to undeveloped territories, especially parts of Africa or South America, where their work would profit Nazi Germany.

"You see, Marc, how hasty you were," Uncle Carl said. "It's all settled in an orderly way. You shouldn't have sided with Ira."

Fritz Alsberg's pale mouth jerked out a reply. "But they will not keep their promises. A promise from a Nazi iss no promise——"

Uncle Carl ignored the man who had entered the conversation uninvited. "This memorandum has been submitted to an intergovernment committee of thirty-two nations. Are thirty-two nations children? Sir Herbert Emerson of Great Britain is going to carry on the work. Mr. Rublee has resigned now that he has everything settled. Is Great Britain a child to be fooled? And the United States too? President Roosevelt has shown the greatest interest in this committee. Those who do not know our country should keep still with their opinions."

Like Uncle Carl, Bertha considered the clipping something which would bring Marc back into Hursch and Company.

"You see," she said, "Marc, everyone will be taken care of."

"In the meantime Rudolph Thalheimer——"

"Marc, you mustn't think he's so important There are two hundred thousand others."

Now Hallie was on Marc's side. She said, "Two hundred thousand Rudolph Thalheimers. Each one is a human being." She looked shyly at Marc. "Marc is right." She crossed the room and stood beside him with her arm through his and her cheek rubbing against his shoulder.

About that time the paper carried a story about three hundred Jews who had got as far as Montevideo when their visas to Paraguay were suddenly canceled. Uruguay was embarrassed. Oscar Hursch was also embarrassed.

Getting dressed that morning, he said to Clara, "I'm ashamed. Every day I pick up a paper and there's a headline about Jews. The Jews this and the Jews that. What will men like Ellinger Lake think?"

He was buttoning his collar, and his face was red from strain and anger.

Clara said, "Perhaps the Jews can't help it. Perhaps it's conditions...." It was more opposition to Oscar's opinion than Clara had ventured for years.

He turned around and for a moment watched the awkward process by which she struggled her body into its clothing.

"Besides," he said, "I think it's wrong for you to go around in those cotton stockings. All this boycott business. *Don't buy from Germany. Don't buy from Japan.* It doesn't look right. The Jews should stay out of all that. How do you think Ellinger Lake feels when he comes into a room at my house and sees every woman there in cotton stockings? You can't settle this by wearing cotton stockings. Don't make yourself ridiculous!"

Clara's lips wavered. "If I don't wear cotton, Hallie is critical. And Bertha. Bertha feels very strongly about cotton. And Ann Bromage, who isn't Jewish at all, feels strongly. And———"

She was trying to tell Oscar that the younger members of the family and even many gentiles were now on the side of the Jews.

CHAPTER VI

WHEN CLINTON FINALLY came home from spain he was gaunt and silent. He walked among the luxuries of his home as a man might walk in a dream. Alice invited Marc and Hallie for dinner and ostentatiously used only her everyday china, reporting that the Spode she had once adored no longer excited her. Laughing, she said that Clinton, who used to eat little, now ate ravenously. She was sure that he had been hungry for nearly a year.

For his father's sake he had taken a quick trip to Jerusalem. Yes, the orange groves were wonderful, he said; the hospital was handsome. The university was very modern. Everything was in striking contrast to the primitive ways of the Arabs. He looked around this spacious dining room with its Venetian blinds, scenic wallpaper, and grilles which dutifully poured in warm or chilled air as commanded.

He spoke only in monosyllables until Ira asked if he had seen the Wailing Wall. Then Clinton raised his eyes from his plate and said, "I saw it three times. Once with a Jewish guide, once with an Arab, and once with a Christian. ... I got three explanations of why the Jews wail there. The Christian guide said they were weeping because centuries ago they had been defeated in battle and lost the Temple. The Arab said they were not weeping but pronouncing incantations. He showed me that they were placing little pieces of paper in the crevices. Said the papers were inscribed with curses, that the Jews were begging the Evil One to harm the Arabs. The Jewish guide also said they were not weeping but praying. He said sacred prayers were written on those papers. The *Shema* .... And that's Palestine, Dad, the Holy Land. Unholy with hate."

Stiffly Ira reminded his son that it was also a refuge for persecuted Jews.

"It won't be large enough. Now that Germany's pulled the trigger and the war has come ..." He looked at the attentive faces of his elders. "You don't see it. You don't see how little time there is. Nor how vicious it will be. And Palestine ... Palestine won't be a holy land or an orange grove. It will be a pipe line for oil and a military outpost—for the British."

"The British are lighting the Nazis," Ira retorted.

"At last. They've finally stopped appeasing. If the British had taken a stand in Spain——"

Later, interrupting his father's comments on the Soviet-Nazi pact, interrupting his own reply about Russia's playing for time, Clinton asked Marc, "Is Herbert learning the arts of war? He'll be going, you know. World War II will be for all of us."

Hallie gasped, and Alice, angered, said Clinton really seemed to have forgotten his manners. Her scarlet lips turned and twisted as she rebuked her son.

When she had finished Marc said, "Yes, Clint, there will be war. For the United States too. For all of us."

When the Japanese dropped bombs on Pearl Harbor the country knew war had come. Though everyone in his heart had been fighting Hitler, help was now given freely to factories. Marc would drop in at the Alsbergs' to ask if they were getting along all right. They always said everything was fine, or if they mentioned any difficulties they were minor, such as the choice they had to make at the Americanization school just after they reached the city. Two sets of classes were offered, one for eastern Jews, the other for German Jews. The Alsbergs said they would join both since they wished to learn a great deal very rapidly. A short woman, a stranger to them, whispered that people of their level of culture must not join with eastern Jews.

Fritz said, "I ended that quickly. I said we had not come to America to continue old quarrels."

Seeing the shadows in Marc's eyes even when he was at their door gaily inquiring about their concerns, as if he had none of his own, the Alsbergs offered him each amusing detail of their naturalization: Marianna's anxiety lest they fail their tests; Eric, at six on the morning they were to receive their final papers, drilling them while still in bed, making them recite the names of vice-presidents, and that evening bringing a bouquet because the judge had praised Fritz's knowledge of United States history and Gretchen's grasp of the function of each branch of government.

Fritz had kept the job Marc was kind enough to get him at Hursch and Company until he saw that his services were no longer needed. Now furniture was not being sold or even made; other factories were begging for workers. Fritz learned to make his numerals in the American way and so had become a bookkeeper at a salary the Alsbergs could live on. They did not need to sell cameras, and besides, the government had decreed that in wartime it was a misdemeanor for those not fully citizens to possess a camera.

Blushing, Fritz said, "Surely the United States must realize we are anti-Fascists."

Gretchen said, "You, yes, but there are also spies pretending to be Jewish refugees. It is even said that some refugees are spying. I am glad the government is careful. To be without a camera is no great sacrifice. Take it. Give it to Herbert."

Marc said, "Britain, too, is careful. Heinrich Thalheimer was interned for three months on the Isle of Man."

He did not send the Leica to Herbert, since he had already given the boy his. Soon after the Alsbergs were naturalized they invited Marc to celebrate with them. There would be coffee and *Torten.*

Marc brought candy and laid their Leica on the table beside the box.

The Alsbergs smiled proudly. "It iss nice to be trusted once more."

Then Marc drew a letter from his pocket. "Our Army needs pictures of German cities. Photographs of factories and railway stations. Of any places which might guide our pilots. Help them to locate themselves." He put the letter down slowly. "You have a great many friends among the refugees. Do you think they have pictures?"

Gretchen said yes, many; the Alsbergs, too, had brought pictures.

She fetched a large wooden box. "Choose," she said to Marc.

Fritz was smiling quick smiles, a habit he had nearly lost. Gretchen said to him, "Yes, the air raids will kill people we know, and smash opera houses where we have heard music, but it will also kill Nazis. It will take from their filthy hands the lovely German country."

Fritz sighed. "It iss only that I hate destruction." Then he jumped to his feet and said, "I will get photographs for you, Marc. I will ring doorbells and ask. On this block and on the next. Wherever refugees live."

"I too," Gretchen said. "At the houses where I give singing lessons. At the grocery store. I will be rejoiced to ask. That Hitler!"

Marc sent Washington so many photographs pertinent to bombing needs that he received a letter of commendation signed by a general. In it he was asked to express the Army's gratitude to Mr. and Mrs. Fritz Alsberg who had gathered the pictures. Gretchen had the letter framed and hung it in the hall where it could be seen before visitors were all the way inside the door.

A scarcely legible letter from Aunt Martha said Rudi and Ilsa and the two little girls had been shipped into Poland. When Hallie's questions forced Fritz to tell more he said Jews shipped into Poland were put to death in gas chambers. Thousands and thousands of them. His manner suddenly shrank. His body shrank. "Rudi ... Rudi ... Never a finer man anywhere in the world ... Brave ... A man who spoke out ... Rudi in a gas chamber ... Rudi ..."

Ellinger Lake II, in the presidential office at the bank, planning to be stern with Marc, did not rise, just mumbled an excuse for continuing to sign letters and indicated by a gesture that Marc was to be seated. Later, glancing up, he saw that Marc was calmly surveying the details of an etching on Lake's wall. Standing away, going closer, his slender body with its narrow shoulders, the left one greatly higher than the right, was acting as if nothing in the world was of pressing importance except that etching which Lake himself could not appraise except by its purchase price and the enthusiasm of the dealer who sold it. Anger and respect mounted in Lake like twin thermometers. He came across the room and shook hands.

"Good morning, Mr. Kleinman. I have asked two members of my board to sit in on this conference. Both good friends of yours."

The two board members were Hart Bromage and Uncle Carl, and they shook hands solemnly.

Hart's usually good-natured face was sobered into furrows. He had suffered, he felt, too much from Jews. What other fellow of his set had so often gone out of his way to stand by them? It was always Hart Bromage who had to be the one to try to get them into private schools and defend them at his club whenever the topic popped up, as it did often enough these days. Many a time he had told himself he could do without their insurance; his income was large enough to take the cut; no, the trouble was that he was still trying to make friends with Marc Kleinman to whom he owed nothing. And was Marc grateful? Did he ever by word or glance show that he appreciated Hart Bromage's efforts?

He did not! Answering his own question, Hart would sometimes rage to Ann, who seemed as much without a social sense as without a clothes sense. Hart thought it came from having been greeted at birth with a huge bank account and no need to bother about anyone's opinion. The most Ann would answer was that she liked Hallie or that Alice said that Marc was an idealist.

That enraged Hart. He would answer, "Yes, an idealist. It's an extravagance no businessman can afford, as he will jolly well find out."

Now, however, Hart spoke with moderation. "We agree with you in theory. No reason on earth Negroes shouldn't be getting better jobs, none. Nice of you, darned nice of you, if you ask me, to want to give them a chance. But it won't work, Marc. A lot of pressure is being brought on our Chamber of

Commerce by the Washington alphabet boys who want them to hire Negroes. Now get this, Marc, they're not going to do it." He repeated that.

"They've been in here complaining. They feel this thing is serious. It would be causing trouble if you were to open up the whole question of whether Negroes can do skilled work and office work and be executives and all that. It would be a crack in the dike. Nobody has a finger big enough. I read that story in school when I was a kid. Leave this to us and gradually they'll get some skilled jobs. It has to be done slowly. You———"

Now Mr. Lake jerked up his chin as a signal to Carl Hursch to go ahead as agreed; so Carl, blushing, told Marc that this thing he wanted to do was bad, risky coming from anybody, but worse than risky, completely impossible, coming from a Jew.

Marc could no longer remain seated. He stood behind a chair, his pale face ashen, his lively eyes anguished, his higher shoulder twitching, both hands white at the knuckles, gripping the back of the chair.

"We are at war," he said.

"But Negroes." Carl shouted. "You will have nothing but *tzores. Tzores* with unions. *Tzores*———" He stopped. He had not meant to use the foreign word before Bromage and Lake. "You will stir up trouble.... All this—all this———" He sputtered and shrugged and murmured privately to Marc, "Remember you are a Jew."

Marc replied aloud: "Each of us remembers he is a Jew in his own way. I remember that Czarist ghettos made Jews, even Jews scorned, and when America freed them they became fine people. I remember Hitler ground the pride of Jews into bits, then ground their bodies into bits."

Uncle Carl exploded: "Such nonsensical talk. What———"

"This," Marc answered, pushing the chair away. "Hitler called the Jews an inferior people. The Jew knows that's a lie. He knows it is also a lie when Negroes are called an inferior people. A man must not live by a lie. All I want to do is to abide by my faith in a man as a man. You and no one else has ever known in advance what a man might become."

Carl was not listening, merely waiting to speak. "Marc, my boy, it is not for the Jew to rush out and fight the Negro's battle for him. It looks bad when a Jew—— Too many Jews——" He frowned at Bromage and Lake. "I told you it would do no good."

Mr. Lake, staring at Marc, repeated, "Why should the Jews do this unwise thing? Many Jewish businessmen have been very successful. You should be satisfied."

Hart Bromage cleared his throat. "Look, Marc, you want a pretty world with liberty and justice for all. Now, damn it the hell, you know that's a lot of baloney when it comes to getting along in business. It's—it's baby talk."

After Marc left, the door again was flat and unseen within a paneled wall and the three men remaining shook their heads and returned to their work.

Uncle Carl would not sit down. He had come to Aurelia's apartment to see Marc about what happened at the bank. In the presence of Lake and Bromage he couldn't say all he wanted to say. Now he stood with one pleading hand on Marc's shoulder, an old man giving advice.

"Marc, for God's sake! Why must you be a *Rechthaber?* No one disagrees with you. Every Jew knows it's true. That a man is a man, and that's all there is to it. Black or white, a man is a man. But we live in a gentile world, and the gentiles don't know it. You can't teach them overnight. Even Jesus couldn't teach them.

Why must Marc Kleinman think he can do better than Jesus? The Negroes are their coreligionists—which we are not—yet they won't accept them. How can a Jew be so high and mighty as to think he can make them do it? It would be better to build the Negroes a country club if they are discontented, but—Marc, you are the discontented one!"

"Yes."

"My God, boy, I wish I disagreed with you. In America the Jew is only halfway up the ladder. The Negro is at the bottom. Rosenwald tries to pull them up with that fund of his. He can educate them and not lose his foothold, but you'll slip. You're not big enough. Your free hand had better go up—up where you can be pulled higher—not down to the Negro. You will fall on your face. If Jesus couldn't make them listen, Marc Kleinman can't either." He paused. He looked attentively at Marc, then at Aurelia. He left, banging the door behind him.

When Aurelia heard that Marc's new desk mate at the map factory where he worked was a Negro she forgot that he was noble and told him he was a fool. "Even Papa—he used to call them poor devils, but he didn't work next to them at one desk."

"There were no Negroes where Papa worked."

"It makes no difference."

They were in Aurelia's dinette.

"A man should behave with sense," Aurelia said.

He stopped eating and began to smoke. Aurelia saw he was wondering whether to try to help her to understand.

"Say it, Marc."

"When this Hitler deal came along I felt as if it was Papa's family they were after, but I also didn't like it when Hitler pushed around the artists and liberals and labor-union fellows.

They were not Papa's family, yet they were my family. Clinton went off the deep end about Spain where there weren't any Jews. There's something else mixed up in it. It's that a man who stands doing nothing while other human beings are being kicked about—well, you go on looking after your own affairs, making a little money, living soft, and after a while, by God in heaven, you know you're not really a man . . . ."

"Refugees, yes, but——"

"So you're proud when your country begins to do something about it. You know you live in a land of men. A little sorry, yes, that all this seemed to begin with Jews in trouble because you know it began much deeper. You walk down the street and you see boys in uniform and it makes you feel good inside that something is being done. But that's not enough. I've got to do something too . . .

CHAPTER VII

THE DAY THAT herbert entered the army was hot, the heat a smothering hand at the throat, a hungerless stirring in the stomach, hammers within the ears, sticky moisture upon the skin, the will to move overpowered by an inability to move which seemed part of the heat itself. Marc and Hallie waited outside the tall white Federal Building in their car.

Hallie was restless, incessantly pulling her blouse forward from beneath her arms, crossing and recrossing her knees, lighting cigarettes and then putting them out. She talked only of practical details. Surely Herbert was mistaken to go in with nearly nothing, no suitcase, no pajamas, no extra clothing. Only his camera. What if they didn't issue him khakis right away? The weather was terrific, and Herbert was so particular, not at all as he was when he was a little boy and used to claim that a bath made him hurt all over.

Marc said that after a few days they would be permitted to visit him at the barracks. It would be the night before he was shipped out, and then they could bring him anything he wanted. Marc planned to take some color film.

Herbert had wanted to go into the Japanese language school. He had passed all the tests. It was Marc who had not passed, for the FBI reported that Marc had been a premature anti-Fascist. He had given money to the Spanish Loyalists. In defense of his father Herbert had retorted, "Do you mean a man of vision?" The fellow at the desk closed the folder. "That's the way it is, son. Sorry." So now Herbert was going in the Army. He had volunteered.

Waiting for him, they listened to radio music and to a newscast. In the midst of it Herbert suddenly was beside them, standing with one foot on the running board, looking like a high school senior. Moisture dotted his upper lip; he said the room in there was packed, hotter than hell, and smelled bad. In answer to Hallie's question he said very likely she hadn't seen him coming because he came out the door on the other side.

"Why, Herbert darling, why, when you knew I was watching this one?" Her voice was querulous, poor Hallie, who was nearly never querulous, and Marc saw that this parting was too much for her.

Herbert saw it, too, and looked at his mother with his eyelids drooping pity. Then he looked swiftly and fondly at Marc, cupped his palm around his father's upper arm, and said, "Dad, swell of you to knock off to take me over, but they want us to go in a bunch. I belong to Uncle Sam now."

He smiled and blushed and tried to conceal his proud happiness from Hallie. Stooping, he kissed her firmly and loped across the street, his arms held up like chicken wings in proper track-team style. Boys and young men were climbing into a truck with a picket-fence back. The last one in, Herbert stood at the center, his small bundle clasped under his arm, both hands gripping the central uprights, his face only a pale oval and a pair of large eyes.

Hallie leaned forward. "My God, Marc, he looks so young."

Marc dropped her hand which he had been holding. He hastened to start the car and get Hallie away quickly.

She was whispering to herself, "They look like little sheep being taken to market—to the slaughterhouse ...."

Then Marc realized that nothing he had said and nothing which had happened had convinced Hallie that her own Herbert should go to war; and that whatever else might come, this moment would remain one of the worst moments of all their lives for them both.

On the day Herbert was to be shipped Hallie left for Columbia, fluttering her eyelids in a new, nervous habit Marc saw she sought to conquer but could not. Her mother's asthma was worse and Jill was nearly out of clothes; the summer session took more clothes than the winter because the heat demanded infinite changes. Hallie would stay just long enough to attend to things.

Kissing her good-by, Marc thought: Poor Hallie needs to look after something and hasn't even a house to look after. Poor Hallie! He promised her he would long-distance at once when a letter came from Herbert.

Herbert was moved from the barracks in Missouri to a fort in Alabama, thence to a camp in Georgia. He sent a great many photographic studies of the men in his company together with amusing accounts of their ways; obviously he was continuing to train himself for journalism. But mostly he became a succession of post cards: "We hiked ten miles today. My dogs are plenty sore. Thanks, Mother, for Grandfather's copy of Plato's *Republic*. Am sending it back. Save it for me. Think we're about to get shipped."

Once he wrote that Clinton was in the same camp and had advised him to keep a diary and to eat plenty now.

Each time Herbert went to a new place Hallie said she thought she ought to go there to see how he was settled. Because the hostess houses for visitors were identical, she would forget which town she was in. When she returned she would tell Marc happily, "I got Room B again. I like B. The other woman in it was there to visit her son too." She kept a suitcase packed and ready. Once she arrived in Mississippi four hours after Herbert had been shipped to Nebraska.

After months in Columbia, Hallie came by taxi to the factory where Marc worked. He was on the night shift. She waited in his car in the dark. She was pale and spoke to him slowly, as if she had drilled herself in what she was saying.

"Marc, I can't go on like this. If we're married, then you must make room in your life for me. If you don't want me———"

She cried in his arms. When she was calm enough to speak she said, "If only I could put you out of my life. If I could stop loving you ... It's not fair even to yourself for you, a brilliant, educated man, to become a laborer."

"America needs maps. Not furniture. It's fair to America."

He stared at the long low wedge-shaped factory shed, the be-windowed walls shining softly lavender against the night.

She was silently weeping, toying with the handle of her pocketbook. When at last she looked up she said, "I keep wanting life to be fun. I keep feeling it's your duty to make life happy for me. I know, darling, it can't be that way. I know .... All I ask is that you never let me leave you again. Nothing has been so terrible as your politeness, the way you let me go as if the whole thing is my affair, not yours."

"Hallie, it's only that I can't beg you to stay."

"Marc," Hallie said a few evenings later. She was looking hazy-eyed at her nearly empty dessert plate, idly poking the fork at what was left. "I must know who she is—why you like her, dear."

"I don't understand."

"The woman—while I was away."

"There was no woman."

"Then what did Mother Kleinman mean? Today I received a letter. Forwarded from Columbia. Mother Kleinman must have written it about the time I left there. Before she knew I was coming."

"What did she say?"

"That if I wanted another woman to have you it was all right to stay away, but if I wanted you for myself, then I must———"

Marc rose. They had finished their meal and others waited for the table.

"We'll go to see Mama," Marc said.

No matter what Marc asked, Aurelia kept repeating, "A man must have a home. Even one room can be a home, but without a wife, a palace is no home." At last she put down her knitting and looked reproachfully at Marc, then at Hallie. "You're too proud, both of you. Pride should be kept for outsiders. It's not something to come between man and wife."

"Mama, what made you think I was going with someone else?"

"I didn't say you were. I said if she wanted another woman———Marc, I want you and Hallie to be together, so— well, every woman, even Hallie, has jealousy. It was all I could do—I couldn't wait. He said I mustn't, so———"

She was chattering as she used to chatter to Hans, saying nothing because what she had to say was too vast for words and she herself too preoccupied and giddy to seek the right ones.

At last, after telling about the fine bridge party The Girls gave that afternoon and showing the knitting bag she won as a prize, she answered their question. The man who said she mustn't wait was the doctor, of course. Who else would tell her that?

Dimpling, she bragged that she had outwitted him, making him wait two extra days because she wanted to go to the bridge, it being the last of the season, the big party when they could invite guests and The Girls would wear their new hats. She rushed out and came back wearing hers.

"What's wrong with you?" Marc demanded.

"That pain in my side." She said it casually, as if she had told him about the pain many times, and in the midst of more talk of hats and why she had at last chosen a bow instead of a feather as trimming, she said that tomorrow was the day she was going into the hospital. She didn't know when the operation would be performed; very likely the doctor had said, but with the bridge party on her mind——Again and again she told Hallie if something went wrong Hallie must remember that this new straw hat was of the finest braid and should not just be thrown out but given to one of The Girls, though she kept changing her mind as to which one.

"What does the doctor think it is, Mama?"

"I didn't ask him," she answered.

Marc couldn't discern whether that was true, but he saw that Aurelia thought she might die, and death to her meant mainly that Marc might be alone.

"It's wrong to fib," Marc teased, pretending he was not worried by her news.

"It's wrong to live one here, one there," she retorted. "That's the greatest wrong of all."

She saw them smile at each other and saw something in the smiles which made her believe them when they said that that was over.

Aurelia sighed, "I hope they let me wear the blue bed jacket Bertha gave me. I hate those hospital gowns. I'll write it myself to Ruth and to Freddy. You two always make so much out of nothing."

She pretended to be annoyed with them, angry at them, completely without affection for them; surely they need never grieve for a woman who had not loved them, who had showed she did not love them, as she was showing it now.

Then Marc was sure the doctor had told Aurelia she was fatally ill; the purpose of the operation was to delay the inevitable, perhaps by a half year.

Some months later the war scalded Marc and Hallie with boiling lava. Herbert—in the mud of France. They staggered forward, each able to remain erect only because it was necessary to keep the other from falling.

When Aurelia phoned each morning to ask, "How are you?" Marc would reply—if it was Marc who chanced to lift the phone—"Thank you, Mama. Hallie is all right." And if Hallie answered: "Thank you, dear. Marc is all right." They did not inquire how she was because they knew that ever since her operation she was often in pain and did not like to be asked.

Except for Marc's hours at the factory, he was constantly with Hallie, and she, waiting in their hotel room after she returned from Red Cross, would be mounting or framing or assorting the hundreds of photographs Marc no longer looked at except politely for a moment when she would say, "See, Marc, what I've been doing."

When they walked in the park it was together. When they wept it was in each other's arms.

Several times Hallie planned to go East to Jill, now in college near Boston specializing in home economics, which seemed to be mostly chemistry with a dash of sociology; but each time Hallie's enthusiasm for the trip at the last moment was insufficient. She would say, "I'm better off here with you."

On the first Christmas of their grief they forbade Jill to come. They reminded her that civilians had been asked not to travel. If she had to get away from the campus, why not visit Aunt Ruth and Uncle Lou in New York?

From Greenwich Village she wrote a letter saying that Ruth and Lou were wonderful, better than college. They got tickets for everything, and Ruth knew next to nothing about cooking, but it was fun to eat out. All the actors and musicians were Lou's friends. His stage-sets were grand, and he had a new commission and Jill was having a marvelous time. Lots of dancing at a canteen at night, and she fell in love with a different G.I. every evening, especially if he was tall.

"Don't worry, darlings, it's just my age. I'm perfectly normal and liking it." And then: "P.S. When I'm in crowds I often think I see Herbert. Are you two really all right? I can come home any time."

If anyone mentioned Jill, Hallie would bring out her letters and read them aloud, skipping all her pompous advice about vitamins. She would read them to Aurelia, to Ann Bromage, to Mamie Lee, to Alice, to Bertha and Clarence, to some of her Red Cross friends. When she was alone with Marc she would say, "We mustn't cling to Jill too much." Agreeing, they clung to each other. The sweetness between them grew more poignant than ever before.

Each Christmas for all these years Marc had received a London *Times* calendar with Kleinman Wolff's card attached. During the war the paper became thinner, but the photographs continued to disclose the charm of English lanes and the placidity of English hills. In April Marc would receive a note thanking him for having subscribed to the *National Geographic* as a Christmas gift for the Wolffs.

Last year, after praising the articles, Mr. Wolff concluded with this: "Fourteen Kleinman cousins are now in London. All doing their bit for the war. Heinrich Thalheimer is a promising physicist." This year in his note he said briefly that their home had been bombed but fortunately no one was hurt. Then: "We lost Albert in the invasion."

When Franklin D. Roosevelt died, Marc, listening at the radio, again lived through his grief for Herbert; again a death was cutting him off from the future.

"I have liked that man too much," he told Hallie at midnight as he sank back into his chair at last, the room strangely empty without the transmitted voices. "When I used to listen to his fireside chats I always felt I was associating with a gentleman. When I read his Four Freedoms I believed they were nearly here."

Hallie wrapped her negligee closer to her body. Her hair hung about her shoulders. She looked very tired, very pretty.

"You have put so much hope in progress, Marc."

"I used to believe the years would pass and progress would come automatically. Well, we'll have to create progress. F.D.R. helped us to believe that we can swing it."

They missed Franklin Roosevelt most when the war ended. All the world longed to hear his rich voice intoning truths with which to make the peace.

When the bomb dropped on Hiroshima they needed someone to reassure them that so much death could indeed give birth to a good future.

When Germany, lying face downward in her own gall, behaved as a ruthless degenerate, Marc felt no triumph for her defeat, only shame for its betrayal of human dignity.

Almost immediately soldiers began to return from overseas. Now they wore blue and gray suits four years old and in each lapel a gold eagle proclaiming their honorable military past. They complained only of their homelessness.

Marc and Hallie went together to see the Buchenwald film. Though Marc asked Hallie several times whether she was sure she wanted to go, she insisted that she did. He reminded her that she always closed her eyes at film brutalities. "These won't be pretty."

"I won't close my eyes. Ann went without Hart. He says the government should not encourage people to be morbid. He says the war was fought and won and now should be forgotten. But Jill wrote everyone should see them. I want to go. I want to go with you, Marc."

It was nearly time for the evening showing to begin when they entered the Auditorium Building. They had not foreseen that they would have to go to the top balcony for seats. Marc saw some fellows from his factory and Hallie saw a friend from the veterans' hospital where she was working now; but people just nodded to each other, distantly. They were in a somber mood.

The heaps of dead, the skeletons arranged like logs in mounds, the stacks of just-dead bodies with one not altogether dead moving a little seared them with horror, but even more appalling were the survivors with great round dull eyes and swollen knees and flayed backs and skeletons clearly defined beneath the glistening skin, moving with slow, ghostlike motions. Watching them, Hallie was shivering and Marc held her hand tightly, begging her to stop.

When the film ended, though it had lasted for a long time, no one got up to leave. A man next to Marc said, "Now we know why we fought the war."

"We had to see this to prove to ourselves that we aren't guilty."

At that Mallie looked toward Marc with surprise, as if he had spoken a truth she had not been aware that he knew.

They walked part of the way home because they did not want to be where they might have to say hello casually or to speak of the film with strangers. They needed to let it become a memory settling itself among other memories. It must not remain a strangling in their throats.

For many blocks they were silent. Then Hallie said, "Marc, we had to part with Herbert."

He had not expected her to say that, nor to hear in her voice serenity. For a moment they were out of step. Then they were as before, hand in hand, walking with one rhythm, a little more briskly now.

"Marc, when I used to run off to Columbia—I was frightened. Terribly frightened. ... I'm not so frightened any more."

"Some of the dreaded things have already happened." He squeezed her hand tightly, as if he thought the little pain might ease the greater.

As they came to the crest of the rise Marc halted so that they might look back for a moment into the gray-violet of the aged section where the tall buildings either were crowded with too many families or, behind shining new fronts, had become salesrooms.

He gestured toward the people in the valley, toward the dead and dying in the film. "The question is whether a human being is important. That's what the whole struggle is about—what it will be about for a long time. Hallie, I have to get in on the making of that decision. Is another man part of ourselves or is he only something we can use to enrich ourselves? If he is ourselves, then each man shares the other's strength and we needn't fear. But if the other man is not ourselves, we'll fight with him and with each other about him and no one will be safe .... I used to worry about Papa's family. There's more to this than saving the bodies of a few exiles. It's wider for me now."

"How, Marc?"

"When I was a kid I used to hear my father praise this country—not as acres and chimneys—but as the land of the free. To the thousands of immigrants coming to America that's what it meant—coming to a place where they would be respected because they were human beings. We mustn't let that idea get crowded into a corner .... And it isn't enough to say we believe that. It has to be part of the way we live. All the little things I see each day which are insults to men as men are for me slaps across my face. I'm not easily aroused to fight. I've waited overlong.

Now I've got to wade in, far in. Hallie, it may not be easy for you."

"Marc, you must decide."

"History hasn't given me a choice. If ever the record made a decision for a man, it's this time."

Glancing up, she saw that Marc was looking younger than he had for years, and very much alive. His voice was rich with feeling as he said, "I'm going to work at this thing all day, every day, with all I've got. If I could plan selling campaigns for davenports and dinette suites, I can plan campaigns for this. I'll care whether this idea sells. Millions of people throughout the world care. It won't be hard to find a place to work or a way of working."

She answered, "I can work for that too. Yes, Marc, with all my heart. But, Marc, even when I lose my nerve, you're to remember that I'm for your side .... I'm sorry I've been so afraid."

"It's only the unimaginative who are never afraid these days. ...."

Later, as they were getting ready for bed, Hallie said, "Marc, I met Gretchen today. They've had a letter from Eric————"

"Sergeant Eric Alsberg."

"He's in Nürnberg. Guarding a Nazi general whose trial is coming up soon."

"You mean Fritz's boy is holding a gun over a Nazi general? Hallie, it's fantastic." His hand dropped a shoe. "I wonder how Fritz felt when he heard that."

"He heard bad news too, darling. All the relatives are dead. His mother. Aunt Martha. Everybody. And all the friends. No one they went with is there. Eric wrote that no one even remembers their names. Perhaps they're afraid to say they remember—or ashamed."

Aurelia lingered over her dying. During those last months she would not let The Girls come to see her because she had grown jaundiced and homely.

Marc came each evening and would sit quietly in the room until Aurelia began to ask questions: "Marc, do you think the Giovannis still keep canaries? ... Marc, Jill always said she wanted the ivory goose-man .... See that she gets it, and my baking pans. I want Jill to have lots of my things. Mamie Lee will know. Let her divide, but before she starts, see that Bertha gets something she wants ...." Later, wearily, "Marc, do you think Ruth gets enough to eat? Do you, Marc? Are you sure? Wasn't it nice of Monica Edgewood to send flowers? ... Marc, do you remember when Papa took you to see——" She would at last doze off.

Bertha remained at the hospital from early morning until Hallie came for the afternoon, leaving only if Mamie Lee arrived for her twice-a-week visit. Aurelia no longer had the strength to say more than a few words, but she enjoyed hearing Mamie Lee's news of Otto's cases and the fine work Frederick was doing, and that one of his children had received an appointment as a principal, and another, a social worker who played Bach as well as boogie-woogie, had received a promotion. Sometimes Mamie Lee spoke of those who had been felled by poverty; then Aurelia would tap the covers in rebuke, to show that she wanted to hear only the good news.

Before Mamie Lee hobbled out, her arthritic hands holding to the wall to help her arthritic knees, she always talked for a while about Freddy Kleinman, whom she called her Freddy.

Once, seeing longing in Aurelia's eyes, she phoned Bertha and implied that a person who liked to boss as much as she did might as well do some good with her bossing, and if she wasn't going to write Freddy to come, Mamie Lee would. Hadn't Ruth and Lou sat up in coaches all night and spent two days with her, making her laugh and convincing her that Lou Ricardo had kept his wife bewitched? They brought her a painting of a bouquet of flowers. Mamie Lee agreed with Bertha that it wasn't pretty, though it was meant to be, and Aurelia liked it because Lou had painted it especially for her.

Fred came by plane and after a few hours left again. He still looked like Freddy, only with gullies instead of folds in his cheeks and less hair and a way of cocking his head quickly which was like Freddy but a new trick. He came twice more, the second time with Celia, arriving on the morning of the funeral.

Bertha arranged all details for the burial, consulting only Clarence and the rabbi. Suddenly she was the one who knew everything, while the others stood bemused and helpless. The services were held in her long neat living room, with The Girls seated together in the sunroom, with Manns and Hursches overflowing up the steps and down into the garden. When the rabbi spoke of Aurelia as a good Jewish mother, Marc stirred uneasily in his chair and Fred lifted a brow as if to ask if anyone knew how being a good Jewish mother differed from being any other kind of good mother.

Out at the cemetery, after "The Lord is my Shepherd" had been recited, the *Shema* spoken, the crushed flower tossed upon the coffin while the rabbi murmured, "The Lord has given; the Lord has taken away," the crowd scattered a little but did not immediately disperse.

Marc paused to look at the nearby stone: HANS KLEINMAN, 1870-1917; then he took Hallie's arm and they walked away from the others, Hallie asking about the six-pointed stars on the graves, Marc replying but only half thinking about what he said.

That evening Marc and Hallie drove Fred and Celia to the airport. The night air was cool and the wind fretful. One minute it would whip at their faces and the next subside.

Waiting, the women stood and talked while the men paced the long concrete stretch. It was in this last moment that Fred inquired about Marc's plans, but only after he had said, "Marc, we must see each other oftener. I've worked so damned hard."

In the dark depths of his eyes stirred the pain of brotherhood, the desire to love and the effort to love across differences, and the bewilderment at being both like and unlike.

Fred's lips set themselves firmly against each other, as if determined not to betray that what he felt for Marc in this moment was also what he felt for that distant part of himself which had been Freddy Kleinman, the little boy, the younger brother, the part he had shoved aside as burdensome to a man becoming a success.

Marc tried to explain. He said, "You remember how Papa used to say, 'When a man is down, he can be stepped on'? Events have proved that——"

Fred drew a quick breath. "I can't do a damn thing about it. If you think you can—Marc, I'll sure as hell be wishing you luck. This anti-Negro, anti-Semitic stuff——" He whistled and shook his head. "That scrap over there in Palestine——" He shrugged his shoulders. He said once more: "I'll be wishing you luck."

Other passengers were entering the plane. While his mouth spoke staccato good-bys, Fred's eyes remained quietly on Marc.

Suddenly making a farcical interlude of his departure, he scampered up the steps, hurrying Celia in a flurry of veils and furs ahead by both her elbows. The door banged, the lock turned, and the steps were wheeled away.

The plane became a roar, a giant insect crawling, running, rising, at last a spot in the sky swiftly fading into nothingness.

For a moment Marc and Hallie, arm in arm, watched the great shafts of light flashing back and forth against a tumble of clouds. Then they walked away in rapid, steady strides, a graceful woman and a thin, nearly tall man with one shoulder higher than the other. Together they leaned forward into the stiffening wind.